FIRE & DARK

The Night Horde SoCal Series
Book Three

Susan Fanetti

THE FREAK CIRCLE PRESS

Fire & Dark © 2015 Susan Fanetti
All rights reserved

Susan Fanetti has asserted her right to be identified as the author of this book under the Copyright, Design and Patents Act 1988.

This is a work of fiction. Names, characters, places, and incidents are a product of the author's imagination. Any resemblance to actual persons, living or dead, events, or locales are entirely coincidental.

ALSO BY SUSAN FANETTI

The Night Horde SoCal Series:
(MC Romance)
Strength & Courage, Book 1
Shadow & Soul, Book 2
Today & Tomorrow, Book 2.5

The Pagano Family Series:
(Family Saga)
Footsteps, Book 1
Touch, Book 2
Rooted, Book 3
Deep, Book 4

The Signal Bend Series:
(The first Night Horde series)
(MC Romance)
Move the Sun, Book 1
Behold the Stars, Book 2
Into the Storm, Book 3
Alone on Earth, Book 4
In Dark Woods, Book 4.5
All the Sky, Book 5
Show the Fire, Book 6
Leave a Trail, Book 7

Always to the Freaks, who are my love and support in life and in art.

Especially to C.D. Breadner, who helped me see what Connor and Pilar's story was missing.

And to Jim, with whom I've come through so much fire and dark.

I look at you
Across those fires and the dark.

~Weldon Kees, "Late Evening Song"

CHAPTER ONE

Two black Range Rovers crested a hill on the horizon, and Connor Elliott stood up. He'd been sitting sidesaddle on his parked bike, feeling both bored and wary. His brothers in the Night Horde MC had been similarly waiting—sitting on their bikes, walking around the dusty field they were parked on the edge of, all of them in that strange place of indolent readiness.

It had been the kind of atmosphere that just about demanded a smoke, if you were of that persuasion—as several of the Horde, including Connor, were. But it was July in Southern California. Smoking out in the wilds was about the most dangerous thing a man could do.

"Heads up. The Queen approaches." He felt the weight of the gun holstered under his arm. They were meeting an ally—their boss, for all intents and purposes—but he'd ridden a long enough road to know better than to let his guard down around a drug cartel, friend or foe.

By the time the Rovers pulled up alongside their parked Harleys, all the Horde on this run—Connor; Hoosier, his father and the club President; Bart, the VP; Lakota, Trick, and Jesse—were standing in a row. As the doors opened, Hoosier stepped forward, and Connor, his Sergeant at Arms, went with him. Bart, too, took a step up.

Four men in suits stepped out of the lead Rover. Three men dressed likewise stepped out of the one behind it. The driver of the second then opened the last passenger door and reached in. A shapely female leg stretched down and set a high-heeled black pump on the scruffy desert floor. The driver stepped back, seeming to lead a small, beautiful woman out of the Rover.

He wasn't leading her, though, as all the Horde were well aware. This was Isidora Vega, known as La Zorra, queen of the Águilas cartel and de facto ruler of the Mexican drug trade.

The Horde had been working with La Zorra for a year and a half. Their reactions to the idea of a female drug lord had ranged at first from skepticism to amusement. None of them was skeptical or amused now. In the time that they had known her, she had crushed one cartel into dust. She had forced a struggling but storied Colombian cartel into a subcontractor position, and she had wrangled a treaty with the entire Mexican trade that had stabilized and focused cartel power over the trade and the country itself.

For years, it had been known that Mexico was essentially run by its drug lords. Now that was factually true.

She had accomplished all that, bringing dozens of psychotically homicidal men to their knees at her feet, with the same will for violence that had always described the drug trade, but she had done it without the manic flair. She'd simply killed, with cold calculation, all the psychos until the men who were left were willing to think and act with logic.

A woman—a small, gorgeous woman under forty—had brought the drug trade to heel. She'd stabilized an entire fucking country. In short, she was a badass of the highest order.

So Connor always felt guarded when the Horde leaders sat down with her. Though these meetings ran like board meetings, despite their unconventional venues, Connor still expected another shoe to drop. She was a woman. Who, in not even two years, had reorganized a country. With apparently little but the force of her will. Even with the evidence of her stability, he found it hard to believe. And he had seen the evidence of her violence.

And she was guarded everywhere she went by seven men. It seemed to him that not even La Zorra herself fully trusted in the extent of her control.

But his father stepped out with his hand extended. "Dora. Good to see you."

"Hoosier." She smiled and shook his hand. Then she nodded to Hoosier's right. "Bart."

"Dora." Bart gave her a nod that had something of the flavor of a courtly little bow.

She turned to Hoosier's left. "And Connor."

"Ma'am." He thought she was about his age, but 'ma'am' felt appropriate. She had certainly earned respect.

Returning her gaze to Connor's father, Dora said, "Thank you for meeting. I know this wasn't in our schedule. But I have some new information and possibly an opportunity, and I'd like your input."

She turned and gestured to two of her men who had moved to the back of one of the Rovers. When one of them opened the hatch, Connor changed his stance, and his hand automatically shifted subtly toward his holster.

But the men pulled out a large, flat gizmo that, after a minute or two of setup, turned out to be a portable picnic table. When it was up, La Zorra turned to Hoosier with a smile. "Shall we sit?"

~oOo~

On the way back into town, they took the freeway. Traffic on the 15 came to a complete halt about ten miles out. They lane-split for the rest of the ride, passing the last remnants of what had obviously been a serious, multi-car accident with injuries. Long, wide streaks of blood stained the asphalt, and the three cars and a parcel truck being loaded onto flatbeds seemed to have been wadded up by a large, angry hand.

Two fire engines were still on the road, the firefighters packing up. As the Horde approached the scene, an ambulance pulled onto the road with its flashers on but no siren, and one lane of the freeway was opened behind it. The Horde rode by what was left of the scene in single file, slowly, with respect for what was very likely at least one dead.

At the Mariposa Avenue exit, the group split off—Bart and Hoosier took the ramp, which would lead them to the clubhouse. Connor, Lakota, Trick, and Jesse went on by. They weren't meeting on La Zorra's new business until the next day, and the four of them were off to hold to their post-run ritual. They rode north, through Madrone and up toward San Bernardino. They were headed to The Flight Deck.

The Flight Deck was a bar laid out in an airplane hangar that had once been part of an Air Force Base. The base had closed about thirty years ago, and its structures had been almost entirely dismantled or repurposed, but Troy Crowley, the owner of The Deck, had bought early and preserved the space.

What he'd made in it was something that Connor was fairly sure was unique in its way. Six bars, a full kitchen, a huge dance floor, with live music three nights a week, a karaoke stage, massive television screens with viewing areas that were like little theaters with sofa seating, a billiards area, and two boxing rings.

Despite its vast size, the place had an almost intimate air. The lighting was low and golden, the sound was abated with excellent insulation, and the staff, barkeeps and cocktail cuties alike, knew all the regulars.

All that, though, maybe made the place unusual but not unique. What really made The Deck stand out was that it was a roughneck bar—that catered to people on both sides of the line. Cops, firefighters, bikers, farmers—you name it, they all made their way here, sometimes in droves. And the place still managed to pull in some of the club crowd, too—straight arrows taking a spin around the wild side.

Connor, who enjoyed himself a good rumble, had been in the ring often, and he'd fought more than a few Sheriff's deputies. The club was on good terms in Madrone and with the San Bernardino County Sheriff, but he still got a kick out of putting a uniform on the mat.

They backed their bikes along the side of the building and walked in. It was too late for The Deck's second happy hour—which was famous for its wide array of all-you-can-eat bar food—but not really late enough for the crowd to get wild. The rings were quiet. It wasn't a live-band night, so the dance floor in the middle of the space was empty. But karaoke was happening. As the Horde walked toward the bar nearest the boxing rings, Jesse slapped Connor on the back.

"You see that?"

He had. A table full of girls, in full club regalia, all high heels and short skirts. Four of them. One of them, a bodacious bottle blonde, had a tall, glittery tiara on her head. In the center, bedazzled in bright purple sparkles, was the number '21.' There were flashing lights across the top.

Score.

Lakota laughed as they sat at a table in clear sight of Birthday Barbie and her friends. "Gettin' long in the tooth for you, brother."

As Trick went to the bar to place their first order—always two pitchers of Shock Top Belgian White and a bottle of Jack—Connor turned to Lakota and grinned. "Twenty-one is still in the easy zone, brother. I'm telling you, you are missing out."

Lakota shook his head. "Nothin' easier than club pussy."

"Yeah, man. But club girls are used *up*. They're sweet and good at it, sure, but they've seen it all. They've done it all. Young pussy is just so…*eager*. And teachable."

"Teachable's my problem with it," Jesse interjected. "I don't want to teach anybody sex ed. I just want to get my rocks off."

Trick came back, and Connor poured out four glasses of beer. Handing one to Jesse, he said, "You, sir, are the perv. Not me. I'm doing a public service, showing sweet young things what sex oughta be." He drank from his own glass and wiped foam from his beard. "And virgin pussy? Fuck, man, there is nothing tighter in the world. Rare enough to find a legal chick still holding her v-card, but if she's where I am, it's because she's looking to turn it in. It's not like I'm scoping out high schools."

Trick tossed back a shot and poured another. "Yeah, you're an asshole, Conman. Spin it any way you want, it all comes up asshole."

Unoffended, Connor flipped him off. Yeah, he preferred girls in the eighteen-to-twenty-two range, for all the reasons he'd said. They were young and firm, they were eager, and they did what they were told. The ones he pushed up on were dazzled by his leather and ink and deliciously willing. Moreover, they were various. They were like a fancy restaurant where the chef prepared whatever was fresh that day. The roster of club girls was like a fast-food menu: quick, easy, and never changed.

Flipping him off right back, Trick grinned and took his second shot. "Are we going to talk about this new job La Zorra wants on our plate?"

"Absolutely not." Connor's answer was firm. With the exception of officer meetings, he didn't like offshoots to talk club business. They were only four, and there were thirteen men who sat at the Horde table. Talking out of the Keep would only lead to fractured loyalties.

But Trick pushed the point. "Not to work out our opinions, Connor. But I have questions."

He shook his head. As SAA, he had rank over the others, so nobody else chimed in. "Not outside the Keep."

The new job was a hit. La Zorra wanted the Horde to take somebody out of her way. But that somebody was the Los Angeles County District Attorney—high profile and risky as shit. It was their distance from L.A. that had her convinced they were right for the job.

His father, Bart, and Sherlock were sitting down tonight and putting together the intel they could. La Zorra had ostensibly given them an option not to take the job, but if they were going to decline, then they'd better have a damn good reason and a viable alternative. They had a stable relationship with her, and she had been nothing but reasonable in all the time they'd been working together. But Connor had seen what she was capable of—what she was willing to do.

None of that needed to be said until it could be said at the table, so Connor knew that the best course was to let the geeks do their thing while everybody else rolled on as usual—hence, sitting here at The Deck.

Trick stared at him, and he stared back. Then the party girls squealed about something, and the little touch of tension broke as all the Horde looked their way.

Connor smirked. The girls were going through the karaoke book. That meant that they'd been celebrating a while and had their inhibitions down. He got up. "Time to send the lovelies a birthday round. I'll send it from all of us—my gift to you, my brothers."

~oOo~

Birthday Barbie's name was Madison. They were always named Madison these days. Or Hailey. The early Aughts had obviously been big years to name a girl Madison or Hailey. Or Caitlyn. Connor figured he'd fucked a round dozen each of those names.

Tonight's Madison was sitting on his lap, sharing shots with him, putting the glass to his mouth and then taking it away to finish it herself. Okay, this part about catching the young ones got a little annoying. The things they thought were cute really just were not.

But his hand was up her microscopic little skirt, her wisp of a thong was out of his way, and she was hairless and soaking wet.

Her friends—there was a Hailey in the group—were arrayed similarly with his brothers, who all seemed to be coming around to his way of thinking.

Except for Trick. Poor Trick had gotten stuck with the Ugly Friend.

Based on Connor's observation, there was one in every group of girls. One girl who was a little less noticeable than her friends. Her hair was a little less styled, her makeup a little less layered. Sometimes she had glasses. Sometimes she was heavier. Usually, she was fine looking, except in comparison.

Trick himself could probably be considered something of an Ugly Friend, in fact. As far as Connor could tell, he was a good-looking guy. But he had a look that wasn't really up the alley for girls like the Barbies—long blond dreads, a long, wiry beard, and some pretty weird ink all the way to his fingers. Barbies wanted bikers, not freaks.

The funny thing was that Trick was probably the least freaky of the four of them. He had a college degree. He read thick books about philosophy and shit and liked to talk about what he read. He was a fucking vegetarian.

Scratch that—as bikers went, Trick Stavros was a total freak.

Trick was talking to Madison's Ugly Friend, and they looked like they were having an actual conversation. Jesse and Hailey were making out. The other Barbie, whose name had escaped Connor, was combing her fingers through Lakota's long hair. And Madison the Birthday Barbie was squirming on Connor's lap. Turning into a pretty good night, all in all.

Madison finished another shot and then let out an impressive belch. She threw her hand over her mouth, her eyes wide, and mumbled, "Bathroom!" Then she was off his lap and reeling gracelessly toward the restrooms.

Lakota and Jesse's Barbies ignored their friend's drunken dash toward the johns, but Trick's conversation partner got up and followed her back.

Fuck. Missed the window. He liked young girls; indeed he did. He liked them perky and naïve, eager and flexible. But he did not fuck a girl, at any age, who wasn't damn sure what she was up to.

Connor poured himself a beer and sat back with a sigh, scanning the rest of the bar. A big group of cubicle-dwellers was on the karaoke machine, and a portly dude with glasses was massacring some kind of chick-bait ballad. Connor didn't think the chicks would be biting.

As it was occurring to him that the pickings were slim here on this midweek night, and he'd end up back at the clubhouse with a regular after all, a big group of guys walked by. He made them quick as firefighters; he'd seen a couple of them here before. His interest was a bit more than casual, because he'd faced the guy up front in the ring not long back. Connor didn't lose often, but that guy had pulled some real MMA bullshit and about broke his leg.

He wanted a rematch. Not tonight, but soon. So he watched while Mortal Kombat and his buddies walked by. When they pushed tables together, Connor saw that there were two women in the group, too. He hadn't realized that there were chick firefighters anywhere local. But they were probably paramedics, actually. He couldn't see a chick bashing in the door of a burning house.

One of them caught his eye—or his ear, more like. She had a bawdy, husky laugh, and when he sought out its source, he was looking a fucking gorgeous firefighter. Long, wildly wavy dark hair and a raunchy smile. Not really his type, but nice to look at nonetheless. He wondered if chick firefighters were held to the kind of fitness standards the dudes were. That could be interesting.

But Madison had come back from the restroom and was trying to get back on his lap. She smelled like puke and Altoids. He reached over and pulled a chair from the nearest table and sat her there. Then he kissed her cheek. Time to let her down gently. "Tell you what, beautiful," he said at her ear. "I think we'll do this another time."

She blinked blearily at him. "What?"

Her Ugly Friend leaned in. "He means you're sloppy drunk and it's time to go home, Maddie. C'mon."

But Birthday Barbie didn't like that idea. "Wait, what? You don't want me?" Her mouth had some trouble forming the words but not the outrage.

Connor put on a soothing smile. Young girls were insecure, no matter how pretty they were. So he lied smoothly, "I want you, puss. Just another time, when you're on your feet better."

Her speech was suddenly perfectly clear. "*You're* rejecting *me*? On my birthday? Oh, fuck you, Grandpa." With that, she stood up and flounced off unstably, her Ugly Friend right with her, the others eventually getting up and encircling her.

Connor watched her go, bemused. *Grandpa*? What the fuck? He was thirty-six years old. *Grandpa*? He turned and found his brothers staring at him. As soon as he met Lakota's eyes, they all collapsed into a communal fit of hilarity that he most certainly did not share.

Grandpa?

CHAPTER TWO

"Hey, Cordero—you with us?"

Pilar blinked and turned toward the voice. "Where else would I be, fucktard?"

"I thought maybe you were dreaming about running off to become a biker bitch, leaving all this glamour behind." Kyle Moore swept his arms wide, encompassing their whole group.

She flipped him off. "Nah, I was just wondering what the odds were you could take that guy again if you actually fought him clean."

In truth, she'd barely been thinking about the bikers at all. She'd noticed them; it was nearly impossible not to notice them. And she'd nearly sprained her eyeballs rolling them up at the sight of the big guy with the little blonde child oozing drunkenly all over him. They were all playing with a bunch of vapid little children—fuck, the one the big guy had was wearing a fucking *tiara with flashing lights*, which pretty much closed the case on her inability to make good life choices. And if Pilar had had to bet, most of those guys were closer to forty than they were to twenty.

So yeah, she'd noticed. And the big guy was totally her type—short dark hair, full but trimmed beard over a nice face, good ink, broad shoulders, huge arms. He'd been in the ring with Moore just a couple of weeks ago, so she knew he was tall and built like a brick shithouse, too, with just the right amount of dark hair over his chest. Dude was all man, definitely. And hot as hell.

Except for his obvious and ridiculous preference for girls half his age. He'd had a Bambi draped over him the night he'd fought Moore, too. That cut his hot points in just about half.

But she'd stopped thinking about him or even seeing him a while ago. Where she'd been was on the freeway, at their last call. That had been a bitch. Four vehicle involvement, three dead on scene, five serious injuries. Nobody in those vehicles had walked away from the scene.

One of the fatalities had been a four-year-old girl. Pilar had been the one to cut her body out of her mangled car seat. Her mother, who'd been driving one of the cars that had been sandwiched between the car that had been stopped short and the truck whose driver hadn't noticed that traffic had stopped, had been conscious, and had screamed when Pilar had lifted the broken little body out of the crumpled wreck of a Honda Civic. The woman's legs had been amputated below the knees, but until she saw her daughter's body, she had barely moaned. She'd been focused on getting her little girl rescued, asking after her constantly, talking to her.

Abbie. The little girl's name was Abbie.

Pilar could still hear that damn scream, and she knew she'd hear it in her sleep. Unless she went to bed really drunk and, with any luck, well fucked.

It was why they were all here, and why they were all rowdy. There was a kind of mania coming off a call like that. When it happened in the middle of the watch, you could work through it in the station with your crew and be okay by the time you went out into the world in your street clothes again. But her platoon had been working their thirty-six watch, and the alarm had come in a couple of hours before the end.

Working a job like this required the ability to control your empathy. You had to care deeply and then stop caring, or turn it way down, anyway, when the call was done. Pilar figured cops and soldiers had to do the same thing—you saw some bad shit in a job like this, and if you couldn't turn off the screen, then your brain would play the Bad Shit Greatest Hits all the damn time.

But some calls wouldn't turn off. Calls like tonight's. Then you found a way to work it out. Booze and sex was how Pilar did it—same with everybody at The Deck with her tonight. The rest of the platoon had either gone home to their families or off to commune with their personal Jesus or whatever they needed to do. But these guys, they were her inner circle—all of them single, all of them on the young side, all of them a little bit wild. They hadn't even needed to say out loud that they were all headed straight for The Deck for their fix of booze for sure, and sex hopefully.

But not with each other. God, no. Gross. You did NOT want to fuck around with a firefighter from your own station. Jesus, you were practically married to everybody anyway.

Moore rebutted her claim about the way he'd fought the hot, shallow biker. "I fought him clean. Not my fault the asshole fights like The Thing. No finesse at all, just those boulders he calls hands."

He was right—dude had big hands. Broad and thick without being fat. Strong hands that had blackened Moore up right good, before Moore had put him down. She focused more keenly on the table of bikers and saw Miss Tiara flouncing off with her friends. The biker watched her go, then his buddies started laughing, and he flipped them off.

Aw, poor honey had gotten turned down by a drunk baby bimbo. He got up and headed toward the nearest bar.

Pilar looked around. "Hey—we need refills. Anybody up for a round of tequila? Patrón?"

Stephanie Perez laughed. "Oh, no. Cordero's locked on. Who's the target?" She scanned the room and lit on the biker. "Oh, looky there. Hunting for bear tonight, I see."

"Eat me, Perez," Pilar answered.

"Fuck, don't tease. Perez and Cordero goin' down on each other? I'd pay real money to see that." At Eric White's statement, the men all turned toward the two women and nodded.

"You don't have the kind of money you'd need, White. You'll just have to jack off to the pictures in your sick head."

"Oh, I do, I do."

Being a woman in a firehouse had its challenges. Pilar was the only female firefighter in San Bernardino County, and she loved the work. There were female paramedics, like Perez, but Pilar rode an engine. She had the respect of her platoon and most of her station, but she'd had to scrap like crazy to get it.

She'd had to figure out a way to be one of the guys and also let the sexual innuendo shit roll off her back. They were always making some kind of comment like the one White had just made. She knew it wouldn't go past that kind of verbal playing around, and she also knew how to stop it if it did.

Early on, while she was still in the academy, she'd learned that if she made an issue of it at all, what she was doing more than anything else was drawing attention to her difference. So she played along. And frankly, it didn't bother her. She'd been raised by a strong woman in a profoundly sexist world. She knew the game.

She lived with these guys. For a huge chunk of her life, she ate with them, worked with them, worked out with them, chilled out with them. She slept with them. Yeah, the women's bunks were separated by a partial wall, and they had a little one-stall, one-shower bathroom of their own, but that was the full extent of their privacy. They had all seen everybody in all their skin. She knew they looked. But hey, she looked, too, and she didn't bother to be any more subtle about it than they were.

The best way, she'd learned, to stop being judged by her body was to stop giving a fuck what they saw of it. It sounded backward, maybe, but it made sense to Pilar: if she didn't care, then she didn't draw attention, and after a while skin was just skin.

It was probably some kind of feminist cardinal sin, but she didn't much care about feminism. It wasn't that she didn't agree with it; she totally did. She just saw it as a political movement, and all political movements were bullshit, as far as Pilar was concerned. Nothing ever changed up that high. The only change she had any control over was her own. So she didn't worry about what was going on with the politicians. She just did her damn thing, and woe to anyone who tried to get in her way.

Instead of a protest sign, she carried a fucking Halligan.

"I'm going for shots." She stood up.

"We won't wait up." That was Pete Guzman, the oldest and quietest of their group.

White stood up, almost knocking his chair back. "Hold up, hold up." He dug into his pocket and pulled out a condom packet. "Always be safe, muffin. We love you!"

Pilar laughed and snatched it out of his hand. She always had a condom with her, but she'd take a free one when it was offered. Unless…"Oh, fuck, this is one of those flavored things, isn't it?"

"Tropical," he smirked.

She tossed it back. "Gross. They're sticky. And they taste and smell like fruit marinated in gasoline."

"No one's ever complained to me."

"Maybe if you were bigger, they'd notice."

On Perez's comment and the roar that followed it, Pilar smirked at White, then turned her back on her friends and headed toward the bar.

The big biker had turned at her friends' commotion, so he was looking her way when she approached. He smiled the kind of smile that said he was used to girls melting at the sight of it.

It was a pretty melty smile, in fact. He had a really good face, and that smile showed straight white teeth surrounded by good lips and a nice dark beard. But Pilar looked past him and leaned on the bar at his side. "Hey, Bill. Round of shots—seven. Patrón Silver."

"You got it." The bartender nodded and turned to the shelves at the back.

"Make it eight," said a gruff voice at her side. Excellent voice. Those hot points were climbing back up.

She turned. "You think I'm buying you a shot? I don't even know you."

"I think I'm buying you seven shots and me one. And I'm Connor. Now you know me."

Bill pushed a row of shots toward her. As she dug into her pocket, her new friend Connor handed a fold of bills over the bar. "Keep it," he said, and Bill nodded his thanks.

As Bill counted the money and nodded, Pilar did a quick bit of math and realized Connor had tipped really well. Another point in the hot column. Unless he'd only done it to impress her—then again, she was impressed, so it had worked. But she liked to make a guy work for his play. He clearly had this whole seduction shtick going on; he'd have to get innovative if he wanted to move up from the JV jiggle squad to the A team.

After she pushed a shot glass toward him, she began corralling the other seven. She'd done her time in the food service industry, so getting seven full shots over to the table would be no big deal.

He laid his hand on her forearm. Yep. Really good hand. "Wait. Do yours with me."

"Why would I? I'm drinking with my friends."

"Because it was my treat. And you haven't told me your name."

"That's not a treat, if you're looking for something back. That's just payment in advance." Oh, this was fun.

He thought so, too. That sex smile widened and showed real interest. "You're a smartass."

"It's been said."

"Well, now. That's interesting. It's been said about me, too."

Before she could answer, she was jostled from behind, and Perez and Ron Reyes were there, collecting six shot glasses.

"Thanks, man," Reyes said to Connor, who dipped his head in a nod.

"Don't break him," Perez said to Pilar, plenty loud enough for Connor to hear. "He's too pretty to scuff up."

"Assholes!" Pilar called after them both.

When they were alone again, Connor picked up one of the remaining two glasses and tapped it to the other one, miming a toast. "We had an audience. Looks like they planned our night."

She looked past him at his table of buddies, who were all watching as if they had money on the outcome. They might, for all that. Nodding in their direction, she said, "Bigger audience than you think."

He looked over his shoulder. "Yeah, they're assholes, too." Turning back to her, he lifted his glass again. "Like to know your name before they marry us off."

"Pilar. I'm Pilar."

"I like it. I don't think I've ever known a Pilar before."

She shrugged.

They did their shots. Pilar swallowed hers first, and as she set the glass down, she asked, "So, we gonna fuck, then?"

Coughing and fighting to swallow, he finally sputtered, "Jesus, girl!" He waved his empty glass at Bill and gestured for two more shots. "That's abrupt, don't you think?"

"Look. I'm not trawling for Mr. Right. I had a shit day. I need tequila and sex. Tequila's been taken care of—and thank you for that. You're hot. I'm horny, and I figure you are, too. Little Miss Tiara rubbed around on your lap for twenty minutes and then scampered off." The next round had arrived, and she picked one up and knocked it back. "I guess if you were into that bimbo, then maybe I'm not your type. But I know things she can't even spell. I'll fuck your brains out and send you on about your life. You in or not?"

He'd started to grin about halfway through her speech. After he tossed his own shot back, he said, "You were checking me out."

"Don't be obnoxious about it. You're hot. You *are* my type. So, yeah. I ogled."

"I feel so violated."

"Will you feel better if we go back to the storeroom and fuck against the beer cases?"

"It's a start. But Troy'll have a shit fit."

"Troy loves me. C'mon. Let's go, big guy." She grabbed his hand and led him to the farthest reaches of the bar.

Damn, he had good hands.

~oOo~

The Deck storeroom was a perfect place for a quick fuck, and Pilar had taken a few guys back here. The hot ones whom she had no history with. She didn't want to take some random guy home with her, and she sure as hell didn't want to go to some random guy's place. She'd been on calls that were the aftermath of that kind of stupid.

Troy had a soft spot for the protect-and-serve types and made a point to get to know those who frequented his establishment, so when he'd come back here once or twice while Pilar was mid-squelch with somebody, he'd just nodded and gone on about his errand.

The storeroom was a semi-private space in a very public place. Safety and convenience. Perfect.

But not, you know, romantic. It was a huge, chilly space, lit with rows of industrial fluorescent lights suspended on long poles from a ceiling which must have been at least thirty feet high. Rows of metal shelving held canned food, boxes of paper supplies, and whatever else an enormous bar like this needed to keep in stock. One wall held a row of deep freezes. She'd fucked on those a couple of times.

But Connor was pulling her up by the stacked cases of bottled beer. Well, she had said they could fuck against the beer. Then he immediately went for her jeans as his head came down, and he planted his mouth right on hers.

And damn, he was a good kisser. His mouth covered hers and his tongue went right for it, sweeping into her mouth. When she met him, her tongue rolling and twisting with his, his hands stopped plucking at the button of her fly and just held on, curling into fists around her waistband, pulling her close.

He smelled fantastic—the booze and the leather of his kutte, which had a kind of well-worn scent, and his skin itself, which smelled warm and, well, *indecent*—and his scent wrapped around all her senses and made him taste just as good. Pilar grunted and arched her body into his, pressing herself against a very hard, very cut chest, just out of reach behind his shirt. He responded to her tighter contact by letting go of her jeans and taking hold of her ass, clutching her hard.

But he could go harder. She wanted him to go harder. To encourage that, she put her arms over his shoulders and grabbed the neck of his kutte in her fists, increasing the ferocity of their kiss. He went with her, grunting along with her, until she bit down on his bottom lip and pulled away. When he pulled sharply back, letting go of her so he could rub at his lip, she dropped her hands and stared up at him.

Fuck, he was hot. His eyes were like a dark grey or something and sheltered under a perfect, strong brow. That little bit of blood smear on his lip made her lick her own.

But when he came back in with a little growl, she shoved him back.

He frowned. "Don't you want this?"

She was practically panting for this guy. In fact, she was literally panting for this guy. But the lingering turmoil from the freeway call was still frothing up her blood, and she wanted more from this encounter than just a quick, thrusty fuck. What she felt like she needed was something she didn't take from strange men.

But she needed it. Or something like it. A bit of it.

"I want it."

"Then what the fuck, Pilar?"

For some reason, that—his saying her name, her given name, in that deep, rocky voice—decided her. "I want you to work for it. I'm no post-teen princess. You gotta bring more game."

At that, he chuckled. "Baby, you dragged me back here. And now you're playing hard to get?" She could see in his posture that he was changing his mind, deciding she was a nutcase and not worth the trouble.

"I'm not playing hard to get. I'm playing make me." For emphasis, she hit him in the chest with the flat of one hand. Not hard, but abrupt.

His brow furrowed, but he didn't react in any other way. "You got a rape fantasy thing, I'm not your guy, puss. Girl says no, I stop."

"Well, aren't you a gentleman."

"Not especially. But that's a line. And a point of pride."

"That's fine. Rape's not my kink."

His eyes flared at the word 'kink.' "What is?"

"Fight me." She shoved at his chest again.

It was a risk, but it didn't feel like one. Though she didn't know him, she felt sure that he wouldn't hurt her. He just gave off that vibe. There was a protector thing about this guy, outlaw biker or not. And yeah, she knew he was an outlaw. He was Night Horde. She'd been on a couple of calls at the Horde's compound. Somebody had thrown a barrel full of burning horse through their window. And a few months after that, somebody had shot their clubhouse up. Those weren't the kinds of things that happened to law-abiding citizens, generally speaking.

He took a step backward. "What? No. I'm a lot bigger than you are."

Indeed he was. "I'm not asking you to hurt me." Though she wouldn't mind it much if there was a little bit of hurt. She pulled her t-shirt over her head. Under it was a sport bra—there was no point wearing silky or lacy anything at the barn; the guys would just make a meal out of it—but it was a nice one, turquoise, with thinner straps that crossed on her back. "I'm asking you to fight me. Let's get sweaty."

He was staring at the midriff she'd just bared. So she flexed those muscles.

"Jesus fucking Christ," he muttered. "Look at you."

CHAPTER THREE

Pilar was standing in front of him with her t-shirt wadded in her hand, wearing a little blue sport bra that wasn't much in the sexy lingerie department but was stellar in the tiny shirt department. But that hardly mattered, because Connor's entire attention was locked on her belly. Jesus fucking Christ. She had as much definition as he did.

No—she had more. He had bulk and breadth, but she was lean, and every fucking muscle in her body looked like it had been etched into her bronze skin with a laser. He'd never seen anything like it, not in person where he could touch.

Which he did now, laying his hand over the sharp planes of her belly. "Do you compete?"

Her abs flexed when she chuckled. "No. But I work out."

"Fuck yeah, you do." He smoothed his thumb over one of the cans of her six pack. Damn.

But she surprised him, knocking his hand away and then hitting him in the chest again. "You don't need to do your seduction act on me. I'm just looking for a good, sweaty fuck."

The hitting him thing was getting old fast. Connor was hot as hell for this chick, no mistake. But wild, rough ruts weren't his thing, not with chicks he didn't know. The downside was way too fucking steep. When he wanted or needed to be rough, he went for club pussy. They'd been around, they knew the score, and they wouldn't scream assault if they came up with a bruise or a bite mark.

What she'd called his 'seduction act'—that was his thing for a random hookup. It was why he liked young girls. He liked to do a little sweet talk, get a chick all dewy-eyed, offer her a ride on his Night Train, then take her back to the clubhouse and broaden her horizons a little. He also knew which girls were prime to be swept off their feet for a night but not want more than that one night. The princesses looking for a walk on the wild side—or what they thought of as the wild side—and then wanted to get back to the car their daddy had bought them and drive home to their safe little suburban life.

Every now and then, one would simper a little, making noise like she wasn't done with him. But he hadn't met a pretty young thing yet who still wanted to see more of him after he'd walked her through the clubhouse on a weekend morning, with its inevitable array of passed-out, naked bodies. Not to mention the stench.

This girl, though, this woman, wasn't remotely like his usual game. She was coming at him hard, and all Connor's warning bells were going of like the fucking apocalypse had arrived. It was one thing to go for a quick rut against the wall back here. But she was asking him to *fight* her? What did that even mean?

At his hesitation, she scoffed and turned away. "Fuck it. Never mind."

Her hair swung as she turned, a fantastic mass of dark, loose, wild waves that cascaded halfway down her back. His hands itched to be buried in that hair, to grab hold of it.

And then he did exactly that. He reached out and took a fistful of her hair, dragging her back until she collided with his chest. She was chick-size, neither tall nor short. He was six-two, and she came up to, say, his chin or so. His body reacted strongly to the contact, his already-hard cock swelling painfully. Before he knew he would do it, he'd thrust his hips against her.

She didn't react almost at all to his force, but when he leaned down to put his mouth to her ear, he saw that she was smiling. "I'm not gonna knock you around, puss. But I'll give it to you hard, if that's what you want." He bit down on her shoulder—not hard enough to mark her, but hard enough to let her know what he meant. She had elaborate ink across the back of her shoulders, one side to the other, done in oranges and reds: some kind of flowers that looked like they were on fire. "Is that what you want?"

Reaching her arm up to hook over his head, she dug her nails into the back of his neck. "Bring it," she said quietly, her voice more growl than whisper.

Jesus. What the hell was he getting himself into?

It didn't matter. With one hand, he yanked up her bra and took hold of a tight knot of nipple, and he shoved the other into her jeans. She was shaved or waxed or whatever, her skin silky smooth and so fucking firm. He had never had a body like this in his hands before.

Her hands dropped and went to her fly. She tore it open, easing his access, and then reached behind her to grab his cock over his jeans, squeezing him hard. He grunted and pushed his fingers inside her, then turned them both and shoved her against the stack of beer cases.

The bottles rattled ominously as they crashed into them. Connor didn't want to create a chaotic mess back here and have Troy up his ass, so he looked around. Finding a likely spot, he yanked her jeans and underwear down to her knees and picked her up. Finally, he'd surprised her. She gasped and went stiff.

He carried her to the row of deep freezes and dropped her down on the one at the end. She smiled and started to turn to her belly, moving to slide her legs off the end, but he grabbed her bare hip and forced her back to her side. Keeping his hand there to hold her still, he dug a condom out of his kutte, opened his jeans, and got the fucker on.

Then he wrapped an arm around both of her legs, holding them tightly together. Keeping her on her side, he yanked her ass to the very edge of the freezer top and pushed sideways into her eager, bare pussy.

Her back arched sharply as he got deep. "Oh, holy shit! Oh *God*, yeah! Bring it hard. C'mon!"

He laughed and shook his head—she was something else. "Okay, baby. Okay." With one arm locked around her knees and the other hand grasping her shoulder, he went hard, pounding into her without preamble, his hips rocking so hard that the freezer shook, one side coming off the ground with every forward thrust.

She was keeping up a constant litany through clenched teeth: "Fuck, fuck, fuck, fuck," over and over, her voice that same breathy growl. She began to push her body toward his, meeting his thrusts in counterpoint. Then she put her hand between her legs and went for her clit with fervor.

"Fuck, yeah," she gritted. "Come on, come on. I need it harder."

Holy hell. Before Connor could figure out how to give her more, the storeroom door opened, and he stilled his hips and turned to see. A bar-back, just a kid, stood there staring at them with his pimply face totally slack and his mouth gaping wide.

Pilar surged toward Connor. "Don't fucking stop!"

Hardly unused to fucking in public, he returned his attention to the very demanding woman on his cock.

A hesitant, young voice squeaked, "I...I...um...need napkins."

"Then fucking get 'em!" Pilar shouted through her labored breath. "Then get the fuck out, perv!"

No one had ever retrieved a box of napkins more quickly.

The interruption had not quelled Pilar's driving demand or Connor's enthusiasm for it. He could feel his finish gathering in his balls, and she was still chanting, "More, more, more." So he threw her legs over one shoulder and leaned over her, pushing his arms under her and hooking his hands over her shoulders. With her bound up tightly and pushed firmly against him, he pistoned into her as hard and fast as he physically could.

"Fuck yeah!" she yelled. She grabbed her tits and twisted her nipples sharply, and then, thank all the saints, she was coming.

He could feel it; her body clamped down all around him, the muscles around his cock, against his chest, under his hands, all of them tensing to marble rigidity. Her face went dark. With all of the talking and yelling she'd been doing, he'd expected fireworks for her big finish, but she was still and silent, as completely clenched as he'd ever seen.

When she finally relaxed, all at once, he stopped holding himself off. Keeping up the same frenetic pace, he went at her until that perfect moment of beautiful, empty-headed ecstasy took him over.

Fuck, that was hot.

When he could pay attention again, he looked down at her. She was completely relaxed and smiling. Her wild hair was spread out around her head like a halo. She had amazing eyes, a brown so light they were almost gold, rimmed with chocolate. Her lashes were thick, dark, and long—naturally or from makeup, he didn't know, but they framed those flashing gold lights and made her look hardly real. If she had been lying anywhere but on the metal lid of a freezer in a bar's storeroom with her clothes bunched and twisted around her, she might have looked like a mystical creature.

But they were here, in the real world.

"That what you wanted?"

She laughed and stretched, that beautiful, sinewy body writhing, and his exhausted cock twitched inside her at the sight. "It'll definitely do."

With a pat to her tight little ass, he pulled out and set her legs down. She sat up, and he pulled off the condom.

As he tied it off, she said, "You're not cut."

"Hmm?" He looked up, not sure what she meant. As an answer she nodded at his uncircumcised cock. Ah. "No. That a problem?"

"Not at all. It's a great cock." She grinned and jumped off the freezer to pull up her jeans. "Really great. I just don't see a lot natural cocks in American men your age."

There were a lot of questions to be asked about that statement, but Birthday Barbie's nasty little *Grandpa* comment kicked him in the head first. Christ, he was having a tough time with chicks tonight. "My age?"

"Our age. You're in your, what, early-mid thirties?"

"Thirty-six." That was feeling older tonight than it usually did.

But she pointed her thumb at her chest. "Thirty. Our age. The whole circumcision controversy didn't really take off until the turn of the century, so it's mostly twenty-somethings who aren't cut."

Connor was damn sure circumcision had never in his life been a topic for post-coital chat. But with this chick, it seemed totally reasonable. "You see a lot of twenty-something dick?"

She pulled her t-shirt over her head. "You see a lot of twenty-something pussy?"

He laughed—a real laugh, from his gut. It felt good. This chick, man. This chick. "Touché."

She was grinning up at him, those golden eyes flashing, her hands on her hips, and he just acted without thinking. He slid a hand around her neck, into her hair, and bent down to kiss her. Not a sex kiss. Just a kiss. Gentle. When he swept his tongue lightly over her lips, she flinched backward a little.

"What was that for?"

He lifted a shoulder in a casual shrug. "Just wanted to do it."

"You don't have to let me down easy, you know. I'm done here."

He grinned. "Good. So'm I."

"Okay."

"Okay." He nodded at the door. "We should get out of here."

She gave him a quick look that was searching, a little suspicious. And then she nodded and headed for the door. He followed her out.

Once on the floor, she drew up short. "Fuck." Her table was occupied by strangers. She'd been left behind.

"You got abandoned?"

"Yeah," she sighed. "How long were we back there?"

Connor didn't wear a watch, so he pulled his phone out to check the time. "Half an hour?" That was his best guess, and once it sank in, he looked down at her and wiggled his eyebrows.

Her eyes widened. "Really? So much for a quick fuck."

"What can I say? Stamina, baby."

She tossed her head back and gave that raunchy laugh that had first caught his ear.

The sway of her hair drew his attention again, and he reached out and let a lock curl around his finger. "You need a ride somewhere?"

"No. I'm my own ride." She nodded at his table, where his brothers were still drinking. "I see your friends are better than mine."

"Never leave a man behind. You're welcome to come over and drink with us."

"Thanks, but no. I'll head out." She turned and held her hand out to him, which was weird. "Anyway, thanks. I'll see ya."

"Don't thank me. That's fucked up." He pushed her hand away and slid his arm around her waist. "I'll walk you out."

With a firm hand on his chest, she held him off and stepped back. "No. I'm good. Have a good night, Connor."

He let her go.

When he got back to the table, Trick lifted his eyebrow at him. "I can't tell whether you just had an epically hot fuck or an ice-cold rejection."

Connor sat down and poured himself a beer from the fresh pitcher on the table. "Both, I think."

When he put the glass to his lips, he could smell her on his hand.

~oOo~

Sherlock moved his finger around on his tablet, and an image went up on the back wall of the Keep: a photograph of a man in a suit, grey hair, slightly balding. Fairly average in just about every way.

"Allen Cartwright," Hoosier said. "L.A. County District Attorney. La Zorra wants him dead, and she wants us to do it."

The men in the room who had not been privy to that information already all reacted in some way—not strongly, though. No one was exactly shocked. Almost every man in the room had killed at least once. But there was surprise, and they all looked at each other or directly at Hoosier. They were not contract assassins, as a rule.

"Why?" Fargo hadn't had a seat at the table for very long, but he'd been vocal from his first meeting. He didn't stir shit, but he was curious and careful, and he asked deep, layered questions. He'd been a sharp Prospect with enough initiative to get his work done and enough savvy to know when not to use his initiative. He had Connor's attention—he was a smart kid.

But Connor knew Hoosier wasn't going to answer his question. They didn't have a clear answer to give. "Personal. She wasn't forthcoming with more than that. We can check into it ourselves, but there's risk there, too. So we'll have to decide whether we care if we know why."

Connor didn't particularly, but he knew some of his brothers, like Trick, for instance, would struggle with killing a man without some sense that there was a valid reason.

But Trick didn't push that point right away. Instead, he asked, "Why us?"

"Distance," Bart answered. "We're not on his radar. Our routes don't cross into his territory, and we've got no beef with him. We haven't drawn heat for our association with the Águilas cartel yet. Since we shut down the Dirty Rats out here, our work has been nothing but smooth and quiet. Fuck, we're just peaceable, law-abiding citizens, except for what's in the trucks we ride with. Dora thinks that makes us perfect for this job."

Muse leaned in, and the projected image moved over his face a little. "And what do *we* think? This isn't the kind of guy we can yank off the street and no one will notice."

Like Connor, Muse was an enforcer. They had four enforcers, including Diaz and Demon as well. Back in the day, they'd needed that much muscle, and they might need that much again in the future. Muse and Diaz were their finesse guys, and Connor knew that they were expecting this job to land at their feet. He didn't think that was the right play, though. He'd talked to his father and Bart, and they agreed.

So he spoke up. "No. We can't grab this guy. This needs to be a straight-up hit." He turned to Trick. "Sniper, if we can make it happen."

Trick sat back with a quiet whistle. "I'm rusty, man. I don't know." Trick had been an Army sniper and had done a tour in the Middle East, until he'd been kicked home on a general discharge for beating the shit out of his commanding officer.

Connor knew the story and knew that it was true, but the Trick he knew was a quiet, mellow guy. He also knew that beating your CO into a hospital bed and coming out with nothing worse than a general meant that the CO had fucking deserved it—and he had.

"Wait," J.R. cut in. "So we're doing this? Is this going to a vote, or are we so bent over to La Zorra that we don't have a choice?"

"We're voting it. Not today. I want everybody to have a handle on the job first," Hoosier answered. "She asked, she didn't tell. But let's be clear. We say no, she won't be pleased. We need a good reason."

"I fucking hate being on a bitch's leash," J.R. groused. It had been adjustment for most of them to deal with a woman with that kind of ferocious power. J.R. was the last one still bitching about it, though.

Ignoring him, Trick asked, "What's the upside? This a paying job or just a favor?"

"A job. Upside is a cool mil."

That shut even J.R. up—except for one word: "Fuck."

Hoosier nodded. "Dora Vega pays for what she values." He gestured at Sherlock. "Sherlock has some more pictures to show us. What I want to do the rest of this meeting is figure out if we have a way to get this job done. If we have a way, then we can decide if we have the will."

~oOo~

When Connor came out from the dorm later that night, his dad was sitting alone at the bar, drinking his typical Jameson. It was mellow in the Hall so far, but it wasn't a weekend night. It would be just the patches and the regular girls. On Friday nights, they opened their doors a little, invited fresh blood—girls who might want to make a habit of banging bikers on call, men who might be interested in hanging around, sometimes a few celebrity tourists. Otherwise, though, it was pretty much just family around the clubhouse. They had a rep for being wild, but really, they were boring most of the time.

That wasn't to say they sat around other nights reading the Bible and singing hymns. It was sex, booze, and rock-n-roll. No illegal drugs, just weed and booze. There wasn't a prohibition on anything, but everybody knew there was no point in inviting trouble. The clubhouse was clean. They didn't get heat from law these days, even with their dark work, but even if the clubhouse were raided, there'd be nothing here to incriminate them.

He sat down, and Jerry, their new Prospect, picked up the bottle of Jameson and poured him a tall glass without him having to ask. He nodded his appreciation and took the glass.

"What do you think about this gig?" he asked his father. "You trust her enough for this?"

Hoosier took a long swallow of his whiskey before he answered. "I think we've been working with her for a year and a half, and she's been straight up with us. She's earned some trust."

"To ice a guy without knowing why, though. That's an assload of trust."

His father turned and considered him. "You got qualms?"

He didn't, actually. He trusted La Zorra enough. She was too savvy and careful to go after a high-pro guy like this DA without an excellent reason, and if she was keeping that reason close to her chest, she had a good reason for that, too. He'd never known a cooler customer. "No. But others at the table will. She is asking a lot. The money won't turn all their heads."

"Yep. Got some work to do." His father narrowed his eyes and examined him. "The money turning yours?"

Connor lit a smoke and took a drag, blowing it out before he answered. "No. The money's great, yeah. But it impressed me more because it feels like respect. She needs a job done, and she pays to get it done, instead of throwing her weight around in threats. I like working with this woman. She has all her marbles. She gets that this is a job."

"Yeah, agreed. She's pulling more and more power, though. At some point, they all start to believe their own legends. That's when the shit meets the fan."

As his father tipped his glass to his lips again, Maria, one of the more established girls, came up behind Connor and slid her hands over his shoulders. "You hanging around tonight, Connor?" she purred in his ear.

He liked Maria; she was a good girl, and she took care of the Horde, in any way they needed. She was hot, too. Normally, on a night like this, when he wasn't planning to go out and catch himself a little bunny, he'd turn right around and take Maria up on her offer.

But tonight, he wasn't into it. He guessed his head was too full of this La Zorra business. And he was restless. He couldn't put his finger on why. It was like he was lonely, or something. But not for the company of Maria.

So he patted her hand. "Don't think I am, puss." When she kissed his cheek and headed off to find company elsewhere, he turned to his dad. "I think I might go to the house, see what Mom's got in the fridge."

Hoosier drained his glass and pushed it away. "Now that sounds like a good night. Let's roll."

CHAPTER FOUR

About eight years earlier, when Pilar was just coming into the department, during a period of relative prosperity for the state of California and with a big tax boon, the county had done a massive restructuring of emergency services. They'd opened new stations, eliminated the use of private ambulance services, and expanded platoon numbers.

But prosperity always cycled with penury, and the state was now coming off a tight couple of years. Many public services had been curtailed and workers furloughed.

That hadn't been the case for emergency services. They'd avoided furloughs, and all the new fire stations had survived, but platoons had been cut and the work schedules at the fire stations had been adjusted to include a thirty-six-watch. After a thirty-six-hour watch, a platoon got three days off. The schedule was a mix of twenty-four and thirty-six-hour watches, with two or three days off between. A thirty-six hour watch could really be a bitch.

There were plenty of watches that were mostly served in the station, doing maintenance and busy work, getting a good night's sleep, eating good meals, working out, taking down time, maybe answering a couple of calls for a fender bender or some dope who'd gotten his arm caught in a fence or something. But there were also times, especially during the wildfire season, where the platoon spent almost all thirty-six hours in turnout gear, neck deep in fire and smoke.

They'd all learned early on to make the most of their off days because who the fuck knew what they'd face on the clock. Even a watch that had been fairly low-key could go to shit at any time. Like the last one.

Sometimes, for Pilar, making the most of her time off meant heading up into the mountains for a hike, or maybe snagging

Moore to go climbing with her at Joshua Tree. Other times, it meant shutting down as much as she could and just being quiet.

After the last watch, Pilar had needed quiet. She'd spent her first day off as a homebody. She'd gotten up, taken her run, then come home to shower and spend the rest of the day in baggy shorts and a beater. She'd done her laundry, tidied up her apartment, watered her plants and then camped on the sofa for the rest of the day reading and watching television.

The next day had been pretty much the same, except that she'd put on actual clothes and run errands and gotten some pampering, too—had her unmanageable mane trimmed, had a massage, went to the market. By that evening, Friday, when White called, she was ready to be social again. But White had wanted to try a new place, and the vibe had been too clubby for Pilar. Too much driving bass from the DJ, too many pretty people. Deciding she'd been wrong about being ready to be social again, Pilar had fended off the complaints and digs of her friends and headed home alone after only a couple of drinks.

She'd lain in bed that night wondering if her life weren't way too fucking small. It seemed strange, or even ungrateful, to have the kind of job she had, a job that made a real difference, that made her a goddamn hero, and then look around and think, *meh*.

She'd never felt it before, not in almost eight years on the job. She was proud of what she did, of who she was. But she spent her whole life with the same people. Her colleagues were her friends—her only friends. Other than her grandmother and brother, she had no one else in her life. In fact, she intentionally shut everybody else out. She didn't date; she fucked. She fucked actively and as often as she wanted, with a couple of fuck buddies or with a random hookup here and there, whichever struck her fancy at the time, but she couldn't remember the last time she'd gotten dressed up to have dinner with a man she liked.

There were reasons for that—she'd seen the stresses that this job put on relationships and families, and she knew why. Nothing about this life was normal—not the hours, not the work, not what it could do to your head. She thought her colleagues who tried to be with normal people and make a normal home were either nuts or stupid.

She couldn't imagine spending a watch picking up burned parts of people and animals and then having to go home and be a loving partner to somebody who'd been sitting in a nice, tidy office all day. All she wanted to do after a call like that was drink, fuck, and be left the hell alone. She was better off sticking with people who got that.

But that Friday night, she'd looked around at her friends, all of whom lived a life like hers, all of whom she loved and would die for without a blink, and thought *Damn. I know everything there is to know about all of you. My whole life is at this table.*

And it wasn't enough.

Abbie's mom was still clanging around in her head—not the scream, though that was there, too, but the complete focus she'd had on her little girl. Despite the woman's own extreme physical trauma—she'd been sitting in the driver's seat, bleeding out, half of both her legs gone—she'd never stopped talking to her little girl, trying to send strength to her, not knowing that Abbie wasn't there anymore to take it. Her little girl. Her own child.

For all the love and friendship Pilar had in her life, she didn't have love like that. Maybe it was for the best—Abbie's mom had had it and lost it horribly. But Pilar was feeling some kind of lack all of a sudden. It was perverse.

After a night spent wrestling those dark thoughts, Pilar nearly threw her phone out the window when the alarm chimed at five-thirty in the morning. She was tempted to pull a pillow over her head and try to sleep in, but she knew the danger in that. Screwing with her sleep schedule on her off hours only made her slow on her on hours. So up she got on this last off day, her mood dark and stormy.

As usual, she jumped up and grabbed the pull-up bar she had installed in her bedroom doorway. She did her fifty, and then, feeling more awake if no more content, she headed to her bathroom to get her morning started.

~oOo~

Her phone rang as she was towel-drying her hair. Draping the towel over her shoulders, she walked nude into the kitchen and checked the screen. Her grandmother. Pilar knew she'd leave a message if it was something important, so she stood at the counter, in the beam of the sun streaming through the bare windows, and waited.

When the alert came up, she checked her voice mail. *Call me,* mija. *Hugo didn't come home last night.*

Fuck. Hugo was her younger brother. Their grandmother called him a troubled soul. Sure, that was one way to put it. Half the slim piece of life she didn't spend at the barn she spent bailing her brother out of trouble.

Pilar returned the call, and her grandmother answered immediately. "Oh, thank goodness."

"What's up, Nana?" She put the phone on speaker and poured herself a glass of tomato juice.

"I'm worried, *mija.* He didn't come home, and he's not answering his phone. He came home from work last night and barely said anything to me. Just changed his clothes and left again."

Hugo worked in at a distribution center for an online retailer, loading boxes onto trucks. It was a decent job, and with his long history of short time on jobs, he'd been lucky to get it. Their grandmother had pulled some favors. Pilar expected Hugo to shit on that soon enough. He took obnoxious advantage of their grandmother, and he had from the time he was just little.

Renata Salazar was their mother's mother. Pilar and Hugo had different fathers, both of them bangers, and both of them dead. When, twenty years ago, the drive-by shooting that killed Hugo's father also killed their mother, Renata had gathered up her grandchildren and moved them to Madrone. She'd worked three jobs to put them in a decent house in a safe neighborhood and keep them fed and clothed. Consequently, Pilar had done a lot of the raising of Hugo.

And she'd done a piss-poor job of it.

He was twenty-five, five years younger than she. Despite the move they'd made to get them clear of the gangs, and despite their grandmother's hard work and strong will, Hugo was constantly on the precipice of repeating the mistakes of a father he barely even remembered. He hated to work, he loved to party, and he was always scamming for the easy buck, the easy high. He was buddies with some of the younger bangers in their fathers' gang, the Aztec Assassins. He wasn't a member, but it was a standing question whether he would be.

By the time he got through high school, actually managing to graduate and still not in the Assassins, they had both thought they'd gotten him through the tough part. But they'd been wrong. It was forever going to be the tough part for Hugo.

She drank down her juice and sighed. "Okay. I'll check around for him. You know if he's been talking to any of his asshole buddies in particular lately?"

"Don't swear, *mija*."

"Sorry, Nana." Pilar rolled her eyes. "Has he been?"

"No. He's been doing good lately—just going to work and staying home with me. I don't know what happened yesterday."

It could be any of a number of things—somebody he owed had come looking for payment, he'd fought with his boss, he'd been rejected by a woman, anything from a big deal to a small deal could set him off and start him burning everything down.

"I'll check around and let you know. Call me if he comes home or calls, *si*?"

"*Si, si. Gracias, mija.* You're my good girl."

Yep. She was the good girl.

~oOo~

After three hours doing the Hugo Velasquez Tour, Pilar found his rusty pickup. From its location, she knew he was with his friend Jaime, and that meant that he was hanging with the Assassins, either up in the roach motel Jaime called home or down the street at the High Life, the bar where the Assassins held their court.

Either way, she was deep into Assassins turf and not a moron. She drove her old Honda Element past Hugo's truck and parked in the lot of a Vons supermarket. For about the thousandth time, she texted her brother, this time saying that she knew where he was and he needed to get his ass out.

Like all the others, that text went unanswered. This wasn't Pilar's first rodeo; she knew that the most likely scenario was that Hugo was high out of his mind, either passed out with the bedbugs on Jaime's rancid couch, or with his head down on the bar at the High Life. But she'd been texting for hours, and it was unusual for him not to respond at all. A thin thread of anxiety wove through her frustration and anger. He could be in real trouble. The kind of people he was hanging out with made real trouble on a daily basis. She couldn't just shrug her shoulders and drive off. She had to know he was okay and get him home.

Alone, though, she couldn't. Jesus, an uninvited woman walking alone into either place would be lucky to be in one piece when she limped out. Hugo wasn't a member, so even if he were in a position to stand up for her, he could offer her no coverage. And if he was in trouble with them, or just passed out? Fuck. No.

She ran through her mental list of male friends, all of them strong, all of them good fighters, and any of them would be willing to help her out. But she'd be asking them to take on possibly life-threatening risk for her reprobate brother when they spent their working life at that kind of risk. She was a better friend than that.

The cops were out of the question—she had friends in law, sure. One of her fuck buddies was a San Bernardino County deputy. But ratting on the Assassins brought the kind of trouble best avoided. Nothing good would come from that.

Fuck. She knew no one who could help her, no one she'd be willing to put at risk.

And then a new thought rolled into her head. She maybe knew one person. Well, not *knew*, exactly. Except in the biblical sense. Connor. He was Horde. And she'd picked up a heavy protector vibe from him. Plus, the Horde had a rep for helping people out around town. Would it be completely loco to see if he could help?

Yeah. Completely loco. Besides, she didn't have his number or his last name or anything.

Then again, she knew where the clubhouse was, and it was only a couple of miles away, back inside the Madrone city limit. They had a big bike shop. If he worked there, maybe he'd be around.

Wait—what was she going to do? Amble in and ask her random fuck from a few nights ago to drop everything and come with her and save her brother from a fucking street gang? Her brother who might well not want to be saved? Yeah, that was beyond loco. That was just stupid.

But what other option did she have?

While she grappled with that question, her phone rang—her grandmother again. Her finger hovered over the "dismiss" button, but instead she answered. "Hi, Nana. I'm still looking." Mostly true.

"Oh, Pilar. I'm real worried now. His boss called the house. He didn't go to work or call or anything."

While Hugo was quick to quit a job and had been fired quite a few times, he never took a sick day, and he was never a no-show. That was a point of pride for him. When he decided he didn't want to go in, he'd call and quit without any notice, but he didn't, as he said, 'puss out' and just bail without a word. So they had the next anomaly in an otherwise familiar search mission.

"Okay, okay. I'm getting close, I think. I'll be in touch soon."

"Okay, *mija*. Call soon."

Pilar put her phone away and pulled out of the Vons lot, headed toward the Night Horde's bike shop. She couldn't remember the name of it, but she knew where it was.

~oOo~

The name was Virtuoso Cycles, and it was a gleaming, beautiful showroom, with gleaming, beautiful custom bikes arrayed across a glossy floor. Pilar had a bike of her own, one she loved, but it was just a stock Victory Hammer. She'd never been to this shop.

It was a Saturday afternoon, but still early enough that they were open, and she could hear the muffled sounds of power tools coming from some point beyond the back wall. The showroom, though, was empty except for an attractive young woman sitting at a reception desk. When Pilar walked toward the desk, the woman looked up and smiled a bright, professional smile.

"Welcome to Virtuoso Cycles. Can I help you?"

Still not believing she was going through with this, Pilar answered, "I'm looking for Connor? Is he around?"

The woman's smile changed a little, took on a knowing tinge. "Let me call back and see if he's available. Can I tell him who's asking?"

"Pilar." No point in saying more; her first name was all he knew—and he'd said he'd never known anyone else with her name.

While the woman made her call, Pilar turned and went to the ring of bikes. God, they were gorgeous. Some were just modified stock bikes, but a couple were obviously entirely unique builds. One was a spectacular black and brass—could it be brass?—piece of art that looked like a Renaissance-steampunk mashup. On the floor in front of it was a plaque that read: *Best of Show, Rat's Hole Bike Show, Sturgis, S.D. 2022. Designed & Built by Patrick Stavros*. On the plaque was a photograph of one of the bikers she'd seen the other night at The Flight Deck, and had seen there a few times, with long, dark-blond dreads and a bushy blond beard. He stood next to a guy wearing an ugly-ass green rat suit, like a debauched Mickey Mouse. The unsmiling biker was holding a big metal version of the ugly-ass rat, which was apparently the trophy that came with the win.

"Hey."

She turned at the gruff voice behind her and wasn't even three feet from Connor. He was wearing a black coverall, opened to the waist and showing a white, v-neck t-shirt, stained with grease. His sleeves were rolled back to his elbows. She'd seen a lot of his ink when he'd been in the ring at The Deck. Much of it seemed to have a Celtic flair, including the big piece on his right forearm, like a leather bracer carved with Celtic knots. In an arc just below his collarbone he had row of different knots. The hair on his chest obscured that ink slightly. Down his spine, she knew, he had the word HORDE in thick, Celtic-looking letters.

Around his neck he wore a gold crucifix, slightly larger than, but otherwise not unlike, the one she herself wore.

Damn, he was hot. Right in her wheelhouse, too: tall, brawny, and just the right kind of furry—the well-kept kind, only where it ought to be. Also apparently Catholic—of the Irish persuasion, she guessed.

Not that that should fucking matter.

"Hey," she answered, the picture of eloquence.

He smiled that melty smile, and for half a second, Pilar just about forgot that she was here because she needed help for a possibly dangerous problem.

"You need something, or d'ya just miss me?"

There wasn't any point in dancing around the problem—it was time sensitive, anyway. So she got to it. "I need something. A favor. Pretty big one."

His eyebrows went up, but he didn't say anything. He simply waited for her to continue.

"Um, okay." She was nervous—well, shit, of course she was. She was about to ask a near-stranger to rescue her idiot brother from the lair of a notorious gang. "I've got a problem and nobody to help me with it."

To that, he did respond. He reached out and took hold of her elbow, pulling her toward the seating area. She noticed that the actual ugly rat trophy was under glass on a square pedestal nearby.

Before he could push her into a leather chair, she pulled her arm back, careful not to be abrupt about it. She didn't need to sit; it wasn't that kind of problem. "My little brother isn't answering his phone, for almost a whole day now. I've been looking for him. I found his truck outside the Cypress Court Apartments."

Connor reacted to that, his head going back in a kind of reverse nod. A sign of recognition.

"You know it?" she asked.

"I do. That's Aztec turf. He in some trouble?"

"I don't know. He hangs around with some of those guys sometimes. His dad was an Assassin."

Again, his dark eyebrows lifted. "But he's not in?"

"No. He wasn't as of last night, anyway."

"When you say 'little brother'…"

"He's twenty-five."

"That's a man. If he wants in, then that's his call, isn't it?"

Yeah, she guessed it was. But Hugo wasn't a man, not really. The calendar didn't matter. He was still a child. "I know. But my grandma is worried, and I am, too. I just need to see that he's okay, and I can't go in on my own."

That earned a dry chuckle from Connor. "No, you can't." He sighed deeply and looked away, out the showroom window. "What help do you need, Pilar?"

She really did like the sound of her name in that gravel voice. "I need to be able to get into where he is and at least make sure he wants to be there. I need to try to get him out."

"You know where he is, or just where his truck is?"

"His friend lives in the Cypress. And the High Life is just down the road from there. He's in one of those places, I'm sure of it." She huffed in frustration and admitted the truth. "But no, I don't know where exactly. Because he won't answer his phone."

"It's on, though?"

"What?"

"His phone—it's on, ringing before it goes to voice mail?"

She thought about that for a second. "Last I checked, yeah." Pulling her phone out of her pocket, she dialed Hugo. It rang five times. "Yeah, it's on."

He nodded and took her phone out of her hand. "Okay. That should make it pretty easy to nail him down, I think. Come with me." And then he took her hand and led her across the showroom and through a black door at the side.

~oOo~

She'd been sitting at the bar in the Night Horde clubhouse, drinking a bottle of beer that Connor had handed her before he'd gone off somewhere.

The room she was in looked like a big, ratty bar. Grungy and a little smelly. The opposite of the high-end gleam of the showroom fifty feet away.

There weren't any guys around except one kid, whom Connor had called Jerry, who was stocking the bar and putting clean glasses away. He ignored her, other than to eye her bottle every now and then, as if waiting for when she'd need another.

Otherwise, she was basically alone. There were a couple of women around, but they were in the kitchen, talking and laughing, and Pilar knew she wasn't invited—not that she would have wanted to be, anyway. So she sat, she sipped, and she waited.

Jerry had just handed her a second bottle when Connor came back into the room, now dressed in jeans and his kutte, and trailing another biker. This one had a heavy, dark beard and inch-wide gauges in his ears. Industrial piercings, too. And a ring through his bottom lip. Kind of punk. Cool. And he had vivid, bluish-green eyes. These Horde dudes were hot.

"Pilar, this is Sherlock." As Pilar and Sherlock nodded their greeting, Connor went on, "He got a lock on your brother. He's at the High Life."

"Fuck." She'd been holding onto a slim hope that he was wasted at Jaime's, playing some stupid video game. If he was at the High Life, then he was wound up somehow with the Assassins, most likely.

"Yeah. You know, we don't have a relationship with the Aztecs. We barge into their house, they'll take it poorly."

She couldn't ask them to do that. She'd just have to go in on her own and take her chances. Her family, her problem. "I understand. Thanks for finding where he was, though. That helps." Intending to go out the nearest door and find her way back to her Element, she slid off the barstool.

But Connor wrapped his big paw around her arm. "Hold on. I talked to our President, and he okayed it, so we're going in. Three of us. I just want you to be aware that this could turn into a clusterfuck, and I don't see a way of keeping you out of there—your brother doesn't know us, so you'll have to go in with us."

Jesus, the whole club was going to help her? That was more than she'd expected—a lot more. It was on the tip of her tongue to back out, to apologize and say she didn't want to put them at risk. And that was true. But she'd come here, and she'd asked, and they'd stepped up. It seemed disrespectful to say 'no, thanks' after all that.

And she needed them.

"I understand. Thank you."

Connor nodded and gave her that smile. "Always happy to help a lady in need." Then he winked.

Normally, she'd have side-eyed a smarmy line like that. But right then, in this moment, this context, while he was sliding a Glock into a holster, and after he'd helped her with a different kind of need a few days before, it wasn't smarmy. It was just funny and charming.

So she laughed and winked back.

CHAPTER FIVE

Madrone was a quiet, picturesque, mostly bland little town. Until urban sprawl and crazy real estate prices had pushed the workers of Los Angeles so far out, this part of Southern California had been little more than desert broken up by a few small towns and the lands of a few intrepid ranchers. Aside from a core area that had been around since the 1800s, when a little one-horse town had risen up around a train depot, and one area on the western edge of town that was on the seedy side, the rest of the Madrone city limits bounded middle-class and upper-middle-class developments, the kind that had gates at their entrances or at least brick pillars holding brass plaques with names that started with "The" or ended with "Estates": "The Commons," "The Meadow," "Mountainview Estates," like that. The commercial district was mostly strip malls and office parks designed to suit the architecture of the neighborhood. A city ordinance required that all signage be low to the ground, so as not to disrupt the view.

Because that was what Madrone had going for it more than anything else: three different mountain ranges rimmed the horizon in three directions. On a clear day, you could stand anywhere in town and feel like heaven itself was in reach.

In the odd way of community development, a couple of towns that abutted Madrone were nowhere near as well-heeled. It was thus possible to cross a street that served as a city limit and leave a tidy, landscaped neighborhood to enter a desiccated husk of a town that had been obliterated by one or more of the cyclical state downturns.

Aztec Assassins turf was in one such area. As Connor, Sherlock, and Diaz rode, taking positions around Pilar's little SUV, they crossed Calaveras Road and dropped about four tax brackets. The view at the horizons was the same, and just as close, though the roads here weren't designed so carefully to make the most of it. The buildings had been erected with a desultory attention, and their care had only dwindled from there.

The High Life was housed in a single-story building at the end of a block that had mostly been abandoned. There was a bakery, a laundromat, and an electronics repair shop, but otherwise the storefronts on the block were empty. A major factor for the lack of vitality was the High Life itself, Connor knew. It wasn't the kind of bar you happened upon. It wasn't on anybody's barhopping itinerary. It didn't attract the kind of people that kept a neighborhood vibrant. Though it ostensibly did business as a bar, it was really the Aztecs' clubhouse, and anyone who drank there was a friend. Everybody else stayed away.

The Horde had no beef with the Aztecs—yet—but they had no working relationship, either. They stayed out of each other's way, letting Calaveras Road serve as a kind of force field. The Aztecs dealt drugs, but those drugs came from a different source, one that had a stable truce with La Zorra.

As Pilar and the Horde pulled up across the street from the High Life, Connor knew that what they were about to do, if it went badly, could ripple out and cause a lot of problems. Beefing with the Aztecs could, if it got bad enough, disrupt a truce between two drug cartels, and that could mean open warfare in two countries.

All because Connor was feeling chivalrous.

That wasn't entirely true; it wasn't just on him. This was what they did, why they were respected in Madrone, and why people looked the other way at some of their less savory activities: the Horde helped where they could. Pilar had come asking, and the club had obliged. Still, this Saturday afternoon was likely to be a lot more exciting than Connor had expected.

As they gathered on the sidewalk, Pilar nodded at Diaz. "Token brown face to meet the spic bangers?" she asked him.

Connor was offended, and opened his mouth to say so and point out that a bitch asking for help like this should try a little fucking courtesy, but Diaz grinned and answered, "Not like that. I volunteered. But it's true that these assholes don't speak Spanish."

Connor and Sherlock both flipped him off.

Pilar made a scoffing sound. "They all speak English in there. They're not just off the truck."

"Yeah," Diaz answered. "But it'd be good to catch any side talk, you know?"

"True, yeah. But *I* speak Spanish." She looked up at Connor, who was still struggling with that spike of irritation. When he didn't respond to her comment, she huffed and added, "So…what?"

He looked at his brothers and then across the street to the entrance of the bar. A tall neon sign with a martini glass and a flashing olive glowed in the nearing dusk. This area had no restrictions on the height of its commercial signs. "We go in. We ask nicely. We work from there." He glanced down at Pilar, who was binding her mane into a lush ponytail at the back of her head. "You stay behind us. Understood?"

She shook her head. "I thought I was going in with you because you need me to talk to Hugo."

He hated having to explain the obvious. Biting back a sigh, he said, "We need you in there. But you're not armed, and you are female. These guys have a bad rep with women. So you stay behind us. We're your cover. Got it?"

Without answering, she turned back to her Honda and hit her fob to unlock it. Then she opened the passenger door and ducked in. When she came back, she was pushing a little handgun into the back of her jeans.

"Now I'm armed."

Connor reached around and grabbed her gun. When she tried to grab it back, he pushed her away. "No way, puss. Last fucking thing we need is you starting some drama waving this thing around. I don't even know if you can shoot."

"I can. I'm good at it."

"Well, someday you can show me. But not now." He tucked the gun into his own waistband.

When she went for him again, Sherlock snatched her and held her back. "He's right, sweetheart. We can't add any more variables to this equation."

Shrugging free of Sherlock's loose hold, she glared at Connor and opened her mouth to say something that would, he knew, be irritating in one way or another. So he grabbed her chin in his hand and closed her mouth. "I know you're all up in your girl power and shit, but you want our help, you do it our way. Got it?"

This time, she did answer that question, with a not-very-convincing nod.

"I want to hear you say it, puss."

"I got it. And don't call me puss."

"You could take a lesson in gratitude, *puss*."

At that, she had the grace to look abashed. "Sorry. You're right. I'm just…"

She didn't finish, but she didn't have to. "I know. Let's see if we can get this done. Our goal is to bring your brother out quietly. If he wants to stay, are you looking for us to make him leave?"

"No. If he wants to be there, then that's his call. I just need to know he's okay."

"Good. If he wants to go but they don't want him to, then we'll do what we can. But that'll be messy as fuck—and that's why you stay behind us. Understand?"

She nodded. "Yeah, I do. I will."

"Shoulda worn vests," Sherlock muttered.

"We go in wearing vests, and they know we expect trouble—so that's what we'd get. We're trying to get out of here without firing a shot." He looked across the street again, unsnapping the guard on his holster. "Okay, let's do this."

They crossed the street. Connor was the first one through the door, feeling the weight of his Glock against his ribs. Diaz came in behind him. Then Pilar, and then Sherlock, covering the rear.

Connor widened his vision to see the entire scene, adjusting quickly to the darker space. The lighting made the kind of gloom that was typical for a place like this.

Hip-hop music played on a jukebox near the door, and a girl danced alone in front of it. Two men sat at the bar. One guy stood behind it, paused in the act of wiping the top. Two men playing pool to the right. In the back corner, at a big round table, five men. Three women, as well—two of them being passed around to be pawed by them all. One woman sat on the lap of the man facing into the room.

Ten men, all showing Aztec colors. No Hugo, apparently. Connor glanced over his shoulder and sent Pilar a silent question, making sure. She shook her head and shrugged subtly.

Okay, fuck. If Hugo wasn't here, then they'd come in with no good reason. The man in the corner was their leader, Raul Esposito. As the Horde walked forward into the room, all the men came toward them, hemming them in. Only Esposito remained seated.

A massive, shaved dude with three teardrops inked at the corner of his eye and an elaborate sugar skull on his throat stepped directly into Connor's path. "You lost, *ese?*"

Connor smiled, keeping it friendly. "No, friend. We're here to ask for some help."

Baldy grinned nastily, and Connor's fingers twitched. Then the guy turned and looked back at his boss. When he stepped to the side, Connor knew that, at least, they'd get an audience.

Some crews in San Bernardino County, and everywhere else, ran like businesses, saw value in their territory and the people in it. The Horde was one such, and they worked with several others in one way or another. But the Aztecs were like the Dirty Rats. Bottom feeders who got off on tearing shit down.

He fucking hated this piece of shit gang that solved every problem with blood and noise. He hated the way they lorded over this rundown turf and never put anything into their community but drugs and death. They acquired their wealth by scraping the last dregs of hope from the people who lived around them, and they flaunted it in front of the same people. He would have preferred to have come in here with two AKs strapped to his back and just strafed the shit out of every last one of these assholes.

But the Aztecs had friends bigger than themselves, and the ripples reached far. He kept his smile plastered to his face and looked down at Raul Esposito.

Esposito was older than Connor—late forties, maybe early fifties. His dark hair was slicked tightly back against his head. A long, wide scar bisected his face at an angle, from his temple, over his hooked nose, to his jaw on the opposite side. When he smiled, it was impossible to believe it could be sincere.

He gave Connor that smile now and pushed the girl off his lap. She teetered off toward the bar. "The great and famous Night Horde Motorcycle Club needs help from some *cholos* down the block? Can it be?"

"I guess so. Our friend here is looking for her brother. She's worried. Just wondering if you might help us find him."

Esposito tilted his head, and Connor took one step to the side, enough to let Esposito see Pilar but not so far that he couldn't cover her if he needed to.

"Pilar. What you hanging with these boys for? You want some bad-boy dick, we can give you plenty right here." He laughed, and his lackeys laughed with him.

Pilar shuddered ever so slightly, and Connor felt his fingers tense and curl into his palms. He sensed the same tension in his brothers.

"Just looking for Hugo, Raul. Is he here?" There was a catch in her voice, and Connor realized that she was scared. Of course she would be, should be, but it affected him more than seemed reasonable.

Esposito leaned back in his chair and dropped his hands into his lap in a dramatic gesture of disappointment. "Your brother, baby girl, is a bad boy, too. He took something from me. He has a debt to pay off." He nodded toward a man at the back. He said something in Spanish, but Connor could barely order a beer in Tijuana, so he had no idea what. Diaz, though, changed his stance, moving into battle readiness.

"The door," he muttered at Connor's side.

Connor pushed Pilar fully behind him, and Sherlock came in tight. They made a circle. And Esposito's man opened the door.

Behind the door wasn't somebody ready to attack them. In fact, none of the Aztecs had moved except the guy who'd opened the door. What was behind it, and was now in full view of the room, was a man Connor assumed to be Hugo. He was stripped to a pair of soiled and bloody khakis and bound to a support beam. His face was grotesquely swollen, and his chest and arms were horribly bruised and striped with bloody gashes. He'd been beaten and whipped.

At first, Connor thought he was either dead or unconscious, but then he lifted his drooping, gagged head. At about the same time, Pilar peered around Connor's side and gasped loudly. "Hugo!" Connor shot out his arm to block her just as she surged toward her brother.

Hugo reacted weakly but emotionally, yelling around his gag and shaking his head.

Connor sighed. This was a problem. Hugo was obviously not okay, and Connor had told Pilar they'd help. But if her brother had stolen from the Aztecs, then he had to pay the price for that. The Horde was not in the business of meddling in other people's business, not even scummy assholes like Raul Esposito. How he was going to get Pilar out of here and keep her out, he did not know, but he wasn't going to start a beef with this street gang over a guy he didn't know getting what was coming to him.

"Yeah, okay. We'll leave you to it, then. Sorry to interrupt your work."

At his side, Pilar said, "What?" and jumped forward again, but Sherlock grabbed her and held on.

Connor turned and took hold of her arm. "Keep chill until we're outside," he gritted at her ear.

But when they took a step toward the front door, the Aztecs closed around them. Nine men.

"I'll keep Pilar," Esposito said behind him. Connor turned again and faced him, and the bastard, still at the table, let that nasty smile slide up his bisected face. "You boys keep to your white bitches with their yellow hair. This one's one of ours. And she's of use to me. Leave her and go."

Connor still had his hand around Pilar's arm, and he could feel every emotion moving through her body in the tension rolling under his palm. He moved his thumb back and forth over her bicep, making an attempt to keep her calm.

She hadn't spoken. In fact, she'd said very little since they'd come in—and that was good. But her eyes were a riot of bad feelings. Still, she was letting him lead.

And he was about to lead them all into chaos. "Sorry, *ese*," Connor replied. "Can't do that. She's with me."

"Greedy motherfucking *gueros* think the whole world is yours for the taking. You leave her with me, or you and me, we have a problem."

Connor shifted his shoulder and let Pilar go so that he was ready to draw. "Then we have a problem."

He felt movement at his back, *on* his back, and he knew what it was. But before he could react, Pilar had pulled her gun from his waistband and aimed at Esposito. Jesus fuck.

Controlling his initial reaction to grab her and disarm her, Connor stood pat and made ready. Right now, she had the floor, and trying to change that would blow this room up. He sent a quick glance to his brothers, conveying to them that they should hold, too.

She was shielded by the bodies of the Horde men, and the Aztecs didn't realize that she'd drawn until she was aimed and still. "Anybody draws, and I'll just shoot," she said, her voice clear and steady. Her head tilted toward Connor. "That goes for everybody."

Despite her threat, the Aztecs around her reached for their weapons, but then Esposito put up his hand, and they all stopped. For a moment, the room was perfectly quiet. Then Esposito made that snaky sneer and turned his attention to Connor. "You let a little girl fight your fights for you, *ese*?"

Connor shrugged. He and his new little friend were going to have this shit out, but not here. "I'm secure enough to take help where it comes."

"I want Hugo," Pilar cut in, her aim still true. "Just let me have my brother, and we'll get out."

Esposito returned his attention to the woman with a gun pointed at his head. They stared at each other. Meanwhile, Connor tried to keep track of the whole room, looking for where the danger would start. Baldy would be his first target. That guy was looking for blood.

But Esposito nodded. "Sam. Cut him loose."

Baldy turned. "What?"

Without looking away from Pilar, Esposito snarled, "Don't fuckin' question me. Cut him loose."

While Sam did as he was told, Esposito cocked his head at Pilar. "You got balls, *chica*." He nodded sidelong at Connor. "More than him. So I'll let you and your pussy friends leave. But you know this ain't over. Your brother pays his debt, or I take it from somebody else." He looked her up and down. "You, maybe. You got some assets I might want."

Sam pushed Hugo toward their little circle, and Connor caught him. The guy was dead weight, barely conscious, so he hoisted him over his shoulder. Fucker stank to high heaven. "Let's go. Back out, puss. Come on."

Pilar nodded without breaking the lock of her attention on Esposito.

Keeping to their wary circle, the Horde, Pilar, and her troublesome brother eased backward out of the High Life and onto the street.

Once outside, they all drew their weapons, expecting the Aztecs to follow. But they were alone on the dark, dead street.

Connor got Hugo into the passenger seat of Pilar's Element. "Where you taking him?"

"He needs a hospital."

"Hospital means questions."

"Look at him!"

Connor did. The asshole was fucked up bad, and he wasn't willing to drag his carcass into the clubhouse. He'd been enough trouble as it was. "Okay. We gotta get moving. You found him on the street like this. By his house, someplace not here. Right?"

Getting it, she nodded. "Yeah, okay." After a beat, she added, "You were gonna leave him."

"I was. If your brother's tangled up with these guys of his own will, then that's nothing I want to meddle in. But I wasn't gonna serve you up to them. Fuck that."

She stared up at him for a couple more beats, just long enough for Connor to shift and prepare to remind her that they needed to beat hell out of here.

But she spoke before he could. "Okay. I get it. Thank you for your help."

"We're not done yet, puss. We're riding you out of here." And he and she were going to have a fucking talk.

"You don't have to—"

"Shut up, and let's ride." With that, he went to his bike and mounted up.

~oOo~

In the ER parking lot, Connor dismounted and put up his hand to hold his brothers off from doing the same. They weren't followed, so the coast seemed clear enough for now.

"You sure?" Sherlock asked.

"Yeah. Got it from here. You get back, catch Hooj up on this shit."

Diaz and Sherlock exchanged a look, then they nodded in unison and pulled out. Connor took off his helmet. After a thought, he shrugged off his kutte, folded it, and stowed it in a saddlebag. Going into the ER with this douche while he was wearing colors could cause problems. Then he went to Pilar's car and opened the passenger door. Hugo was unconscious.

He hoisted her brother back onto his shoulder.

"I can take it from here," she protested.

"Too late. And we're still not done. We need to have a serious talk. So let's get him seen to."

~oOo~

Connor sat in the ER waiting room and did what the room was there for. He waited. Until he could grab Pilar and get some information and set some parameters, he wasn't going anywhere. He'd fielded a couple of calls from his father, but since he didn't have any more information yet, Hoosier had stopped calling.

It was a pretty sure bet that they were now beefing with the Aztecs, and they had to control the ripple effect to every extent that they could. But there were a lot of unknowns yet—several of which had to do with Pilar and her brother. The club had to decide whether this one foray into helpfulness was the last favor they'd do for them, or if they'd taken them on as a responsibility. To know that, they'd need to know how the fuck Hugo had gotten himself into the position they'd pulled him from.

Pilar came through the doors to the treatment room once, but she ignored Connor. Her attention was devoted entirely to a small, thin woman who'd been standing at the reception desk. The woman was older—elderly, in fact—but her back was straight and her hair and clothes were stylish. Pilar hugged her, hard, and after a few exchanged words, they went back through the doors.

And Connor kept waiting.

Finally, both Pilar and the woman Connor assumed was her grandmother came back through the doors, and this time they headed his way. He stood and met them in the middle of the room.

Pilar spoke first. "Nana, this is Connor. He and his friends helped us today."

The older woman smiled and held out a spotted hand. "Thank you, Connor. So much. I am Renata Salazar." Like Pilar, her grandmother had almost no accent. Just a little linger over her Rs.

He took her hand and gave it a light squeeze. "Happy to help, Mrs. Salazar."

Smiling at the respect, she patted his hand and then let go and turned to Pilar. "I'll stay with Hugo. You have done enough for him today, and you have work in the morning. You go."

"No, Nana—"

"Go, *mija*. I mean it."

And just like that, the demanding, rebellious woman Connor was getting to know dropped her head and nodded meekly. "Okay. Keep me posted, though."

"Of course." Renata Salazar squeezed her granddaughter's face between her old hands. "*Te quiero, mija.*"

"*Te quiero,* Nana."

With a pat to Pilar's cheeks and a nod to Connor, Renata went back to the ER treatment rooms.

Connor and Pilar stood in the middle of the waiting area. It was Saturday evening, becoming Saturday night, and the place was filling up. He put his hand on her shoulder. "How is he?"

She shrugged. "Still out, and a fucking mess. But he'll heal. And then I'm going to kill his stupid ass."

Knowing she was exaggerating, he chuckled a little and squeezed her shoulder. "We need to talk, puss."

"I really hate that you call me that. So stop. But yeah, I know we need to talk." She looked around the crowded room, gnawing on her bottom lip. "I live here in Old Towne, just a few blocks off. Want to come over?"

He grinned—that offer had surprised him. "To your place? You sure?"

Her eyes narrowed. "To *talk*. But I'd say you've earned some trust."

"Okay, then. I'll follow you."

CHAPTER SIX

Pilar opened the door and stepped through, making way for Connor to follow. As he came in, she flipped a light switch, and a floor lamp came on, illuminating her living room in a warm glow.

He looked around, taking in her collection of mismatched stuff she thought of as 'vintage funk'—which sounded better than 'thrift shop cheap.' Actually, she was proud of her place. She liked to fix up old furniture, and had done just about all the different treatments she'd ever heard of, from decoupage to crackle.

He ran a hand over a table she'd painted three different colors. "Cool place."

"Thanks." She closed the door and turned the deadbolt. "You want a drink or something? I've got beer, tequila, vodka, some others. Oh—I could make coffee, too."

"You got Jameson or Jack?"

"Sorry, no. I think there's some Jim Beam." Doug, her deputy fuck buddy, was a Jim Beam fan. He'd brought a bottle over a while back.

Laughing, he shrugged out of his kutte and laid it over the back of a worn, red-velvet chair. "Not the same thing, pu—ilar. But it'll do."

With a smirking nod, she acknowledged his attempt not to call her 'puss'—which had been making her want to punch him in the throat—and went into the kitchen to serve up drinks.

"You want ice or water or something?" she called while she filled her own glass to make a vodka on the rocks with lemon.

Tequila made her horny. Vodka chilled her out. On this night, chill was vastly preferable to horny.

"Nah, just straight," he called back.

When she came back in, Connor was staring at a painting hanging over her sofa. She went over and handed him his glass. "You like it?"

He took a long drink before he answered. "I don't know. It's kinda fucked up."

She looked at the piece in question: an acrylic painting of a monochrome skull with a near-photorealistic dark red rose growing through an eye. Her tattoo artist had done it; botanicals were his specialty. "Why fucked up?"

He made a noncommittal grunt and turned away. "I don't know. Feels dark. We need to talk about your brother."

Yeah. Great. She indicated the sofa, and he sat. She took the damask chair on the other side of the glass-topped table with the driftwood base that served as a coffee table. "Okay. Let's talk."

Not knowing for sure what it was he needed to know, Pilar sat and waited for him to ask a question.

"You got any idea what your brother's into with those guys? You said he was friends with them—they didn't seem so friendly."

"He hangs out with some of the younger guys. His buddies weren't there, though." It had occurred to her that Jaime and the others could have served Hugo up to Raul.

"Esposito said he took something. You know what?"

"No. No clue. And Hugo wasn't awake when I left. I'm sorry I dragged you into all this, but I swear I don't know what the hell he's fallen into here." A little stream of worry trickled through her, wondering if he was safe at the hospital, if her grandmother was safe with him. But she also knew that those guys wouldn't stir up trouble there. Too many people, too many cameras, too much security. Besides, Raul had let him go. They'd let him heal and then they'd come for him again. In the meantime, they knew he wouldn't rat.

"You said *his* dad was an Aztec—you don't have the same dad?"

"No. But mine wasn't much better than his." She decided that the trust he'd earned warranted some disclosure on her part. "Mine was an Assassin, too. It's complicated—and anyway, they're both dead. Our mother, too. Our grandma raised us from the time I was eleven and Hugo was six."

He cocked his head like he was understanding more of the picture. "That's what Esposito meant when he said you were one of them—it wasn't just a Hispanic thing."

"No. We're family whether we want to be or not, and they like to keep the family close. They've been on Hugo to go in since he was fifteen."

"Why didn't he? No offense, but he's not coming off like a guy who's strong enough to hold them off."

"He's not. But Raul's got a thing about our grandmother. She doesn't want Hugo in, so Raul lays off him a little."

"What do you mean he's got a thing? Like a crush?" His surprised puzzlement turned his face into a caricature.

"God, no! Ugh! No—he's, I don't know, a little scared of her. She took care of him when he was a kid. My mom and dad and Hugo's dad and Raul all grew up together. They were close. Like I said, it's complicated."

Connor either wasn't interested in the bizarre family soap opera that she'd just hinted at, or he wasn't shocked by it, because he didn't ask more about it. "Not scared enough to back off you all completely, though."

"It's worse lately. The last couple of years. I stay out of Hugo's shit, except when I'm cleaning it up, so I don't know all he's into. But he's a taker. Like a fucking sponge. Maybe he decided to try to get over on Raul."

"That'd be pretty stupid."

"That'd be my brother."

She was done with her drink and wanted another. Connor had emptied his some time back; she stood and went to the sofa. "Want another?"

"Sure, thanks." He held up his empty glass. When her hand went around it, over his hand, he pulled back a little—not enough to take the glass back, just enough to pull on her slightly. "The Horde is in this, now. That scene tonight is gonna play out some way."

"I know. I'm sorry."

He shook his head, his eyes holding hers. "No need. We knew going in we could be beating a wasp nest. We'll deal. Your brother's safe while he's in the hospital. They won't make a scene there. But Raul's sniffing at you now, too. You need to watch your back."

Now Pilar shook her head. "I know how he works. He's not as interested in me as it looked. I'm just a *puta* to him. He was stirring you guys up. He saw you shielding me and knew going for me would get you aggressive. He was picking a fight with you."

She could see that Connor hadn't run that probability. He sat back, his gears spinning, and let go of the glass. "Fuck. You're right."

"I know. And I'm sorry. I didn't know that would happen."

He gave her a wry smile. "I could use that refill."

"Yeah. Just a sec."

While she refreshed their drinks, Pilar let her brain run loose over the events of the past day. She'd spent most of it searching for her brother. She'd ended up dragging a whole fucking MC into her family's problems and had made an even bigger problem for them.

As frustrated as she'd been that afternoon, being told to be quiet and meek and let the men handle things, as angry and determined as she'd been in the High Life, she'd also noticed and appreciated the way Connor had been attuned to her, keeping his position relative to hers all the time, shielding her. That attention had gotten him and his club into some trouble.

But the most potent part of that whole fiasco had been the way he'd gone with it when she'd taken her gun back and pointed it at Raul's head. Connor hadn't tried to assert himself then, and he had yet to try to shove it down her throat that she'd been out of line. He'd simply adopted what she'd done into his plan, and he'd been impervious to Raul's taunts about standing behind a woman. He'd let her lead.

They'd managed to rescue Hugo fairly peacefully, at least in that moment. Now her brother was in the hospital, beaten half to death, but rescued. And Connor the Protective Biker was sitting in her living room.

It had been a very long time since she'd had a man over whom she wouldn't have already called a friend. Somebody she trusted to know her.

This was her space, where she lived, in more than simply physical terms. Half her life was spent in the barn, but that was a different Pilar, or at least a particular side of her. That Pilar was a tough-ass bitch who talked smack with the boys and could sling an unconscious man over her shoulders and carry him out of a burning building. That wasn't Pilar at all. That was Cordero.

Here, she could be more than that. Or less; maybe it was *less* that she needed to be at home. She could be vulnerable. She could pretty up her furniture and talk to her plants. She could watch the *telenovelas* she loved. She could go out to get her hair and nails done, to get a massage, to shop for ridiculously fancy shoes she'd never wear. She could be a girl. She could be Pilar.

She didn't let many people see that person, and she wasn't sure she wanted to show her to Connor. But she did like that he was here.

She took the refilled glasses back out to the living room. Connor was on his phone; he turned to her and smiled as she brought him his drink.

"Yeah, Dad. Makes sense. Okay. I'll just see you tomorrow, then." He ended the call and put his phone away. "Interesting day, huh?"

When he took his glass, she said, "I *can* shoot, you know."

"I saw your stance. I believe you now. But then it was a variable, like Sherlock said. You gotta control the variables in a situation like that, as much as you can." He took a drink of bourbon. She was still standing over him, sipping her drink, watching his throat move under his beard as he swallowed. With a curious look, he added, "You gonna stand there staring down at me? You want me to go?"

"No." She didn't. And she didn't like that she didn't. It wasn't booze or adrenaline or any of that making her horny. This guy right here, sitting on her sofa, big and brawny without being some he-man pig, was doing the job all on his own. She didn't like the way she liked him.

She put her knee on the sofa and straddled his lap.

His smile at that was of the melty variety, and he opened his arms to make way. "Well, hello."

She sat down on his thighs and finished her drink, turning to set the glass on the table behind her. "Hi. This okay?"

His smile lost no heat as he said, "I'm usually the one asking that question."

"Is *that* okay?"

"Sure." He finished his drink, and she took the glass from him and set it next to hers.

"I'm up at five-thirty, and I have to be at work at seven. You can't stay the night."

"Understood." He slid his hands up the outside of her thighs and over her hips. "You really just go for what you want, don't you?"

"Flirting is a waste of valuable time."

"I don't know. I like to flirt. It's part of it, like verbal foreplay. If I can get a girl wet with just my voice, that's hot for both of us."

"I'm already wet. And I can tell your motor's revving." She rocked her hips over his erection to prove her point.

He chuckled and fed one hand into her hair, holding her head. "Jesus, Pilar. Slow down. It's not that late."

She didn't want to slow down. She didn't want to flirt. She wanted to fuck. And she had the answer to her earlier internal question. As much as she liked the sound of her given name in his gruff voice, it was safer to keep Pilar away. "Most people call me by my last name: Cordero."

"Is that what you want me to call you?"

"Yeah."

With his hand in her hair, he brought her close while his other hand slid up under her shirt. His callused fingers played over her skin. "Well, Cordero. You got a bed in this place? I want to get naked this time." Without waiting for an answer, he kissed her.

He had a great mouth and a fantastic tongue, and the feel of his beard against her skin made her moan. As their tongues slid together and his hands moved up her back, under her shirt, she rocked on him, dragging the ridge of his hard cock over her core.

Fuck, she was hot for this guy. Too hot for him. Things were getting complicated, in her head, if nowhere else.

But she couldn't bring herself to care. She wanted him to stay, at least for a little while.

She lifted his t-shirt and scratched her nails over his chiseled belly until he groaned and tore his mouth away from hers. "Bed, baby. I want to strip you naked and fuck you in your bed."

He didn't wait for her to respond. He just grabbed her hips and stood up, taking her with him. "Point me in the right direction."

Not liking to be carried, she squirmed, kicking her legs free of his hold and landing on the ground where she belonged.

He lifted a dark eyebrow at her. "Most girls like that."

"This woman doesn't."

"Fuck, Cordero. You're wearing me out while my fly's still zipped." He slapped her ass—that, she liked. "Fine, then. *Lead* me in the right direction."

Grinning, she grabbed his big hand and led him to her bedroom.

Once there, she turned and grabbed at his t-shirt, pulling him close. He reached back to pull it over his head from behind, and once he was free of it, he bent down to kiss her again. He took her mouth firmly, and she pushed him away and then came back, taking the control for herself. In that way of give and take—or, really, take and take—they tore their own and each other's clothes off, casting pieces aside carelessly.

When they were standing naked before each other, Pilar put her hands on his chest, partly to hold him off for a second, and partly just to have her hands on him. He was her perfect type, and she ran her hands over his chest, his shoulders, his arms, his belly, loving the feel of hair and muscle smoothing past her palms.

She skimmed over his hips, his thick, muscular thighs, the glorious rod between them. *¡Madre de Dios!*

He stood and let her touch all she wanted, a small, enigmatic smirk crinkling the corners of his eyes.

Her hands dropped down his arms, and she focused on that forearm tattoo, the bracer. Smoothing her thumb over the entwined Celtic knots, she asked, "Is this a warrior thing?"

He shrugged and turned his arm in her hold. "Covers an old tat. It was big, so the coverage needed to be bigger. But yeah, I'm the club SAA. You know what that is?"

She did. There was a patch on his kutte that said as much. And that was hot, too—she understood the Protector vibe he had going. "Sergeant at Arms. Club badass, basically."

He laughed. "Close enough."

"Are you Irish?" She picked up his crucifix with her other hand. "Irish Catholic?"

"I guess so. My old man is Irish and Scottish—by way of Indiana. But he's into his roots. Me, I just like the knots. And my old man." He shook her hands off and pulled her close, pushing his erection into her belly. "Baby, you said you didn't want to waste time. If we're gonna play the get-to-know-you game, can we do it later? Because you standing here in nothing but that fine body is making it tough to think about who I am."

Taking his hands, she walked backward to the bed. When she bumped up against it, she dropped his hands and slid up onto the mattress, keeping eye contact as she did so.

He followed right with her, easing up along her side, one hand sliding up her body as he settled next to her. "Fuck," he murmured, clutching her thigh. "You are like nothing I've ever felt before." He dipped his head and sucked a nipple between his teeth, and at the same time he slid a hand between her legs, groaning as his fingers moved slickly through her ready wet. He pushed a finger inside her, and when she moaned and rolled her hips toward that touch, he added another, pushing into her with some force.

The way she liked. She spread her legs wide, encouraging him, and whispered, "Fuck yeah, come on."

Pulling his fingers out, he turned his attention to her clit, rolling and rubbing and pinching with his rough fingers until her nerves were frayed and on fire. All the while, he suckled her breasts, moving back and forth, his beard lightly abrading her skin. When she knew she was on the express to an orgasm and she'd thrown her arms back and grabbed her wrought-iron headboard in her hands, he released her nipple and lifted up to look down at her. She met his eyes, and at that moment, he slid his fingers back inside her and fucked her hard and fast—*so* hard and fast—with his hand.

"Oh my fucking *GOD!*" she gasp-screamed, the sound practically inhuman even to her own distracted ears.

"You like it hard, baby?" His eyes glittered with heat.

"Yes, fuck yes," she grunted. And then he went even harder. He took her right up to the point of pain, her favorite place to be, and when she came, she flailed and shook so hard that the headboard slammed into the wall over and over. As the orgasm finally crested and crashed, she curled into Connor, grabbing at him, biting down on his shoulder.

When it was over, she had trouble making her body unclench. With that gravelly chuckle he had, Connor eased her off of him and back down to the bed. "You okay?"

Before she could answer, there was a violent knocking on the wall, and Connor looked up at it, surprised.

But Pilar laughed. "That's Mrs. Lee. Our bedrooms share a wall. We probably woke her up."

He looked back down at her, his brow creased. "This isn't a house?"

"Duplex. She's got the back half."

"Ah. Sorry, Mrs. Lee!" he yelled.

She laughed and slapped his arm. "Stop!"

"Well, it pays to be polite." He licked the fingers of the hand he'd fucked her with. "Mmm. You taste great, Cordero."

She liked the sound of her last name in his voice even more than her first name. Damn. As hard as he'd just made her come, she was ready to go again. But when he moved downward, headed for a more complete taste, she grabbed his head. "No. I want cock."

Again with the sex chuckle. "You got it. Just need a condom."

She grabbed his arm before he could move off of her. "In that drawer right there."

Nodding, he reached over and opened her nightstand drawer. And his eyebrows went up.

She wasn't surprised; she knew what she was letting him see, and it hadn't been a mistake to let him.

He pulled the box of condoms out and peeled one off the strip. "Oh, baby. I think I want to see more of you. Because I'd like to root around in that drawer."

That was okay by her. But for now, she simply smiled and spread her legs.

When he got the condom on, he lay between her legs and fed himself into her right away. And then he gathered her up and rolled over, putting her on top. It surprised her; he'd been take-charge in all their fucking so far. She pushed up, away from his chest, and he closed his hands around her hips.

"Ride me like you stole me, Cordero." With that, he smacked her ass. "C'mon. Giddy-up."

Still take-charge, then. But she liked it. Damn. She was getting into deep woods with this guy. She knew it, but it felt too good to care.

She rode him hard, using his cock shamelessly to bring herself off in another crashing explosion that had Mrs. Lee pounding on the wall again. When Connor made an enormous growling sound and tried to sit up, she pushed down on his shoulders and held him there, fucking him harder, finding another peak for herself.

He stopped trying to sit up, and grabbed her breasts instead, pulling sharply on her nipples, and she did come again, this time with him. He left her breasts to grab her hips again, and his head bent back, and the muscles of his neck and shoulders bunched hugely. Her hips ached from the pressure of his fingers.

By the time they were both finished, Pilar was completely fucking exhausted and practically fell off of him, dropping over to the side, leaving her legs in a tangle with his. They lay there, their panting breaths loud in the room.

As they calmed, she could feel a familiar but still strange tension coiling into the air. The post-coital tension of the casual fuck. Another reason she didn't bring casual fucks home—it was obvious that the end of the fuck was the end of the encounter when they were up against a wall in a bar restroom, or back in the storeroom at The Deck. In her own house, though, that line wasn't so clear.

But what if Connor wasn't a casual fuck? Was he? She wanted to see him more. And he'd made noises like he wanted the same thing.

"I'll get out of your hair in a sec," he said, taking a deep breath and patting her thigh.

"You can stay if you want." Fuck, saying that scared the shit out of her. But it was what she wanted, and she made a point not to quibble when she wanted something.

He lifted his head. "You sure? I thought you had work."

"I do. You'd have to get up and out when I get up. But if you want to crash, I'm good with it."

With his head still up at that odd angle, he stared at her. She was uncomfortable and getting defensive before he smiled.

"Okay, Cordero. I'll crash with you."

CHAPTER SEVEN

The sound of an old-fashioned alarm clock, the Big Ben kind with bells on the top, dragged Connor out of a deep sleep. Cracking one eye open, he saw the fuzzy image of a woman sitting up and reaching for something.

The noise blissfully stopped just as he recognized Pilar and remembered that he was sleeping in her bed.

An unusual development, to wake in the morning in a woman's bed. Usually, he made a point to bring his little bunnies back to the clubhouse. This chick was rocking his world a mite.

She turned to him and pushed his hip. "Hey. You awake?"

Opening his eyes fully, he stretched and reached out to twist a hank of her wild hair around his finger. "Yeah. Morning."

"Morning. I got to get going. So you do, too." With that, she pushed his hand away, tossed the sheet back, and stood up. She grabbed at something on her nightstand and then put her hands in her hair—oh, she was pulling the mop back into a ponytail.

The next thing she did shook the last of the sleep right out of Connor's head. Naked, she walked to her doorway and leapt up, catching a bar installed near the top. Her house—duplex—was old, with high ceilings and tall doors. That bar was pretty high off the floor. She had decent ups for a girl.

As he lay there, watching, she started doing pull-ups, totally naked. Christ almighty, she had muscle tone. Her back and shoulders flexed and rolled in ways he'd never seen a woman's body do before. His hand eased over his belly, under the sheet, and grabbed hold of the part of his body that found her exertions most interesting. After a few seconds, he realized he was jacking himself off in rhythm with each pull-up.

He hadn't noticed before now, but she had another tattoo, at the small of her back. On any other woman, he'd call ink there a tramp stamp. But Pilar—no, she wanted him to call her Cordero—Cordero had a firefighter's cross there. That cross had a particular name, and Connor knew that somewhere in the reaches of his head he knew it. To distract himself—he wanted to see if he could get her to let him in before he left, and he didn't want to fuck up her sheets—he searched for the name.

Maltese Cross. That was it. Cordero had a Maltese Cross at the small of her back. Too badass to be a tramp stamp. But Connor grinned at the irony of putting a symbol of that kind of strength—of heroism—in the place of a so-called 'tramp stamp.'

Unwilling to let go of his cock, but needing more distraction, he looked around her bedroom. She had eclectic taste, for sure. All of her color choices were bold, and a lot of her furniture was just plain weird. There was a table in her living room that looked like photos had been glued all over it and then shellacked. And a chest in here had the rough texture of raw granite, but it was clearly made of wood.

Both the living room and the bedroom were painted a warm yellow. All the woodwork trim was white. Her iron bed, with ornate headboard and footboard, was painted blood red. Dark reds and blues seemed to feature prominently. She had lots of strange and funky knickknacks and artwork. It was a cozy, weird little house.

Finishing her set, she dropped back to the floor and turned around. She wasn't breathing heavily, but her bronze skin had a faint sheen to it.

First thing she noticed was what Connor's hand was doing. When she lifted an eyebrow at him, he let go of his cock, which was near to screaming for some relief. "Wanna help me out with that?"

She walked to her dresser. "Dude, no. I told you. Up and out. I need to get a run in and shower before work. You need to go." She opened a drawer and pulled out some clothes.

As she shimmied into a pair of form-fitting running shorts, he sighed. He could almost feel his balls turning blue. Rubbing his hand over the empty space in the bed where she belonged, he said, "I could work you out right here."

"Contrary to popular belief, sex isn't that great for exercise."

"The way we fuck, it is."

She stopped in the act of grabbing one of her sport bra things, with her hand still in the drawer, and grinned at him. For second, his cock got all hopeful. But she shook her head. "No. You gotta go."

"Fine," he sighed, and stood to look around for his jeans. They'd tossed their clothes all over the room last night. He found them and stepped into them, wedging his protesting cock down into the denim, and Cordero bent over and dug a pair of running shoes out from under her bed.

Damn, that ass. He couldn't resist—he reached out and gave it a swat, and she jackknifed up and swiveled around. He gave her an impish grin, and she returned it. "*Dios mio.* Get dressed, you fool."

Seeing her resolve, he got dressed.

She walked him to the door, on her way out for her run. Before she opened the door, though, he caught her hand and pulled it around his waist. "I want to see you again."

At first, her eyes went soft, and she smiled a smile he found encouraging. Then something moved across her face like a shadow in shifting light, and she stepped back.

"This is nothing, right? We're messing around is all."

He didn't like that she'd said that, and he didn't like that he didn't like it. When his reaction pulled him up a bit, it took him a half-second too long to respond. Just enough for her to take another step back and give him a wary look.

He caught her hand before she could move any farther away. "Yeah, absolutely. I want to fuck you again, play with some of the toys you've got in that drawer, but that's it. In fact, I'm probably going to grab some pussy as soon as I get to the clubhouse. I got me a set of blue balls this morning, thanks to you and your Playboy Centerfold Workout. How many reps was that, anyway?"

Her smile returned. "Fifty."

"Nice. I could top that, of course. Double it, even."

"Yeah. We'll test that theory someday. But not now. C'mon, dude. Time to go." She pushed him to the side and opened her door.

He was on his bike and headed back to the clubhouse before he realized that they hadn't exchanged numbers. Exchanging numbers wasn't a thing he did, so it hadn't occurred to him.

Oh well. He knew where she lived and worked, and she knew the same about him. They'd figure it out.

In the meantime, he definitely needed to grab some club pussy, if anybody was still around and conscious from last night. He needed to get both of his heads straight this morning.

~oOo~

Meeting on a Sunday was unusual. The shop was closed on Sunday, and the Horde tended to use that day to chill out and recover from the weekend. But they had big business to discuss—on more than one front.

So the club was arrayed around the table, several of the guys looking like they could use a nap. Connor felt pretty refreshed, however. He'd been up early, but he'd slept hard. Cordero's bed was comfortable, with a nice, firm mattress.

And when he'd gotten back to the clubhouse, he'd found Fawn, one of the newer girls, in the kitchen, cleaning up. She'd reset his heads nicely. After he sent her on her way, he'd slept another couple of hours and had a hot shower. There was something to be said for rising early.

Not a lot, but something.

"Let's get to the business we all know about first: La Zorra's job. Trick—you got anything for us?"

Trick sat forward. "Yeah. I went out to Demon and Faith's place and knocked the rust off. I'm sharp again. With my M25, I can hit the center of the ribbon on a can of PBR at nine hundred yards."

"Nine hundred yards?" J.R. interjected. "That's…about half a mile!"

"Yes, it is," Trick's answer was matter-of-fact, despite the staggering impressiveness of his claim. "Of course, I was in the desert, no obstacles. I won't have the luxury of that distance in downtown L.A."

"From a rooftop, though, we could set you up a couple of blocks off." Sherlock swiped his fingers on his tablet and put a map of the Los Angeles financial district on the back wall, which they kept blank and white for that purpose. "In about a week and a half, Cartwright is going to be speaking at a lunchtime event in Pershing Square, which is this green space here, just on the southeast edge of the financial district." As he spoke, a red line circled a little rectangle of park on the map. "Here's where they'll set him up." A new picture came up as an inset overlaid on the map, showing an odd, purplish-blue monolith with green space and concrete benches around it. A short red line appeared as Sherlock indicated where Cartwright would stand.

"This building"—another photo came up over the map, this of a tall, but otherwise nondescript glass box of a skyscraper—"is four blocks away. Well within your range, T. Here's the line of sight from its roof." The photo that came up this time showed a direct view to the park, apparently from that weird building. The next photo showed the same view on zoom, with a red 'X,' which was apparently where Trick's target would be standing.

From his seat near the head of the table, Connor could see Trick studying all the images closely. Trick looked back over his shoulder at Sherlock. "You got a street view of that distance, too?"

"Hold on." The projected image went dark, and Sherlock swiped and tapped at his tablet. As he worked he said, "You know there's no clear shot from street level."

"I know, Trick answered. "Not what I'm interested in."

After a couple of minutes, the back wall lit up again, and Sherlock put several images up in a grid. "Best I can do—street view of the route between the points, and the view in all directions around the building."

"Good. That's what I wanted." Trick leaned forward and studied the images. The rest of the Horde sat quietly and looked, too. Connor assumed they were doing what he was doing: trying to figure out what Trick was looking for.

Finally, shaking his head, Trick turned back to the table. "There are cameras everywhere. We're being spied on every time we turn around, and people just let it happen. We should be burning the place down over shit like that." Connor could sense the general eye-roll around the table as it seemed like Trick had a rant building, but he let his quiet outrage drop and looked at Sherlock, asking simply, "Can you do something about all those?"

Bart was the one who answered him. "To an extent. We can loop dead space into some and obscure others, but if we interfere with too many, that itself could raise a flag. It's the financial district. Those fuckers are paranoid. Typical crooks, always sure everybody else is crooked. So we need to get you close before we start messing with the surveillance."

"Which is where we hit our first snag," Sherlock added.

Seeing the problem, Connor laughed. It was a real problem, but it was also funny as hell. When everybody turned to him, he explained, "It's you, T. You stand the fuck out."

And then everybody turned to Trick and took him in: long, thick, dark blond dreads and a bushy, wiry, dark blond beard. The tats that covered his arms and hands they could deal with, but they couldn't exactly give him a head transplant. And it was July in Southern California—August at the time of the hit. He would stick out more in a ski mask than he did looking like fucking Medusa.

Hoosier cocked his head toward Trick. "How about a trip to the barber, brother?"

Every head swiveled back to Trick. That boy loved his hair. Had Connor not known Trick, he'd have expected that head of his to smell bad. It looked unwashed. But Trick was fastidious about his hair and hygiene. Sometimes it took the guy almost an hour to get himself ready in the morning. When he worked or rode, he wore his mop tied back with a piece of hemp, but otherwise, like now, he left it loose to drape down his back and over his shoulders. He was practically a girl about that hair.

Connor's mental observation was reinforced when, reacting to Hoosier's question, Trick did a protective sweep and flip over those thick snakes and looked, for a brief second, like the world's ugliest princess.

But his eyes were wide with shock. He was distraught at the suggestion.

"Hair grows, T," Connor said, trying to sound reassuring. "You can grow 'em back."

Trick turned hot eyes on him. "I haven't cut my hair since I got kicked from the service. Ten years. It's more than just hair. It *means* something. This..."—he turned to Hoosier—"are you shitting me?"

Connor's father spoke calmly. "We don't have another sniper, brother. I know what we're asking. I get it. But there's nobody else can do it, and you are easily identifiable. Our goal here is to get up and out and none the wiser."

"We haven't even voted on the fucking job yet!" Usually, Trick was calm and quiet, but this discussion had him agitated.

Still speaking in that careful, steady voice, Hoosier said, "We agreed we'd set a plan first and then vote on the job. Now we know the plan. You can vote against it, no judgment at this table. But this is the plan we're voting on, and it requires you to get military sharp again."

Again, Trick put his hands protectively to his hair. This time, though, he caught himself doing it and dropped them to the table. "Fuck me."

When he didn't say more, Hoosier turned to Bart and Sherlock. "Okay. Let's hear the rest of the plan. Then we vote."

After all the details were laid out, with more photos and maps projected onto the wall, Hoosier called the vote. When it came around to Trick, there was a weighty pause, and then he said, "Aye. And fuck you all."

The vote was unanimous. They were doing the job for La Zorra, taking out the District Attorney for L.A. County. Without knowing why she wanted him dead.

When that business was finished, Hoosier said, "We have a new issue, too. Most of you know, but let's lay it out. Connor, Diaz, and Sherlock had an interesting afternoon yesterday. Connor, let's hear your take."

Connor described the scene at the High Life, and Diaz and Sherlock added bits as they saw fit. He left out the part that Pilar and Hugo were Aztec family. He didn't think it was pertinent to the Horde's specific problem, though it was certainly pertinent to Pilar's.

When the story was told, J.R. spoke up. "I'm not clear—why were you charging into Aztec turf? To do a favor for some piece of ass you don't even know?"

A surprisingly strong bolt of anger went through Connor's head at that. Before he could retort, though, Muse leaned in. "She asked for help. We help, right? That's how we keep the citizens friendly. They know they can come to us when they can't go to Sheriff Montoya."

J.R. shook his head. "Yeah, but we help with petty stuff. We don't get involved in internal trouble on somebody else's turf."

"It's not internal trouble. Her brother isn't in." Connor could feel the kind of tension coming on him that usually needed a fight before it would dissipate.

And J.R. leaned in and poked some more. "But he did something to piss them off. That shouldn't be our problem. This is about you chasing some sweet Latin pussy and dragging us all with you."

"I want you in the ring after this," Connor snarled. He was angry because J.R. was suggesting he'd dragged the club into trouble over a chick. He was sure that was the source of the anger. He was sure he wasn't feeling some sense of protectiveness for Pilar's honor. That wasn't it. Couldn't be.

J.R. blinked—he was slight, and Connor could break him in half if he had the will to do so—and if this kept up, he might. But then J.R. grinned. "Fine by me."

Hoosier cut in, slapping his hand down on the table. "Fight it out in the ring if you want. But on the point that matters in *here*—I okayed their field trip yesterday. There wasn't time to vote it, so I made a call. Now we might have a beef brewing with the Aztecs, and if so, then that's on me. They're not much of a problem on their own. Esposito is a cocky S.O.B—he could've just been popping off. The bigger issue is that he's bent over to the Fuentes cartel. I don't want to be the cause of shit rising up in Mexico. La Zorra has a truce with them. If what we do here fucks that up there, we will have a problem. So be sharp and pay attention."

He sat back in his leather chair. "That's all I got. If J.R. is set on being an idiot, then by all means, you two go fight it out. But brother, you're in the wrong. Also, you pissed him off and he's got five inches and sixty pounds on you. Maybe you should just fucking apologize while you can still walk."

Connor just smiled.

~oOo~

"Can you take Lana for a minute?" Demon's wife, Faith, leaned over the back of the sectional and held her daughter out.

Connor set the television remote down and took the pretty little infant into his hands. "Sure thing. Come see Uncle Conman, cupcake." He settled her on his chest, and she immediately went for the cross hanging from his neck, pulling on several hairs as she tried to shove it in her mouth. "Ouch. That's mine. Have this instead." He put his hand up to her mouth, and she sucked on one of his rings, and his finger, instead.

As Faith led Tucker, Lana's older brother, down the hall toward the bathroom, Connor looked back. "She's changed and all, right?"

"Yes," Faith sighed theatrically. "I promise you won't have to do anything but be charming."

"Good. I got that down." Connor loved babies—when they were dressed and quiet and didn't stink. He didn't mind them when they weren't quiet, either, up to a point. He could deal with a little squalling, as long as they settled down when he turned on the charm.

He loved all the club kids. But this little girl was the sweetest thing he'd ever known. Maybe because she was Faith's, and Faith had been special to him since they were kids. She was like his little sister. He'd felt it hard when she'd run away back in the day. But it wasn't until she'd come back home, about a year and a half ago, that he'd fully realized how much like a sister he'd felt her to be.

Her daughter was like a perfect little doll, with wisps of pale hair and huge hazel eyes. And she hardly ever cried—not with him, anyway. She was a watcher. Not even four months old yet, but Connor could tell. This little miss took things in and thought about them before she made a decision.

They were all at Connor's parents' house for dinner. It was a thing that his mom, Bibi, had started doing not long after Demon and Faith got married. She wanted her family together at least once a week. Horde family came and went all week long, to drop in for a bite, expected or not, or to help out with some home repair, or just to hang out. But this core group—Connor and his parents, and Faith and Demon and their kids—Bibi wanted them to sit down like a family. Both Faith and Demon looked on his folks as parents, too, which was fine with Connor.

He felt closer to Faith than to Demon. He and Demon had met when Connor was a Prospect and Demon had started hanging around the club, back in the day, when they'd still been in L.A. So they'd started off with Connor thinking of him as inferior. And then right after Demon got his patch, there'd been that whole bullshit with Faith and her father, and it was just tough not to think about all that.

He loved Demon as the brother he was, and they had an ease together, but they weren't confidants. When Connor needed to bend an ear, he went to Trick. And Demon went to Muse.

Demon came into the room now and sat on the other side of the sectional. "You good with her?" he asked.

"You know I am, brother. I love this sweet little thing." His hand was dripping wet with her drool now, though, so he shifted her into the crook of his arm, and Demon handed him a teether and a cloth diaper. "How's Tuck doing?"

Demon grinned like the proud papa he was. "He's real good. That preschool is helping. He's catching up. When they took him from Kota, he was about a year behind in everything. Now he's almost on target."

It had been about a year and a half or so since the state had taken custody of Tucker from Demon's junkie ex. "That's great. That kid's been through some life already."

His grin fading, Demon nodded. "Yeah. But it's good now. Faith's adopting him, and he loves his baby sister, and it's good. Life is good."

"Yeah, it is."

The young boy in question came in just then and put his hands on his hips. Tucker was nearly four, but he was small for his age, the byproduct of being born to a junkie mom and being stuck in her barely-conscious 'care' for his first two years. All of his problems could be put down to that. And his recovery since was due to the loving family that now surrounded him.

"Pa!" Tucker nearly shouted. "Granny say wash your hands and come eat."

Demon turned and smiled at his son. "Okay, Motor Man. Just me?"

Tucker thought about that and then shook his head. "Unca Con, you eat, too. But not Lala. Mommy gave Lala a boob already."

Laughing, the men stood up. "What should I do with her, Tuck? Should I put her on a shelf?"

"No! Unca Con! She's a baby! Babies don't go on shelves!" Again, he considered the problem. Connor and Demon exchanged an amused look and let him think. "Give Lala to Pa. Pa knows what to do. Right, Pa?"

"You bet, buddy. I got this."

Demon took his daughter and set her in the portable swing, where she would sail happily through the meal, probably sound asleep in about five minutes.

When they were sitting around the table passing bowls around to fill their plates, Connor took a minute to think about what he and Demon had said. Life was good. They had the club family, and it was tight. And they had this family, sitting around this smaller table. His mother and father. His sister and brother. Their kids.

His relationship with his parents had always been good. He'd needed no rebellion, because they'd always respected him for who he was, and he'd always wanted to follow Hoosier into the club. His mother was nigh to perfect, as far as he was concerned. Sure, they'd all had their fights, but they were rock solid and knew it even while they shouted.

Neither Faith nor Demon could boast an upbringing as stable as his, which was how they'd come to be welcomed into his little family. And now he got to be Unca Con.

He was a lucky son of a bitch.

The main reason he was living in the clubhouse at thirty-six years old was that he didn't want to live alone. He wanted family around him. He was too old to live at home, so he'd done the next best thing.

But sometimes he wondered if he might someday want a table like this of his own.

CHAPTER EIGHT

Fire Station 76 was located deep in the heart of Old Towne, the neighborhood that had, in the days when California was a frontier territory rather than a state, been the entire town of Madrone. In those days, the town had been little more than a depot, a few rough-hewn blocks of commerce surrounded by dusty ranchland.

That small town had not officially expanded its borders into the desert floor of the foothills until the latter half of the twentieth century, when the first middle-class stragglers began to flee the booming growth of the Los Angeles area, a sort of mini-reversal of the westward expansion that had fed the state its residents for decades. In the late twentieth century, when real estate values had exploded into absurdity, picturesque Madrone burgeoned into the quiet, tidy commuter community that it was.

Most of the town, then, was shiny and new, full of gated developments and landscaped, irrigated green spaces. The Chamber of Commerce renamed the original Madrone 'Old Towne,' adding an 'e' for flair, and exploited the rustic, Wild West feel of the clapboard buildings and wooden walkways.

Station 76 was housed in what had been the old livery stables. The emergency vehicles lived on the first floor of the livery. The sleeping quarters, showers, and rec room were above it. An addition had been built on in the Eighties to expand the kitchen and include administrative space and a gym. During the restructuring of the fire district a few years back, another building had been added to garage the brush unit and ambulance.

Station 76 didn't have a ladder truck. The layout and architecture of Madrone was low profile, and few buildings were taller than two stories. The whole district had two ladder trucks, both at the same station. When a ladder was needed, Station 58 was called in.

Pilar rented a duplex only a few blocks from the station, in the small residential area that had been the home of the shopkeepers and bank tellers back when Old Towne was just Madrone. It was one of the only parts of the town that didn't look, to her eyes, like every other part of the town. While the houses in almost all of Madrone were stucco faux villas in neutral tones with composite tile roofs, Old Towne was mostly wood-sided cottages with a faint Victorian flair. The trees and gardens were less uniformly landscaped. People took pride and care, but they weren't so worried about perfect lines and patterns. The people, and their homes, were just more interesting in Old Towne, as far as she was concerned.

As close as she was—she ran by the station on her morning runs—she always drove or rode to work, because she never knew whether she'd go straight home or head out somewhere at the end of the watch. Even a twenty-four hour watch, like the one she was on now, which would end at seven o'clock in the morning, didn't mean she'd go straight home.

After she'd pushed Connor out her front door so she could get ready for work, she'd showered and dressed, then she'd mounted her Victory and ridden the half mile or so to the station. She hadn't bothered with breakfast, because nothing she could make herself at home would be as good as what was waiting for her at the station.

It was a stereotype and a cliché that firehouse cooking was great, but it was a true stereotype and cliché. Firehouse cooking was fucking awesome. Every watch had at least one, usually two or three, fantastic cooks. Her watch had Ron Reyes. That man knew what he was doing with a spatula. Her best buddy Kyle Moore was good, too—he was their master griller—but Reyes, man. They were always pushing him to try out for one of the cooking shows, but he was quiet and shy and simply shook his head.

That morning, with Connor slowing her down, she was one of the last ones in the barn. Everybody was already around the table, though Reyes was still at the range, and Moore and Perez were laying trays in the middle.

Perez was the first to greet her, turning with a serving spoon in her hand and asking, "So? Did you go back for seconds of bear meat? How was it?"

White backed her up with, "Must've been juicy—Cordero's never late!"

Guzman stopped in the act of pouring orange juice. "You been at it with that guy since last watch? How're you walking?"

Pilar simply flipped them all off and went to the counter to pour herself a mug of coffee. Moore came over and hip-checked her gently. "Come on, girl. Spill. You know we won't let you up until you do."

Her mug full, Pilar turned and went to her place at the table. "Get your thrills in your own lives, *chismosas*."

"Don't talk spic to the *gringos*, Guzman rejoined. "They don't get it when you're dissing them."

Most of the firefighters spoke Spanish, but Guzman knew that and was just throwing shade at the Caucasians in the room. "I was dissing you, too, *ese*. I'm not talking about my sex life with you trolls. When have I ever?"

Just then their Captain came in, and they all stood. He waved them down and sat at the far end of the table with them.

Clayton Harrison had been Captain of Station 76 for all of Pilar's years there. As Captain, his job was mainly administrative, and he hardly ever put on turnout gear anymore, though his was prepped to go just like everybody else's. As leader of the station, he had the luxury of scheduling himself for a Monday-to-Friday, eight-to-five job, but he didn't. He worked at least one weekend a month.

Pilar liked him. Everybody did. He wasn't friendly, necessarily, but he was fair. And he respected his firefighters.

They didn't talk smack around him. It was like their father had walked into the room.

"You want coffee, Cap?" Scott Nguyen, Perez's paramedic partner, asked.

Harrison shook his head and reached for the pitcher of orange juice. "No, thanks, Nguyen. I've shot my limit already this morning." As he sat back with his glass of juice, he grinned and said, "So, anybody got news *besides* Cordero?"

Pilar could have hugged him. Usually, she didn't mind all the smack and banter, but she was feeling defensive about Connor. She knew why, too. She liked him. A lot. He had a wry sense of humor and a devil-may-care attitude. That could come off as superficial, and it had, at first. But he was smart, too. And thoughtful.

And he was smoking hot and a great lay.

Though she thought she'd covered it well, she'd been pissed when he'd said he was heading to the clubhouse to grab some pussy. She'd been more pissed at herself, however, that she was pissed at him.

Nothing serious. She wanted nothing serious, and neither did he. That was a good thing. A perfect scenario. It was *fine* that he was getting more pussy. It meant that she didn't have to worry that he'd want more from her than she could give. He had no more to give than she. A good thing.

She didn't have a life or a job that made room for a serious relationship. Every watch, there was a chance she could get killed or fucked up. She literally lived half her life at her job. Yeah, there were people in the barn who had families, but she didn't have the temperament for it.

It was a spiel she knew well, and it was running through her head on a loop this morning.

So Pilar was very glad when Captain Harrison filled his plate and they all sat around the table and spent the rest of the meal talking about the weather and the drought.

~oOo~

After breakfast, they did their daily checks and assignments, making sure the equipment was in shape and the supplies were stocked and the barn was clean. It was Sunday, so they didn't have training or public service to do. Weekday watches often included trips to schools or school trips to the station, blood drives, and a variety of other kinds of community engagement obligations. Pilar and Perez spent a lot of time on those details—they were two of the very few women in this job at all, and they made good press.

Especially Pilar, since she was the only woman in the county whose primary job wasn't medical.

All the firefighters were EMTs, it was a requirement of the job, but there were two paramedics on every watch, and they took the lead in first-response medical calls. Pilar's primary job was rescue. She was often the first into a burning building—or second, behind Moore. They were a team.

For a woman, Pilar was fairly average in size: just shy of five-seven, about one-twenty-five. For a firefighter, she was small. But she was strong; those one hundred and twenty-five pounds were solid muscle. She was agile, too—and fierce. The package helped her excel at rescue. She could get places a man could not, even in full gear. And she could lift well more than her own weight.

Moore was much bigger than she was; in fact, he was one of the bigger guys in the whole station. About Connor's size. He was her brawn. Those places too tight even for Pilar to get into, Moore and she could clear together.

When people told her she was brave, she normally corrected them, at least in her head. She didn't think she was brave. She preferred the term 'fierce.' To be brave, one needed to overcome fear. Pilar didn't feel fear. She had respect for the risks, and she knew her job. She did her job. She barely noticed the danger. When she was on scene, fire was just something to be dealt with.

She trusted her training and her instincts, and she did the thing she was there to do.

The truth was, though, that burning-building calls were the least common calls they went on. Much more common were the accident calls—vehicular or otherwise—and medical calls or public safety calls like gas leaks or water main breaks. There was a reason a structure fire made the news. It didn't happen all that often.

In California, especially in the summer, though, they went on plenty of fire calls. They had an actual wildfire season, the way the Midwest had a tornado season. Though the Forest Service had its own firefighters, all firefighters were trained in wildfire management and took calls to assist, and the department jumped on brush fire calls like they were harbingers of Armageddon itself.

Because they well might be.

This summer, so far, despite the dry winter, the fire season had been quiet. But it was still early yet, really. As the dry season progressed, everything got more precarious, and August and September were often the worst months. There was always an extra layer of vigilance over every watch in the summer and early fall. One cigarette butt tossed out a car window could destroy hundreds of thousands of acres of forest and brush. It happened all the time.

And those fuckers were nearly impossible to fight.

But the watch on the Sunday after she'd been with Connor was quiet. The truck and ambulance went out on a vehicular call about eight hours in, but the only injury had been a driver whose airbag had made meat out of his face. Both cars had been obviously totaled, so they'd kept the truck around to block the lane. They'd milled about for an hour or so, directing traffic until the tow company could get the wrecks onto a flatbed and out of the way.

Then they'd gone back to the barn and run their checks again.

After dinner that night, Pilar and Moore were on cleanup detail, so they were alone in the kitchen while everybody was upstairs in the rec room watching the Dodgers game.

While Pilar loaded the dishwasher, Moore put away the cooking supplies. Reyes was a great cook, but a real slob at the counter. Leaning over her to put the spices away in the cupboard, Moore asked, "You got plans tomorrow? Want to head to Joshua and do some climbing after watch?"

It sounded like a plan to her. "Yeah—but I need to check on my brother first. Can we make it an overnight, ride out in the afternoon and climb in the morning?" It was too hot to climb past noon in the desert. "Indian Cove should be pretty light on a Monday night. Not too many tourists."

She and Moore were both rock climbing enthusiasts; their friendship was based as much on their off time as it was on the teamwork on watch. They weren't close in a 'share-our-deepest-secrets-and-braid-each-other's-hair' way, but they understood each other without that kind of sharing. They'd come into the station within a year of each other, Moore after Pilar, and had hit it off right away. They experienced the world in similar ways, most of them physical. But they'd never been physical together, despite countless camping trips sleeping in the same little pack tent.

They'd come close once, a couple of years ago, when they'd been up on Big Bear and an unexpected rain had driven them into the tent early. They'd spent the night drinking terrible wine they'd picked up at a convenience store on their way up, and they'd ended up making out for about three minutes.

At which point, they'd dissolved into drunken giggles and then passed out. So no. They weren't into each other. It would be like fucking her brother. If she had a brother she actually liked.

"How's he doing?"

Pilar had told Moore about Hugo, giving a highly edited version of the story—no showdown at the High Life, no Night Horde shield, no threat to her personally. But her friend knew enough about her brother to know that he was always in some kind of shit soup, so she'd told him that he'd gotten in bad with the Assassins and had landed in the hospital because of it.

"I called Nana earlier. He's awake and doing okay. They're keeping him for a couple of days, and then he'll be home moaning for Nana to wipe his ass, but he'll live. Probably lost his job, though. That was the best job he'd had for a while."

"I'm telling you, that kid needs to join up." Moore hadn't served in the military, but his younger brother, Jude—who also had his challenges getting along in the world—had enlisted in the Army a couple of years out of high school. The main reason he'd enlisted had been to hurt their mom when she'd tried to put her foot down. He'd succeeded at that. But actually serving had turned him around.

"He's not a kid. He's twenty-five."

"Not too old to enlist."

"Unless we can roofie him and throw him on a C-5, I think it's not going to happen. Besides, it'd kill Nana. She thinks he'll straighten out. As long as she keeps Assassins ink off of him, she thinks he'll find his way."

While Moore took a sponge and wiped down the counter, Pilar took the special cleaner to clean the table. It was a big, oblong pine table. The emblems of their station, of their district, and of their profession had all been carved into it, with the founding date carved at the head. 1913, when the livery stable first housed a fire engine. They didn't wipe that table down with just a wet sponge.

"She's wrong, you know. If he's not turning around yet, he's going to keep going in the direction he's in. And that's down."

Pilar knew that. Of course she knew that. And deep down, her grandmother knew it, too. But it infuriated her that an outsider was standing there with a lime-green sponge in his hand and handing down judgments. Even an outsider that was closer to the inside than any other. Maybe he was too fucking close.

"Butt out, Moore. Didn't ask for your opinion or your help."

He glared at her through the hanging pots and pans for a second, and then he nodded and went back to his work.

~oOo~

The next morning, after a quiet night without a call, Pilar and Moore made plans to meet up in the afternoon, ride out to Joshua Tree, and set up camp in preparation for an early-morning climb. No hard feelings had lingered after their terse exchange in the kitchen; by the time they'd turned out the lights and headed up to the rec room, they'd been fine. They understood each other, and they didn't take their disagreements to heart.

After the new watch came in, Pilar changed into her street clothes and rode to the hospital. When she got up to Hugo's room, her brother was having breakfast, and their grandmother was fussing around, unpacking an overnight bag.

Hugo noticed her right away and set his carton of milk back on his tray. "Hey."

"Hey." She came into the room and closed the door. Hugo looked terrible. His face was a swollen mess, and he had sutured lacerations across his nose and along his chin. His chest and arms were wrapped in bandages. Pilar knew he had a serious concussion, too, but he looked alert, his eyes focused inside his swollen, darkened face.

"I'm glad you're here, *mija*. Dolores brought things from home, but I need to run out for some things Hughie wants. Can you stay with him?"

Dolores was their grandmother's next door neighbor and good friend. "Sure. But if you'd called, I could have picked it up, whatever it is." But she wouldn't mind a chance to talk to her brother alone. They had some things to get straight.

"You know I hate to bother you at work. I don't mind. I'd like to get out in the sunshine for a bit."

Pilar picked up a wedge of white toast from her brother's tray. "Okay. Take your time. I don't have plans until later. Kyle and I are going out to Joshua Tree tonight."

"Oh, that sounds fun. Kyle is such a good boy. And handsome, too."

"Yeah, yeah, Nana. You should ask him out, since you're so into him."

Her grandmother put her hand on her hip in a saucy little pose. "Don't think I won't. I was quite the beauty in my day. Your *abuelo* used to brag about what my legs could do."

"Ugh! Nana, no! That is not something I need to have in my head." Their grandfather had died long before Pilar had been born, but their grandmother had lots of stories. He sounded like he'd been a cool dude. And yes, Nana had been a great beauty. She still was.

She laughed and patted Pilar's arm. "I'll take Kyle. You take that furry one from the other night. Connor, right? I like him, too."

"Okay, okay, go get your sunshine. I'll babysit the brat."

With a gentle kiss to Hugo's swollen cheek and a promise to be back soon, their grandmother left them alone.

And Pilar turned on her brother. "You fucked up in a big way, *pendejo*."

Hugo finished his milk and sat back against the pillows. "Opening with the lecture. Great."

"I pulled your ass out of the back room at the fucking High Life, Hugo. What do you expect? Raul says you owe him. What the fuck did you get into?"

"None of your business."

"It is my business. You drag me into it, and my friends, and now I'm on Assassins radar."

"We're always on their radar. Both our fathers died wearing Assassins colors. I didn't ask for your fucking help, Pilar. And didn't ask for you to find me or save me or anything. Whatever trouble you're in now, that's on you."

"Nana asked me to find you! And they were killing you!"

"They weren't. It was a beating. They won't kill me. I'm family. And, anyway, I haven't paid my debt yet." He twitched, like he'd realized that he'd given her an opening.

And she took it. "What does he want?"

Sighing, he pushed the table over his bed away. "I was supposed to move a brick for him. I found a buyer with a better price. I figured I'd sell to him, bring Raul the money he was expecting, and pocket the rest. But the *hijo de puta* paid me in counterfeit bills."

She sat hard in the chair next to the bed. "Jesus, Hugo. A kee? That's like, what, thirty grand?"

"Thirty-five. Guy paid me fifty. In funny money."

The parts of the equation were starting to find their proper place. "So you didn't bring product to Raul's customer. You sold that product to somebody he doesn't know. And he paid you in trash." Hugo didn't answer, but he didn't need to. "Oh, you stupid *culo*. What does he want to put you even?"

"I don't know. He was still at the working out his rage part when you showed up. And with bikers, right? I'm remembering that right? The Horde?"

"Yeah."

"Raul hates those fuckers. You bringing them into his house…yeah, that trouble's on you. I'll deal with my shit. You deal with yours."

"You won't deal with your shit, Hugo. You never do. Until the day you die, you'll be looking for somebody to take your heat for you. It's what you do."

Hugo turned on the television and focused his attention there, away from her. "Well, maybe Raul will kill me after all and make your life that much better."

That broke her heart. When Hugo was born, Pilar had been ecstatic. A little brother. Someone to care for and play mother to, someone to sit with her stuffed animals and take her lessons. As he'd gotten older, they'd continued to be close. He'd followed her everywhere. Then his father and their mother had both been killed in much the same way her father had been killed, and they'd been moved away from the home they'd known, out of Assassins turf.

They'd had only each other. Their grandmother had slaved to be a good provider and a good nurturer, both. She'd done as well as she could, and Pilar had picked up the slack, getting Hugo to school, making his meals, trying to help with his homework. She'd loved him so much. From the day he'd come home wrapped in a knitted blue shawl.

She still loved that little boy. But she didn't know the man he'd become. And she knew it was her fault, at least in part, that he'd turned out as he had. In middle school, when he'd started to drift, she hadn't known how to steer him back on course. All she'd done had been to shout and fight.

That was all they'd been doing since. They didn't like each other much anymore. But she still loved him. She'd still die for him.

She sat and watched television with him. She'd told their grandmother she'd stay.

So she stayed.

~oOo~

"Cordero, here! I'm open!"

They were getting in some fitness time on their next watch. Pilar wasn't much good at basketball, but this wasn't really much of a basketball game. The rules were fluid. They split into teams and shot baskets and blocked shots until they were bored or worn out. It got physical.

Pilar turned, pushing back on Moore, and threw the basketball to Reyes, who sank the basket. Moore grabbed her around the waist and hoisted her up, pretty much tossing her out of his way.

"Foul! Foul!"

Moore laughed. "That's your pussy talking, sugarplum. You need to toughen up."

She punched him in the solar plexus.

"Ow! Fuck!" He doubled over, clutching at his chest.

"Now who's the pussy?"

Moore picked her up and threw her over his shoulder, then caught a pass with one hand and heaved it at the basket. He missed, probably because Pilar was punching him in the kidneys.

"Put me down! You're getting your man slime all over me!" He was shirtless and sweaty and smelled like a horse. Some men's sweat smelled sexy—Connor's, for instance. Not Moore's.

While she was still hanging upside down, there was a pause in the action.

"Uh, Cordero?" Perez said. "Got a guest."

Moore set her back on her feet. When her vision settled, she saw Connor standing near the corner of the building. His arms were crossed over his chest. He was wearing dark sunglasses; the lenses had an iridescent blue tint.

She didn't like the fluttery thing her belly did when she saw him—or the faint sense of guilt she felt, either, compelling her to step away from Moore.

She started toward Connor, but Moore pulled her back. "I got this."

"Fuck you, asshole." She jockeyed to get in front of him, but he muscled her back and got to Connor first.

"Hey, man." He held out his hand. "Kyle Moore."

Connor looked at it for a second. Then he stood tall and shook hands. "Hey. Connor Elliott. We've met."

Pilar got the sense that Connor was pissed—like, jealous. She liked it.

Moore grinned. "I know. I kicked your ass."

"Just surprised me with those pussy dance moves."

"Kickboxing, not the tango."

"Whatever. Gimme a rematch, I'll take you down."

Moore's stance changed now, too, got more aggressive. "Friday night at The Deck? About eight o'clock?"

"Make it nine. I got plans before that."

"You're on."

"Good."

"Good."

"Okay, okay. Rulers away, boys." Pilar grabbed Connor's arm and dragged him forward, around the building and to the driveway at the front of the station. "What are you doing here?"

"You banging that guy?"

"What?" The man who'd gone for pussy straight from her house was asking who she was fucking? Yeah, no.

"You two were rubbing all over each other. Do you fuck him?"

"First, who the fuck are you to ask? And second, what the fuck are you doing here?"

For enough seconds that she almost left him standing where he was and went back to deal with whatever shit her buddies were ready to ration out, he just stared down at her, his eyes shielded by his sunglasses. Then he shook himself a little and smiled. Watching his face, Pilar got the sense that the smile took effort. But once it was on, it was sincere—and smug.

"You look good, all sweaty and in that tiny shirt."

He reached out, but she knocked his hand away. "What. The fuck. Do you want?"

The smile faded. "To see you. We never exchanged numbers. I was riding by and figured I'd see if you were around. You were. Doing basketball porn."

"Don't be an asshole. Give me your phone." He pulled it out of a pocket and handed it to her, and she keyed in her number. Then she called herself. Her phone was in the barn, but it didn't matter. "There." She handed his phone back. "Now we've exchanged numbers and you've made a hot date with Kyle. Did you get what you want?"

"Have dinner with me."

"What?"

"Dinner. Evening meal. Let's go out to eat Friday."

"You said you had plans. And you've already got a date to get your ass kicked on Friday."

"That's not how it's going down. But a man's gotta eat, doomed or not. The plans I have are with you. I figure we eat, I hand your buddy his balls, and then I take you back to your place and fuck you with all your interesting toys."

Oh, that was a good plan. "I'm back here Saturday morning. We won't have time to use all my toys."

And the grin was back—the melty one he used when he was getting his way. "We'll get a start. So you're in, then?"

The thought of watching him in the ring was enough to make her want to jump him right there on the driveway. The thought of playing with him and her toys wasn't making her any calmer. And she liked this jealousy thing he seemed to have. She shouldn't like it; warning bells should have been going off like crazy, but they were strangely silent.

"You want to take me on a *date*?"

He shrugged. "Call it a date if you want. Eat, drink, fight, fuck—just sounds like a Friday night to me."

Pilar laughed. It sounded like a great date to her. "Yeah, I'm in. Pick me up at seven. You know where I live."

"Yes, I do. I'll see you then." He bent down and kissed her cheek, brushing his beard over her skin as he moved his mouth to her ear. "Wear something slutty."

And then he turned and walked back to his bike.

Pilar watched him mount up and ride off. She had no choice; she felt cemented to the spot.

CHAPTER NINE

Cordero opened her front door as Connor walked up to it. She stood in the doorway with one hand on the jamb.

And damn, she looked fine. He'd told her to wear something slutty, but he had not been prepared for what she was wearing: a tiny black dress that looked like it had been painted on her skin. Short, the hem just a couple of inches below her perfect ass, and plain, just stretchy black fabric that clung to her like Saran wrap. It had longish sleeves, below her elbow, and the neckline was off her shoulders. Her hair was loose, her wild waves cascading darkly over her bare shoulders. The only jewelry she wore was a pair of thin gold hoop earrings and that little gold crucifix.

He didn't know how the crucifix wasn't burning itself right into her chest, because that dress was pure sin. The urge to just grab her and take her back to her bed right the fuck now was so strong that he stepped up onto the threshold.

Then his eyes traveled the length of her bare, bronze legs, shapely with muscle. And on her feet were a pair of bright pink fuck-me shoes with heels about five, maybe even six inches high.

He lifted his eyes back to hers to find her giving him a look full of laser-sharp derision. "You get your eyeful?"

"Hot damn, Cordero. You clean up right. It's not even slutty. It's just pure sex."

She grinned, and he could see that he'd pleased her. "I don't dress like this much."

"You should. Every day." He himself was dressed in good jeans, a white button-down shirt, and, currently, his kutte—though he wouldn't wear it into the restaurant. This was about as dressed up as he knew how to be. "I was just going to take you to The

Bunkhouse. They have the best steak. But you're too fancy for that. We could go to Blue Sky instead." He wasn't much of a fan of Blue Sky, which was probably the nicest joint in Madrone. He'd been there once. The food was good, but it was the kind of place where the waiter wanted you to taste the wine first, and she'd probably want wine. He hated all that pomp and circumstance over some damn grape juice.

"I love The Bunkhouse. That sounds great."

"Cool." He felt ridiculously awkward, probably because he hadn't been on a date in more than five years. Then he recognized another snag: her outfit. "I can't have you on my bike like that. Too dangerous."

"No problem. I'll drive." She turned to the side and picked her keys up out of a glazed ceramic bowl that sat on a nearby table. When she turned, he saw that the heels on those pink shoes were covered with faceted pink spikes, all over. They glittered in the light. Holy Christ.

"I don't ride bitch. But I'll drive your car." He held out his hand, expecting her to hand him her keys.

She crossed her arms, keys firmly in her fist. "I don't ride bitch, either. Not in my own fucking car."

They stared at each other. Connor hadn't ridden bitch with a woman behind the wheel since he was old enough to drive. Even his mother had handed over her keys as soon as he'd had a license.

His hand was still out, waiting for the keys. He pushed it forward a little. "C'mon, Cordero. It's not that big a deal."

"You're right. No big deal. So I'll drive. Or I'll meet you there." When he still hesitated, she huffed. "Dude, it's like you don't want this to happen. If you don't, it's cool. I'll just see you at The Deck later and watch Moore serve you up your ass."

Connor wanted the date. He wanted her on the back of his bike—and failing that, he wanted her at his side, with that little dress hiked up. Since that night in the storeroom at The Deck, he'd been thinking a lot about this demanding woman with the Ironman body.

He sighed. "Fine. Drive."

She nodded and pushed him gently until he stepped down from the threshold. Then she followed and locked her door. As they walked to her Element, she said, "That was the first stupid he-man thing you've done with me. It knocks your hot score down. Just sayin'." She pressed her fob, and the doors unlocked automatically.

As Connor opened the passenger door, he spoke over the roof of her Element. "I'm guessing my score can take a couple of hits. And I'm not used to a girl digging her heels in like you do."

"You need to start spending time with more *women*, then." As she put her foot in the car and prepared to slide in, she stopped. "Play your cards right, though, and I'll dig these heels in deep later."

Damn.

~oOo~

The Bunkhouse was Madrone's best steakhouse. There were a couple others, but they were franchises of big chains, and neither their food nor their atmosphere was as good. This place was locally owned and had been in Madrone for decades. Its décor was consistent with its name and the Wild West heritage of Old Towne, where the restaurant had originally been located until an earthquake in the Nineties—which hadn't done much more than knock things off shelves in most buildings—had put a huge crack straight through the restaurant. Restoration of the historical building had proved too expensive, so The Bunkhouse had moved to the commercial district of Madrone. But they'd kept the rustic feel at their new location.

The new site was near the Horde clubhouse. Thus, Connor knew the place well and had become friends with Rusty, the owner.

It was Rusty who greeted them and led them to a booth set back in a dark corner. They sat facing each other and opened their menus. Then Becky, a waitress Connor knew...well...came over with his usual glass of Shock Top. She had nothing for Cordero, not even a glass of water, and she didn't even look at her. Great. He hadn't calculated female drama of this kind into his night.

"Hey, Connor," she said sweetly.

"Hey, puss. Becky, this is Pilar."

Reluctantly, Becky turned to Cordero, who clearly had not missed the vibe. "Hi. Getcha anything?"

Cordero didn't smile, but she wasn't aggressive, either. "I'll take a Shock Top, too, thanks."

"Got it." That was all. No assurance that she'd be back to take their order, no spiel about specials.

As she turned, Connor grabbed her wrist. "Sort yourself out, puss. Right now."

She blinked at him and then pulled her wrist away. "I'll be back with the drink and to take your order."

"Good girl."

When she left, Connor turned back to Cordero, who was staring at him like he'd grown a horn in his forehead. "What the fuck was that?"

"I know Becky."

"Yeah, I got that. Sheesh, have you fucked your way through all the blondes in Madrone?"

He laughed. "I like redheads and brunettes, too. Even had a chick with a shaved head once."

"You are a ho."

Not the first time he'd been called that, so he wasn't offended. He just lifted a shoulder. "I love sex. But most chicks bore me. So I just want sex. You dragged me into the storeroom five minutes after we met, so I'd be careful throwing that rock from your glass house."

She frowned. "Maybe if you weren't after girls barely more than half your age, you'd find women more interesting."

Again, he gave a halfhearted shrug. "Interesting women are complicated." A case in point was sitting across the table, looking at him like she regretted being here with him, all because little Becky, whom he'd fucked a total of twice, months ago, had decided to preen her feathers. He felt invested in this date they were getting off wrong at every turn, so he gave her a little more. "Look, I didn't come to this way of being by accident. I've had girlfriends. I've even been in love before. Women who don't bore me don't want to live my life, but they don't figure that out until they're *in* my life, and then it fucking hurts when they leave. Little girls walking on the wild side for a night are easier. End of story."

That look of contempt had left her face, and what had replaced it was softer. Compassion. "I'm sorry. But why did you ask me out, then?"

That was a good question, but he knew the answer. He hoped he did, anyway. "Because you *are* interesting, but you want what I want. Right? Just messing around, like you said."

"Yeah. Yeah." She didn't look as comfortable with that answer as he'd been expecting. He needed her to be comfortable with that answer.

Seeing her the other day playing basketball with her buddies, he'd been jealous—and not just a twinge of it, either. He was looking forward to meeting that Kyle guy, whom he'd been calling Mortal Kombat since they'd fought before, in the ring. Because he wanted to Picasso his face.

Connor knew that he could get more attached to this girl—woman—than he should, if he let himself. He was relying on her reserve to keep himself in check. She didn't want more than fun, and she routinely made that clear. Good. Neither did he. Because he could sense that things could get real complicated between them if they didn't keep to their emotional corners.

Becky came back with Cordero's beer, behaving now like a normal waitress, and they ordered. Connor was pleased that she ordered a filet, rare, with baked potato and salad. She ate like a human being. He got his usual T-bone and fries.

After Becky left again, Cordero took a drink of her beer and leaned in. "How'd you get into your life, anyway? Did you always want to be a biker?"

He took a drink, too, and wiped the foam from his beard. "I've never known anything else, so I guess so. I grew up this way. My dad's the club President."

"You always like it?"

"Sure. I'm close with my folks, my brothers. This is the way I know the world."

Nodding like she thought that answer made perfect sense, she thought for a minute. And then she asked, "Can I ask if you've done time?"

His antennae twitched. "Can I ask why you're asking?"

"Just curious."

Believing her, he answered straight. "Not much, but yeah, I have. Did eleven months about thirteen years ago or so. Assault."

She grinned; he liked that reaction. "Did the guy deserve it?"

He grinned back. "He did." When she didn't ask another question, Connor filled in the space with one of his own. "How'd you end up a firefighter? You said your dad was an Aztec, too, right? Doesn't seem like the same straight line I had."

"It's straighter than you think. I grew up on Assassins turf. Until I was eleven, and my nana took us out of there, they were our family. Everybody I knew hated the cops. Even people like Nana look sideways at the law. They never helped make anything better. When they came at all, they just made more trouble. Or that was how I saw it, how everybody saw it."

That was his take on law, too. "You see it differently now?"

She spun her glass on the table as she spoke. "Yes and no. I know a lot of cops. We work together on calls pretty often. And I like a lot of the cops I know. They're just working stiffs like everybody else. But they're working stiffs with guns, and there are enough power-drunk *hijos de putas*"—she stopped. "Sorry. That means—"

"I know that one. Sons of bitches."

"Yeah. There are enough sons of bitches on the force that there's reason to be suspicious if you live in a world like the one I grew up in."

"What does that have to do with you being a firefighter, though?"

"I wanted to do something important. There was no money for real college. I got an Associate's degree, but that doesn't get you far. If you want to make a difference and don't have any money, you can join the military or go into public service. Everybody loves firefighters. We're not like cops. We're heroes, straight up. We don't judge, we don't hurt. We just help. It's about the most important work you can do when you can't afford to be a scientist or whatever."

Interesting women were complicated for Connor because they were interesting. A woman like this, who was strong and thoughtful, who did work like she did and had an answer like that for why? That lit a fire in him. She could have looked like the Elephant Man and still have been somebody he wanted to hang with. But Cordero did not look like the Elephant Man. She was fucking beautiful.

Everybody thought he was shallow. With very few exceptions, he let them think it. Even people he loved. What he was, though, was careful. He wasn't good at losing what he loved. It made him an asshole. More than that, it made him dangerous, and not in the controlled way that was his job. It was much easier and safer not to let his feelings sink in deep.

So, feeling rocked by the way he and Cordero—Pilar—were talking, the ease and depth of their conversation, knowing that they were on the precipice of something significant and afraid to make that jump, he responded to her thoughtful explanation of her career choice with his oiliest grin. "Well, it makes you a badass bitch, that's all I know."

Her gold eyes darkened, and she sat back abruptly.

And they were back where they belonged.

~oOo~

Cordero's friend, Kyle or Moore or whatever, was almost as big as Connor was. And he knew how to fight; he'd proved that last time. But Connor was leaving the ring tonight one of only two ways: a winner or unconscious.

The Deck had a ref in the ring who'd call a fight if it got too intense, regardless of whether anyone had tapped. That was how Connor had lost to Moore the last time—he'd had his legs kicked out from under him and then been caught in some bullshit submission hold. He wasn't that kind of fighter, he was more of the 'keep hitting them until they stop moving' school, but he felt sure he would have been able to break the hold if he'd been given the shot. He hadn't tapped. The ref had called it.

Tonight, he'd paid the ref off to let the fight go to tapout or knockout.

The fight started out like any other. They'd come into the ring barefoot and stripped to their jeans, their hands taped and gloved. Cordero had his clothes and boots at their table. She was sitting there in that sinful little dress, looking gorgeous, her face lit up with amusement. He winked down at her just before the ref set him and Moore loose on each other.

Moore did a little flitting like a butterfly, but that wasn't Connor's style. Especially this time. Knowing that the guy liked to use his feet, Connor went in fast and hard, taking a combination to Moore's gut. He put his back into it and laid the fucker out.

Flat on the canvas, gasping, Moore glared up at him. "What the fuck, man?"

Connor grinned. "It's a fight, asshole. You out already?"

"Blow me." Moore rolled to his knees and stood.

Connor waited until Moore faced him and then took the same combination right back to him. This time, Moore kept his feet and came back with a hard uppercut to Connor's face. His jaw cracked dangerously, but he could tell it hadn't broken. It would swell, though.

Moore obviously had expected that blow to stun him, and tried to capitalize on that. He spun, bringing in some of that Jackie Chan shit he liked so much, but Connor caught the leg coming at him with both hands. He pulled and put Moore on the mat again, so hard his head bounced.

"Told you, asshole. All you had going for you last time was surprise." Too smart to follow Moore to the mat and set himself up for one of those holds, he waited for him to get back up to his feet.

And then Moore abandoned his flashy tricks and flew at him. Connor didn't take the time to laugh, but it was exactly what he'd wanted: to piss the shithead off. Make him stupid.

After that, it was a mutual bludgeoning. Moore got his shots in, and Connor was feeling it, but he knew he had the advantage. Cordero's bestest buddy's face was ground meat. Still, neither of them showed any signs of letting up, and the ref was giving them what Connor had paid for.

It was Cordero who stopped the fight. She came up to the ring and started yelling at the ref, and when that didn't get her anywhere, she started yelling right at them. Connor, who was well trained to pay attention to what was around him even when he was taking blows to his head, noticed and disregarded her.

"Stop, you fucking idiots! Moore, you have to work in the morning! Connor, back the fuck off! What are you doing? STOP!"

Moore stopped. They were on their feet, so he said, "Yield. I yield, motherfucker." And Connor backed off.

"Good fight," he said, spitting blood onto the canvas.

"Fuck you." Moore's words had gotten pretty mushy.

Okay, then. There was no fanfare to winning a fight at The Deck, and none of the Horde were there—it was a Friday night; they were all at the clubhouse. So he just nodded and climbed through the ropes. Cordero was right there, and he grinned and reached out, but she turned from him and went to Moore instead.

Connor stood there and watched as Cordero went to her friend and took his face in her hands, checking his wounds. She brushed her fingers over his profusely bleeding eyebrow.

Connor had taken his share of blows, too, and it pissed him off to be standing there bleeding, on their date, while she fussed over her friend.

Fuck this shit. He took a cheap towel from the stack at the side of the ring and wiped his face and chest, then threw the bloody, sweaty towel into the plastic bin provided for that purpose. Then he went and pulled his shirt back on.

She'd driven, so he didn't have a ride. He'd have to call his father; his brothers would be too wasted by now to pick him up. Great. Fucking great.

"What the hell, Connor?" She was standing right behind him.

He turned and faced her. Behind her, Moore was headed to the table full of firefighters. "It was a fight. We were fighting."

"You were fighting like it mattered."

"All fights matter."

"Well, that's bullshit."

He was too tired, and sore, for another fight. "Whatever. You know what? This is a bad idea. Go tend to your buddy. I'm out." He left his shirt unbuttoned and bent to pull his boots on.

"Out where? I drove."

"Yeah, and that was a mistake. Don't worry, puss. I can sort myself out."

If she reacted to him calling her 'puss,' he missed it. "Your kutte is in my car. You at least have to go out there with me to get it."

Fuck. "Fine. Then let's go get it."

~oOo~

When they got out there, he reached for the door handle, but she hadn't unlocked the doors yet. He turned and stared at her, waiting.

She walked up to him. "What the fuck happened?"

"You pitched a bitch fit. Think that sums it up."

Balling up her fist, she popped him in his right arm—which was feeling the effort of the fight. Ow. "Fuck you. If anyone was a bitch in there, it was you. Why'd you go at him so hard?"

"It was a rematch. Payback. That's how I fight." He forced himself to laugh. "What, you think it was about you?"

She didn't take the bait. "Wasn't it?"

"We're just messing around, right? Why would it be about you?"

Of course it was about her. Before he'd gotten in the ring, he'd known it was about her. He'd known standing outside her station that he wanted to fight the guy again not just to win but because he'd had his hands all over Cordero, and that had pissed Connor off.

Instead of answering, she grabbed his head. In those crazy high heels, she was only a couple of inches shorter than he was, and when she pulled him close, she was right there to plant one on him.

He was still reeling with adrenaline from the fight, and with anger from what had happened after. He was jealous—and mad about that, too. He was fucking hot for her even as he was furious. So when she kissed him, he grabbed her and turned them both around, shoving her up against her car.

With a gasp he caught in his mouth, she yielded to him completely, and her body softened and molded to his. This was a thing he was figuring out about her—she was a tough bitch and fought tooth and nail with him at first, but it was like she was making him fight for the right to have his way with her. She was a bottom who came on like a top. It was electrifying, the fight and the surrender.

And he could not have cared less in that moment about the anger he'd been feeling. All he wanted now was to be inside her.

His shirt was still open, and the feel of her writhing against his chest made his balls tighten. Pushing his hand between their bodies, he dragged the top of her dress down; she wasn't wearing a bra, and when her firm, naked tits pressed to his chest, he groaned and turned the heat up on their kiss, knowing that he was being rough, and knowing, too, the way she was responding to his demands.

Then he moved his hand and dragged the bottom of her dress up until it was bunched at her hip. She was wearing a wisp of a thong; he pushed it out of the way and plunged his fingers inside her.

She was so goddamn wet.

She tore her mouth from his and cried out, but she didn't stop him—far from it. Instead, she flexed on him, picking up his rhythm, and sought his mouth again, her nails digging into the back of his neck.

His face was sore from the fight, and he knew his lip was bleeding freely as they kissed, but he didn't care, and neither did she.

Nor did they care that they were in the middle of The Deck's brightly-lit parking lot, leaning against her car, all but fucking right then and there. He had every intention of actually fucking her right then and there.

He took his fingers out of her and grabbed a condom out of his pocket. Without breaking their kiss or even slowing it down, he opened his belt and jeans and pulled himself free.

Once the condom was on, he grabbed the backs of her thighs and lifted. She helped right away, hooking her legs around him. And then he shoved into her. Again, she cried out, but he didn't let her mouth go, so he took all the sound into himself. Those studded heels pushed at his loosened jeans and dug into his ass, and he pounded into her, grunting into her mouth, slamming her body into the side of her car again and again until it rocked on its wheels.

There was too much intensity, too much heat, too much need. It wasn't going to last long, and they both knew it. She wanted it as fast as he did—he could tell because even pinned as she was, her body rocked and writhed, urging him on.

Pushing his hand between them, he found her clit and worked it until she arched back and went stiff and still. Recognizing her finish, he let himself complete, too, pounding wildly until pleasure burst in his gut and he tore his mouth from hers and practically howled.

Before he could catch his breath, she was squirming to get loose from him. He obliged her, pulling out fast enough to make them both wince.

She started pulling her clothes back to rights quickly, and she didn't look at him. As he pulled off the condom and tied it off, he asked, "You okay?" Maybe she was regretting the direction their fight had taken them.

"Yeah. Just—let's get in the car." She looked around the parking lot, something like guilt or shame playing over her face.

Ah. He got it, and he grabbed her hand before she could pull away. "You don't like fucking in public."

"Not my kink." Then she looked up at him, and her expression calmed. "It was hot, though." She smiled and brushed her fingers over his sore lip. The touch moved him more than it should have.

"What *is* your kink, Cordero?" What he'd seen of her drawer of toys was too much of a cornucopia to have offered much insight.

"Come home with me and find out."

CHAPTER TEN

They didn't talk at all on the ride back to her place.

Pilar's brain was grinding its gears, trying to make sense of the night—the strange dinner, which had been fun and illuminating and irritating and confusing, all in a disorienting cycle; the bizarre scene at The Deck, with Connor and Moore trying to kill each other, and the ref letting it happen, as if he'd been paid off or something.

Oh, fuck. That was it. One of them had paid him off.

Connor. It had to have been Connor.

Stopping at the end of the off-ramp that would lead them to her home, Pilar turned and studied the man in her passenger seat. Mostly, she saw the back of his head, because he was staring out the side window. But she knew his face was pretty messed up. Moore looked a lot worse, though. Only one man had gone into that ring with an agenda beyond competition.

Why?

Because of her. He'd denied it, but it was true. He was jealous. She'd known it at the station, and she'd liked it. Well, tonight had been the consequence. And she still kind of liked it.

Hence the rabid fucking in the parking lot. Public sex was a line for Pilar. She didn't like it, she didn't think it was hot, she didn't want to see or do it. Getting walked in on was one thing. She wasn't shy; half her life was spent living with men who saw her naked often enough that she no longer cared. But she wasn't looking for an audience. Sex, even casual sex, was intimate, and it deserved at least a semblance of fucking privacy. Something in her life should be private.

But she'd loved what they'd done, at least while they'd been doing it. It had been all dark need and fire, and for that it was one of the hottest encounters she could remember. She'd never had even the slimmest thought to stop.

They needed to talk. Like, real talk.

He turned, his brow creased with a frown. Yeah, his face needed some attention—in addition to the swollen jaw and bruised cheek, there was a cut over one eye, blood smeared and caked around it, and another through his bottom lip. She'd tasted that one in the parking lot. For all she knew, her own mouth was streaked with blood, too.

Okay, first things first: she'd fix him up, and then they'd talk.

And then, depending on how that went, maybe she'd show him her kink.

"Problem?" he asked, and she realized she'd been stopped at the intersection for too long.

She checked for cars and then made her left. "We need to talk."

He didn't answer, just turned back to look out the window.

~oOo~

The garage door was open; Mrs. Lee had a tendency to forget. They shared the two-car space, Mrs. Lee's old Ford Taurus on one side and Pilar's Element on the other. She parked her Victory against the back wall—and usually left her Element on the side skirt of the driveway, because as a two-car space, that garage was a joke, and Mrs. Lee had to open her door all the way to get her arthritic legs out of her car.

She parked in the driveway now. As they got out, she hit the remote for the garage door, and the door began to roll down. Connor looked over and then sort of tilted his head.

"Who rides?"

"What?" She met him at the back of the Honda.

"There's a bike in there. Whose?"

"Mine. I ride."

The way his expression shifted told her that he'd been set to be jealous again. There was an uncomfortable second as that feeling warred with the one brought on by her answer, and then he smiled, wincing when his lip spread. "Nice. Didn't catch the make—but not a Harley."

"No. Victory Hammer."

"Nice."

He seemed impressed, maybe even pleased, but Pilar didn't want to talk bikes. "Come on. I've got first aid stuff inside."

Once inside, she led him to her kitchen and sat him down on a chair in her little dining nook. Then she got her kit and some other supplies. When she came back, he was sitting with his elbows on her table, resting his head in his hands. He looked up as she set the kit in front of him.

"You feel dizzy?"

"Nah. Just tired." He reached for the kit, but she brushed his hand away.

"I got it. Just be still." Stepping between his legs, she lifted his head. He never had buttoned his shirt, and his broadly cut, perfect chest was right there. It made her mouth water.

First she wiped his face with a wet washcloth. He closed his eyes and let her, his face relaxed even as she pressed down to clean the blood from his cuts.

"You paid the ref or something didn't you? To let you fight as long as you wanted."

He opened his eyes but didn't answer. Not saying 'no' was answer enough.

"Because you're jealous of Moore."

He shook his head.

"Bullshit."

"Pretty high opinion of yourself, puss."

She pushed his chin away and dropped the washcloth. As she rifled for an antiseptic wipe, she snarled, "I fucking hate it when you call me that. I could tell the first time I heard it that you call all the women you don't care about that—and the waitress at dinner proved me right. It's just short for 'pussy,' isn't it? Because that's how you see all women." She was wiping his lacerations with the antiseptic, and this time, as she dug at the cut over his eye, he winced and pulled back.

"Not all women, no."

Guessing what he meant, she rolled her eyes. "All women but your mother, then."

"What does it matter? Why do you care?"

She shied away from that answer and instead asked another question. "Why did you come home with me?"

"What? You invited me." He grabbed her wrist and pulled her hand away from his face.

"Yeah, but you got your fuck, and we're pissed at each other. Why'd you come?"

He stared. "I'm not pissed."

"Well, I am." She set the wipe aside and got a butterfly bandage from her kit. As she affixed it over his eyebrow, she asked, "What are we doing, Connor?"

Again he stared, but this time his eyes moved, scanning back and forth over Pilar's face, as if he were looking for something she was hiding. But that was the point of her questions—she didn't want to hide. She'd decided she wanted something—someone. Him. And not just for fun. She could feel their chemistry, their connection, and it fed something inside her. Maybe a guy like this would get her and would give her room for the life she lived.

Then a mask seemed to slide over his face, and he answered her latest question. "I thought I was here to fuck you."

That hurt. As at dinner, when just at the moment she'd been feeling most connected, he'd said something cavalier and a little bit shitty, she felt almost like he'd literally pushed her away.

There was going for what you wanted, and there was throwing yourself into an emotional blender, and Pilar knew that the line between the two was coming up fast. But she was just figuring all this out herself, and she knew she was changing the terms, terms she'd been the first to set up. It had been *her* pushing *him* back until tonight.

She brushed her fingertips over a cheek that was swollen but not cut, and his eyes fluttered closed for a second. "You don't want more than that?"

His hands grabbed her hips, and for a second, Pilar thought he was going to pull her onto his lap. Instead, he pushed her backward and stood up.

"I told you. I don't like complications. I like you. I like hanging out, and I love fucking you. But no. I don't want more than that."

She knew that was bullshit. She *knew* it, could feel the truth of it. But she didn't call him on it. He was going to leave. When he buttoned his shirt and pulled his kutte off the back of the chair, she simply watched.

She wasn't surprised when he said, "I'm going. I'm sorry about the parking lot. I don't make a habit of fucking women in ways they don't want."

"I wanted it."

He chuckled without humor. "Okay, then. Thanks for the medical attention. I'll see you around."

I'll see you around. He was done. Fuck, Pilar did not want that. She wanted to explore what they were feeling, why they were feeling it. There was something between them. There was, damn it! "Connor, wait."

She reached out, but he grabbed her hand before she could touch him. "I thought we understood each other, Cordero."

For the first time, her last name sounded wrong in his voice. "We do. That's my point. I think we understand each other."

"Not what I meant." He dropped her hand and turned from her, and he headed straight to her front door. She followed him to the doorway between the kitchen and her living room and saw that he didn't even pause before he opened the door and went away.

She was still standing in the same spot, gripping the jamb with one hand, when she heard his big Harley chopper roar and then fade away.

There'd been a window somewhere in the little time they'd known each other. Maybe it had been the morning here, after he'd spent the night, when he'd said he wanted to see her again. Maybe if she'd done something other than back away from him, the window between them would have stayed open.

But she hadn't. What she was feeling had surprised her, and that morning had been too early to see what she really wanted. She'd let the window close.

Fuck.

~oOo~

"Station 76 on two-story stucco residence, heavy fire and smoke, multiple exposures, heavy brush twenty feet. Report of two missing, assumed at risk. Using super booster, next company in bring a line."

Pilar heard Guzman's call for backup in her headset and filed it away in her head. It was nothing she didn't already know. She and Moore prepared to enter the structure, a house at the end of a cul de sac. Off to the side of the scene were a mother and two children, getting medical assistance from Nguyen and Perez. They were distraught. The father was in the house; he'd been trapped by the fire while trying to get their third child out.

This was a hot one, but unless it was fully involved, a fire could usually be navigated by someone who understood it and had the right gear. The mother had reported that the little boy had been in the kids' bathroom upstairs. Her husband had gone for him.

Now, the staircase and hallway were engaged. And that was the puzzle. Every rescue had one; the thing that kept a citizen trapped was the thing that the rescue team had to solve. In this case, it was getting to an interior room on the second floor when the only staircase was already involved. They'd tried a ladder into a second-floor window, but the involvement blocked that option completely. They had to climb.

And there was no human sound coming from above, no sign that anyone was hoping for help. That could be a good thing—the father could have had them on the floor away from the heat, knowing to save their oxygen.

Or they could have been incapable of calling for help.

While Moore called for a line, Pilar stood at the foot of the stairs and watched the fire. She put her hand on the wall; her gloves had sensors in the fingertips and palm that read out information onto her face shield about the environment—temperature, oxygen content, etc. The data glowed green and seemed to float over the wavering reds and yellows and whites in the fire.

"I see it. I'm going up." She tightened her grip around her Halligan and put her boot on the first step, right against the wall.

"Cordero, fuck! Let's get it wet down."

That would turn smoke and vapor into dense fog. "I won't be able to see, then. I got it."

"Fuck. I'm right behind you." He hit his mic. "We need a unit on the line in here. Rescue going hot to the second floor."

"Belay that. Line coming in."

Pilar heard the order and ignored it. Fire moved fast. She saw the way through, but it wouldn't be there long.

She could hear Moore huff into his mic. "No go. We're up already."

Then he was right behind her, following her path. When they got to the top, the blaze looked impassable, but Pilar had seen the break in it. She crossed just as water spumed up from below, and smoke and vapor filled the air.

They moved into the hallway, where flames were burning straight up the walls but staying close to the baseboards on the floor. Fire was a lazy bastard and always took the easiest path; Pilar turned and met Moore's face shield, the best they could do for a meaningful look. Investigation wasn't their field, but they both thought this looked like accelerant. On the second floor.

That was somebody else's problem; they were on a rescue mission. Half the doors on the hallway were open. They checked each room, Pilar laying her hand on the closed doors and reading the stats before knocking them in. They found fire licking up the walls, blocking the windows, creeping onto the floor space in an oddly controlled way.

Toward the end of the hallway, on the interior side, Pilar laid her hand on a closed door and found a temperature read that suggested no fire—probably because the oxygen content was so low. Smoke must have filled the room. Nothing about this fire made sense.

With so little oxygen, there was little danger of backdraft, so she tried the knob. It turned, but the door didn't give. It was blocked, and Pilar he thought she knew why. She rapped on the hollow, interior door, high, then moved downward, getting a sense of the block. It was low and thick. A body, then.

She turned and gestured to Moore, signaling what she intended. Then she raised her Halligan, meaning to hit high and rip the door in half. She could grab the kid, and Moore could get the dad. With luck, they were just unconscious.

He nodded.

And then the ceiling collapsed behind him. As fire fell from above, he lunged forward, into Pilar, and they tumbled to the floor. They were surrounded by flames.

Still lying on top of her, Moore yelled into his mic, "Structural collapse. Repeat, structural collapse. The ceiling is down, second floor. Full involvement. We are flanked." He looked around and then rolled off her. They had about six feet clear around them. If help didn't come from below soon, they were fucked.

"We need to get in there."

Pilar nodded. "Aim high."

Moore stood and swung his irons at the door. When he pulled out and took another swing, the water arrived and settled the fire.

Scalding fog filled the space, bringing the temperature up to brimstone intensity. Moore ripped the door open. Father and son were on the floor on the other side, unconscious. Moore reached over what was left of the door and grabbed the father, muscling him over his shoulders. Then Pilar grabbed the boy. They picked their way through the debris and headed to the staircase.

Outside, three engines and a tanker were now on the scene. And, joy of joys, a satellite news truck. The brush at the back was involved now, and that was a potential crisis, a wildfire waiting to break control. Moore and Pilar met paramedics at the edge of the safe zone and handed over their rescues.

Reyes ran up to them. "You okay?"

"Yeah, yeah," Pilar answered. "Lucky break."

Moore laughed and pushed at her shoulder. "Only you could call that a lucky break."

"We're whole. That's lucky."

He nodded, and they went back to work.

~oOo~

It was daylight by the time they got back to the barn. They were on a thirty-six watch, so they still had several hours on the clock. After they ran their checks, some grabbed a bite, but most hit the showers and then their bunks.

Perez was one who'd headed to the kitchen, so Pilar had the tiny women's bathroom to herself. She stood under the cool shower and let the fire wash away.

Father and son were alive. They were in bad shape, but they were alive.

They'd killed the brush fire in a few hours and had kept further exposure contained. And she and Moore had escaped that collapse alive.

All in all, it had been a good call.

But that fire had been weird. It hadn't behaved like it should have, not entirely. But it had been familiar to her, too.

She hadn't been completely honest with Connor when he'd asked why she'd wanted to be a firefighter; there was more to the story. When she was eight, she'd been staying overnight at a friend's house. There'd been a fire in the middle of the night, and she and Mia hadn't been able to get out. They'd been rescued by firefighters, carried out bundled up in strong arms, and she'd known her first heroes. She could still vividly recall that night, the way she'd felt waiting in a room filling with heat and smoke, the way the firefighter's arms had felt.

They'd learned fire safety in school, and they'd remembered to stay low, so they'd been lying on the floor in Mia's room, holding hands and waiting. Pilar had watched the flames, the way they'd danced, the way they'd seemed to follow a path they knew.

At the time, of course, she hadn't known how fire ate a food it loved, an accelerant. Now she did.

Somebody had set the blaze when she was eight, and somebody had set the one tonight. They'd gone through the whole house, top to bottom, to douse it in fire food. While the family had slept.

The way tonight's fire resounded in her memory, that must have been the reason she cared so much, felt so rocked—she'd done her job, gotten the victims out, delivered them alive to paramedics. She and Moore had come through their excitement unscathed. It had been a good call.

But she felt lonely. So fucking lonely. She wanted someone to give a shit that she could have died tonight. She wanted someone to bundle her up in strong arms and let her feel rescued for a little while.

It was stupid, and she didn't understand how an ancient childhood memory and a weird fire tonight had tangled up and made her lonely. But that was the feeling she felt most strongly.

Connor had turned and left her house more than a week earlier. She missed him. They'd barely gotten to know each other, but she felt keenly that something important had been lost. That he was somebody who might get her, might get her life, might make room for it, since his own was outside convention, too.

But he didn't want to try.

She should already have called Doug or Charlie, her fuck buddies, and fucked herself straight, but she hadn't had an appetite for either of them, or for a random hookup. Ironically, sex without strings felt too complicated. Or she was already gone for the biker who only wanted to play. Either way, she was lonely.

When Perez came in, Pilar shut off the water and grabbed her towel.

"You leave me any hot?"

"Yeah. I didn't want hot tonight. Already had plenty." She dried off and pulled the clothes she wore here to sleep—loose sweatpants and an old t-shirt—on, then braided her unmanageable thicket of hair. She didn't feel like undertaking the fuss to get it dried decently. "I'm gonna try to crash for a few."

In the bunkroom, at the corner between the men's bunks and the little nook they'd made for the women, Moore was waiting. He, too, was freshly showered and dressed in sweats. The blackout shades on the windows were drawn against the morning sun, and the room had the eerie blue glow of midnight.

"You okay, *chica*?" He reached out and picked up the braid lying over her shoulder. His face had healed some since the fight with Connor and now was mottled in faint, aged-looking pastels of yellow and green.

"Yeah, why?"

"Your force field is up." That was what he called it when she was in a difficult mood.

She pulled her braid out of his hand. "Just tired. I'll catch a couple, then I'll be fine."

He squinted at her, then nodded. "Yeah, me too. Assuming we stay quiet, I'm on the grill for lunch."

"Cool." She patted his bare belly and moved past him, then dropped to her bunk. She really was exhausted.

And so fucking lonely.

CHAPTER ELEVEN

Connor walked out of the dorm, escorting a little twenty-year old education major to the front door. Mingling aromas of coffee and bacon filled the air, and Connor's stomach rumbled. He needed to get…Kristy…out of here and get some grub before he showered and headed to the shop.

He'd already called her a cab. She had the wide-eyed look of a girl who was regretting some recent decisions. As she scanned the Hall, though, she settled a little. It was a Wednesday. The Hall was just a room, and as clean as it ever got. A couple of girls in the kitchen, and Trick slouched in a chair, dressed in his shop coverall, rubbing a hand over his newly-shorn head and holding some tattered paperback in his other hand. But he wasn't reading; the giant television on the wall was showing the morning news, and Trick was focused there.

Connor opened the front door and led her into the early-morning sunshine, and the cab was just pulling up. "Okay, Kristy. You have a good day now." He leaned in to kiss her cheek, but she jerked back.

"It's *KEARsty*. I totally told you like a million times."

He was losing his appetite for young chicks. Jesus, they were insipid. No pussy was tight enough to compensate for that whiny way so many of them had of talking, the way they turned up the last syllable of every sentence so that it sounded uncertain. "Okay, puss. Okay. Get on back to your life now." He opened the cab door and guided her in, then leaned in the front window and paid the driver.

Then he turned around and went inside.

There was hot coffee in the machine behind the bar, so he went back and poured himself a big mug, then added a light splash of milk from the bar fridge.

"You want a cup, T?" he asked Trick.

Trick didn't answer, so Connor padded over in his bare feet and sat on the couch facing the television. On a Wednesday morning, bare feet were safe in the Hall. On a Saturday morning, that was a risky choice.

The screen showed a reporter standing in Pershing Square in L.A.—the scene of Allen Cartwright's death a week earlier.

That hit had gone smoothly, and exactly as planned. Trick had taken a position on the rooftop Sherlock and Bart had cased, and he'd made a bullseye, dropping Cartwright with a bullet in the forehead from about five hundred yards away.

They had no connection to Cartwright, and Trick had been sure to leave no trace of himself or his assignment behind. If a crime could be perfect, that hit, it seemed, was it.

He sat for a second and listened to the news. The reporter had thrown the story to footage of a press conference, several men in uniforms and bad suits lined up behind a podium. The man at the mic was obviously a Fed. They all just had a look about them.

... investigators have determined that the shot came from a distance, estimating at least four hundred yards. We are searching every building within a thousand-yard radius of the incident...

Connor turned to Trick. "Anything to worry you?"

His friend's attention finally left the television. "No. They're nowhere. And I left nothing. I'm sure of it. They'll probably eventually figure out that the cameras were hacked, but Sherlock and Bart erased their tracks. I've played the scene out in my head about a thousand times in the past week, and it went just the way I'd played it out in my head beforehand. We didn't leave a trace."

He leaned back. "That guy had little kids. A wife. Sure the fuck wish I knew why La Zorra wanted him dead." He rubbed his head again; he'd been doing that, like a nervous tic, since he'd had his dreads and beard cut off.

There was no point turning over the matter of La Zorra's motives, so Connor changed the subject and nodded at Trick's head. "How you doin' with that, Velcro-head?"

Trick lifted his middle finger, flipping him a lazy bird. Then he answered the question. "My head doesn't feel like it's full of helium and about to float off anymore. And I almost recognize myself in the mirror. Still sucks, though."

"So grow 'em back."

"I guess. I don't know. The point is lost now. Turns out, I am who they trained me to be. A drone who kills without question." Making a disgusted sound, he picked up the paperback on his lap and tossed it onto the table at his side. It was black, with a black and white picture on the cover, like one of those medieval etchings or something. Connor took a closer look, and the picture was pretty involved—and also pretty deranged: people hanging from chains and ropes. The title of the book was *Discipline & Punish: The Birth of the Prison*, by Michel Foucault.

"That some fetish shit?"

Trick scoffed. "No, asshole. It's not 'fetish shit.' It's a critique of the prison system, and it has some stuff about soldiers, too. Soldiers are a lot like prisoners. We all are, actually. Everything we do is scrutinized and judged, every way we act is because of it. We all live in the panopticon." At Connor's frown, he shook his head. "Don't worry about it. I'm in a mood."

Trick was always reading some thick-ass book that put him in a mood. Connor considered him his best friend, and vice versa, but they were very different men. Aside from their physical differences—Trick was fair and lean, while Connor was burly and dark—they were different in interest and temperament as well.

Trick had a college degree. Connor had managed to get himself through high school without getting expelled. Trick was a voracious reader, who liked to Think Big Thoughts and have deep conversations about books and politics and current events. Connor thought politics was a crock of shit, and he had never been a reader. Reading meant sitting, and he didn't like to sit. He liked to do.

He was a problem-solver, a fixer. Trick was a problem-seer, an analyst. Where Connor tended to be loud and was quick to fight, Trick was quiet and always measured in his responses.

Maybe that was why they got along so well and, ironically, got each other without trying. They were opposites, and they filled in each other's gaps. They complemented each other.

While Connor was thinking that, the television caught his eye again. The screen was full of flames, showing a fire that had happened during the night. He saw the '76' on one of the trucks and knew Cordero's station was there. He didn't know if she'd been working last night, but he watched intently, looking for her. Why he thought he'd be able to recognize her, he didn't know. All the firefighters looked the same, buried in heavy gear.

But then two came out of the burning building, carrying bodies. One firefighter was considerably bigger than the other and had an adult over his shoulders. The other carried a child.

That was her. He knew it. His chest tightened. Fuck, she was impressive. An actual hero, carrying a child literally through fire to safety.

Ever looking for the 'human interest' story, the cameraman zoom hard toward the scene of the firefighters handing over the victims to the paramedics, laying them on stretchers.

And then Connor's attention shifted from Cordero to the man on the stretcher. "I know that guy. That's Marshall Bridges." A glance at the text on the bottom of the screen, showing the street name, settled it.

Trick leaned in and studied the television, but then a firefighter blocked the camera and pushed the crew back. "I didn't see. You sure? The Bridges Motors guy?"

"Yeah, yeah. He bought his oldest a Low Rider for high school graduation last year, had me pimp it out. He was a pain in the ass about it, and I had to talk to him a lot. He said some stuff that got me twitching, so I asked Sherlock to study him up. He didn't need to—he'd already known. The guy has three chop shops across SoCal. That's how he makes his real bank. And that means he's hooked with some crazy *cholos*."

"You think this is something, then?" Trick waved at the television.

Connor shrugged and stood. "Don't know. Probably not. It's interesting, though." He rubbed his bare belly, which was really starting to complain. "But right now, I'm more interested in breakfast."

~oOo~

"Hey, Mom!" That afternoon, Connor closed the front door of his parents' house. When his mother, Bibi, didn't answer, he walked through the entry and headed to the kitchen. The faint aroma of baking bread made his mouth water. He was going to raid the larder before he left.

"Mom? You around?"

He knew she was—her Cadillac was in the garage, and the overhead door was open. But when she still didn't answer, and the kitchen was empty and pristine, two loaves of fresh bread cooling on racks on the granite counter, his heart sped up a little. "Mom!"

That fire at the Bridges' house the night before had him extra twitchy, and without a solid reason. Yeah, Bridges bought stolen cars from the Aztecs—and every other gang in that biz in the bottom half of the state. Yeah, Cordero had worked the fire. Yeah, he, and by extension the Horde, was connected to Cordero and her problems with the Aztecs. But those were all coincidences. Correlation did not imply causation. The Horde had nothing to do with Bridges, except for tricking out his spoiled kid's bike. Whatever trouble the Horde might have with the Aztecs, last night's fire was irrelevant.

But he was twitchy anyway.

The Aztecs had done a couple of drive-bys past the clubhouse and bike shop over the last couple of weeks, since the Horde had meddled in their affairs. Nothing more than that, just literal drive-bys, slowly down the street, but Esposito was waving his dick around, and the Horde were waiting for them to do something more.

They had to wait, at least for now. La Zorra had not been impressed by the news that the Horde had any kind of trouble with the Aztecs. She shared their opinion of the gang as scum and generally beneath her notice, but she didn't want to weaken her truce with the Fuentes cartel. Plus, her attention had been on the L.A. District Attorney.

La Zorra was pleased with the hit, and the Horde had brought in a huge stack of cash. But neither she nor they needed law to turn toward them over the Aztecs. She had asked Hoosier, Bart, and Connor to stand down until there was aggression, and they had agreed it was the best course. So they were waiting, and letting Raul Esposito wave his dick around. Connor wanted to cut it off.

And those assholes went for family all the time. If the Horde were sitting on their asses while a loved one got hurt, Connor would tear the whole fucking town apart.

He had asked Sherlock to check in on Cordero's brother. Hugo was home with his grandmother, and so far, it didn't look like the Aztecs were pushing on him to make his debt right. That was that, then, as far as Connor was concerned. He and Cordero, whatever had been going on between them, however she'd fucked with his head—that was dead. So Hugo and his sister were on their own. He needed to worry about his own family.

Good plan. Except he couldn't stop thinking about her. The few times they'd fucked played in a loop all night, every night, whether or not he was with a Madison, Hailey, or Kristy—no,

KEARsty. Whatever. But more than that, he thought about their dinner at The Bunkhouse, sitting across from her while they ate and talked, seeing her in that cardinal sin of a dress.

He'd been right to walk away. She'd changed things up between them, and he hadn't wanted that. But she was still in his head.

Right now, though, the only thought in his head was his mother. He pulled his phone out, but before he called her, he tried one more time, yelling, "MOM!" at the top of his voice.

He dialed, and her phone rang in the house.

Fuck!

At the moment that his concern blossomed into fear, the French doors to the back yard opened, and in came his mother, wearing a floppy straw hat, her gardening gloves, and bright yellow rubber boots. "What the hell, Connor? Why are you in here roarin' like a big ol' grizzly?"

Relief exploded his heart, and he grabbed her and lifted her off the ground. "Jesus fuck, Mom. Thank God!"

She pushed on his shoulders, and he set her down. When he looked down at her face, she was giving him this look she had, one eyebrow up, her eyes a little squinty, like she was reading under his surface. Since he could remember, that look had made him feel naked—and guilty, whether or not he had something to hide.

"You know I'm not gonna ask why you're scared. You just tell me if I need to do anythin'."

His mother had been an old lady for a very long time. She knew the score. "Just keep your phone close. Let me or Dad know where you are when you leave the house."

"I was in the back yard, honey. Your dad already talked to me about checkin' in. So that's it?"

"Yeah, yeah. Nothing new. I'm just…jumpy, I guess."

She reached up and cupped his jaw in her hand. "It's not like you to be jumpy, Connor. There anythin' you need to talk about?"

He sighed and dropped into a chair at the breakfast table. "I don't know."

Toeing off her rubber boots, his mother said, "I roasted a turkey breast yesterday and sliced it up for sandwiches, and I made a couple of loaves of white bread this mornin'. Did you have any lunch?" She pulled off her gloves and hat and set them on top of her boots. "And you can tell me what the fuck is up your ass."

He laughed. His mom was an interesting broad. Trick liked to say that she was like the daughter of Gaia and Ares: the perfect mother, with a warrior's heart.

"I love you, Mama Bear."

She came over and kissed the top of his head. "You're my baby. Now talk." As she headed to the counter, without turning, and with a deceptively casual tone, she asked, "Anythin' to do with the girl your dad told me about?" She opened the fridge and pulled out a beer, like she hadn't just dropped a grenade in his lap.

"What?"

She popped the cap and brought the bottle to him. "Dad was just tellin' me that y'all helped a girl out a while back, and you seemed kinda protective of her."

"I *am* protective. That's what I do. In general." He took the bottle, and she lifted an eyebrow at him and then went back to the counter and started making sandwiches. In his head, he flipped through the very few opportunities his father would have had to form an opinion about him and Cordero.

The Keep. He'd gotten huffy at J.R. for calling her Latin pussy. Goddammit, Dad.

"I'm just thinkin' it would be nice to have you close enough with somebody to bring 'em over for Sunday dinner. Fill out the table, you know. You haven't brought a girl around in years."

"Jesus, Mom. Don't nest. I'm not gonna bring anybody home. You want family and grandbabies, you got Deme and Faith for that."

In the act of smearing mayonnaise on a slice of bread, she stopped and turned to him. "Honey, this ain't about what I want. It's about what you want. I know you want that in your life—a woman, children. Why don't you look for it?"

"I did. Tried a couple times. Didn't work out."

"So you just give up? Connor Jerome Elliott, you are not that weak." She slapped the knife across the bread with force and then stabbed it into the mayonnaise jar.

"It's not weak to understand that my life and women don't mesh."

"You do see that you're talkin' to a woman who lives this life, right? Forty-two years and countin'. Standin' here healthy and strong."

"You haven't always been."

Her head jerked up, and her complexion paled. "We don't talk about those days. And I came through it. Right?"

The reason Connor was an only child was because his father had always lived a violent life in a violent world—just as they both did now. When Connor was four years old, his mother had been taken hostage by an enemy of their old club. He hadn't even been a member of that club at the time; he'd been patched into a support club. She'd been beaten and raped for three days before they'd found her. She'd been horribly hurt. And unable to have any more children.

Connor hadn't known any of that at the time, of course; he'd been too young. He'd learned the story much later, as a young man.

Most of what Connor remembered of the year that followed his mother's trauma was absence and silence. His memories of that year were like the old silent movies—monochrome and without sound. And all of his memories of his mother during that time were like still photographs. She sat, and she stared. Faith's mother, Margot, his mother's best friend and another member's old lady, had done most of the raising of him then.

Margot had been pregnant and then had had an infant daughter of her own, Faith's older sister, Serenity. The only happy times he remembered in that year had to do with that tiny little girl. Margot had let him hold her, play with her, sit at her cradle and rock her. She had smelled so good—when she hadn't smelled like shit or puke, anyway. Her first smile had been at him.

Serenity and Connor had ended up not being all that close. Sera was a straight arrow and had wanted nothing more from their life, from the time she could grasp what it was their fathers did, than to be away from it. Connor had wanted to follow his father from the time he could grasp what it was their fathers did.

When he'd learned about his mother's trauma, the knowledge had drawn him closer to the life, not driven him from it. He'd wanted to be strong, to fight, to protect. Not to flee.

Faith, seven years younger than he, had been the sister who'd become his sister.

"Connor." His mom set a plate with two sandwiches and a wedged tomato in front of him and sat next to him with a plate of her own—one sandwich and a tomato. "I got through it. I had love, and I got through it. Everybody's got shit to deal with. It don't matter what job you have. Ditch diggers, secretaries, doctors, outlaws, we all got shit. You look for the one who'll carry you through it, and who you want to carry through."

Still caught up in those old memories, he didn't answer. He picked at his sandwich for a second, his appetite gone.

His mother put her hand over his. "You're young, honey. Don't give up so quick. If you want somethin', go find it." With a sharp pat on his hand, she sat back. "Now eat up. I need you out back to carry that big potted tree to the other side of the yard. I made you that meal, and now you owe me."

He laughed and picked up a sandwich. "You're awesome, Bedelia."

"Yes, I am. Good you know it."

CHAPTER TWELVE

Pilar parked her Element on the street in front of her grandmother's house. Renata Salazar lived on the 'wrong' side of Madrone, in the only neighborhood in the city limits that didn't look like people cared. Even so, it was about five steps up the affluence ladder, and completely across town, from the neighborhood she'd moved them all from, where the Aztec Assassins ruled.

Pilar had parked on the street because the driveway was full of Hugo's truck and their grandmother's old Corolla. The garage had never been a place they'd kept cars. Their grandmother had a lifetime packed away in there—boxes and furniture and who knew what. All of their mother's things were there. Every last knickknack. Even her toiletries from the bathroom.

When Pilar and Hugo's mother had been killed, they'd been living in a rickety two-bedroom apartment. But it had been filled with expensive crap, especially electronics. Pilar had been just old enough to begin to understand why—to wonder no longer why there were holes in the walls and cockroaches in the cupboards when the living room was a sea of leather furniture and sleek black boxes.

By eleven, she'd figured it out.

She understood what was happening when her stepfather, Little Jay, would sit in that living room with his buddies, all speaking in low murmurs, while their mother, Olivia, stayed back with them in their shared room and read them stories.

Or she thought she'd understood. Little Jay was like her father had been. A man who always had a gun under his shirt. A man people were afraid of. Then, as a child, she'd been proud. She'd thought fear and respect were the same thing. She'd thought they lived like they did because Little Jay and his crew stayed in their home neighborhood, even when they could afford more. They stayed with their people, didn't abandon them. She'd thought it made them Great Men instead of Bad Guys.

Neither her father nor Little Jay had been bad fathers. They had usually been gentle with Pilar and Hugo, even indulgent. And Pilar's memories of her mother were all good—a sweet, pretty woman who dished out hugs and kisses freely, who kept the best house she could under the circumstances, who made delicious food and chatted freely with the neighbors. Who fought for her children and protected them fiercely.

Her own father had been shot down in the street the day of her fourth birthday party. By the time she was five, she had a stepfather and a baby brother. She'd been too young at the time to wonder at that timing. By the time she was eleven, she hadn't remembered enough of her life before Little Jay to wonder about how he'd come to be in her life.

By the time she was old enough to reflect on it, her mother, father, and stepfather were all in the ground, and it no longer mattered. So she locked the question away.

Little Jay and Olivia had been killed much like Pilar's father had been—a drive-by. Two others had been killed, both Assassins.

Renata had her apartment and theirs packed, and they had moved, in what had seemed then like a matter of mere days. She'd left Little Jay's things behind and had taken every single thing that had been their mother's. Almost all of it was still in the boxes she'd packed in that rush. The gold crucifix Pilar wore was the only thing of her mother's she had, though she supposed she could dig through the garage and rebuild her mother's life entirely.

Now, her arms laden with shopping bags, Pilar walked alongside the cars in the driveway and went in the side door of the house. Her grandmother didn't like people coming in through the front and traipsing the outside inside through her living room. She was the kind of woman who left the plastic covers on her lampshades. The living room was for 'company'—which she never had.

They'd all done their living in the kitchen and the little 'family room' in the back, which was really just an enclosed porch with a window air conditioning unit.

"*Hola,* Nana. I went to the market." Pilar stepped into the kitchen and set the bags on the white-tile counter. As she started unpacking groceries, her grandmother came in from the family room.

"*Gracias, mija.* Did you get the plantains?"

"Yep. They were on special, so I got a whole bunch. If that's too much, I'll take some home with me. Oh, and the deli had that fruit salad Hugo likes, so I got that, too." When Hugo didn't come into the room, to help or even to say hello, Pilar called out, "Hugo! Come on!"

Putting a carton of milk in the refrigerator, her grandmother said, "He's not here, Pilar."

"What?" It had been almost three weeks since he'd been beaten, so he was healed. But he'd been milking it, lazing around, lapping up their grandmother's nursing. Hiding from the Assassins.

"He said he had a line on a job."

"But his truck's in the driveway. And it's five o'clock in the afternoon. And Friday."

"A friend picked him up. I didn't recognize the car. Maybe it's night work?"

"Nana..." The only kind of 'friends' Hugo had were the kind that brought trouble.

"I know, *mija.* But what can I do with him? Lock him away? He's a grown man."

"Maybe if you'd treat him like a grown man, and quit wiping his ass for him all the damn time, he'd act like a grown man."

Her grandmother slammed the fridge door. "I do the best I can. I know his troubles are my fault. I didn't get your mother out of that place after your *abuelo* died, and she got taken in by that gang. And I lost her. I got you and Hugo away as fast as I could, but it costs a lot to live here. I had to work so much. I couldn't be in two places at once!"

Pilar pulled her agitated *abuela* into her arms. "Shh, Nana. It's okay. You did good. You took care of us. We both always felt your love. You don't have to try to make up for doing the best you could to keep us safe. But you're right. Hugo is a man. He should be, anyway. Maybe it's time to let him go. Maybe he needs to know we won't fix his fuckups for him anymore before he'll try to fix them himself."

Her grandmother sniffed and relaxed on Pilar's shoulder. "Don't swear, *mija*."

"Sorry."

"I love him. I love you both." She stepped away from Pilar and went back to unpacking groceries. "I can't sit back and let him suffer. I just can't."

Sighing, Pilar pulled the plantains out of the bag and set them in the wide, shallow bowl her grandmother kept for fruit. "I know, Nana. I know."

A thought occurred to her as she was packing the empty bags together. "What did the car look like?"

"You know I don't know from cars. It was an old sporty one. Like from that old show with the talking car." She waved her hand. "Long before your time. But it had a bird on the hood. A painting of a big bird."

"A Trans Am?" She took her phone out and found a picture online. "Like this?"

"*Si*. But black, and the wheels were gold."

She knew the car. She'd seen it parked outside the High Life the night they'd found Hugo. She'd driven by that place a couple of times since and had seen the driver get into it once. It was Sam's—Raul Esposito's main thug. "Fuck."

"Don't swear, *mija*."

"Sorry, Nana." She didn't say more, and her grandmother didn't ask—in fact, she seemed to have made a firm decision not to ask. Pilar didn't know what to do with the information that Hugo had gone off with a high-ranking Assassin, or whether to do anything at all.

Let him go. Let him make his mistakes and clean up after himself. Their grandmother couldn't, but did that mean that Pilar couldn't, either?

So she kept her mouth shut and let her grandmother have her denial.

~oOo~

It was Friday night, and Pilar was off on Saturday, but she was in a foul mood and shrugged off Moore's call to join them at The Deck. She hadn't been there since the last night she'd seen Connor, and she was fairly certain she wouldn't be going back.

Fuck, she could not stop thinking about that guy. Talking to her grandmother earlier, realizing that Hugo was falling back in with the Assassins in some way, apparently voluntarily, had everything about the night they'd found him spinning around in her head. The way Connor had helped, and pulled his club into it, too, simply because she'd said she needed help. The way he'd shielded her and stayed with her until he was sure she was safe.

The way they'd fucked that night. How comfortable she'd felt sleeping with him.

Those thoughts pulled into a frenzy all the others that were normally floating around in there already, and she could barely be still.

There was something between them. And she'd missed the window.

Fuck, she was lonely. Fuck.

Then she thought, *You know what? No. Why am I not going for what I want?*

She had no good answer. If Connor wanted to be done with her, he was going to have to make it a lot more clear than 'See you around.'

It was after nine on Friday night. Without bothering to change, without even bothering to brush her hair, Pilar grabbed her keys and went out. She walked past the Element and opened the garage.

Where she was going, she wanted to ride.

~oOo~

Night Horde parties were well known. Every Friday night. They partied other nights, too, maybe even most nights, but on Fridays, they opened their doors. It wasn't totally open, you ostensibly had to have been invited, but it wasn't like anyone was checking a list at the door.

Pilar backed her bike in at the end of a line of bikes on Mariposa Avenue. These were guest bikes, she knew; the Horde parked in the side lot, which was fenced with eight-foot-high chain link.

People—the men mostly heavyset and heavily bearded, and the women mostly busty and in bedazzled black, everybody inked—milled about on the sidewalk outside the front door to the clubhouse. Music thudded heavily against the walls—Stevie Ray Vaughn.

She was noticed, but other than some cordial nods in her direction, which she returned, no one interacted with her. She opened the door, and the music poured into the air. Then she stepped into the Horde clubhouse.

It wasn't her first time, of course. Connor had brought her into this room when he was arranging to help her. But then, it had been almost empty. Now, it was packed to the rafters with people. Weed and cigarette smoke filled the air. It wasn't even ten o'clock yet, but people were well on their way to blind drunk. They were laughing, playing pool, or pinball, or in various stages of getting busy. No wonder Connor hadn't thought twice about fucking her in the parking lot. There was a lot of nakedness going on around her, and nobody but the people involved even seemed to notice. Except her.

She stopped looking at that and started looking for Connor.

He was standing at the end of the bar, and a little redhead was rubbing all over him, wearing shiny red booty shorts and a miniscule silver lamé halter top. She was unbuttoning his shirt. He smiled down at her, that fucking melty smile, then he turned his head and put a cigarette to his lips.

Pilar hadn't known he smoked. She wasn't a fan, but she could deal. What she couldn't deal with, however, was the little redhead, who now had his shirt completely open and was scratching long, red talons over his nipples.

When his hand went to Red's ass and he bent down to kiss her, Pilar...well, she lost her shit. A little. She had no right to, but that hardly mattered.

Clearing the remaining distance in about four strides, she grabbed Red by the shoulder and yanked her back. "Sorry, *chica*. Connor's got plans tonight."

But Red wasn't one of Connor's little teeny-boppers. She was young, but she wasn't naïve—she had the cold look of a chick who'd seen some shit. She turned on Pilar, hauling off and punching her right in the eye. "Fuck off, bitch!"

Pilar hadn't expected that, and it hurt. But she could throw a punch, too—which she did, right into Red's bare belly. Pilar felt the chick's navel jewelry dig into her knuckles. Red doubled over, coughing.

The room's attention was pulling to the scene, and Pilar could sense that Red had friends, girls heading into the fray. She could fight, but not if she was heavily outnumbered. And some of the guys looked excited, like they couldn't wait to see a bitch brawl.

But then Connor grabbed her, hooking his arm across her chest and pulling her back against him, and he caught Red's hand as it swung again.

"Okay, ladies. I'm flattered. But enough. Tina, I'll catch you later."

'Tina' looked furious, but she didn't challenge Connor at all. In fact, she forced the anger from her face and put a smile on instead. "Okay, Connor. Whenever you want me."

Pilar scoffed and side-eyed the bitch. What a whore. With a venomous look at Pilar, Tina sashayed off, and a couple of girls rushed up to check on her.

Connor leaned down and put his mouth near her ear. "I don't know what the fuck you're doing here, or what your problem is, but you're coming with me right now or I'm gonna let Tina and the girls have what they want with you."

His voice sounded different from what she knew of it—heavier, thick with threat. But she'd come in here like every cliché of a jealous woman rolled into one, and she'd started it all. Plus, she did want to be alone with him; it was why she was even here.

She nodded. "Okay, yeah."

He moved his arm, turning her and hooking his huge hand over the back of her neck. Then he led her through the room and down a hallway. At the end of the hall, he stopped in front of one of the several doors that lined both sides, and he unlocked it.

"Get in."

She went in, and he closed—and locked—the door behind them. Then he hit a switch, and the overhead light, which was part of a ceiling fan, came on.

They were in a bedroom. His bedroom, she assumed. It was obviously not for public use—there were personal items everywhere, and the bed had the kind of linens that people had for themselves—tan with brown and blue stripes. Not basic motel linens. It was a small room, not especially messy, but obviously lived in.

"You live here?"

"I'm asking the questions. Sit." He indicated an elderly armchair in the corner of the room. She took the seat, and he sat on the bed. "What the fuck, Cordero?"

When she'd left the house, she'd been operating on instinct, want, and loneliness. She had no plan, no intention beyond being with him. There might have been the fantasy of walking in and finding him alone, and just going straight up to him and kissing him, him wrapping her up in his arms and kissing her back.

Yeah, that would have been best case.

But while she'd been unable to want anybody else—which, she was sure, wasn't helping her on the loneliness front—he obviously had no problem getting his knob polished. Seeing him getting pawed at, and enjoying it, had made her nuts.

Nuts enough to want to break somebody's face. Which Connor had done to Moore.

Of course, *she* had reason to be jealous. He did not.

Except that they both had the same reason to be jealous. There was something between them. Something real.

The problem was that she was the only one willing to admit it.

So that was her plan. Get him to admit it, or make herself accept that he simply would not. Start something with him or move on. That was the plan.

She'd waited too long to answer his angry question. He huffed and asked another. "Are you in trouble?"

Oh, yes. She definitely was. But that wasn't what he'd meant. "No. I wanted to see you."

He chuckled sarcastically and looked away. "Well, you did that. Made a fucking entrance, too. Why?"

"Same reason you beat the shit out of Moore."

His head swiveled back, and he looked at her with narrowed eyes. "You fight Tina before? Need a rematch?"

"Fuck, Connor. Please let's just be straight with each other. We are not kids. Can't we just be honest?"

He crossed his arms over his chest, his shirt still open from Tina's seduction, and for a second Pilar was distracted by the sight. God, he was gorgeous. He was also angry; his breast heaved with it. "I've been nothing but. I told you what I wanted. I thought you wanted it, too. I'm not the one who fucked up a good thing."

"You're fucking it up right now." All at once, Pilar was just too weary. She felt self-conscious and exposed, rejected and awkward. She'd nearly started a brawl over this guy, and he wasn't even strong enough to admit that he felt something for her. It had been stupid to come here.

And anyway, she had her answer. He wouldn't admit it. So it was time to move on.

She stood. "Okay, Connor. You win. I'm sorry I barged in and interrupted your night. I'm gonna go. I'm sure Tina's motor's still revving."

He said nothing. She crossed the small room and went to the door. It took her a second to turn the lock. By the time she was opening the door, he was right behind her. He slammed his hand on the flat wood and forced the door shut.

For a second, two seconds, three, four, five, neither of them moved or spoke. Pilar's heart was pounding so hard she could feel it in her jaw.

"I don't like to lose," he spoke low, his head looming over hers. His voice was little more than a growl.

"I know. Me, either."

"You said you didn't want this."

"I know. I was wrong."

She could feel tension leaving him slowly; she could see it—his hand relaxed just slightly on the door. "The life I lead…I break the law every fucking day. My life is violent. *I* am violent. I end plenty of days washing blood away. People I love have been hurt because of what we do. You could get hurt. This life *is* the wild side."

Pilar resisted the urge to lean her head on the door in pure relief. She wasn't sure there was even a name for the emotion that was swirling through her veins. It wasn't love; it couldn't possibly be love already. But it was the thing that eventually became love, whatever that was.

"I know, Connor. I know who you are."

He laughed bitterly and bent down, his mouth right at her ear. "No, you don't. You can't know who I am unless you're in my life. But don't you fucking tell me you want in and think you can say that and then leave any time, when you decide you were wrong. Don't jerk me around like that."

She turned and leaned back on the wall next to the door. "I'm telling you *I know*. I grew up on the wild side. We haven't even started, so I can't tell you it's forever right this second. Maybe *you* won't want it to be forever. Maybe I won't. But can't we even try? If we end, it won't be because I ran away in fear. Your life doesn't scare me. I know what you do—more than most. And I know you could get hurt or killed."

He was staring down at her with such intensity that her face felt warm. She put a hand on his bare chest, over his heart, and he blinked, once, slowly, and then the heat of his gaze was even stronger.

She had more to say, though. "Does *my* life scare *you*? Every shift is a night I'm away from home. Every day I clock in could be the day I never go home again. Can you handle that?"

As an answer, he kissed her.

His mouth came down and covered hers ferociously, and his hand left the door and snagged hold of her hair. His beard strafed her lips, chin, cheeks. He leaned in, onto her, and devoured her.

And oh shit, it felt good.

Reeling from the surge and swirl of too many emotions, Pilar at first simply let him kiss her. She couldn't catch up—but then she did. Her hand was still on his chest; she pushed it up over his shoulder and around to grasp at the back of his head

Her other hand she slid into his jeans, loving the sound he made as her palm skimmed his hip and then his ass. He rocked his hips, pressing his erection on her belly, and deepened the kiss, forcing her tongue to twist and curl with his.

And then he broke away, panting. "You work tomorrow?"

"No," she gasped. "I go in at seven Sunday morning for a twenty-four."

"Thank fucking Christ. Stay here tonight."

So excited she almost shouted YES, she caught herself just before the word left her lips. "I can't"—before she could finish, he pushed away, his forehead creasing angrily, but her hand was caught in his jeans, so he didn't get far. "Wait. I can't just fuck you. I'm already feeling…involved. I can't do fuck buddies with you. Are we more than that?"

He cocked his head, the anger leaving his face again. "Isn't that why you came here?"

"Yeah. But you confuse me. I need to be clear. Are we serious now?"

"*I* confuse *you*?" He laughed and brushed the backs of his fingers over her cheek; it was a little tender from Tina's fist, but not bad, and his touch was light. She thought maybe this sweep of his fingers was the first simply gentle touch they'd had. "Cordero, I'm in fucking knots. Yeah. We're serious."

"Exclusive, then. Just you and me. No more girls."

He cocked an eyebrow at her. "No more handsy firefighters, either."

She actually stomped her foot. "Fuck! I don't fuck Moore. We never have. We tried once and it was just weird, like macking on a sibling. He is no threat to you."

"Well, that's true. I could tear that bastard into quarters." She hit his chest in frustration, and he laughed. "Okay, I get it." He reached for her belt buckle and started undoing her jeans. "So nobody else. Exclusive. And you're away half the week. Awesome."

As he started to pull her jeans off her hips, she grabbed his hand. "You can deal with that, right?"

"Can I stop by for a fuck on a fire engine? Saw that in an old movie once—up on the hoses."

Fucking *Backdraft*. "No, we are not going to fuck on an engine."

"That's not your kink, either, huh?"

"No." He was focused on her jeans again, so she lifted his chin and made him look her in the eyes. "My kink is I like to be hurt a little."

He went still. "What?"

"Relax. Nothing crazy. I don't want to get beat up or bruised or cut or whatever. But you already know I like it rough. I like hard touch, especially when I've got bad shit in my head—it's why I tried to get you to fight me that night in the storeroom. I like to be moved around. I also like to be tied up and…well, I have some toys I like when I am."

"That hurt you."

"That are hard touch." Shit, was *that* the thing he couldn't deal with? "It's nothing I need. Just something I like."

He shook his head. "Everybody needs to fuck the way they like. Especially if you need it to come off bad feelings."

She stood straight, ready to pull her jeans up. Her stomach lurched in the tempest of emotions she'd been sailing through all night. "Is that too much for you?"

"No." He answered right away, but not like he was jumping the gun; that was something. "I just never…I saw vibrators in your drawer. I've used those on women before. That's about it." He pulled her hands from her jeans. "But I'm a quick study."

With that, he pulled her jeans and panties down to her ankles and knelt at her feet. With her jeans binding her, she couldn't spread her legs, but that didn't stop him. He circled his hands around her knees and pulled, getting her to unlock them. Then he grasped her hips and leaned forward, sliding his tongue between her folds, over her clit and then back again.

"Fuck, Cordero, you taste sweet."

"Pilar. Call me Pilar."

He looked up. "What? I thought you wanted me to—"

With a shake of her head, she stopped his words. "Not anymore."

"You are one confusing chick. But okay. Pilar it is. Again." He grinned. "I like it, by the way. It's sexy." Before she could respond, he leaned back in and went to work.

He had no trouble locating her clit and stayed right on it, flicking the tip of his tongue and dragging its flat surface over that small knot of nerves again and again, varying the touch in ways she couldn't predict. She shot up like a bullet to the brink, and then he perched her there, kept her on the precipice, his fingers digging into her hips, his beard rasping over her thighs, her mound. She trembled there for an eternity, until her body was literally trembling. And then, with a chuckle, he stopped playing around and got her off. He flicked his tongue firmly over her clit, with fierce determination, until she thought she might die, and then the release finally came.

She grabbed hold of his head as sparks of pure pleasure fired her body. She could hear her moans and squeals—oh God, there were squeals; she'd be embarrassed about that later—resound in the room. She rarely made noise when she came; she tended to get quiet. She must have had a lot of pent-up need. Well, hell yeah, she did. She hadn't been fucked in two weeks!

As she settled, she expected him to stop. She needed him to stop. But he didn't. He kept going, paying the same dedicated, forceful attention to that tiny, painfully over-stimulated cluster. His hands were clenched so tightly around her hips that they ached. Too much. Too much. Oh shit, too much.

But she didn't stop him. Because she knew this thing, how it would play out, what the discomfort she was feeling now, the way her body tried of its own will to escape him, rocking back against his tightening hold, what it all would lead to. So she held on to his head and let him continue.

The pain really was, for those first moments, nearly unbearable. But then it wasn't. And immediately after the pain was gone, an orgasm twice as intense as the first landed on her like an anvil.

She howled, a feral, insane sound. And this time, when her body had completely escaped her control and she collapsed on him in a spasming heap, he stood and kissed her again, filling her head with her own taste and scent.

Then he picked her up and dropped her on the bed in another heap.

He stripped, laying his kutte over the chair she'd been sitting in earlier. When he came naked back to the bed, she hadn't moved. She was too exhausted. It was possible that she hadn't even had a thought.

So, still without saying a word, he stripped her, pulling off her boots and socks, her jeans and underwear, her top and bra. She lay and let him move her. When he rolled her to her belly and pulled her hips up high, she pushed her knees under, presenting her ass to him.

He left her to go to his dresser. With her head on the bed, she watched him dig out a condom and roll it on. When he returned, he squatted at the side of the bed, face to face with her. "You have to tell me what you don't want. I've never thought about how to do something like this. I'm just making this up as I go."

"I'll tell you. But you know what to do. Just…go hard."

"You have a whatever—safe word or something?"

She laughed into the covers. "How about 'stop.'"

He laughed, too. "The old standard. Right." As he got up, he kissed her shoulder. Then he went to the end of the bed, leaned over and grabbed her wrists. He pulled them behind her and crossed them on the small of her back. She could feel him wrap one of his big hands around both her wrists.

"Oh, yes," she gasped. "Yeah, this is good."

She heard his chuckle as he pushed his cock over her totally exposed pussy, letting it brush up and down a few times. "You are fucking amazing, Pilar."

With that, he pushed into her—one motion, balls deep. He was big, and balls deep for him was really fucking deep. Pilar gasped and clenched around him, and he made that growly sound again, deep in his chest. Then, with his free hand, he reached out and grabbed her hair.

Holding her like that, one hand restraining her arms, the other pulling her head sharply back by her hair, he began to thrust. And he went for it from the first thrust.

He drove into her again and again, so hard she had to close her eyes, because the sight of the room bouncing around made her woozy. The room was alive with sound: the slap of skin as their bodies slammed together, the wet suck of his cock moving in and out of her grasping pussy, his wild, vicious grunts every time he landed deep, her rough gasps echoing his.

Her scalp ached where he had hold of her hair. Her hands tingled from his punishing grip, and her shoulders protested the way they were wrenched back. She could still feel the impressions of his fingers on her hips.

And oh, God, oh fuck, oh sweet Jesus, it was so motherfucking good.

"Connor, fuck—fuck—" she wanted to say something to let him know how fantastic he felt, but she couldn't think enough words.

He froze. "Okay?"

"Yeah, yeah," she gasped. 'I didn't say stop. God, keep going."

His laugh sounded strained and desperate. "Fuckin' hell, baby. You got me crazy." He released her hair and pushed her shoulders to the bed as he began again, moving even faster now.

When Pilar came, she felt it in every joint and muscle, one huge clench and release that had her chewing on the bunched covers. She felt her juices running freely from her, through her folds, down her legs.

"Thank fuck! Jesus God, you're tight when you come!" With that, Connor came. She felt him arching back, his hips pressing against her, his cock as deep as it could possibly go.

When he was finished, he let her hands go and pulled slowly out of her. As he disposed of the condom, Pilar rolled to her back and stretched out, rubbing her wrists and rolling her shoulders.

"Did I hurt you?" he asked as he sat on the bed at her side.

"Only in the good ways." She smiled and brushed her hand over his thickly muscled thigh. "You have a fantastic body."

He laughed and sat back against the wall at the head of the bed. "Thanks. You know what I think of yours."

"We should work out together sometime. Do you run?"

"Only if somebody's chasing me. I lift. Do some core shit, knock the heavy bag around some."

"No cardio?"

With a grin and a shrug, he answered, "People chase me often enough."

She laughed outright. When she raked her hand through her hair, he caught a hank of it before it fell back, and watched as it coiled around his finger. It wasn't the first time he'd done that—that, in fact, had probably truly been the first way he'd ever touched her with real gentleness. "I'd like to watch you lift."

He met her eyes. "Likewise. We got a weight room here. Nice and close to this bed. For after."

"You're on. Not tonight, though."

"No, not tonight. I'm not letting you out of this room or anywhere near clothes until breakfast. But soon."

"You can show me how many pull-ups you can do." She raised an arm and bent it in a flex, tightening her muscles.

He wrapped his hand around it. "Nice. But I can do more than you." He flexed his huge arm, thick as her thigh.

"Care to wager?"

He rolled over on top of her and propped on his elbows. Those biceps swelled on either side of her. "Stakes?"

She thought for a few seconds. "If I win, you have to do karaoke at The Deck. In that Karaoke Idol thing at the end of the month"

"What?" His eyes went wide.

"Scared? Not a lot of confidence in yourself, I guess."

"Fuck you. You're on. But if I win, we fuck on the fire engine."

She shook her head. "We really can't, Connor. In that movie, remember, a call came in while they were up there? They played it funny, but it's actually really bad. It could slow the line down, get somebody killed."

"Okay, okay, hero." He kissed her, pressing soft, light kisses to her lips, her jaw, her throat. "If I win…you have to…do that karaoke idol thing at The Deck."

That deserved a slap, so she whacked his shoulder. "Lame."

"Wait. I wasn't done. You have to do that song about touching yourself."

"What?"

"You know, that old thing, 'When I think about you…'" He sang the line—in a nice, smooth baritone.

"The Divinyls? No fucking way. How do you even know that song? I can't imagine it's your genre."

"My mom liked it when I was a kid. She used to sing it around the house. When I understood it, I was retroactively traumatized." Full of gentle touches now, he brushed her nose with his. "Scared? Don't think you can beat me?"

"If I have to sing that one, then so do you."

"Ah-ah-ah. I already agreed to your terms. You didn't specify, so I get to pick. If you lose, you have to sing that one. To my brothers."

"Jerk." But she was smiling as she said it. She was happier and more relaxed in this moment than she'd been in a while.

"You could just concede the point."

"No way. I'll take your bet, because I'm gonna win."

"We'll, see, baby. We'll see."

She could feel that he was hard again. Bringing her knees up along his hips, she whispered, "Show me something else right now."

He shifted until his lips hovered over a nipple. "I can show you that all night."

That confidence, at least, was not misplaced.

CHAPTER THIRTEEN

When Connor woke the next morning, he experienced an unfamiliar sense of disorientation. And he was sore, too—his thighs and back particularly. He opened his eyes carefully, trying to figure out where he was and what had happened.

He was in his own room. So why was his whole body on alert? What the hell?

And then his brain woke up. Fuck—Cordero. Pilar.

She was lying on her stomach at his side, the cover slanted over her back and hip, her hair fanned out in a dark, wavy mass.

His cock was extremely happy to find her there.

But he needed to think. So he closed his eyes again and lay still, ignoring the complaints of his body. At least now he knew why he was sore, because damn. They'd done some Olympian kind of fucking.

And now she was his girl? Just like that? He needed to think.

In this head, he turned over the events of the night before. Just a typical Friday night. He'd been in a foul mood most of the day, and he'd almost bailed on the party and just gone to his folks' house to crash there in the quiet. His dad had left just before nine, as had become his custom over the past year or so.

He'd been sitting there at the bar, watching the crowd, trying to decide if he had really come to the point in his life where he was leaving a party at nine on a Friday night. Because that would have been a depressing state of affairs.

There had been some new girls, but for the first time in a long time, the thought of playing the seduction game with a nineteen-year-old just made him feel tired. And old. Also a depressing state of affairs. But then Tina had slunk up and handed him a fresh beer. She was still fairly new but had been around long enough, and consistently enough, to be considered under their protection, on the roster.

He'd decided that what he needed was a simple, straightforward, uncomplicated fuck.

Then Pilar had stormed into the Hall, and those adjectives had become meaningless. Nothing about what had happened after that was simple, straightforward, uncomplicated.

And now she was his girl.

He opened his eyes. She hadn't moved, and he fought the urge to reach out and sink his fingers into that wild hair.

She was his girl. Did he want that?

After a couple of aborted attempts at relationships, each of which ending dramatically, with the woman he loved, or thought he could love, deciding he was a monster and running as fast as she could from him, Connor had put some effort into building a life that didn't require that kind of connection. Allie, the woman he'd actually loved, had *really* loved…fuck. She'd left in the middle of the Perro bullshit. The club had had to threaten her. She hadn't known much; Connor was of the mind that club women should not ask questions. But she'd known enough to know that a threat to go to the cops would get a rise out of him. He and his father had forcibly moved her away and threatened her family to keep her quiet.

That was the kind of man he was. The kind of man who would threaten a woman's family to keep his own safe.

But Pilar insisted that she knew him, knew his life. That she understood. And that was the thing: he wanted her to understand. He wanted to believe that she could. He couldn't get her out of his head.

So now the question: did he want to lay himself open like that again? For this woman?

She was demanding and argumentative. She had a troublesome family, a troublesome history. She was strong and smart. She was funny. She was cynical, but she believed in heroes. She fucking *was* a hero. She was hotheaded. She was gorgeous. She wanted to be hurt, overtaken, but she was proud of her own strength. She was fucking complicated, a puzzle through and through, from the wavy hair on her head to the little, horseshoe-shaped birthmark on her ankle.

She was his bottom that came on like a top.

She was his girl. No—she was his woman.

Did he want that?

Yeah, he did.

He scooted closer and put his arm around her. She stirred, moaned quietly, and then rolled to her side, pulling his arm more tightly. Curled around her in that way, Connor felt relaxed and cozy. He felt trusted.

So he ignored his swollen cock. He closed his eyes, tucked his head against his woman's shoulder, and went back to sleep.

~oOo~

He woke again in the middle of an intensely erotic dream, so vivid that his body was moving, and even after he woke, he could feel the touch of soft hands on his cock.

No…no…that was no dream. Pilar had turned to face him and had been jacking him off in his sleep.

Oh, Christ, he was close. He groaned and clutched her shoulder.

"Hey." Her voice was sultry and smiling. "Finally. I thought you were gonna come and never even wake up."

She didn't need to know how close that was to true. He smiled and brushed her hair back from her face. "This is assault, you know—taking advantage of me while I sleep."

"You want me to stop?" The sincerity of her question was compromised by the way her hands clenched and pulled.

"No, no," he groaned. "Assault away."

Shifting, she pushed him to lie on his back, and then she moved downward on the bed. When she took his cock into her mouth, sucking him down, he reached up and grabbed the pillow, taking handfuls on either side of his head.

Just as he thought he was going to go, she backed off and attended to his balls instead, laving them with her tongue, sucking each one fully into her mouth. His muscles twitched and contracted as though an electric charge had been applied, and he could feel his sack tighten against her tongue. He couldn't take this.

"Baby, come on."

"You want to come?"

What did she think? "Yeah. Fuck, yeah. Come on."

He wasn't going to come unless she was on his cock directly. Even as a kid, he'd never had wet dreams. He'd had crazily erotic dreams and woken up feeling like he was having a dick hernia or something, but he'd always had to jack off to get relief. So while she was down there smiling up at him, lightly licking his balls, all she was doing was making him absolutely fucking crazy.

"How bad do you want it?"

He lifted his head off the pillow. "What the fuck?"

She grinned, seemingly unaffected by his distress. "Beg for it."

"What?" Even to him, his voice sounded almost panicky. What was her game?

"Say please."

Oh. Sure, yeah, okay. Whatever. "Please. Please, baby."

Her grin was utterly debauched. She shifted again, moving over to kneel between his legs. Hovering over him, she pressed her tits together around his cock and rocked back and forth, bending her head to suck and lick at his tip as she jacked him off with her tits.

It wasn't the first time a woman had gotten him off that way. There had been a club girl a while back, Ember, who'd been known for it. But there was something about seeing Pilar like that that…Shit-Christ-Fuck-GOD. He came explosively, his back arching, but she moved with him, stayed on him, finishing him completely.

When he relaxed, she smiled up at him, a drop of his semen at the corner of her pretty mouth. And that was the hottest thing he'd ever seen in his life.

Then her tongue darted out and lapped it up, and THAT was the hottest thing he'd ever seen in his life. He was already hard again.

When she noticed that, she cocked an eyebrow at him.

He sat up, grabbed her, rolled them over, and fucked the absolute shit out of her.

~oOo~

They were lazing together after that, catching her breath, when Pilar said, "We didn't use a condom."

Connor rose up on an elbow and looked down at her. "Damn." She was right. He never forgot a condom, but he had this time. It hadn't even occurred to him. He should at least have noticed the different feel, but he'd missed that completely. It had been a raw, fast, hard, mindless fuck. Fuck. Fuck.

"It's cool, don't panic." she said, brushing her fingers over the furrows in his brow. "I'll go by the pharmacy on my way home. But we should talk about health. Do you get tested? I do—it's a thing with my job, because we come in contact with bodily fluids. I'm clean. How about you? You've stuck your dick all over town, so please tell me you get tested."

He felt defensive and insulted. "I always use a condom."

"Not always, you don't." Pilar pushed him back and sat up. "Jesus, Connor. Seriously? You don't get tested?"

"The girls here do. And I wrap up."

"You don't just fuck the 'girls here,' whatever that means, though. And we just now didn't use a condom. God! I can't believe I just gave you head!"

Now she really was insulting him. He got up off the bed and turned to glare down at her. "I'm not fucking dirty! This is the only time since the last time I had a serious thing that I haven't wrapped up. And it's not like I've been slamming every skank in the Inland Empire. Jesus Christ!"

She stood up, too, and they stared at each other across the bed. They were both naked; Connor felt naked in more than just his body. What the hell was happening here?

But then Pilar took a deep breath. "Okay. Okay, I'm sorry. I didn't mean to be mean. I'm just freaking out a little now. I don't forget the condom."

"Like I said, neither do I." He gave her a wary look; he felt wary.

"Will you get tested? Please?"

"Will you get on some other kind of birth control? The Pill or something?"

"Yeah. That's a good idea." She smiled. "I wish I'd been paying more attention—I bet you felt amazing without the condom."

He was still mad, but he couldn't help it: he smiled, too. "How'd we miss that?"

Sweeping her hands down the length of her naked torso, over her firm tits, her sculpted belly, her tight hips, Pilar answered, "I guess you're just that hot for this bod."

Indeed he was, and his anger evaporated. He grabbed his stiffening cock. "And you for this one."

They stared at each other, touching themselves, and the bed between them seemed to take on a magnetic pull. But then Pilar shook her head. "I can't go again. I need a break. Like food and water."

Laughing, Connor checked the clock on his dresser. "It's 10:30. There's probably breakfast out there. But there are probably still passed-out bodies, too."

"If there's coffee and maybe a piece of bread, it'll feel like Thanksgiving." She tipped her head to the side and gave him a hooded look. "Then a shower after?"

"You're on. I'll scrub you up good."

~oOo~

Surprisingly, the Hall was fairly empty. Jesse and Tina were sleeping on a sofa in a mostly-naked heap, and Fargo was passed out alone in a chair. Keanu, the most recent patch, was awake, playing a video game with the sound low. Empty bottles and full ashtrays lay everywhere, but for a Saturday morning, it didn't look too bad.

Connor had noticed this happening: the Horde were settling down. Of fourteen patched members, six—Hoosier, Bart, Diaz,

J.R., Muse, and Demon—had old ladies, and he hadn't known any of them to stray. Well, J.R. and Diaz made use of the run rule—what happened on a run stayed on the run—but that didn't count. Those men tended to leave most parties early and sober. And he guessed he was joining their ranks—though it was too soon to be sure. That cut the available Horde in half.

Pilar looked around as they came into the Hall, but she didn't seem more than vaguely curious. He turned and led her straight into the kitchen, where there was hot coffee, some kind of muffins cooling in trays, and the sizzle of bacon frying.

His mother ran the clubhouse and the women on the roster. He'd never really bothered to understand how and why women were available to the members. He knew that there were women who were considered part of the club, 'on the roster,' as they called it, and he knew who they were, mainly because somebody always had some gossip when a new girl joined. They were fair game for the men. Most of them had jobs, but they had responsibilities here, too: in addition to putting out exclusively for the Horde, they cooked meals and cleaned the clubhouse, dorm and all. They weren't paid. They got club protection and a place to be, and that was it.

This morning, Marie, who was kind of his mother's assistant manager, and Sharon were in the kitchen. Sharon was a friend of Tina's, and she gave Pilar a nasty look. Connor stopped and stared at her until she met his eyes. Her look went from nasty to nervous, and then her eyes shifted away. Good.

"Hey, Connor," Marie said, looking over her shoulder from the stove. "Hungry?" She didn't address Pilar; she wouldn't unless Connor made it clear he wanted her to.

"Yeah. Smells great. Marie, this is Pilar." To Pilar he said, "Help yourself to breakfast, baby."

Marie and Sharon both stopped and gaped. Then Marie recovered and gave Pilar a smile. "Hi. We have a big vat of great coffee, the muffins are fresh blueberry or cinnamon crinkle. And there's OJ in the fridge. Bacon's up if you like it floppy. Couple more minutes for crisp."

"Uh, thanks. Thanks." Pilar turned to Connor. He got the sense that she wasn't comfortable talking to the girls. "Coffee, I guess. Mugs?"

He squeezed her hand and let it go. "I'll hook you up. Grab a muffin and have a seat." As he headed to the coffee pot, he nodded at the big island, one side of which was lined with stools.

While they ate and drank, not doing much talking, Trick came into the room, dressed in baggy track pants and nothing else. He rubbed his hand over the blond scruff on his head, which was growing out a little. Wouldn't be able to call him Velcro-head much longer. "Morning."

"Hey. You sleep here alone last night?"

"Nah. Just sent her home. She was trying us out last night."

"And you're the one gave her the tour?"

"Fuck you, man. Chicks dig me."

"I can see that," Pilar interjected. "You've got the brainy-hot thing going. And a real nice ottermode look. And the ink and piercings are cool." Trick had a pierced ear and a pierced nipple, the freak. Pilar squinted, and Connor was about to protest that she was looking too fucking hard, but then she sat back. "Some of the ink looks like etchings from old books."

Trick grinned. "They are. Most people don't see that."

"They're cool. I'm Cordero, by the way."

"Cordero?"

"Last name. Most people I know use it."

Connor turned and looked hard at her. Should he have introduced her to the girls as Cordero? The name thing confused him. Even something small like what to call her was complicated.

Holding out his tattooed hand, Trick said, "Well, good to know you, Cordero. I'm Trick. I've seen you around, at The Deck." As they shook, he turned to Connor. "Will we be seeing her around here more?"

He fought to keep a stupid grin off his face. "Think so."

"Well, goddamn."

~oOo~

A few days later, Connor led Pilar into the Horde weight room. He'd made sure that the Hall was empty. Most of the guys were working one job or another, and he'd sent the Prospects off on a bullshit errand. He did not want an audience while this chick, his woman, with that body, got sweaty in tiny workout clothes.

Because all she wore to work out in were tight little shorts and one of those sport bra things.

After spending that Saturday together, mainly fucking and resting, and an errand to CVS, they hadn't seen each other since. She'd worked two days, and the other two days, the Horde had been on a run to Oakland for La Zorra.

He'd used one of his days home alone to do what she'd asked—to get tested. Though he'd been sure he was fine, it had been a strange thing to wait even a day for the proof. Being tested pried open the door to a question he'd never bothered to consider before. But he was clean, as he'd known he would be.

And Pilar was going on the Pill. A few more days, and he would be paying better attention when he fucked her naked.

Her job was yet another complication. Besides not seeing her enough, now that his dick had a leash, all their talk about forgetting the condom, and emergency contraception, and the Pill had caused him to realize that a pregnant firefighter—hell, a firefighter mom—was problematic. For him, at least.

Now that he was in, he was in. And if they did stick, he wanted kids. No way he was bringing that up yet, though. For now, he was just glad to have some time with her.

After he won this silly bet and proved to her that a strong woman was awesome, but a strong man was stronger, he was going to spend the rest of the day in bed with her, using up the rest of his condoms. Because he wouldn't see her again until she was, as he'd joked to her, childproofed.

He'd asked Trick to be in the weight room with them, because, according to Pilar, they needed an impartial witness. Like she didn't trust him. He felt like he should be insulted that she was so sure his best friend wouldn't be on his side, but she was right—he'd be impartial.

Pilar insisted on warming up, so he swung his arms around a few times while she went through a whole stretch routine. And then they were ready. "Ladies first."

"Fuck that. You really think I'm dumb, don't you? Whoever goes first sets the mark. Going second is like home field advantage."

"Okay, then, I'll go first."

"No. It should be straight-up fair. I don't want you saying you let me win. We should flip. Trick, you got a quarter or something?"

Trick dug into his jeans pocket. "Yeah. Cordero, you call it."

"Tails."

He tossed the coin and caught it, then clapped it onto the back of his other hand. They all looked when he lifted his hand. Tails. "Connor, you're up first."

Connor jumped and grabbed the pull-up bar, and then he got started. They'd agreed on underhand style. He wasn't stupid, so he didn't show off. She was a cocky little shit, and he was serious about showing her her limits. So he just did pull-ups, ignoring everything around him. To their credit, both Pilar and Trick stayed quiet.

Fifty was no big deal. He routinely did sixty when he worked out. He started feeling it at seventy-five. By ninety-five, his arms were on fire. He was pulling up two-hundred-twenty pounds of muscle. By one hundred, he was shaking and puffing.

Then Trick and Pilar both starting cheering him on. That pissed him off, so he got some mileage out of it.

He hit failure at one-thirteen. And dropped like a rock to the floor. "Fuck. Beat that, baby."

"Damn," she said. "I'm impressed."

He had trouble getting his arm up to get water to his mouth. "You concede?"

"I didn't say that. I'm just impressed." She stretched a couple more times and then jumped to the same bar.

He knew fifty barely broke a sweat for her, so while Trick counted, as he had for Connor, Connor sat on a bench and just relaxed and enjoyed the view of that amazing body, flexing with effort. In their relative positions, he could see her face, and it was nearly blank with concentration. She'd simply gone away.

At eighty-five, she looked exactly the same, and he started to worry a little.

Trick came over to him. "Eight-nine"—He leaned down and muttered, "Damn, bro. This woman is something." Then he stood back up—"Ninety."

Yeah. She really was.

She was past one hundred before she looked noticeably fatigued, and Connor knew he was screwed.

At a hundred and eight, she broke her rhythm and struggled to get it back, and he stood up, reclaiming the possibility that he'd win—and also kind of worried for her. Each pull-up after that, she struggled, her arms shaking, her face tense and red. And he found himself cheering her on, as she had him.

She hit one-fourteen and beat him. And then she hit one-fifteen. And one-sixteen. When she was still trying to drag herself up to one-seventeen, he went over and wrapped his arms around her thighs. "Enough already! You beat me. Point made. Now it's just sad."

She let go of the bar and sagged into his hold. "Ow."

His tired arms weren't exactly thrilled with holding her this way. Letting her slide down his body, he caught her again so she could wrap her legs around his waist. "Not everything has to be a competition, baby."

"You're one to talk." She grinned. "But I win! And now you owe me karaoke."

Trick came over. "Wait. What? That's the wager? The Conman is singing karaoke? Oh, please tell me it's true."

"Fuck you, asshole," Connor snarled. He had almost a week before the stupid Karaoke Idol thing. Maybe he'd die before then. He could hope.

"Haha! That's brilliant. Cordero, you have restored my faith in humanity."

Connor ignored him. Setting a triumphant Pilar back on the floor, he bent down and kissed her, keeping it light, knowing she didn't much like an audience. "Come on, baby. We both need a hot shower." He considered sweeping her back into his arms and carrying her to his room, but just the thought made his muscles ache more.

And anyway, as much as she liked getting *thrown* around, she didn't like getting *carried* around.

So he took her hand. She linked her fingers with his, and they walked to his room together.

CHAPTER FOURTEEN

"I hope you like steak. We're a steak and potato crowd around here." Bibi filled a glass with red wine from a box and handed it to Pilar.

"I eat anything, and this all looks delicious. Is there something I can do?" She was standing in the middle of Connor's mother's kitchen, and Bibi and Faith, who was a family friend or a relative or something, were both doing cooking things, moving around the kitchen in a rhythm that seemed well practiced. Faith's baby girl was sleeping in a swing off to the side. The men—Connor and Hoosier, his dad, and Demon, Faith's husband or old man or whatever, and their little boy, Tucker—were all in the back yard. Connor had introduced her, tripping over whether to call her Pilar or Cordero. He'd landed on Pilar, and she hadn't corrected him.

She had to get her head around why she was getting all weird about her name. Normally, when she first met someone, she introduced herself as Pilar. Like a normal person. Her friends were the only ones who called her Cordero. But since she'd decided she'd wanted Connor to call her Cordero, and then wanted him to call her Pilar again—which was odd as hell, she knew that—the use of her given name felt more intimate. She was developing a complex about it.

She wasn't going to figure all that out here and now, though. So she hadn't fussed when he'd introduced her as Pilar, even though it made her twitch inexplicably. And then he'd grabbed a beer and abandoned her to the women.

This was not a situation she was comfortable with. She got along better with men; she always had. Most women found her hard and bitchy, and she found most women vain and insipid. In her heart of hearts, she liked girly stuff, sparkly things and pretty clothes, but there was only so long she could talk about shoes.

She looking longingly out the French doors to the patio, where the men were sitting, drinking, talking, and grilling. Tucker sat on the patio amidst their feet, rolling cars over the stonework.

She was at Connor's parents' house for Sunday dinner. Barely more than a week since they'd decided to be serious. Pilar's head spun thinking about the change in him. Once he'd decided they were trying this, he was immediately and fully serious. He'd even said as much: *If I'm in, I'm in.*

Even though she'd gone for him, the speed they were moving now freaked her out a little. Everything about him, at first glance, even second glance, read shallow and lighthearted. He should have been the perfect fuck buddy—volcanic sex and nothing else. But almost from the first, she'd felt that there was much more to him than met the eye, and that…essence…she couldn't see had captivated her. Now she was learning that that core of his self was steady and serious—and not buried as deeply as she'd thought.

Bibi poured Welch's grape juice into a wine glass and handed it to Faith, who was apparently not drinking. Faith answered the question Pilar had asked. "Everything's about done. We usually eat a little earlier."

She'd just come off a thirty-six—had come straight here, in fact. "Sorry about that."

As Faith said, "No, no," Bibi waved her apology off. "Please. You were workin'—and important work. We're happy to wait a little to have you with us." She checked the range. "Green beans are about done. Would you mind settin' the table? Everythin's stacked on it already."

"Not at all." Pilar felt stilted and strangely defensive. She was not good at this meet-the-family stuff.

When she'd been a little girl, family of one sort or another had been everywhere. There was always a party, always a dinner, at their apartment or their grandmother's, or that of one of the Assassins—they'd been a highly social crowd. The birthday party at which her father had been shot down had been boisterous. Her memory of that day was nothing more than a few faded, random images, but every one of them was full of people: kids clamoring under a pink *piñata* shaped like a puppy; a crowd watching her father sit her astride the Barbie two-wheeler that had been her best present.

People shouting and running out of the yard. Her *abuela* grabbing her up and running into the house. She never saw her father again.

After that, life had quickly picked up where it had left off, the only change the man who sat at their table in the morning. She'd had friends, family. Lots of people she called *Tia* and *Tio*. But when Renata had moved them away, it all stopped. From the time she was twelve, birthdays were celebrated at home, with just Hugo and Nana. There had been no more parties. There had been few friends. And certainly no expensive *quinciñera* when she turned fifteen. Nana had circled the wagons.

She hadn't missed any of that, not really. Her attention had been on Hugo and on helping her grandmother. Hugo had missed it much more and found ways to seek out the social interaction he'd needed, but Pilar had been content, or at least resigned, to be the responsible one.

But she didn't know how to stand in a kitchen with women and socialize. She'd actually been thrilled to get the job of setting the table, because it gave her something to do. She drank down her whole glass of wine and hurried in the direction she'd been pointed.

She could only imagine what the talk about her would be later tonight: *Wow, Connor really picked a winner there. Real charmer, that one.*

She was not good at this stuff.

~oOo~

Once everyone was around the table, it got easier. This kind of conversation—around a big, full table—she was used to. And these were not formal people. Hoosier had dropped a big plate of steaks in the middle of the table. There were twice-baked potatoes and a green bean casserole, a big basket of rolls, and corn on the cob. It was a redneck feast.

She laughed to herself as she watched the men reaching across the table to grab food. Connor, the tray of potatoes in one hand, lifted an eyebrow at her. "What's funny?"

Not about to say out loud what she'd been thinking, she shook her head. "Nothing. I'm just enjoying myself." And that was almost true now.

Tucker was at the table with them, and Demon made him a plate, cutting the portions into small bits. Rather than eat, though, Tucker drove his roll around his plate, making engine sounds.

Demon took the roll out of his hand and set it next to his own plate. "C'mon, Motor Man. Don't play with food. Eat your meat."

"How can you have any pudding if you don't eat your meat?" Connor said, smirking.

Tucker stopped trying to get his roll and stared across the table at Connor. "Pudding? I want pudding!"

"Asshole," Faith muttered at Connor's side.

"Sorry, Bambi." He didn't look the least bit sorry.

"Double asshole." She looked at her son. "There's no pudding, Tuck. Granny made cookies. We have cookies for dessert."

"I want pudding with Unca Con!" Just then, the baby, Lana, still in her swing, started to cry, and Tucker's budding tantrum was averted when his head spun around in the direction of his sister. "Uh-oh, Mommy. Lala needs a boob."

Everybody laughed—Pilar loudest, probably because she was the only one who'd been surprised by that. Tucker grinned, looking proud and a little confused. Then, at another cry from his sister, he scowled. "Mommy!"

"Thanks, buddy. I'm on it." Faith set her napkin on the table and went to her daughter. While she was gone, everybody went back to filling their plates. Demon got Tucker to take a bite of steak.

Around a mouthful of steak, Hoosier asked Pilar, "Connor says you were working a thirty-six-hour shift today. That's a long stretch. How's it work?"

Before she could answer, Faith returned with Lana and opened her shirt at the table, setting the baby to nurse. Pilar saw Demon give Connor a pointed stare and then, when Connor shrugged and put a forkful of steak in his mouth, Demon stabbed at his dinner. Hoosier made note of Faith, too, his eyes sliding in that direction and then skittering away. He shook a little and then refocused on Pilar.

She laughed again. Men.

They did community outreach at the station, so she had pat answers to pretty much everything any regular person ever thought to ask about firefighting. "It's not thirty-six hours of nonstop work. We do a lot more than go out on calls. We maintain the barn and the equipment, do public service and community outreach, training, fitness. But we also bunk during that time, unless we have a busy watch. We eat meals, have rest periods. This watch was pretty quiet. We worked a school fair yesterday. And we only had three calls, all of them pretty low-key. So we got our eight in the bunks."

"You ever been on a fire a whole shift?"

Pilar chewed and swallowed before she answered that one. The food was really good. She took a drink of wine—not that good, but okay. "Yeah. Wildfires. The Forest Service leads those, but we can get called in on all-unit calls, and then you're there until it's contained. Five minute breaks every four hours."

"Jesus," Faith said, sounding a little bit in awe.

"Fire moves fast."

"It's a badass job." Demon smiled at her, and she smiled back.

Pilar thought so, too. But she knew it was rude to say so, at least in this company. So she smiled and said, "It's not boring, that's for sure."

The conversation moved on from her, but with that little interview and the familiar chaos that had preceded it, Pilar had found the rhythm with Connor's family. No longer feeling defensive or stilted, she asked questions of her own. It was a good night.

By the time she and Connor left, Pilar had learned that Faith was an artist—and also a pretty cool chick. She'd learned that Faith and Demon lived not far at all from Joshua Tree, which was also Demon's favorite spot in the world, and that they had a big property with a menagerie of orphaned animals.

She got invited to see said menagerie and accepted the invitation.

She'd seen that Hoosier and Bibi still had mad, NC-17 love for each other, after more than forty years together, and seeing that gave her some insight into Connor's initial reluctance to commit and new enthusiasm for it. His parents had taught him how to love, and he was holding out for what they had.

That had been a heady realization.

She'd learned that Connor was a mama's boy, but in the totally hot way of loving and respecting the good woman who raised him, not in the creepy way where she still did his laundry.

The club girls did his laundry. The whole 'club girl' thing was a little squicky, to be honest.

As they stood at his big bike, strapping on their helmets, he leaned down and kissed her. "Thank you."

"What for?"

He stopped and frowned a little. "I don't know. I just…it was good to have you here. And I feel grateful, I guess."

She grinned and grabbed hold of his kutte, giving it a shake. "That's weird."

"Yeah," he laughed, "it is." He kissed her again. "Let's go fuck."

~oOo~

Three nights later, the night before her platoon was scheduled for their next watch, Pilar sat at The Deck. Her firefighter buddies and Connor's biker 'brothers' were sitting with her, together for the first time, having shoved a bunch of tables into a group. The joint was hopping; it was time for Karaoke Idol. Trick had told everybody in the Horde about her bet with Connor and that she had won, and now there were eight mostly large men in leather sitting with her, drinking and being rowdy.

She hadn't told Moore and the others, but she hadn't dodged the question about where she'd be tonight, so her usual suspects were all accounted for, too. When Connor had swallowed down a pint of beer, kissed her, grabbed a backpack from under the table, and headed behind the stage to the crows and hoots of his brothers, only then had her crew put it all together.

It was safe to say that their misshapen collection of tables was the rowdiest area in a rowdy bar.

Pilar didn't know what he was planning to sing or why he'd needed a backpack—or even where it had come from; they'd ridden here together on his Harley, and he hadn't had it then. She expected him to get up on stage and mutter into the microphone for a few minutes and try to act like he just didn't give a fuck—she knew what the macho cover for embarrassment looked like. She'd had a few twinges of guilt to be causing that embarrassment.

But then she'd remember what his terms had been for her side of the bet, and the guilt died off.

This was Karaoke Idol, so it wasn't just random drunks wandering over to the signup sheet. People had had to register ahead of time. A lot of them rehearsed and had little stage shows. The grand prize was only a hundred-dollar gift card to Blue Sky, but some people took this straight-up seriously.

Connor wasn't first up. Four people went before him, two of whom, both young women, obviously thought they were the shit, because they really belted it out like pop divas—not nearly as well, but they gave it their all. Then there was a singer-songwriter type guy who did an ancient Harry Chapin song. And then a lithe, strikingly beautiful Latina around Pilar's age got up and did an old Selena song about lost love.

Everybody at their table got quiet. She was great. Like, amazing. The kind of voice that gave you goosebumps. When she was finished, there were a few seconds of heavy silence. And then the audience erupted. Connor's brothers pounded their fists on the table.

All of them but Trick, who was just sitting there, watching the singer take her bow. Pilar took a second and watched him watch her. She couldn't really tell if he was entranced or just didn't want to participate in the riot around him. He was hard to read.

At her other side, barely audible in the din, Moore said, "Damn. Damn." Pilar turned and saw that he, too, was quietly watching her.

She laughed. It was definitely interest she was reading on Moore. If Trick was interested, too, then her poor friend could possibly end up facing another Horde man in the ring.

Men. She loved 'em, but they were so predictable.

Speaking of which, it was Connor's turn. The stage went dark, and then the guitar intro from "Sweet Child O' Mine" started playing.

"No way." He was going to do Guns N' Roses? Connor, with his raspy baritone, was going to sing Axl Rose? Oh, God, this was going to be excruciating.

Moore leaned back and put his hands on the back of his head. "Is this him? Oh, this is going to be *excellent*."

"Be nice, *pendejo*."

The stage light came up and...fuck, no. No way.

Connor was wearing a long blond wig with a red bandana wrapped around it. And—and—was he wearing *chaps*? Yes, he was. Pilar put her face in her hands. She couldn't watch this.

Trick leaned over and grabbed her arm. "Sack up, Cordero. You need to see this."

Just as she dropped her hands, he started singing. And...damn—he was good. He had a decent low falsetto.

And the best part of the whole deal: he had completely owned the Axl impression. Working the mic, he swiveled and rocked his hips, flipped his fake, blond tresses, bounced and gyrated.

Connor didn't remotely resemble Axl Rose. He was brawny and bearded. But he could move, and he was working it, and the effect was both hilarious and impressive.

The crowd was eating it up. Even Moore was clapping.

When Slash's guitar solo started, Connor danced around the stage. Then—spontaneously, as far as Pilar could tell—Trick jumped up and went to the stage. He hopped on and started doing air guitar. Connor turned and grinned at him, and they started working it together.

Sherlock went up next. And then another whom Pilar had only just met: Jesse. Four Horde men. Four scary outlaw bikers, up on a karaoke stage, singing and being a mostly terrible air cover band for Guns N' Roses.

Connor hit the last note on his knees, leaning back and singing to the ceiling.

It was fucking sublime.

When the song was over, there was no heavy pause in the crowd. People had been cheering while he sang, and they just kept it up. Pilar realized that he could win the thing.

His 'band mates' jumped down and came right back to the table, but Connor went behind the stage—for his bag, she assumed. Trick returned to his seat, leaving Connor's empty between them. "What'd you think?"

"Holy shit! It was good! He was good! You guys sucked, but he was good!"

Connor's friend laughed. "Yeah, he was. That boy is not shy. He wouldn't've chosen to do it, but he wasn't going to half-ass it. That's why I knew it was a great bet. Connor doesn't do anything half-assed. Or halfway."

Still grinning stupidly, Pilar nodded. She was learning that that was true.

He came around the stage, looking like himself again—his kutte on, the chaps, bandana, and wig gone. Without planning it or completely knowing it, Pilar jumped up and went to him. There must have been a look on her face, because his expression went from momentarily leery to just plain happy. He dropped his pack and opened his arms, and they hugged right there in front of the stage. He bent down and kissed her hard.

That got anther round of cheers from their friends—and, by the sound of it, the rest of the crowd.

She looked up at his grinning, gorgeous face. "Oh, my fucking God, that was fantastic! I am going to fuck you so hard tonight!"

Shaking his head, he bent to her ear. "No, baby. I'm gonna fuck you."

Her muscles twitched, and her heart raced. "Can we just get out of here now, then?"

"What? And miss the awards? No, you got me up there, now you gotta wait to see it play all the way out." He ran his tongue lightly over her ear. "But if you want, I'll finger you at the table."

Not in front of her friends and his. Besides, she was wearing jeans, and she didn't even want to contemplate how he thought he'd get that done. She was getting the impression that his kink was public sex, but she needed to work up to that. Since he hadn't asked outright, she figured she had some time to do so. She shook her head.

He chuckled and kissed her forehead. "Too bad. You'll just have to wait until the end. Because I'm gonna win this fucker, and I want to be here for that."

"Gift card to Blue Sky? You don't even like Blue Sky."

"There's a *trophy*. I'm going to make you keep it at your place. So you can see every day that I still owned you in the end."

"If you win."

He cocked his eyebrow at her. Laughing, she grabbed his hand, and they went back to their tables, where Connor got himself a hero's welcome from bikers and firefighters alike.

~oOo~

It turned out that Connor was disqualified because he'd only signed himself up, and when the other Horde got onstage, that broke some rule of the competition. The Latina with the beautiful voice, Juliana something-or-other, won. Pilar thought she probably would have won anyway, but Connor's confidence and enthusiasm was…alluring.

When he was in, he was indeed all in.

Now he was in her bedroom, and he had her up against the wall. On the ride back—he'd left the backpack with Trick—she'd felt him up as much as she could, and they'd started tearing at each other's clothes before she'd had her front door unlocked, then they'd wrestled their way back to her bedroom. He must have been tweaking on the adrenaline from being on stage or something, because he was fiercer and more demanding than ever.

She loved the feeling of his rough body against hers, the way the hair on his chest rasped against her nipples, the way his callused hands left traces of sensation behind as he caressed her, the way his strength dwarfed her own. There was nothing in the world hotter than wrestling around with this guy until he just overwhelmed her and took over.

He'd had to work to get her here, but now had her hands pinned together to the wall, one of his hands holding them firmly, while his other wandered brusquely all over her skin—her breasts, her belly, her hips and ass, between her legs—and his mouth and tongue claimed hers.

She bit his lip and bucked, shoving him off of her. He wasn't even surprised, not anymore. Now, his reaction was a grunt and a sneer, and then he flipped her to face the wall, and he pinned her again. His huge cock dug into her ass and lower back, rock hard and insistent.

As he pushed a hard hand between her legs, his voice rumbled at her ear, "I want to play with your toys, baby. Do you want that? You want me to tie you up and make you come until you soak the sheets?"

Moaning at the very thought, Pilar nodded. In the week and a half that they'd been a real couple, they'd gotten into her drawer a couple of times. A lot of what she had in there was stuff she used alone, but some of it was couple play. Until Connor, only her cop fuck buddy, Doug, had earned enough trust to play with her. In fact, Doug had been the first one to restrain her, which had been a revelation.

It occurred to her then that she needed to tell Doug that their fucking days were over, but she put that thought out of her head for now.

Though he'd been enthusiastic about the cuffs and other bindings, Connor had been unsettled by some of the things she had in that drawer. The little leather riding crop above all. In the two times that they'd played, he'd stuck to tying her down and having his way.

Which had been fine with Pilar; he paid her lavish attention. If he never wanted to get more adventurous than that, she could be happy forever.

He picked her up and took her to the bed. Then he opened her drawer and rooted around until he came up with her linked cuffs. Before, he'd bound her spread wide on the bed, but if he was going for those, he had something else in mind. She cocked an eyebrow at him and rolled away, but he grabbed her, as she'd known he would.

She made him fight for it; that was among the best parts for her, the struggle, the way that he could move her even when she used her energy against him, and now that he'd finally accepted that the struggle was foreplay, that the display of both of their strength made her even hotter, even wilder for him, and that she would stop him if he was too rough, he was fully, eagerly involved.

He got her cuffed to the headboard, her wrists together above her head. Then he took the loose cuff set that Velcro'd to the bed and tied her legs spread-eagle to her footboard, pausing to press his lips to each ankle, just above the leather band. He slid up her body, between her legs, kissing, licking, and nipping until he'd reached her pussy.

With a brush of his nose through her folds, he murmured, "I love your smell. There's something about it that just nails me, right in my gut. When you're wet like this, I just want to drink you."

She arched up toward him. "Jesus, come on and fuck me." He liked to talk, do the seduction thing, and she had to admit that it could be cool. His low, rough voice got even lower and rougher, and it was sonic sex. But Pilar had never been one to dally. Once they were naked, what she wanted was a good, hard fuck, not soft words.

Chuckling, he nipped at her clit, and the quick, intense burst of sharp pleasure made her hips twitch. But he didn't eat her out. Instead, he continued his journey up her body, kissing and licking, nipping lightly at her nipples, his coarse hands smoothing over her skin like fine-grain sandpaper.

When he was face to face with her, he pressed a chaste kiss on the corner of her mouth—and then got off the bed completely.

"Connor, fuck!"

"Hold your horses," he laughed. "I'm taking my time. And what are you gonna do about it, anyway? Pretty sure you're at my mercy."

Bound to the bed, she *was* completely at his mercy. And now she was also curious.

He opened her drawer again, and she heard the musical rattle of a light metal chain. She knew what that was, and at the recognition, her pussy clenched hard and she flexed and moaned, alone on the bed, deep in need. Fuck, she hoped he was getting those out.

"Please," she whispered, not aware she'd spoken until the word was in the air.

Smirking, he pulled the chain out of the drawer, hooked over his finger, until the little, rubber-tipped clamps dangled freely. "You want these?"

She nodded. Her favorite toy in there.

"I've never used them before."

"They don't need an instruction manual, dummy. And they're already set for me."

"Maybe not wise to call the guy who's got you tied down a dummy. Just a helpful tip."

"Sorry. Please."

"Hold on, hold on. I'm not done." He reached in and pulled out her Magic Wand vibrator. "I've wanted to try this one. A vibe that plugs into the wall. This fucker's got to be intense."

He had no idea. The mere anticipation of what he might have in mind had her halfway to climax already. His curiosity about her toys was surprisingly innocent for a guy like him, she thought. He was hardly inexperienced with women. But it did make some sense. This kind of play wasn't something to do with just some person you'd grabbed for a fuck. It took trust and intimacy. So if his couple of past girlfriends hadn't been into toys, Connor wouldn't have had any reason to know about this stuff.

At long, long last, he came back to the bed. Sitting at her side, he dangled the chain of the clamps over her breasts, letting it drag lightly back and forth across her nipples. When the skin tightened as much as it possibly could, he leaned down and kissed each peak. Then, as she watched and shivered with want, he pulled lightly on one taut nipple and attached a clamp to it.

She whimpered loudly, and he looked up at her eyes. When she nodded her encouragement, he clamped the other nipple, and she cried out and arched upward.

There was no sensation quite like that perfectly steady, balanced pressure, a pinch that fingers or teeth could never duplicate. It hurt, no question, but the pain was pure, erotic heat. When he tugged gently on the chain until both nipples stretched upward, Pilar bit down on her lip to keep from simply shouting in need. Fuck, she was glad he'd picked them.

While she was still focused on the fire in her nipples, Connor got back off the bed. She barely noticed. When he returned, she heard the heavy hum of her wand. He must have plugged it in.

She guessed what he intended, and she was so close to climax already that stillness was impossible.

He settled again between her thighs, first on his knees, so that he could flick his tongue back and forth over each pinched, distended nipple until she was wailing and grinding on the bed. Then he arranged himself so that his legs were under each of hers. He was limber for such a muscular guy. His cock stood up, evidence of his own need, but he seemed to be ignoring it completely.

Holding the vibrating wand in his hand, he brushed his knuckles over her clit and through her folds. She hissed at his touch, the way the shake of the vibe came through his fingers.

"So wet," he murmured. "You already soaked the sheets, baby."

She was barely even listening. All she could think of was that vibe, right there. "Come on, come on," she muttered.

With one hand, he spread her folds wide. With the other, he laid the rounded head of the vibe directly onto her clit.

The fire he'd been stoking exploded into an inferno, and she came immediately. Her body went rigid; her hands became fists, and her toes curled. For long seconds, she forgot to breathe.

She couldn't come down, because he didn't let up. Her lungs finally demanded air, and she took in a great, shrieking gasp. Connor took the hand that had been holding her open away, but he left the vibe where it was, following the gyrations of her body.

"Ow, ow, ow," she breathed. This part was too much to bear for long.

"You want me to stop?"

"No. Keep going."

He grinned and hooked a finger around the chain between the nipple clamps. Her back came up, following the pressure as her nipples stretched gloriously. And she came again.

The next time, he fucked her with his fingers while the wand worked its endless magic on her clit. That time, she shouted out her climax while she tried in vain to curl up. She wasn't sure how much more she could take, but she wasn't ready to ask him to stop.

But then he took the vibe away and turned it off. As she lay breathless, exhausted, he freed her ankles from their bindings. She expected him to move to the head of the bed and undo her wrists next, but instead, he grabbed her thighs and flipped her onto her belly.

"I need to fuck you, baby." Animal need had turned his voice to gravel.

There was just enough play in the chain between the cuffs that had her wrists that it could twist without hurting her. But now she was face down on the bed, still wearing nipple clamps she'd had on for a long time. The pain was intense.

"Wait!"

He stopped. "Too much? What do you need?"

With a calming breath, she considered the state of her body before she answered. The first blast of agony had ebbed, and now she was just rocking on the edge between pleasure and pain.

"I'm okay. I'm okay."

"Sure?"

"Yeah. Fuck me."

With a gentle kiss to the small of her back, he picked up her hips and entered her. He started slowly, making sure she was okay. Damn, it was good without a condom. She'd gotten so used to them that she hadn't realized how much that latex really changed the way sex felt. Without it, everything was hotter and smoother, and just…more *present*.

The movement of her body on the bed pulled at the clamps and the chain just enough to make her whimper. Then he sped up, and in a few thrusts he was going with savage speed and force. The bed slammed against the wall as Connor slammed into her, and she was coming again, this time screaming into the pillow.

As she came down from her latest explosive climax, Connor bellowed and leaned forward to grab her hair. He came, yelling and clutching her brutally. When he finished, he let go of her and pulled out with a sigh.

Mrs. Lee banged on the wall.

"I'm done. I'm done, Connor. I'm done. I need to be done." Fuck, she hurt.

He moved quickly, flipping her onto her back again. First he released the clamps, and she nearly screamed as blood rushed back. With the lightest of touches, he brush his thumb over each nipple and then kissed each one, too. Then he freed her wrists.

"I hurt you." He frowned down at her, brushing hair from her face.

With her tingling fingertips, she soothed the furrows from his brow. "I wanted it. I just needed it to be over when it was."

"Maybe we do need a safe word."

"You stopped when I needed to stop. I think we communicate just fine. That was pretty much perfect fucking, if you ask me."

He laughed quietly and caressed her face. "I don't know where you came from, Pilar Cordero, but there's nobody else like you."

Feeling spent and fragile, feeling exposed but not vulnerable, Pilar snuggled into the crook of his body, where he was propped on one elbow. "I'm falling in love with you."

He flinched and took hold of her chin, turning her head back so he could look straight down into her eyes. "What?"

Though she felt a little anxiety, she didn't back away from what she'd said. "You heard me. Does that scare you?"

His grey eyes were dark, and his scowl was not encouraging. "Don't you fucking play me, Cordero."

Pilar could have gotten defensive at that, but she had just been very well fucked, so she was mellow, and she knew where his words had come from. "We decided to be serious. You brought me to family dinner. We fuck like we do, and we talk like we do. You can't tell me you're not feeling it, too. I'm being honest. And I already told you I'm not keeping my eye on the emergency exit." She smiled as his scowl shaped itself into something much more open, but still wary. "Okay, I lied a little. I'm not falling. I already landed. I love you. There. Now I'll always be the one who said it first. I win."

He laughed, and his expression became simply calm and pleased. "Every damn thing is a competition with you, woman." His smile faded, but his expression didn't darken. "Yeah. I think I do. I love you, too."

No man had ever spoken those words to her before. To hear this man say them—her eyes began to burn. Pilar did not cry. In the life she led, the things she'd seen and would yet see, there was no place for tears. It was a second or two before she realized what the burning was. She blinked it away before tears happened, but Connor had watched that all play out on her face. She could see the knowledge in his eyes.

He smiled. "Well, isn't this somethin'."

CHAPTER FIFTEEN

"I'm not doing that." Connor stared up at the rocky cliff face and shook his head. "It is absolutely not happening."

Pilar put her hands on her hips and made a theatrical and entirely unnecessary scoffing noise. "Dude, since you're standing there in jeans and fucking biker boots, I didn't think you were. I can't believe you won't wear shorts. It's going to be ninety degrees out here soon."

"No shorts. You're lucky you got me out here." Pilar, on the other hand, wore a pair of khaki shorts that did fabulous things to her ass and made the bronze tone of her skin glow. He thought she might look hotter in those shorts, climbing shoes, and her almost-sheer t-shirt than she had in that black dress.

No. The dress was hotter. But she looked good now.

"You told me you've camped a lot."

"Biker camping is not this. Biker camping is passing out on the ground next to your bike. But I'm here. I'll..." He was going to say he'd take a ride, but that would leave Pilar out here alone being a daredevil on that stupid cliff face. "I'll just wait here."

She'd dragged him out to the desert to camp, enticing him with stories about fucking under the stars and sleeping coiled together in a sleeping bag.

The night before had been fantastic. They'd ridden out side by side, Pilar on her little orange Victory and him on his big black Harley. As soon as they'd gotten clear of traffic, she'd revved the throttle and torn off, turning the last leg of the trip into a race. He'd let her win—the view had been superior behind her.

They'd stopped at a little market near the park for firewood and dinner, then arrived at camp in the late afternoon. It was midweek in September, after school was back in session, so there weren't many people around. They'd made camp, had a rustic dinner of bread, cheese, fruit, and booze, and made a fire.

That had surprised him—he'd expected her to be anti-campfire. She wasn't, but she was particular about fire safety, so they hadn't bedded down until it was completely out and cooling.

Hence the fucking under the stars. And what stars they'd been. Several of Connor's brothers came out to the desert often, but he never had. He'd ride out here—the roads were great for riding—but he'd never been interested in the landscape, which was brown. Every season, every day, brown—light, dusty brown. He preferred the variety of the mountains or the coast. But last night, he'd gotten a sense of the place's allure, and not just because the sex had been fantastic. Their sex was always fantastic. But the canopy of stars in a sky that seemed to swirl with dark color had been breathtaking.

Pilar's little backpack tent had a screen sunlight at the top. While she'd slept in his arms, he'd lain and stared through the tent at the stars for most of the night. He'd felt small and infinite both at the same time. And perfectly content.

And he'd known he was going to mark this woman. End of story. It had only been about a week and a half since they'd first used the word 'love,' and far too early to bring it up, but that night, staring up at thousands of stars in a purple and blue sky, he'd seen his future.

Now, he was watching his future climb the side of a rocky cliff with no gear but her funky shoes. He sat on a rock and watched, trapped between his fascination of her ability; his lust for her sinewy body, the muscles in her legs and arms rippling and glistening, her thick, fluffy ponytail swinging; and his bone-chilling fear as she climbed higher and higher. Up a cliff, without a rope. Rocks littered the foot of the cliff. He imagined her broken body lying on them.

Every now and then, she'd stretch wide and put her foot somewhere, then let it drop back, and each time that happened, he'd clench, sure that she'd lost her footing. But then she'd find a better hold and climb some more. By the time she got to the top, he was halfway to a heart attack. Then she waved and disappeared down the other side. She'd told him there was a way to walk back down.

He sat where he was until she made her way back to him. She'd been right—he was getting hot sitting in the desert sun in his jeans and boots. But he was also finding some of the same kind of peace he'd felt the night before. Like his life had settled on its track. He hadn't even known he'd been derailed.

When she approached, he stood up. "I can't believe you climb cliffs for fun. Tell me you don't come out her on your own."

"Dude, that's not a cliff. That's barely a hill. Just a bunch of rocks. Someday I'll show you what climbing a cliff looks like. And no, I don't come out alone. I usually come out with Moore."

She dropped that and looked up at him, and he could see the challenge in her eyes. Well, fuck, yes, he was jealous of that guy. Kyle Moore was her best friend. She spent as much time with him as she did with Connor. Moore slept in the same room with her as often as he himself did, too. He was in love with a woman who might actually be able to deal with the life he led, and he shared fifty-fifty custody of her with another guy. It sucked.

And they were handsy with each other. He got that there was nothing between them. He did. He believed her, and he got it. He wasn't threatened. He was just jealous—of their time together, their friendship, whatever. He'd work it out eventually.

So to answer her now, he just grunted.

"You gotta let that go, Connor. I'm not giving up my best friend."

"I'm workin' on it. Give me time."

She slid her arms around his waist. "You're all hot and sweaty. Me, too. Wanna ride?"

He grinned and kissed her. "Now *that* sounds like fun."

~oOo~

That night, they sat by the campfire, watching it gutter out. Pilar rested between his legs, against his chest. She played absently with the rings on his left hand. With his right hand, he combed his fingers through her loose hair. And they talked. Alone in the desert night, they talked. For hours, until the fire was dark and cold.

In the tent, before they slept, he fucked her slowly, gently, telling her what he wanted from her body, what he wanted to give her from his. Seducing her to patience.

Yeah, he saw his future.

~oOo~

Two days later, Connor, his father, and Bart sat in a hotel suite in the suburbs of San Diego. Dora Vega and her two closest associates, Luis Torres and Matias Cruz, sat with them. The six of them were arrayed around the living room of the suite, and Dora had provided light spread of hors d'oeuvres and drinks.

Usually, the Horde met with business associates in a less polished atmosphere—in an out-of-the-way dive bar or just some abandoned building. But La Zorra preferred to maintain a sense of decorum in her business meetings. Even when they met in the middle of nowhere, she came supplied to approximate a business meeting.

She always dressed like a business executive, too. Most of the boss-type men they worked with dressed with some degree of flash. Even those who wore suits would have stuck out in a downtown executive suite. But Dora dressed conservatively. Today, she wore a slim black skirt and a light blue silky blouse, unbuttoned just to the point that it was impossible to forget that she was a dramatically beautiful woman. Her simply-styled hair, the little bit of gold and diamond jewelry she wore, her plain black high heels—the whole package was a balance of power and poise that Connor couldn't help but admire.

She was a conscientious hostess, too. Each man had a glass in his hand filled with his favorite drink: Connor and Bart had Jack, and Hoosier had Jameson. As they took their first sips, Dora asked, "Has there been any—what's the word you use—*blowback* from my special request?"

She meant the Cartwright hit. His father answered, "No. Bart and Sherlock are keeping track, but it's been five weeks, and they have nothing. Case is going cold."

Bart picked up. "It's not cold yet. They're still working it hard. But if we had left any trace, they would have found it by now. The chatter we're finding says they are looking overseas, at terrorist organizations. Homeland Security has it now."

"Ah," Dora said, and Connor thought she looked pleased.

"That doesn't get us out of the woods just yet. DHS could look south if looking east doesn't pan out."

"I understand, Connor. Thank you." She sipped daintily at a gin and tonic. "I'm impressed by the quality of your work. I'd like to meet with the man who got it done."

Trick was having trouble dealing with having gotten that job done. He was a quiet and thoughtful guy, but that didn't necessarily mean he was always diplomatic. He tended to answer questions posed to him with bald honesty. Connor wasn't sure it would be such a great idea to have La Zorra speak with him directly.

But his father said, "I'll bring him when we meet next."

Thinking about his friend, Connor asked a question he normally would let lie. "Now that the job is done, can we get some idea about why you needed Cartwright gone?"

Her lieutenant, Luis, said, "She would have told you if she'd wanted you to know."

Holding her tall, clear glass in both hands, Dora Vega contemplated Connor over its rim. "As I told you, the reason is compelling."

Connor held her brown eyes. He wouldn't push with words, but he wouldn't be the first to look away, either.

They stared at each other until Dora's mouth lifted in a slight smile. "Luis, Matias, step outside for a smoke, please.

"*Señora...*" Luis protested.

"Please." At her simple, firm word, a command in a plea, her men left the suite.

The most powerful woman—no, the most powerful person—in the Mexican underworld picked up from a tray a dainty cracker laden with some kind of black goo. "I assume you did some research, Bart."

"Only enough to get a read on the target. We didn't dig into you." The Horde officers had discussed that at some length, but the protection around her was state-of-the-art, and both Bart and Sherlock had said that they could get in, but not without her knowing. The risk, therefore, was too great. They did all they could around the edges.

"Thank you. And what did you learn?" She bit into the cracker.

"Cartwright was District Attorney for three years. He worked as an Assistant U.S. Attorney before that. With the Feds, he worked a lot of drug enforcement cases, but he never sat first chair on any of note, and none of the cases intersected with your interests. He got his J.D. at UC Irvine. He's an L.A. native. Married with two kids."

"And before he got his law degree?"

Bart shook his head. "His trail fades out there, and we didn't have a lot of time to dig deeper. We went back as far as we had to to get a sense of him and then focused on the intel we needed to plan the job…" His last words drifted off. "He worked for the Feds before he got his law degree, didn't he?"

"He did. Homeland Security, in fact. It wasn't work he was made for, but he was a field agent for three years."

"And they obscured his record. Which they do for undercover agents. This is about your ex-husband." Connor spoke the words to Dora and then turned to his father, who was nodding; he'd put it together, too. And Bart.

David Vega was, or had been, a Special Agent with the Department of Homeland Security. He'd been deep undercover with the Perro Blanco cartel and had risen to stand at Julio Santaveria's right hand. He'd also taken an interest in one of the young women Santaveria kept as clerks, a pretty young thing named Isidora. They'd married and had three children, all while Vega was living his double life.

"My husband, yes. In that way, it's personal. It also bears on business, of course. Mr. Cartwright worked with my husband. He was also a greedy, corrupt man. Shortly after I took over the Águilas, he made overtures to me, suggesting that we might work together. When we couldn't come to terms, he made threats." She finished her fancy cracker and lightly brushed her hands before she picked her drink up again. "It is not easy to be a woman in my world. The men who live in it do not respect women. They think I can be bullied. I've achieved what I have because they are wrong. I answer every threat in the same way: I ensure that the man who makes it will not make another."

"He made threats?" Hoosier asked.

But Dora shook her head. "The specifics aren't important. Let it suffice to say that Mr. Cartwright thought that my feelings about my husband were a vulnerability. They are not."

Bart leaned forward and set his empty glass on the table. "Can I ask…do you know what happened to your husband?"

"You may not ask, no."

Connor's antennae pinged like crazy. She did know—moreover, now he was sure that Vega was alive, and that she was in some kind of contact. What the fuck did that mean? A drug boss and her Fed husband? What the fuck? They needed to get out of here and talk.

He cast a glance at his father, who met his eyes briefly, but that look was enough. They were on the same page.

His father turned to La Zorra. "Dora, I respect your need to protect your secrets. But I need to protect my family. What's our exposure here?"

"From this, if you did your job, then your exposure should be negligible if not nonexistent." Her expression sharpened. "But this trouble in your own yard—that's another story. This beef you have with the Aztec Assassins. That's an inconvenience. This is not a time for my peace with the Fuentes to be disrupted, and that gang is an important supplier for them. I need that resolved."

"We agreed to sit back and let that cool off. It's cooling. They're beneath our notice."

Connor was surprised at his father's assertion, but he made sure not to show it. The Aztecs were *not* cooling. They weren't escalating, but they were poking. Trying to get the Horde to make the first move. Looking for a fight. His read was that the Fuentes had given them the same instruction, or advice, that La Zorra had given the Horde—stand down unless there was aggression from the other side.

So they needed some attention. They were not beneath the Horde's notice, even though they should have been.

"Good." She gave them a wide, pleasant smile. "Then are we ready to talk new business?"

~oOo~

They stopped at a roadside diner on their way back to Madrone. Once the waitress had their order, Connor was the first to raise the key issue. "I don't like this. Vega's alive and she's in contact. That's what I got from her kicking back that question. If he's still a Fed, that's all kinds of twisted. I don't like how many variables that puts in play."

"Connor's right," Bart said. "Even if he's not still a Fed, and they witpro'd him, we need to know what it means if he's back in play. What team is he on? Fuck, what team is *she* on?"

Hoosier tugged his beard. "She just had us hit a D.A. She's on our side of the line."

"Vega killed on the other side of the line," Bart reminded them. "He killed Hav. And who knows who else."

Sighing, Connor's father leaned back. "I don't think killing Cartwright was some kind of setup. But you're right. Something's off. We've been working with this woman for two years. Things've gone smooth. We're making bank, she's getting her product out, it's been a good relationship. But she's starting to say 'I' a lot more than 'we' lately. She's starting to tell instead of ask. I don't have a problem working with a woman, but I do have a problem being anybody's bitch."

Connor had noticed that, too. When they'd first started working together, Dora Vega was new on the scene. She'd made an impression as a ruthless leader and a cool-headed businessperson, but she'd still been making her mark. At the same time, the Horde SoCal charter had been working straight for more than three years, since the charter had been founded on the ashes of a defunct club. Though that old club had held a lot of power as notorious outlaws, their years of quiet living had seen most of that power fade away.

In the two years since, Dora had embraced what had been intended as a dismissive nickname. She'd become La Zorra, and she all but ruled Mexico on both sides of the line. And the Horde had reclaimed their place among outlaws. Together, they'd killed a charter of another MC, the Dirty Rats, and crushed the Castillos, an upstart drug cartel. Now La Zorra had the Zapatas, one of the original Colombian cartels, who had been working with the Castillos, under contract. She was the queen.

But she was acting less and less like she considered the Horde her partner and more and more like she thought of them as employees—or subjects. That was going to be a problem.

"So where do we go from here, then?" Connor asked.

"I gotta dig into her, I think," Bart answered. "Me and Sherlock. She'll probably see us coming—her guys are as good as we are—and that'll cause a problem, too. But we need to see what she's not telling us. I know you trust her, Hooj, and we've had two good years, but I think it's a mistake to give that much trust to anybody that doesn't wear the Mane. She's got her thumb on the scale."

"Yeah, she does. Goddammit. Why can't anybody just be an honest outlaw anymore?" He sighed again, sounding old and weary. "Okay. You and Sherlock see what you can see. Connor, I want to poke back at the Aztecs—not a pissing match, but we need to get control of that message—to them and to Dora, too. No more joy rides past the compound for our brown friends."

"Should we take that to the table?" Connor asked.

"No. Like I said, I just want to push them back to their side of the city limits. Pest control. But this is our problem to handle as we see fit. Dora's truce with the Fuentes is her deal, not ours."

It was a bold move that could put them at odds with a powerful woman, but Connor was relieved. He'd been feeling hamstrung, too, by La Zorra's 'requests' regarding the Aztecs. He was not one for whom sitting back came easily.

Hoosier continued, "I don't want to come back at them with the same schoolyard bullshit they're throwing at us, though. I think we should hit their business, let 'em know what they risk with this game."

Bart and Connor both nodded their agreement. Bart said, "I don't think we should push harder than a message, though. Not yet."

"No," Hoosier agreed. "A clear message, but no more."

Connor nodded. "I'll bring Muse and Diaz in on it, make a plan."

His father dug into his roast beef sandwich, thinking as he chewed. "I don't want an enforcer approach to this, son. Esposito and La Zorra both need to know that we handle our shit, but if we go in hard, we could start a battle before we have a map of the field."

As Connor considered the problem, another idea occurred to him. It was underhanded, when he preferred a direct approach, but his father was right. They needed to stay back until they had a sense of the lay. "Bart—can you dig dirt on the High Life? They gotta be using it some way to front their drug business."

"Yeah. What're you thinking?"

To answer Bart, he looked at his father. "You say you want to hit their business. What if we can tip off Montoya, get it shut down. Maybe suggest he seize the place—everything he can? That could give the Sheriff a win and put the Aztecs in trouble with law and the Fuentes, both."

Hoosier shook his head. "That's a lot more than just a message. It fucks with how the Fuentes move their product. It could cause trouble with the peace. I don't want Dora stirred up until we understand better what's going on with her."

"So it's not a message. We don't sign this. Let Montoya have it. The most important thing is shutting the Aztecs down, right? They don't need to know who did it." As the idea flowered in his head, he relaxed back in his chair. "Hell, maybe it even helps the Queen if Fuentes can't move that weight. She could take it over. If this works, we'll be doing everybody a favor."

He sat and let the President and Vice President mull that over. It was a good plan. Not flashy, no guns blazing, but a good plan.

And they knew it. His father nodded at Bart. "You can find what we'd need to give Montoya?"

"No question. There'll be something. Those guys aren't careful enough to hide from me. So yeah, this could work. It could be a big move, though. Even if the Aztecs don't figure it out, Dora will know. Could tip the scale with her either way. We should vote it."

"Agreed. And I want her to know." His father pulled his beard. "It's not our style, ratting anybody out to law, but those roaches are taking too much of our time lately. Let's let Montoya take out our trash, and let's keep our focus where it matters. We need to get on top of this Vega thing and show La Zorra that we are not her fucking lackeys."

Despite the heaviness of the topic, Connor grinned. His father had dropped ten years of age from his face and posture since they'd sat down at this worn table. He'd always chafed at working *for* anyone. Connor had heard dozens of drunken rants over the years about how working for someone ran against everything he believed in, the very reasons he wore a patch at all. What Hoosier liked about working for Dora Vega was the partnership. Over the past several months, and especially in the weeks since they'd done the hit for her, she had clearly begun to see the partnership as significantly less equal.

He only hoped that they would find a way to equalize the situation. Because the naked truth was that that woman was now a lot more powerful than they were. If they ended up opposed to her, they'd lose. No question.

So they had to find a way to stand their ground and keep her allegiance. As a partner.

CHAPTER SIXTEEN

Pilar reached out from under the covers and grabbed her phone, swiping off the alarm. Before she could turn the covers back and sit up, though, Connor's arm tightened around her waist.

"No. Stay." His voice was thick with sleep, even gruffer than usual. When he pressed his cock against her ass with a grunt, she moaned and rocked backwards.

"I can't. I go in this morning."

He kissed the back of her neck. "Not till seven. Don't run this morning. Let me fuck you instead. I'll get your heart rate up."

As tempted as she was, feeling his big, warm, hard body tight against hers, his beautiful cock sliding against her ass, his teeth nipping lightly at her shoulder, Pilar hated for her routine to get screwed up on work mornings. "Connor…"

He sighed. "Come on, Cordero. This is our only time together for the whole week, because you're going off on that stupid trip and taking two days we could have had." His voice lost the petulant edge it had picked up, and he nuzzled behind her ear. "Baby, let me fuck you so you feel it all weekend long."

As he spoke, his hand slid over her belly and between her legs, and she decided she could skip her run. She wasn't ready to let him up so quickly, though. "Babes Ride Out is not a stupid trip. It's one weekend a year, every October, and I love it."

"I don't know why I can't go. It's only Joshua Tree. What are you gonna be doing out there, anyway? Some kind of lezbo orgy?" The way his hands moved over her body was distracting, but not so much that she missed his whiny jerkiness entirely.

She reached back and bopped him on the head. "You're such an ass. No. But it's *Babes* Ride Out. You are not a babe. And it's just a party. Music. Booze. Camping. The usual. And you're going to be in *Vegas* when I get back, so come on."

"That's work, though."

"Funny how often you come back from 'work' smelling like expensive whiskey and cheap perfume."

"Hey, now. I'm true. You know that. I can't help if a chick pushes up on me, though."

"I'm just sayin'—your work looks a lot like play sometimes, and it keeps you away from me. So let me have this one weekend."

"I don't know why you have to have a rally of your own. Seems pretty sexist to me." He slid his fingers inside her, and she wanted this conversation to be over.

"Because women are just tits and pussies at your rallies. Shut up and fuck me already."

His chuckle rumbled low in his chest, and he grabbed her thigh and dragged her leg backwards. She reached between her legs and took hold of his cock, pushing it against her until he was inside. "Oh, fuck," she breathed as he filled her up.

For a few minutes, they rocked slowly together, both groaning. Connor's pace gradually intensified, until the bed rocked and Pilar clutched at him, writhing against his hold.

He surprised her by rolling to his back, carrying her with him so she was lying on him. Then he grabbed her hips and lifted her up, driving hard into her from below. Jesus, he was strong.

And *Jesus*, the feel of him, hitting the deepest, most tender part of her, making her nerves writhe and quiver. It was always so fucking good with him.

The loud, rhythmic clap of their meeting bodies rattled the air. She leaned her head back on his shoulder and grabbed a breast with one hand, plucking and pulling at her nipple. With her other hand, she reached between her legs to feel him pistoning wetly into her.

"Fuck, baby!" he grunted in her ear. "Fuck, you feel good."

"Shut up and make me come."

"I'm gonna make you come until you're too sore to ride. I'll keep you with me one way or another."

As if to underscore that claim, he shifted them a little to the side, letting her body rest on his and wrapping her up in his arms. He barely broke his rhythm or his force, and then his hand was under hers, on her clit, and she was done for. His sandpaper fingers on her clit, her hand on his, his cock slamming into her, his heavy breath in her ear, the feeling of his strong body supporting hers, it all charged at her and sent her over the edge. She arched sharply up, her whole back leaving contact with his chest, and came until her head hurt.

Before she was completely done, the room spun as Connor moved her quickly, dropping her to the bed, looming over her and shoving her legs up to her chest. Then he was inside her again, kneeling at her ass, his chest against her shins, his hands closing around her waist. She was bound up tight, with the pressure of half his body and half of hers bearing down on her midsection, and he was pounding into her, his hands digging into her flesh.

Sweet fucking holy Christ. Nothing they'd done had felt like this, even after two months of playing with her toys. She didn't even know why, but *God*! "Connor! Oh, fuck! Oh, fuck!" She grabbed his arms, feeling her fingernails digging into the meat.

"Don't come, Cordero. Don't come."

"What?" She hadn't quite noticed when he'd started using her first and last name both; it was just something that had started to happen. And not quite interchangeably—she had a faint idea that there was some kind of meaning to be sussed out about when he used which, but this particular moment was not the time to worry about it.

"Don't. Look at me, and don't come." She could hear in the strain of his voice that he was close, too. She could see it, the need, in his intense grey eyes, the way his brows drew down. "Look at me, baby. Look at me."

She did—while he made her body spark and throb, while every fiber in her swelled with the need for release, she stared up into his eyes and saw something much bigger than the wild need firing her core. It was too big even to understand. It was terrifying. And she wanted it. Needed it.

"Connor, please," she gasped, not knowing what she was asking for.

"I want to come together," he panted. "Don't come until I'm ready." That was something she'd have been more likely to say to a guy, rather than the other way around, but Connor had stamina, and she was fucking *there* already. He kept up that steady, driving rhythm, hard and deep, a sweetly punishing beat.

Their eyes still locked together, she nodded, but whimpered, "Please, please." Then he moved one hand to her clit. "Connor, fuck! Please!"

"Not yet, baby." The words came through gritted teeth; he was holding himself off, too.

"Fuck!" She threw her arms over her head and grabbed her headboard, trying to draw her attention to the discomfort in her hands clenching around the iron curls.

"Okay. Okay, baby. Fuck, now. Oh, shit. Come with me." He yelled incoherently then and sank into her, as deep as he could be, and froze, then went savagely at her clit, and she let go, swinging her arms down to clutch at his shoulders, shrieking like an animal. He yelled again and pushed even deeper, and she came until she realized she was crying, and even after. She couldn't stop coming.

He relaxed and let her legs go, settling on her, his hips moving again, gently now. He was still hard, and she was still coming.

She wrapped her legs around his waist and bent her head up to press against his hot, heaving chest. Fuck, she was sobbing—out-of-control, ugly crying. She could not remember the last time in her *life* that she'd cried.

His hands tangled in her hair, holding her head, he kissed her neck again and again, and then her cheek, whispering. "Easy. Easy, Pilar. I love you. Shhh. I'm sorry. I'm sorry."

"No," she gasped, finding some kind of control as her body finally began to find its own. "I'm okay. I just…fuck, dude." She sniffed and swiped at her eyes. "Fuck. I love you." She turned to find his mouth, and they kissed deeply. His beard was damp from his sweat, and when he pulled back, she saw that he looked as dazed as she was.

And the tears overtook her again. What the hell? Still inside her, still hard, he gathered her into a tight embrace and just held her until she could finally be calm.

She was late to the barn. And she was sore—a deep, full soreness that would last for days.

The sated ache in her heart would last much longer.

~oOo~

It was dark when she rode back into Madrone that Sunday night in October, but it wasn't late. It had been a great weekend with friends she only saw in person this one time a year. She'd partied hard. She had to be at work in the morning, so she wanted a quiet night. But Connor was in Vegas, and the thought of being alone at her place made her feel lonely. So she headed toward her grandmother's house. Nana would be watching television, and maybe Hugo would be around, too.

It had been three months since she and the Horde had pulled Hugo out of the High Life, and she and her brother hadn't spoken much since. As far as she knew, he still didn't have a job—not one he could tell their grandmother about, at least. He was gone a lot, and at strange hours. And sometimes, unpredictably, he'd come home with a bunch of groceries—or, for Nana's birthday in September, a big television.

He'd forgotten, or ignored, Pilar's birthday.

She knew what was going on. He was doing something with the Assassins. He hadn't been beaten again, and he wasn't wearing colors, so she didn't know how he'd made his debt right or how deep in he was. And he wasn't talking. But she knew he was in with them somehow.

But it was his trouble. She was struggling to get to that place in her head, where she stopped fixing his shit up for him. She wanted to be able to love him without letting him lean so hard on her or Nana.

She pulled up in front of the unprepossessing little house and cut the engine on her Victory. Hugo's truck was in the driveway, blocking their grandmother's compact sedan in. Good. They were both home.

She dismounted and locked her helmet down, then walked up the drive, along the left side, toward the side door of the house.

As she passed Hugo's truck, she noticed that the dash lights were on. Then she saw that Hugo was passed out behind the wheel.

"Fuck!" She lifted the door handle. It was unlocked, and she tore open the door. The smell of piss made her step back. He had been badly beaten, but not like before. This was all fists and feet. His shirt was open, and blood had dried in streaks down his chest and belly.

Blood and ink. In the middle of his chest was a new tattoo: a highly stylized, feathered snake. Quetzalcoatl, the Aztec god, and the mark of the Aztec Assassins.

Hugo had finally been jumped in.

After checking his eyes—pinpoint pupils—and his pulse—rapid and thready—Pilar slapped her brother hard in the face. It worked; he roused, a little, and then flinched, fighting weakly against her grip.

"Hugo! Hughie! It's me. It's Pilar, Hughie. It's okay."

"Pilar? Oh, God. Oh, God. I'm so sorry. I can't stop it. I tried. I promise I tried. But I can't stop it. I'm so deep now. I have to. I don't have a choice. I'm so sorry. Don't tell Nana."

All she felt in that moment was pity. Sorrow and pity. So she pulled her baby brother into her arms and held him while he cried. "Okay, bro. Okay. Scoot over. I'm taking you to my place. Nana can't see this." She shoved at him, and he slouched across the bench seat. When she climbed behind the wheel, trying not to think about sitting where her brother had pissed himself, she pulled her phone out of her pocket and dialed Moore.

He picked up on the first ring. "Hey, Cordero. You done running with the wolves?"

She didn't even bother to acknowledge his old joke. "I need you."

"You got me. Tell me how." This was the kind of friend he was—the kind who asked first how he could help, not what the trouble was. There was nothing and no one that could compel her to give that up.

"Hugo's in trouble. Found him passed out in his truck outside Nana's house. I'm taking him to my place and cleaning him up. But my bike's here, and if she sees it and not me, she'll freak. Are you close?"

He lived a couple of miles away, and he rode, too. He had a big Kawasaki sport bike. "I'm sitting in my altogether on my couch, killing aliens. I can be there under ten."

"Thanks, bro. My gear's still strapped to the back. I'll leave my key in it."

"Already got my jeans on. See you in a few. Hey—you okay?"

"They jumped him in."

"Oh, damn, Pilar. I'm sorry."

Moore never used her first name. She knew why he was now. Because this was a crisis. "Yeah. We'll talk."

"Out the door."

~oOo~

Moore had her bike in her garage while she was still struggling to get Hugo in the bath. He was semi-conscious but still babbling wild apologies and pleas for forgiveness. Pilar just shushed him, stripped off his bloody, soiled clothes, and got the tub filled. As she was helping him into the warm water, she heard her front door open.

She brushed her fingers through her brother's hair, which was stiff with blood and sweat. "You just try to relax, Hughie. I'll make you some tea. And when you're out of the tub, I'll fix up your cuts, okay?"

He nodded and laid the washcloth over his face.

Pilar closed him in and went to the kitchen, where Moore was getting himself a beer. When she came in, he opened the fridge again and handed her one, too.

"Thanks." She twisted the top off and drank half down at the first go.

"So tell me."

"I don't know anything yet. All he's done is cry and say he's sorry and he didn't have a choice, and whatever. But they beat the shit out of him, again, and he's got a big feathered snake right"—she slapped her own chest—"here. He's in."

"Renata is going to lose her mind."

Pilar nodded and looked out the window at the end of her kitchen, into the empty black of the night. "It's her ultimate failure. That's what she'll see. It's the exact thing she was trying to get us away from all those…" Pilar's words faded out as other thoughts emerged. She turned back to Moore. "Fuck. What's the date?"

"Um, the twenty-seventh. Why?"

"Jesus. I didn't think. Oh, fuck. Oh, Nana, why didn't you say anything? Fuck!" She slapped her forehead, hard, and Moore reached out and grabbed her arm, pulling it away.

"Hey, stop. What's wrong?" He kept hold of her arm.

"It's the twentieth anniversary of our mother's death. And his father's. I didn't even think about it!"

"You think the Assassins guy—"

"Raul."

"Raul. You think he thought about it? Brought Hugo in today on purpose?"

"Yeah. He's poetic like that. And he was tight with both our fathers."

"Jesus, Cordero. This seems bad."

It was about as bad as she could imagine. But it was Hugo's bad. The bed he'd made. Not her, not their grandmother. Him. He was lost to them now. "Yeah. But it's on him. I can't pay for his fuckups anymore."

"I wish you didn't have to."

Pilar turned at the weak sound of Hugo's voice. He was standing in the doorway, a towel around his waist.

"Hey, Kyle."

"Hugo. You look rough, bro."

"Yeah. Hey, sis. I feel better. But I don't want to put those clothes on again. You got anything around here that'll fit me?"

"A pair of your sweats that made it into my laundry last time I did it at Nana's. And…I can lend you one of Connor's t-shirts."

He got a strange, furtive look at the mention of Connor, but it left his face quickly. Pilar figured it was all part and parcel of the same problem: her brother was an Assassin now.

"I don't think that'll work."

"It'll be fine. It's just a black t-shirt. I'll grab it." She went and got the clothes. When she came back to the kitchen, neither Hugo nor Moore had moved.

"Oh—I told you I'd make tea and fix you up. Have a seat."

He took the clothes and dropped the towel right there to pull them on. "Nah. I just want to go. I'm solid. I can drive."

"Hughie, you need to sleep it off."

"No. I need to go."

"No, you need to stay. I have your keys, and I can't let you on the road in your condition. You could hurt somebody. Yourself or somebody else."

"I'm clear. I told you."

"Not gonna happen, bro."

Without warning, he backhanded her so hard that she lost her feet and fell to the floor. "I SAID I NEED TO GO!"

Then Moore had him by the throat against the wall. "You put your hands on her again, and you will lose your fucking hands."

Wiping blood from her mouth and nose, Pilar stood and dug his keys out of her pocket. She threw them on the floor at her brother's feet. "Take them and get the fuck out."

Moore looked over his shoulder at her. "Cordero..."

"I want him gone. Out of my life. As of now."

Moore released her brother. Hugo scooped up the keys and hurried out the door, out of her life.

Pilar watched. When the front door closed, she turned to her best friend. "We need to follow him, at least make sure he doesn't hurt Nana. I'll take you back to your bike. Thanks for this."

He hugged her hard. "I got your back, you know that. You sure you want Renata to see what he did to your face?"

She ducked and checked her reflection in her stainless-steel toaster. Her right cheek was turning interesting shades of purple already. "Yeah. She should see this. And I should see her today. I can't believe I fucking forgot what day this was. C'mon. We need to make sure he stays away from her tonight."

~oOo~

Most of the next watch was quiet, and that was good, because Pilar felt slow and thick. She'd spent the night at her grandmother's. Nana had been grieving alone, both happy and sad that Pilar had forgotten such an important date—happy because it meant Pilar had truly moved on from that life, and sad because it meant she herself was alone in her loss. Pilar had found her sitting in the family room, going through a box of her daughter's things—just a random box, with nothing of importance in it. But it was all important.

So she'd spent the rest of the evening sitting and letting the woman who'd raised her, loved her, taught her how to be who she was, tell old, familiar stories about the woman who'd wanted to do those things for her.

In the end, she'd lied about her face, said she'd fallen in the desert. She didn't tell her grandmother about Hugo's new future. It had been the wrong time, the wrong date, for news like that.

They had a school tour at the station during the day, but otherwise, the watch was quiet. Everybody noticed that Cordero was off her game, and they all saw her face, but Moore got between her and any questions. She bunked down early, after dinner and the evening checks, while most of the platoon was hanging out in the rec room. Moore caught her hand and gave it a quick squeeze as she left the room to head for her bunk.

The call came in just after oh-one-hundred hours. Everybody was up almost in unison and down the brass pole. Their station was an old one and still had a pole. They weren't supposed to use it anymore, some bureaucratic circle-jerk had decided that poles were unsafe, but theirs hadn't been taken out because it was 'historic.' So they all used it. They were firefighters, dammit. They came down the pole.

As Pilar was getting into her turnout gear, she had her attention focused on the information coming over the speakers. They were getting called in to a fire in progress. Third alarm. Residential location, multiple-structure involvement, brush at risk. And then the address: Mountainview Estates, Nutmeg Ridge Drive.

She bobbled her helmet. "*¡Dios!*"

That was Connor's parents' street.

CHAPTER SEVENTEEN

The Horde had no charter in Vegas, but their old club had. Ronin had been a member of that old charter, and they still had contacts in the area. The new Brazen Bulls charter was based in Laughlin, which wasn't far from Vegas. And it was a point on their eastbound route for La Zorra. Besides, it was Vegas. It was an excellent place to hold a meeting.

They'd been leading the eastbound route for almost a year now, and yeah, it had occurred to Connor, and to all the Horde, to everyone with a sense of that history, that La Zorra and her Águilas cartel were replicating the routes and reach of the Perro Blanco cartel. Hard to miss. She was taking over what that dead cartel had left behind.

That was just good business; in the years since the Perros had been taken down, those routes had mainly been left to fade out. What had filled in the gaps had been a hodgepodge of less organized and established 'entrepreneurs.' The cartel culture in Mexico and Central and South America had stabilized, but the trade in the north had become erratic—still profitable, but much less predictable. A free market.

A place where bands of hotheaded idiots like the Aztecs had thrived.

La Zorra had not announced it as her intention, but it had become clear nonetheless: she was bringing the trade under control. Her own kind of regulation and standardization.

Which was why she'd been pleased and impressed with the way the Horde had handled their Mexican cockroach problem. It had taken a few weeks for Sherlock and Bart to gather intel and for Sheriff Montoya to get his ducks lined up, to take that intel and turn it into a raid, but when law had gone in, they'd gone in big. Almost the entire crew had been hauled in, and their property—

the building and all their cars and bikes—had been seized. Permanently.

Keeping their distance, the Horde hadn't been able to be present for that beautiful sight, but it had made the local news, and Montoya had provided Hoosier with a report.

They'd caught them with their inventory showing. Sherlock had tracked some kind of a pattern somewhere—Connor didn't understand all that computer whiz-bang crap and didn't care to—and had been able to suggest a date when a raid would be most productive. And the Aztecs had had a back room full of heroin and crystal, all packed neatly in a shipment of flour and sugar, ostensibly for the bakery next door.

Esposito had made bail quickly and gotten most of his guys out within a few days—everybody but Sam, whom they'd nailed on a rape and murder charge, using DNA they'd collected after the raid, and who was being held without bond—but their property was gone. The bar, all of it.

Since then, the Aztecs had been silent—possibly destroyed. That could have blown up in the Horde's face; the Fuentes cartel relied on the Aztecs to move their product in and beyond their turf. But Connor had clued in another crew, rivals of the Aztecs, and they were stepping in—at a lower cut.

The Fuentes were appeased, La Zorra had not been 'inconvenienced,' the Aztecs were crushed, and even Montoya was indebted: that raid was a magnificent feather in his cap. His name had made national news, even.

The Horde could have taken credit in their circle, if they'd wanted. But they'd decided to keep their name out of it. Despite the reach and impact of the coup, it stuck a little wrong that they'd used law to fight their battle. They were satisfied with the result, not proud of the play.

Connor was a little proud. It had been his idea, and it had had a lot of nuanced parts. Nuance wasn't usually his approach. He had a—well-earned—rep for going hard and full-frontal at a problem. He saw a fight in all its dimensions, but he preferred the direct approach. Sitting back and waiting to hear that Raul Esposito, a fucker Connor truly hated, had been *arrested*, and that that was the sum total of his punishment for threatening Pilar...not easy. Connor wanted to feel that bastard's blood on his face.

But still, the plan had been intricate, had gone off without a hitch, and had had much better impact than a beatdown on Esposito would have had. So he felt a little pride.

Sitting in a party suite at a high-end Vegas strip club, drinking whiskey from a bottomless bottle, watching stunning women dance, Connor felt well satisfied, even when he gently set aside a third girl offering a lap dance. He was on a run, and a lap dance wasn't cheating, anyway, but he'd never really understood the appeal of a lap dance. Getting all worked up with no finish? And the point was...?

"Conman! What is up, my brother? You're batting pussy away like you got it to spare." Eight Ball, the President of the Brazen Bulls mother charter in Tulsa, plopped down next to Connor on the ornate, leopard-skin sofa.

Connor laughed and finished his whiskey. Before he could set the glass down, a nude, sparkly girl came up and refilled it. "Not pussy, Eight. Just the suggestion of it. I'm happy to look."

Eight Ball shrugged as a girl came up to him. He spread his arms, and she started her routine. As she writhed on him, he turned to Connor. "Thought I'd see Hooj at a meet this big."

Connor took a drink from his refreshed glass. "Yeah, he planned to be. Got laid out hard with some kind of flu bug. Bart's on point, though. Why—you got something more to bring up?"

"Damn. That's too bad. Yeah, I do, actually." He paused as his lap dance got more intimate, and when the girl moved away from his head again, he continued, "The Bulls are thinking about expanding again, starting a charter in Northern Cali."

That had Connor's attention. The Bulls Nevada charter was still pretty fresh, not yet three years old. But the Bulls had never stopped being outlaw. They had a small but healthy gun-running business that had been going for a couple of decades. "Why NorCal?"

"Our Russian friends are looking to move product into Canada, and they asked us to vet partners. We're thinking why pull in a partner if we can set ourselves up out that way."

Connor nodded. "Makes sense. What's that got to do with the Horde, though?"

Eight Ball patted the girl's ass. "That's enough, sugar tits." When they were alone again in their corner, he turned to Connor. "They're also wondering if your hot Latin Queen might be in the market for some Russian steel."

Ah. "I'll talk to Hooj and Bart. We'll bring it to her." Connor could already see the complications in making the routes two-way. Everything got bigger—the payoff, the danger, the risk of exposure, the interest of the players. Connor liked it as it was. They were all making good bank, and things were running smooth as clockwork. It wasn't his call, though. The Brazen Bulls were friends, and La Zorra was an ally. If they wanted to work out an arrangement, then an arrangement would be worked out. But he had a question: "Did you bring it up with Bart?" Bart was the senior officer here in Vegas.

Eight Ball gestured around the room. Bart was back at the hotel; strip clubs hadn't been his scene for a long time. "Hard to find him havin' a quiet moment."

"Yeah," Connor chuckled. "Our boy is tied down hard."

"Looks like you might be, too, brother. I know we don't see each other much, but I don't think I've ever seen you turn in by yourself before. You've been passing on some prime-quality booty."

"Happens to the best of us." Connor finished his drink and waved off the eager girl with the replenishing bottle.

Eight Ball watched her go. "And you're turning in now, ain't ya? Damn. It's barely midnight."

He shrugged and patted his old friend on the shoulder. "Pick up my slack for me, Eight. I'll see you in the morning."

Pilar was at the station and hopefully sleeping; he knew he couldn't call her now. But he could call it a night and jack off to the memory of the freaking *incendiary* sex they'd had the morning he'd last seen her, and that was worlds better than any random hookup, no matter how prime the offerings in Vegas were.

Sweet fuck, that had been intense. He'd never felt anything like it. Their sex was always great, pretty much always the best sex he'd ever had, often the most inventive, too. But that had been…emotional. And not just because she'd ended up crying, something he'd not seen her do before. Hell, he'd almost been brought to tears himself.

He loved the fuck out of that woman—and that scared the fuck out of him. He was lost to her, and if she bailed…

But she wouldn't. He'd seen that in her eyes the other morning. She was as gone as he was.

And he'd been jacking off to that memory for the past three days.

He was in his room, settling in to do just that when his phone rang—once, then was silent. That got his attention: their code for an emergency was a single ring, then a call back, to let the receiver know to drop everything and answer, even if they were on the road.

He had the buzzer and the tone on; when the second call came in, he picked it up as soon as the phone started to move. "Yeah, what's wrong?"

"It's Sherlock. Brother, you gotta get back. Right now."

He sat up. "What is it? My dad sick?" It was just the flu, just a bad flu. His dad was getting up there, past seventy, but still hearty. He was fit like a man fifteen or twenty years younger.

"I got an alert for the alarm at their house." Sherlock was patched in to everybody's home security system. It was all custom shit that went to him, not to any company, and not to emergency services until he pushed it through.

He was up and grabbing his clothes. "Break-in? They okay?"

"Not a break-in. A fire. The whole neighborhood is going up, and the woods behind. Connor, listen. There are casualties. I'm on the scanner. There are dead at the scene. I don't—fuck, I don't know more. I don't know if it's them. I can't reach them."

Dead? His parents? "GET THERE. JESUS FUCK! GET THERE NOW."

"Lakota and Fargo are on their way. Just get back, Con."

"Call everybody else. I'm out." Connor hung up and grabbed his shit. Feeling panic and desperation massing at the base of his skull, he forced his brain into work mode, narrowing his focus on the task at hand: get home. On his way down the hall, be passed Trick's room. He paused. He needed to get on the road, but he...fuck, he wanted his friend. This was too big to deal with on his own.

Before he could decide to knock or to go, the door to Trick's room flew open. Trick was there, in open jeans and nothing else. "Con! Jesus. Gimme two minutes, and I'm with you."

Connor only nodded and stepped out of the way when a half-dressed girl cleared out of his friend's room.

~oOo~

They were back in Madrone in less than three hours—all the Horde. By the time Connor and Trick were pulling out of the hotel parking lot, Demon, Muse, Ronin, Bart, and J.R, everybody else who'd gone on the run, were running to their bikes, too.

Before they'd crossed into the Madrone city limits, Sherlock had updated Connor, and he knew that his parents had been taken away from the scene injured but alive. They were headed straight for the hospital.

He also knew that Pilar had been called to the fire and was still working it. He didn't know if it had been her who had saved his parents.

The blaze was still raging. Six homes had been consumed, three of his parents' neighbors were dead, four others injured, and the crippling drought of the summer and fall had turned the field and woods that abutted the neighborhood into a wildfire.

He spared a slice of his worry for Pilar, hoping she was safe. But she was well-trained and tough as fuck. He had faith in her. He turned all of his attention, all of his worry, all of his fear to his parents.

They met Lakota, Jesse, Diaz, Fargo, and Keanu at the hospital. Faith, Sid, Riley, and Veda, all the old ladies but Diaz's, were there, too. The Horde family filled the waiting room. Connor didn't bother to wonder who had the kids—they were probably at Riley's with the housekeeper or something. He didn't care.

Faith got to him first. She'd been crying. Oh, fuck, why had she been crying? He grabbed her shoulders and shook her. He didn't know why he was shaking her, but he couldn't stop. And then Demon was there, trying to pull him loose. He knocked him away and grabbed Faith harder. "What happened? How are they?"

Demon shoved him back, his face darkening. "Back off, Con. You hurt her and we have another problem."

"It's okay, Michael," Faith said. "I'm okay." She reached out and grabbed Connor's hand. "We don't know much yet. They're both in surgery, but nobody's told us much. You need to tell them you're here. They've been asking for next of kin."

Trick was at his side, his hand hooked over his shoulder. "C'mon, Con. I'm with you."

Feeling so full of emotion he was numb, he nodded and let Trick push him toward the nurse's desk. The woman behind the desk looked up and asked if she could help him.

He had no idea. "I'm Connor Elliott. My parents, Hoosier and Bibi—um, I mean, Jerome and Bedelia—Elliott...were in the fire? They're in surgery? Somebody's been asking for me?" Everything he said was coming out a question. Nothing felt real enough for certainty. He barely felt like he was even present.

The nurse nodded and picked up a phone. Connor stood there and watched her, not registering what she was saying into the receiver. When she hung up, she gave him the kind of smile you gave someone who was about to get very bad news. "They're sending someone out." She gestured at a row of empty seats nearby. "If you want to have a seat?"

He did not want to have a seat, so he paced instead. About five or ten, or a thousand, minutes passed before the steel double doors swung smoothly open, and a woman in full scrubs walked out. She glanced at the desk and then came right to him. "Mr. Elliott?"

"Yeah." Trick still stood right at his side. He could sense the others approaching, too. And then a small hand slid into his, and he looked down at his other side and saw Faith. "How are my parents?"

"I'm Dr. Sugarman. Why don't we sit?"

"No. Just talk."

Dr. Sugarman looked surprised and intimidated. She nodded. "Okay. I've been assisting Dr. Philpott, who is operating on your father. He sent me out to give you a quick update and ask a couple of questions. I have information about your mother, too. I'll start there. Your mother is stable." The breath Connor took then felt like the first since Sherlock had called him in Vegas.

"She has a badly broken left arm, and she's in surgery to set it. She has some first- and second-degree burns on the left side of her body, and some mild smoke inhalation effects. But she is stable. Her prognosis is excellent."

He felt Faith squeeze his hand, and he smiled a little at the doctor. "Thank you. Thank you. And my dad?"

When Dr. Sugarman took a long breath before she answered, Connor's knees felt weak. It was bad. He knew before the doctor said another word. "Your father experienced severe head trauma, second- and third-degree burns, and his smoke inhalation sickness is much more pronounced than in your mother's case. Dr. Philpott is working to alleviate the pressure and swelling in his brain. We're doing everything we can for him. But I'm afraid his condition is grave." She paused and took another of those ominous breaths. "This is a difficult thing I need to ask you, but your father's organ donor information isn't listed. In the event that—"

"Jesus fuck! Shut your bitch mouth!" Connor's fist was clenched and his arm cocked before he realized it. Trick grabbed it and held on.

"Chill, brother." Trick turned to the doctor. "I know you gotta ask shit like that, but not now. Do your job and save him."

Dr. Sugarman nodded, her eyes wide. "I'm sorry. We are doing everything in our power. But think about that question. If I have to ask it again, there won't be much time for an answer." She stepped back. "I need to get back. Dr. Harris will be out to speak to you when your mother is in recovery, and Dr. Philpott will come talk to you after your father's surgery is complete."

Connor only nodded. The doctor turned and went back through the steel doors.

When Faith pulled on his hand and led him to sit among his family, he went. But he needed Pilar. He needed her, but he couldn't have her. He couldn't even call her.

She was being a hero, and he was alone.

CHAPTER EIGHTEEN

Moore pulled up at the hospital entrance. "I'll park and come up, okay?"

Pilar opened the door of his truck. "Yeah. Thanks." She jumped out and ran inside.

It was a brightly sunny morning. They'd worked past the end of their watch, but they'd finally gotten the fire contained before it had become a full-fledged wildfire. The brush and about a hundred feet into the woods at the back of the neighborhood were charred and dead, and six homes had been completely leveled. Three others were damaged. Four people had died, and five, including Connor's parents, were injured.

Pilar had seen the path of the fire. Like the one back in August. That one, it had been determined, was arson; the accelerant used had been isopropyl alcohol. She was sure that this fire was the same. It wasn't her job to be sure, but it was her job that made her sure.

She felt anxious about that, like there was something she should understand, something just beyond her grasp. Something she shied away from grasping.

As she headed toward the bank of elevators across from the hospital gift shop, her phone buzzed. She'd texted Connor twice on his personal but hadn't heard back. Hoping it was him calling now, she pulled her phone out. But no—it was her grandmother. She'd ignored a couple of calls from her already, so she answered now, pulling to the side of the elevators.

"*Hola*, Nana."

"*Mija!* You always call after a fire. I've been so worried!"

"*Lo siento*, Nana. I didn't have a chance. *Todo bien*." She'd been so worried about Connor that she'd barely given anybody else a spare thought.

Her grandmother sighed into the phone. "*Bueno*. Any word from Hugo?"

"No, Nana. Not since Sunday. Let him go."

"Pilar, you know I can't."

Thinking about Hugo made her weary. "Well, I have to. Nana, I gotta go. I'll call later, *si?*"

"*Mija...*" She stopped and sighed into the phone. "*Si*. Please."

Feeling guilty, Pilar hung up and called the elevator. Moore trotted up just as the doors were closing, so she reached out and stopped them, and he stepped in with her.

"I thought you'd be up there by now."

"Nana called. I took a sec to talk to her. She hasn't heard from Hugo. She wants me to care like she does, but I can't anymore."

That was an untruth, though. Pilar cared about her brother—she cared deeply. The thing was that she wanted to stop. She wanted to be able to throw up her hands and leave him to the mess of his life. She wanted to stop feeling responsible, to stop feeling culpable, for the choices he made.

Her friend put his arm around her. "Just focus here for now. That's what you want, right?"

She nodded. The guilt and responsibility she felt for her brother's downward spiral was infecting every part of her mind and heart. Guilt had racked her head and even her body when she and Moore had handed Connor's parents off to paramedics and then turned around and kept working. It had been the right thing, the only thing, to do, but she'd thought of Connor alone, finding out how badly his parents were hurt, maybe that his father was dead, and keeping her focus on the fire in front of her had taken all of her will.

Then the elevator doors opened again, and she realized that Connor had not been anything like alone. There were so many people in black leather in the waiting room that they spilled out into the corridor. Men and women, all of them somber.

And none of them Connor.

As Pilar and Moore headed down the corridor, Connor's friend Trick stepped out of the milling mass and came straight for her, surprising her by sweeping her up into a tight hug. "Hey, Cordero. You okay?" He set her down and turned to Moore, holding out an inked and be-ringed hand. "Hey. I'm Trick."

They'd been introduced and had even talked on the night of Karaoke Idol, but Trick didn't seem to recall that. Understandable. "I remember. I'm Kyle." Kyle grasped Trick's hand, and they shook.

"Ah. Right. Sorry."

Kyle waved off Trick's apology.

"I'm fine, Trick." Pilar answered the question Trick had asked her. "Where is he?"

"With his mom. Hooj is still in surgery. It's been, fuck, seven or eight hours, I think." He looked them both over. "Did you…was it you who…?"

She knew what he was asking. "Yeah. Moore and me both. We're a team. But I want to talk to Connor before anybody else."

Trick hugged her again. "Thank you." He looked at Moore. "Thank you both."

Moore nodded and asked, "They're gonna be okay?"

"Bibi is. His mom. Hell, everybody's mom." Trick's eyes filled, and he cleared his throat. "She's going to be okay. We don't know about Hooj. Nobody who knows anything has been out in hours, and the one doc who came out then wanted to know about organ donation, so…fuck."

He dropped his head, and Pilar put her hand out and squeezed his arm. "Where's Connor?"

"With Beebs. C'mon, I'll take you back."

He held out his hand, and she took it and let him lead her down another corridor. He opened the door, but he didn't follow her in.

It was a 'semi-private' room, but the other bed was unoccupied. His mother, Bibi, was sleeping. Her left arm was set from her fingers to a few inches above her elbow. Soft bandages covered the left side of her neck, her left shoulder, and, Pilar knew, the left side of the rest of her body. Some of her hair had been burned away, too. A cannula at her nose was helping her get oxygen.

She seemed comfortable, sleeping deeply. She looked elderly, though. Pilar had only seen her a few times, but she was a youthful, vivacious, beautiful woman who took her appearance seriously. She looked nothing like her sixty-or-so years. Until now, at least.

At the side nearest the window, Connor sat on a chair next to his mother's bed. His elbows were on his knees, his head in his hands. He didn't seem to have noticed that the door had opened.

Pilar paused, her heart thumping in her throat. Connor looked so…lost, so devastated, and she understood that all those people waiting outside didn't matter. They were family, and they loved him and his parents. No question that they were strong, steady support. But here, in this room, in this moment, in his own head, he was alone.

She walked to his side and laid her hand on his shoulder. He jumped and lifted weary, sad eyes up to her.

"Oh God, baby! Baby!" He turned abruptly and grabbed her, pulling her between his legs, locking his arms around her waist, resting his head on her chest. "I'm so glad you're here. Oh, God."

And he began to cry.

Stunned at his naked vulnerability, her heart aching, Pilar slid her fingers into his dark hair and held him. After a long moment, she whispered, "I'm here. I'll always be here. I love you, Connor. I'm so sorry."

He heaved a breath, quelling his tears. "Are you okay?" Looking up at her then, his eyes narrowed, and he took hold of her chin. "What happened to your face?"

She didn't want to get into anything about Hugo or what had happened between them. Hugo was irrelevant. So she refocused on the more crucial matter at hand. "I'm fine. Fire's contained. Their house, though, it—"

"I don't care about that." He turned and looked at his mother. Then he stood and leaned over the bedrail, pressing a kiss to her pale forehead. "Let's step away. I want to know everything, but she needs to sleep."

He took Pilar by the hand, but before he moved toward the other side of the room, he pulled her close and kissed her—a fierce, desperate clash of his mouth with hers. His fingers tightened hard around the hand he still held, and his other hand clasped her neck hard enough to make her blood pound in her ears. Then he broke away with a heavy gasp. "I love you so fucking much. Don't leave."

The scope and intensity of his words overwhelmed her as much as his kiss had. Gasping herself, she reached up and brushed his wet lips. "I'm here."

"You smell like fire."

She smiled. "I barely took the time to get my turnout off. I didn't even grab my keys or anything. Moore drove me here."

At Moore's name, Connor winced a little, but Pilar decided to ignore that. She'd enjoyed his jealousy at first, but now she was tired of that carousel, and this wasn't the time for their boring round-and-round about it.

He said nothing about it, though, and pulled her to the other side of the unoccupied bed. "What can you tell me? What happened?"

Her report mode kicked in, and the first thing she thought to say was that the fire had gone to seven alarms. But that wasn't what he wanted to know. She turned her hand in his so that she was leading him, and pushed him to sit on the bed. Then she sat at his side. "Their house was the origin point. That was obvious. We were the third unit in, and it was fully involved. The wind was bad, though, and the fire was not in control. No one had been able to get inside yet, but they were finally getting it knocked back enough that Moore and I could get in." She took a breath and closed her eyes, seeing the scene again. "Your dad was in the hallway, back from the front door, near the kitchen. Your mom was in a bedroom—theirs, I guess. A wall had collapsed, but it wasn't fully engaged. Her arm was pinned."

"Her hair is burnt off on one side. And—they said she was burned."

"When we got to her, the fire was close, but hadn't reached her. Sparks caught her hair. But otherwise I think heat, not flame, burned her. The air itself gets hot enough to burn."

"My dad…"

"He was in the heaviest part of the fire." Pilar recalled the track the flames had followed, remembered the sense she had that the path had been drawn from one point of egress to another, as if it had been meant to block all means of escape. What had saved Hoosier, she thought, if he had in fact been saved, was that he'd fallen on ceramic tile. The heat of the tile had burned him badly, but the fire had chased an easier path. If there had been accelerant near him, it had evaporated. Isopropyl alcohol evaporated quickly. "His head was bleeding heavily." Had been torn open and dented, in fact. "I don't know why. He was clear of debris."

Connor stared at her and then looked away, over his shoulder at his mother. "He was supposed to be with us in Vegas. He got sick, and I convinced him to stay back. My mom would have been alone." She laid her hand on his thigh, and he turned back to her. "Did somebody do this?"

"Connor, I'm not an investigator."

"But you told me you knew about that fire before. The Bridges house. You said you could tell by the way it acted that somebody set it. Could you tell?"

Yeah, she could. And it was the same. But something kept her from saying so; she didn't know why, but it felt wrong—dangerous—to say it. That anxiety she felt, that thing that was just out of her reach. "I don't know, Connor. I'm sorry."

He nodded and then simply sagged. Pilar pulled him close, bringing his head to her shoulder. "I'm so sorry."

"I wish somebody would fucking tell me about Dad."

"You want me to see if I can find somebody?"

His arms came around her. "No. Stay with me."

Feeling sick with sadness and love, she held him and kissed his cheek. "*Te amo mucho.*"

After a few minutes of that quiet, the door opened, and Bart came in. Not seeing them near Bibi's bed, he frowned and then turned their way. "Hey. Sherlock's here. We need you out here. We got something you need to see." Pilar thought the look he turned on her then was odd, guarded or suspicious, but he didn't say anything.

Not seeming to have noticed that, Connor stood and took Pilar's hand. He cast a long look back at his sleeping mother, and then they followed Bart out and down the corridor to the waiting room.

More people were giving her that strange look—not hostile, but wary. It made her neck prickle. Something was wrong, and Pilar began to get the sense that, somehow, all the wrong things prickling her neck and teasing her brain were connected.

Still, Connor didn't seem to notice. He went right for Sherlock, who'd set up a little computer station in the corner.

"What've you got?"

Sherlock motioned him around to see the screen, and Connor kept her hand, so she went, too. Sherlock met her eyes and stuck there for an extra second, like he was evaluating her or trying to tell her something. What the fuck?

"I've been combing the security logs and recordings, looking for anything. I think I found something. I stitched some grabs together. First, there's this. Starting four days ago."

He tapped the screen and a digital, night vision image showing Nutmeg Ridge Drive and the Elliotts' front yard came up. A grey pickup drove slowly up, pulled over and stayed there, then drove off. Pilar's heart picked up an extra beat.

"Three days ago."

Day, this time. The grey pickup, now in color, was faded red. Odd blossoms of rust covered the side panels, and the hood was oxidized. Pilar began to feel truly sick. Connor turned to her, his brow furrowed and his grey eyes dark. He said nothing.

Sherlock said, "Two days."

The same truck. Pilar understood the suspicious stares now, and the fragments of worry and wariness she'd been feeling began to come together and find their fit. She lifted her eyes from the screen and sought out Moore, who was standing back. He cocked his head and mouthed, *You okay?*

She shook her head, and Moore took a step toward her.

"No truck on this feed last night. But I patched into the camera at the entrance to the development. At eleven-forty-three, there's this."

Hugo's truck, turning into Connor's parents' subdivision on the night that their house was burned to the ground and they were almost killed. The night that their whole street had been destroyed and four people *had* been killed. Her brother, recently wearing Assassins colors. Her brother, for whom Connor and the Horde had started a beef with the Assassins.

No, not for him. For her.

Sherlock tapped the screen, and the image froze, showing the front of the truck. A driver and a passenger. Pilar recognized only the driver. Sherlock directed his attention to her when he said, "Good shot of the plates from this angle. I ran 'em. Hugo Velasquez. Some of us have met Hugo."

Connor let go of her hand. "Pilar?"

From the corner of her eye, she could sense Moore approaching, and she knew he was getting ready to have her back. But they were surrounded by outlaw bikers, men who were angry and hurt, worried for loved ones. Loved ones her brother had been involved in hurting. Had he? Had he really? Could Hugo have done something as horrific as this?

She kept her eyes on Connor. The man she loved. "I don't know."

"What do you mean you don't know? That's him. Right?"

"Yeah, it's him. But...Connor, I..." She didn't know what to say. She wanted to say that Hugo would never do something like this, that he wasn't that far gone, that he was a fuckup, not a killer. But she didn't know if that was true. She remember his fevered, fervent apologies, half-incoherent, when she'd found him passed out in the same truck. She'd thought he'd been sorry for joining the Assassins. But maybe he'd been sorry for something he'd known he was about to do.

She reached up to Connor, wanting to touch him, but he knocked her hand away with a feral shout. Then he dragged his own hands over his face. "The fucking *Aztecs* did this? To my parents? My *mother*? This is all because we helped that little asshole. Because we helped you."

He turned away from her and back to Sherlock. "Get his 20. Then call me." He shoved past her, through his brothers, and stormed toward the elevators. Several Horde, including Trick and Demon, followed right behind. She ran after him—if he found Hugo, he'd kill him, and Nana couldn't handle that. Not another funeral. Pilar didn't think she herself could handle that, either.

They had to be wrong—those images looked bad, but there had to be some other explanation. There *had* to be. Hugo hadn't fallen so far as this. Not this.

She circumvented the men and came around to get in front of Connor and grab his arm. "Connor, wait!"

"GET OFF ME!" He shoved her hard, knocking her back. She would have landed on the floor, except that Moore was there and caught her. Connor saw them both, Pilar in Moore's arms, and his face twisted into a nasty, terrifying sneer, and then he and the Horde turned the corner toward the elevators.

Moore set her on her feet. "What the fuck happened? Hugo set that fire?"

"I don't know. Looks that way." She turned to her friend. All around them were Horde family, those who hadn't joined Connor on what she knew was his murderous mission. She dropped her voice. "I have to find him before they do. It'll kill Nana if they get him."

There was another question looming in Pilar's mind, bigger and darker than her grandmother's pain: Could she love a man who'd killed her brother? The enormity of that question was too much, so she pushed it aside. The answer was not to have to confront the question.

"I'm in. Do you know where he is?"

"I know where to look. Moore, it could be fucked up. He's inside the Assassins now. I don't know what I'll find. You should stay back."

"I'm. In. Jesus, Cordero, you can't go alone. I'm in. Let's go."

She turned and looked back at Connor's family. There hadn't even been any word yet about his father. But Connor was gone. After her brother. The rest of them were watching her, the expressions on their faces ranging from angry to worried to, maybe, sympathetic. But they didn't matter. They weren't her family.

Maybe they never would be.

~oOo~

"There's his truck. Pull over."

Moore did, but he didn't kill the engine. He ducked his head and scanned the area. "Where the hell are we?"

"My old block. We used to live in that building." She pointed at the sad, stucco building that housed six apartments and probably at least thirty people. Her memories of the life she'd lived there were warped and faded. Mostly, when she'd been a child, she'd been happy—that was how she remembered it, anyway. But the understanding of hindsight had pulled childhood recollections into more menacing shapes. Her childhood had been immersed in a manic breed of violence.

Her brother's, though, had not. They'd moved before he was old enough for many memories to set and last. His childhood had been safer and quieter. This was not his home, their parents had not been his family. Their grandmother was his family. Pilar was his family. They were his home.

If he was here, they had truly failed him.

"Hugo came back home?"

At her friend's question, Pilar sighed. "No. He doesn't remember this place. But Raul lived next door. He had his man cave above the bar, but I'd heard he'd kept his old apartment, too. Friend of Nana's complained about it a couple of times. He uses it like a safe house or something."

"So your plan is to go up to the angry drug dealer's safe house door and knock?"

It was just as likely—maybe more—that she'd end up tortured and killed as that she'd pull Hugo clear, but she had no other ideas. "You got a better one? I have to get Hugo out of there. Connor's gonna kill him—and I'm not exaggerating for effect. I can't let that happen."

"I know. But...are you gonna give Connor up? Tell Hugo and whoever they're coming?"

"No! What—" Pilar sat back. She hadn't thought about what she'd tell Hugo to get him moving, or how she'd get Raul to let him go. It had to have been Raul who'd ordered the fire; it was Raul Connor should direct his anger toward. Even if Hugo had set it, he'd had no choice.

But he'd had a choice. He'd had lots of choices, lots of chances not to get involved with the Assassins.

Still, she had to save her brother. Not for him, not for her. For her grandmother. She was innocent in all of this, and she would suffer most. And Hugo didn't deserve to die. He was a fuckup, maybe a lost cause. But not a murderer. He wasn't. The boy Nana and she had raised was *not a fucking murderer*.

She slammed her fists on the dash of Moore's truck. "Fuck! I just have to go and figure it out. Connor's gonna find him any minute. You stay put, though. I don't want you dragged into this shit."

"Fuck you. We're a team. Always been a team. You go, I go. So let's just go." He opened his door and stepped onto the street.

Pilar got out, too, and they headed toward one of the many dilapidated buildings on this dilapidated street in the heart of Assassins turf.

CHAPTER NINETEEN

Connor rolled the door of the storage locker up. Before he stepped in, Muse grabbed his arm. "Brother, what are we doing?"

He shrugged Muse's hand away and walked into the locker. "I'm gonna kill that fucker and every fucking Aztec in the state."

"Okay. But we got no word from Sherlock yet. We don't know where he is, what we'll face, nothing. You need to take a beat."

Connor turned on the older man. "Don't pull that 'count beats' shit with me. I'm not Demon. I'm not losing my shit." Demon was standing right there, but Connor didn't give a fuck if he offended anybody.

Muse shook his head. "Yeah, you are."

He hauled off, but Muse caught his arm in mid-swing. He said no more, just lased his blue eyes at Connor. Finally, Connor relaxed, and Muse let go of his hand.

"I gotta pay this back." He didn't give a shit that Hugo was Pilar's brother. If that waste of oxygen was still drawing breath by the end of this day, *then* Connor would lose his shit.

This was all his own fault, and he had to do what he could to make it right. He'd gotten wrapped up in Pilar. He'd been pleased and flattered that she'd come to him for help, and he'd taken her Hugo problem to his father and gotten the whole club involved. And now his father might be dying. And his mother, who'd already been horribly hurt once because of the life her men led, had been hurt again. All because he was involved with Pilar.

Had been involved with her. No more.

His fault.

Muse was talking, responding to the last thing Connor had said aloud. "No question. But we don't know yet what we need. Give Sherlock a minute to get the intel."

He was right. Connor wheeled around and kicked a box. "Fuck!" He looked around at the men who'd come with him: Muse, Demon, Trick, Lakota, and Diaz. They were six men. Enough to wage a battle, if they needed to. But not without some idea what lay ahead. "Okay. We wait."

They waited maybe ten, fifteen minutes, and then Connor's phone buzzed. It was Bart. He answered. "Bart—word on my dad?"

He didn't answer right away, and Connor's head began to throb with desolate anxiety.

"Bart! Fuck!"

"Sorry." Bart cleared his throat. "He's out of surgery and in the ICU. He alive. But it's not good, Con. You should get back here."

Connor squeezed his eyes shut and made himself focus and breathe. "I can't. Not yet. I need to pay this back. You got anything on that?"

"Yeah. We got a 20. 5728 Mission Street. Deep in Aztec turf. It's a freestanding apartment building. Six units. We can't put you closer than the building, Connor. But one of those units is rented to a Carlita Hernandez d'Esposito. I'm thinking she's blood family to Raul. Unit 1B. Be careful, Con. The whole fucking crew could be in that building. Ready for you."

Connor was counting on it. He wanted to take the whole fucking crew down. "What about the other units?"

"Rented to civilians. You gotta go in easy, brother."

There was no easy way to go in. It was broad daylight, and he meant to kill them all. "Okay. Thanks, man. How's my mom?"

"She's awake. The women are in with her now. She's worried about you and Hooj."

That made Connor smile a little. His mom was always looking out for everybody. "Tell her I'll be back soon as I can. I'm gonna make this right."

Another pause, and then Bart said. "Okay, brother. Keep me looped in."

"I will." Bart was the head of the club now. For now. Until his dad was back on his feet. Only until then.

Connor hung up and shared the news with his brothers.

When he was finished, Trick said, "We can't go in hot, Con."

"They burned my parents. My dad might be dying. *My mom got hurt*. Did you see her? I want them all dead."

"Brother, I hear you. Now you hear me. If you want to go now, before noon, in an apartment building, then we need to try to do it quiet."

"Nobody on Mission Street ever called a cop in their lives," Diaz added. "We don't gotta go in that quiet."

Trick turned on him. "It's more than that. How many people live in that building? You think the Aztecs are going to give a shit if kids get caught in our crossfire?"

"So what's your plan?"

Lakota stepped up and flipped his dagger in his hand. "If we can get the jump on them, we can do it quiet."

Connor sat down on a metal chest in the locker and forced himself to think. They were planning a battle in an apartment building. If they could go quietly at all, it would only be at the beginning. They might be able to take down any posted guards. Once inside, though, it would be chaos. No way to avoid it.

Trick had his phone out. "Here's the street view of the building. Six units. Three floors. So two units each floor. One door into the front of the building. One back door, but there's a balcony on the back of each unit, with fire escapes."

Connor took Trick's phone and studied the images. "We need at least two guys at the back. That leaves us with four going in the front. Do we know how many Aztecs there are?"

Trick added, "And do they have families? Kids? What's the outside number of people we need to be ready for? And what are we doing with the women and kids?"

Diaz answered that. "They got one still locked up, but if they brought Hugo in, there'll be seven members. Esposito's kids are grown—his boy is a member. I don't know about the others."

Standing back up, Connor moved to the back of the locker. "Keep sharp out there." It wouldn't do to be seen pulling weapons out of a self-storage locker. "We go in with small arms and suppressors. And we suit up." He heaved a stack of Kevlar vests out of a chest he'd uncovered. "We deal with what we find. We try to keep our bullets where they belong. But I'm not taking the weight for what those shitheads do to their own people. Let's shut the fuck up and move."

~oOo~

It was a couple of days before Halloween. The weather was warm and bright, the cloudless kind of day that got boring in Southern California. Kids were in school, and people who had jobs were at them, so the street was quiet. A few cheap, indifferent Halloween decorations sat on porches, were taped to doors and windows. But this wasn't the kind of neighborhood where people let their kids trick-or-treat. This was the kind of neighborhood people took their kids away from to trick-or-treat someplace safer, with better candy.

They pulled their bikes up around the corner from Mission Street—not too far for a quick getaway, but far enough that their engines wouldn't announce their arrival. They were already suited up and armed. Connor gestured a reminder of the plan, and they headed out.

Demon and Muse would cover the back. Connor, Trick, and Diaz would come through the front. Lakota would keep watch, guarding the large front window, in case somebody came through that way.

Connor led the way up the front, tight to the buildings to keep their profile low. About two doors from their target, as he scanned the street with one eye, he pulled up short and gestured for the others to stop.

Trick was right behind him. "What is it?"

He nodded to a late-model GMC truck parked directly in front of the building they were up against. Trick looked, then looked harder. He turned back to Connor, frowning. Then his head swiveled hard back to the truck.

"Fuck me. Is that…?" There was a sticker on the rear passenger window of the extended cab. A Maltese cross.

"Yeah. Fuck." That was Moore's truck. If Moore was here, then Pilar was, too. Those two were joined at the goddamn hip.

Diaz leaned forward. "What's the holdup?"

"Con's old lady might be in there."

Connor shook his head. No. Not his old lady. Maybe that was the way they'd been headed—who was he kidding; yes, they'd been headed that way—but he was shutting that shit down. It had never occurred to him that it might be *he* who'd be the one who couldn't deal, but he couldn't. Watching that footage, seeing that her brother had fucking *burned his parents' house down with them in it*, burned their whole neighborhood, and seeing the look in her eyes, the way she'd tried to protect her brother, even after what he'd done, that she had chosen that piece of shit over him—he couldn't deal with any of it.

And now she was here. To protect her brother. From him.

So he shook his head. "Doesn't matter. Let's move."

~oOo~

They got to the door of the apartment without incident. An old woman had stepped out into the hall and then, seeing them, had stepped right back in and locked her door, but otherwise, as far as they knew, they hadn't been seen. Connor had called Muse; he and Demon were in place.

It was go time.

He could hear music and talk beyond the door. He checked the seams around the jamb. It was possible, if you knew what to look for, to make a good guess about how many locks on a door were actually engaged. Connor knew what to look for. This door had three locks, but only one deadbolt appeared to be engaged. With the assumption that a chain guard might also be engaged on the other side, he stepped back and aimed his heavy boot.

The door came in on the first kick; the whole jamb tore away. Connor made quick, instinctual note of the scene: nine men, including Moore and Hugo, and three women, one of whom was Pilar. No kids he could see. Without taking any more time, he fired at the nearest head, a grey-haired Aztec with a scaled wing inked on the side of his face. The man fell dead, and Connor prepared for chaos.

For about thirty seconds, chaos happened. They had caught the Aztecs unawares, and by the time those men had their weapons out, the Horde had already ended three of them.

Then Esposito grabbed Pilar and shoved his gun into her face, the barrel pushing savagely into her mouth, and Connor threw his free arm out to stop his men. "Hold!"

He cared. He shouldn't—he should let whatever was going to happen to her happen, as long as he got to her brother, but he cared. Hugo had hurt his family, his *parents*, and Pilar was here, had chosen her brother over him. But he couldn't turn off his heart. He loved her like he'd never loved anyone. Even now. Even here at the scene of her attempt to betray him. He wouldn't forgive her, but he couldn't stop loving her. He felt rent in two.

Now, Esposito laughed crazily and wrapped his hand around her throat, still shoving the gun against her lips, and Connor saw that she'd been bound—her hands were tied behind her back. "Hugo, *hermano*, you're a popular guy." He looked at Connor. "You here to save him again, too? His sister thinks she can bargain him back out. Or are you looking for his head? He did a good job for me, I gotta say. I'm thinking he's due for a promotion already."

Pilar struggled harder, and Esposito squeezed her throat more tightly. She uttered a pained, stilted groan. Unable to stop himself, Connor took a step toward her, and Esposito grinned, sliding one hand from her neck over her shoulder to grab a breast and squeeze.

Pilar's pain and tension was obvious, but Connor forced himself to keep his focus on her captor, who leered as if he had won something. "Or maybe it's *her* you're here for. Maybe you just want this fine piece of ass right here? She's got her mother's looks. *Dios mio*, Olivia was somethin' else. Shame she got caught in the crossfire. I meant to make her mine."

Hugo and Pilar both reacted to that. Pilar stopped struggling, and Hugo turned and faced Esposito. "What's that supposed to mean?"

Again, Esposito laughed that madman laugh. "You don't got much upstairs, do ya, *Hughie?*" Again, he directed his attention to Connor. "You boys drop your guns right now."

Connor was in the lead, a step ahead of his men. He hesitated, trying to make his brain ignore Pilar and take the fucking shot right now.

Esposito nodded, and a blast exploded. Trick flailed backwards and landed, unconscious or at least badly dazed, on the floor. At the same time, Hugo flew forward, toward Esposito.

"NO!" Connor shouted, but then the room went stormy with gunfire, and he was driven to the floor. A bullet caught his arm, slicing through as he fell downward. Diaz landed on top of him and then rolled off, firing.

When Connor came up into a crouch, Pilar was on the floor. Hugo was on the floor. Trick was down. Moore, too.

Esposito pointed his gun at Pilar. Still in his crouch, his dominant arm hot and numb, Connor didn't think, he didn't aim. He brought up his weapon and fired. The shot caught Esposito in the leg but didn't knock him down. Connor stood and fired twice more. As Esposito finally fell, Connor felt like he'd been punched by the fist of God. He landed on the floor again, and the world spun and faded.

"Con!" Diaz was one his knees at his side, pulling at his shirt. "Can you get up?"

Connor had been shot in the vest, low on his ribs. Fuck, that hurt. "Yeah." He struggled to his feet and saw Trick doing the same, his hand clutching at his chest. "You good, T?"

"Yeah. Jesus, that hurts."

"We whole?"

Muse and Demon were in the apartment now, too. Demon nodded. "Yeah. You and Trick took the brunt. All hail Kevlar."

No shit. But Pilar was still on the floor. Fuck! Forgetting the pain in his ribs, he climbed over Aztec bodies and dropped to his knees at her side. He snatched his blade and sliced the tape holding her wrists together, then rolled her over, checking for the bullet wound. Her head was bleeding, and at first he thought his heart was going to stop dead, but it wasn't a bullet that had made her bleed. She had a gash over her temple and cheek. Esposito had hit her with the gun, not shot her with it.

"Thank God. Come on, baby. Wake up." She didn't, and he clutched her to his sore chest and looked around. All the Horde were inside now. The two Aztec women were cowering in a corner; Diaz was talking to them in Spanish. Moore had sat up; he'd been hit in the shoulder. His wrists had been bound, too; they still had the torn tape stuck to them. Hugo lay on the floor in the middle of the room, not far from Esposito's body. His eyes were open and unseeing. A small, singed hole marred his cheek. He was dead.

All the Aztecs were down. When one moaned at Muse's feet, he aimed down and ended the man. And then all the Aztecs were dead.

The entire gang lay dead at the Horde's feet, on the floor of this shitty apartment. All but Sam, the one who was locked up, facing charges for rape and murder.

"We need to clean this up." Trick's voice was still strained, and he hadn't managed yet to stand straight up.

"Yeah, we do. Lakota, call Bart. We need the service up here. We need the van, and we need J.R. at the clubhouse. We got wounded. Trick, can you ride?"

"I'll manage. Let's get Cordero and her buddy some help."

When Trick said her name, Pilar stirred and struggled in Connor's arms.

She opened her eyes, and Connor felt a painful rush of relief and love. He knew that he would forgive her, after all. He loved her too much not to. "It's okay, baby."

"Connor? Oh God, I'm sorry. I'm so sorry. I'm sorry. I didn't know he was...I didn't know." She turned her head then and saw her brother's body. "Hugo? Oh, no, oh Hughie! Hughie!"

Pushing away from Connor, blood dripping down her face, Pilar crawled to her brother and picked up his head. Connor saw then that the back of his skull was gone, but Pilar didn't seem to notice or care.

She didn't cry. She rocked him, moaning, "*Lo siento, Nana. Lo siento, lo siento.*"

Connor didn't know much Spanish, but he knew enough to understand that she was apologizing to her grandmother. And then he thought he understood everything else. Why she'd been so protective of her shitty brother, why she'd tried to save him from Horde retaliation. She hadn't been trying to save him. She'd been trying to save her grandmother the pain of losing him.

Still on his knees, he went to her and wrapped his arms around her. "It's gonna be okay, baby." He should have said he was sorry, that was the thing you said when somebody lost a loved one, but he wasn't sorry. The only thing he was sorry about was that it hadn't been his bullet that had ended the bastard.

No—he was also sorry that Pilar was hurting.

He tightened his hold around her, meaning to offer her comfort, but she fought him.

"It's not okay! My God, it's not! This is going to kill her. He was my responsibility, and I fucked everything up." She looked up then and saw her friend. "Fuck, Moore! God, you're hurt!"

"I'm okay. Help's coming." Moore looked pale, but he was clear and coherent.

Setting Hugo's head gently down on the floor again, she pushed Connor off again and went to her friend.

Connor sat there alone in the middle of the aftermath, his fists clenched, his ribs aching, blood running freely down his arm, and he watched Pilar check Moore's wound. He fucking hated that guy.

~oOo~

After J.R. had him stitched and taped up, and he'd spoken at length with Bart, Connor went to find Pilar. She was with Moore—fucking of course she was. J.R. had already stitched the cut on her face, and he was wrapping Moore's shoulder up.

"I talk to you, Cordero?"

She turned at his voice, and she frowned when she saw his arm. "You were hurt, too?"

It was the first she'd noticed. "Just a scratch. I'm fine. I need you, though."

He took comfort in the fact that she came right to him. She wrapped her arms around his waist. He winced and groaned, and she flinched back. Scowling at him, she lifted his t-shirt. "Jesus! What happened?"

"Caught a bullet in the vest. Cracked a rib or two."

"You got shot?"

"The vest caught it. I'm okay. But I need to get back to the hospital. I want you with me. Please. I haven't seen my dad yet."

She looked back at Moore, away from him, and Connor almost said fuck it all. He could not deal with that shit. But fuck, he *needed* her. So instead, he reached out and grabbed her arm, glad for the way the pulling pain in his ribs gave him focus. "Jesus Christ, stop picking people over me. Fucking stop it."

She turned back to him, her eyes wide. "What?"

"Your brother, your job, your grandma, your friend. When am I first?"

"Connor, you *are* first. I love you. But you're not only. I have other things in my life."

He was sore and tired. He was angry and afraid for his parents. The part of him that saw the big picture knew he was behaving like a petulant brat, but if ever there was a time for him to come first on the list of things in her life, he thought it should be now.

Or maybe not. Her brother had just been killed. Her grandmother hadn't been told yet. Her friend had been hurt and was in the middle of the Horde clubhouse, which wasn't necessarily the most welcoming place for him, especially since Connor had had a drunken gripe or two about the guy.

So, okay. If she said no, he'd find a way to deal. At least until things calmed down again and they could talk it out like grownups.

They still needed to talk about everything that had happened today. Later, though. After things calmed down.

But she didn't say no. "I love you, Connor. If you want me at the hospital, then I'll be there. Let me just tell him that I'm leaving, okay?"

Relieved, he kissed her, and then he let her go to her friend.

CHAPTER TWENTY

Pilar needed to get to her grandmother.

Her brain was so stuffed full that she could barely think at all. She felt slow and numb, and a voice in her head kept trying to convince her that she was stuck in a dream. She'd pinched herself, slapped herself, whatever, and had not been able to wake up. Because this was no dream. This was all happening.

Her brother was dead. Fuck, Hugo was *dead*. He had killed people, hurt Connor's parents, destroyed a whole street of houses, acres of wild land.

He'd had a part in it, anyway. His first task as an Assassin.

God, the things she'd learned on this day.

Now she stood next to Connor and tried to listen, to focus on what the doctor was telling him about his father.

Connor was crazed. She couldn't keep up with his changing, charging moods: his need for her this morning, his fury and rejection of her later, his comfort of her in the aftermath, his demand of her in the clubhouse, his omnipresent jealousy.

She understood why, understood that he was going through so much so fast, that people he loved most were teetering on the edge, but she couldn't understand what he needed of her. She was going through shit herself. God—where was Hugo's body? What had the Horde meant about 'calling in a service'?

How the fuck was she going to tell her grandmother?

Connor's hand clenched harder on hers, and again she tried to focus. Behind them, around them, were several of his Horde family, also listening to the doctor's monotonous voice. They were all standing; Connor had refused the doctor's suggestion to sit.

"I need you to speak plain English, doc. I'm hearing a lot of syllables and no sense."

Dr. Philpott nodded and cleared his throat. "Yes. Apologies. Your father experienced a severe brain injury—"

"I got that. You lost me in the rest of it."

"There's a considerable amount of swelling. To give the brain its best chance to heal and recover, we removed a section of the skull."

"You took his head apart? The fuck?" He raked his free hand through his hair, and Pilar resisted the urge to try to liberate her hand from his demolishing grip.

The doctor winced at Connor's aggressive tone, but he went on in that same cool, level voice. Every doctor Pilar knew was capable of the same detached way of speaking, used to talk to families, to tell hard news in a way intended to keep emotions in check. "We need to give the brain room as it swells. The compression against the skull would be devastating." When Connor only heaved a breath without interrupting again, Philpott continued. "We've implanted the skull segment into your father's abdomen to keep it alive until we can put it back where it belongs."

"Again, doc. You're telling me that you put my father's skull inside his gut?"

"Part of the skull, yes. Under the skin. This is common practice for traumatic brain injuries like your father's."

"Jesus. What else?"

"The respiratory system experienced trauma from the heat and smoke. There is some permanent scarring, which will limit breathing function for the rest of his life, but if he survives, he should have enough function to live fairly normally in that regard."

Connor's hand, and his whole arm, were as rigid as steel. He was crushing her hand. "And his burns?"

"These are the least of the injuries. There are second- and third-degree burns on the right side of the body. There'll be scarring, but there's a chance grafts won't be necessary. For now, our attention is on the brain injury. We'll make a further determination if he begins to recover."

"If you say 'if' again, or keep talking about my father like he's a thing, you're going to end up with a traumatic brain injury of your own."

Philpott paled and flinched, and Pilar put her free hand on Connor's chest. "Calm down, honey."

Connor looked down at her, and his expression almost made her flinch, too. He was scatter-bombing his anger, and she was catching some shrapnel.

The doctor had regained his composure. "I assure you that your father is getting the best possible care. For now, we need to wait and monitor him, see how his brain responds to the surgery and the medication we're administering. The next hours are crucial."

"Can I see him?"

"He's in the ICU, and he'll be comatose for at least the next two days. Understand that his appearance might be…alarming at first."

"I don't care. I need to see him."

The doctor nodded. "I understand. Only you, and no more than five minutes. He's being closely monitored. He's in Room 2." The doctor looked past Connor and Pilar at the rest of the men and women who'd been hanging on his words, and he paled again before his attention returned to Connor. "Do you have any other questions?"

When Connor shook his head, the doctor nodded and turned away. Pilar had the clear sense that he was escaping.

Connor squeezed her sore hand again. "Come with me."

"He said—"

"Fuck that. I need you."

"Let's go, then."

He lifted her hand to his mouth, his grip relaxing as he kissed her fingers. "I love you."

She loved him. The way she felt about him was so strong it freaked her out. But her head was numb and overfull, and she couldn't get the words out. He wanted to be first in her life, and she was here, setting aside her own family, the violence that had been done to it, to stand with Connor while he grappled with the violence that had been done to his. For which she was, to a large degree, responsible. She was torn, and she felt it as a tearing pain somewhere inside.

But he needed her, and he'd asked her to choose. She'd chosen. Fuck. How would she, could she, ever make anything right for her nana? Or for Connor? For herself?

It was too much to think about right now, so she didn't. Her whole life, she'd been good at setting aside the need for introspection. Some questions became more troubling when they had answers.

She stepped close and leaned her forehead on his chest, and she felt him dip his head and press his lips into her hair. For several seconds, they simply stood like that. Then he took a step back and led her toward the Intensive Care Unit.

The ICU was arranged in a circle, with the round desk of the nurse's station in the center. A large bank of electronics dominated half the desk. The glass-walled patient rooms faced inward so that the patients could be constantly monitored.

When Connor, tense and angry, big and brawny, wearing his heavy boots and dark kutte, led her toward Room 2, the three nurses behind the desk looked up, but they didn't stop them. They simply watched.

He drew up so short when they went into the room that Pilar ran into his broad back.

"Holy fuck. I can't"—he turned, and his eyes were wide with shock and fear—"I can't…"

She grabbed his arm. "You can. I'm here."

When Connor nodded and turned back toward his father's bed, Pilar saw what had him so upset. His father looked small and as pale as the sheets beneath him and the bandages around him. His long, grey beard was gone, and the thick tube of the ventilator filled his mouth. His head was wrapped in a thick swath of bandages, as was his chest and right arm. Dark bruising circled his closed eyes.

He wasn't a young man, but when Pilar had been around him, he had exuded a kind of eternal youth that rejected his age. Now, though, he looked ancient, his body shrunken and empty.

"Dad." Connor's voice broke as he went to the bed and put his hand over his father's left arm. "I'm so fucking sorry." After a moment, he turned back to Pilar. "Your brother did this."

She nodded. "It wasn't just him, but yes. He was part of it. I'm sorry." The words sounded anemic. Insignificant. Powerless.

"Who else was in his truck?"

"You want to talk about this now? Here?"

When he only stared at her, she dropped her head and took a deep breath. "Freddy Macias. He was Assassin. O.G. From before even my father's and Raul's time. He was inside for almost twenty years, for murder and arson. Got out a few months back. You killed him when you came into the apartment this morning." He'd set the Bridges fire in August. His big comeback.

And he'd burned her friend, Mia's, house when Pilar was a girl. All of it Assassins vengeance. Her childhood had been steeped in more violence than she'd even been aware of.

"What—your brother was his fucking apprentice or something?"

Just the stooge sent to help out. "It was how he had to pay Raul back."

He stepped away from his father's bedside and faced her. "Why were you there today? They had you tied up. You and Moore. What the fuck happened?"

"I went to find him. I had to."

"To keep him away from me." His expression took on that vicious sneer that had shocked her earlier, when they'd first learned of Hugo's involvement.

This was their breaking point, she knew. If he couldn't be made to see, to forgive, then nothing would save what they had. "Connor, you have to understand. Please. He's my little brother."

He took a deep breath, and Pilar could see it calming him a little. "I guess I do. I'm trying to. I'm trying to get past it. But you understand me: he had to die."

There was a part of her that agreed, and another part of her that even thought it might have been for the best. The rest of her at least understood why it was true for Connor and the Night Horde. "I know. And I had to try to save him."

He looked back at his father. "What happened?"

It was too much to explain. Pilar tried to find a way in her head that would sum up those minutes—it hadn't even been an hour—in the Aztec apartment. "I knew it was stupid to just go there, but I couldn't think of anything better. I wanted to try to get him home, find someplace safe so I could talk to him—and then I would have come to you. I wanted to try to find another way to end all this." At that, Connor made a scoffing, bitter sound, but Pilar went on. "I wanted to know that we were wrong, that he couldn't have done it. But they grabbed us before we even got to the apartment door. Raul started…using me to fuck with Hugo. He wanted to make Hugo hurt me. But he wouldn't. Connor, I know you don't believe this. You don't have any reason to. But my brother wasn't a bad guy"—emotion broke her voice, and she stopped and took a breath. "Not deep inside. He was fucked up. But he was just—he was afraid more than anything else. Everything overwhelmed him, all the time. From the time he was little. I think hanging with the tough guys made him feel stronger."

Connor only stared at her, unmoved. So she repeated, "He wouldn't hurt me. They were starting to knock him around and threaten him when you came in, but he was fighting back."

She shut her eyes against the memory of Raul's hands on her, of the things he'd said to Hugo. What they'd tried to make him do to her. The sound of Moore's shouts and Hugo's protests, of Assassins' laughter.

They'd tried to force Hugo to rape her. When he'd refused and fought, they'd muscled him down and threatened to take his dick off and rape her with it anyway. That was what the Horde had broken in on.

Deciding not to tell Connor any of that, she pushed it all away and opened her eyes.

Connor's expression had not changed; he remained stoic and determined. "Did he burn my folks? It's all I care about, Pilar. Did he do it?"

Maybe if she told him about what had happened in that apartment, he'd care more. But the story made her a victim, and she couldn't stand that. So she told him what he wanted to know, what he wanted to hear.

Freddy had gone into elaborate detail about what had happened in the Elliotts' house. They knew Pilar's connection to them, and they had all enjoyed the story. "Yes. Like I said, he helped. He didn't think he had a choice. It was Raul's order, Freddy's plan. Raul was yelling about how the Horde tried to take them down, but the Assassins would rise from Horde ashes. They didn't know your dad was there, and I guess he surprised them. Freddy hit him. That's how his head was hurt. I don't know with what. But he was laughing about the sound it made." She closed her eyes, shuddering at that memory, and then she steeled herself to say something more. "It was meant to be a message, that the Horde had a lot to lose in a fight with them."

"Fucking hell." Deeper understanding dawned in his eyes. "They knew my mother was there. They thought she was alone. They meant to kill her."

Pilar couldn't say the answer to that out loud. "I'm sorry, Connor. I know it was me who brought all this down on you."

"Yeah. It was us. I got caught up in you. I should have...I don't know. Fuck, I don't even know if I'd do it differently if I could."

"Where does this leave us?"

He stepped away from the bed and leaned back heavily against the wall. "I love you. I thought before that I wanted to be done, but I don't. I can't. I need you."

"We're okay, then?" The thought that they had found their breaking point had shaken her badly, and the hope that they hadn't was shaking her more. She went to him and slid her hands under his kutte. She'd never needed someone this way before; she'd never felt so afraid to lose a connection. It made her feel weak and afraid. It hurt so deeply that it buried the conflicted, confusing pain of losing Hugo and the electric anxiety of what she faced when she told her grandmother. Right now, the most important thing in her life was to be solid with this man.

Connor's big, heavy hands wrapped around her arms. "Do you love me?"

"Yes. So much it hurts."

"Then I guess we'll be okay."

Will be. Meaning that they weren't yet.

Afraid and exhausted, she leaned into him and took what comfort she could when his arms enclosed her and pulled her close. Snaking her arms around his waist, she tried to give him the same comfort back.

She had given herself to this man, her real self. Pilar, not Cordero. Or both of them, really, all of her—the strong and the weak, the fierce and the vulnerable. She needed him to keep safe what she had never given to anyone else.

~oOo~

Pilar's grandmother worked as an office manager at an accounting firm in San Bernardino. She'd been the receptionist there when Pilar and Hugo were children, and she'd worked her way through the administrative ranks. When she'd moved her grandchildren to what she'd meant to be a safer life, she had picked up a second job, cleaning the offices of the very same building she spent her days answering phones in.

She'd also worked weekends at a little boutique. When Pilar became a firefighter, she was able to help out with bills, and being able to cut back to one job had been almost like retirement for her grandmother.

Pilar hated the idea of breaking this news to her while she was at work, but she had no choice. Connor had told her that the Horde's 'cleaner' was dumping the Assassin bodies with the ink intact. They would be quickly identified, and Pilar didn't want her to hear it from some fucking detective who thought the Assassins were all scum.

It had to be her, and it had to be now. Staying with Connor this long had delayed the news too much already.

So she walked into the building, still wearing the uniform she'd jumped into from her bunk, answering the call of the fire on Nutmeg Ridge Drive. How long ago had that been? Hours? Days? She didn't even know anymore. A lifetime ago.

She took the elevator up to the fourth floor and went into the office. A young receptionist sat at a desk that was far larger than was practically necessary. Pilar rarely visited her grandmother at work, so she didn't know many of the people she worked with.

The woman smiled up at her. "May I help you?"

"I'm here to see Renata Salazar?"

"Is she expecting you?"

"No, it's not business. I'm her granddaughter. It's a family matter—an urgent one."

"Oh, I'm sorry. One minute." She picked up the phone and pressed a button. "Renata? Your granddaughter is here to see you."

Hanging up, the girl smiled again. "You can go back. Do you know her office?"

"I do. Thanks." She went back.

'Office' was a fairly optimistic term for the room that her grandmother called her own. Small and windowless, two walls dominated by shelves of office supplies, it was more of a closet. But she had a desk and a phone of her own, and a door that set her apart from the cubicles that took up most of the office suite, and she was proud of how far she'd advanced.

She was standing at the door when Pilar went back, and she looked worried. "What is it, *mija*? It's Hugo, isn't it? He's hurt again?"

Pilar took hold of her hands. "Can we sit, Nana?"

"Oh, no. Oh, no. He's dead. He is, isn't he? Oh, Hughie, ah, *mijo*, no."

The workers in the cubicles were starting to notice this little family scene. "Nana, let's go in and close the door. Please."

Pilar had never been someone who cried, not since she was a little girl. It wasn't that she didn't feel emotion—quite the opposite. She felt it so much that it became inexpressible. She turned tearful emotions into focus, in the same way that she had shut her fear down. She had learned to channel feeling into focus. She got intent, single-minded, but not emotional.

Except with Connor. Her emotions broke her control and focus all the time with him. She recalled the last time she and Connor had been intimate, when she'd bawled hysterically. She hadn't yet had taken the time to figure out what had happened then to loosen pipes that had been dry for years—another question that might be better left unanswered.

Still, feeling her grandmother's aged hands shaking, seeing the fear and sadness in the beloved brown eyes behind her bifocals, Pilar was spun.

She led her grandmother into her tiny office and closed the door.

~oOo~

It took weeks for the coroner to release her brother's body. By the time Pilar and her grandmother could bury him, November was half over.

They had planned a traditional funeral for him, with a Mass before the burial service. Renata went to the church every day for more than a week beforehand to light a candle and to pray the rosary. She was a deeply, quietly religious woman and always had been, but her tenacity regarding Hugo's end made Pilar think that their grandmother was trying to will him into God's grace.

Pilar didn't join her for those daily trips; she had long ago left behind most of the trappings of the religion she'd been born into, though when asked, she still readily identified as Catholic. It was hard to leave so much tradition and belief behind entirely.

But the rituals didn't give her much comfort. Hugo was dead. Despite their grandmother's efforts to save him from the life of their fathers and their mother, he had swirled down the same drain. Pilar had escaped it, for the most part, and in the weeks between Hugo's death and his funeral, she embraced that truth. She went back to her life, away from Mission Street and the High Life, away from the Aztec Assassins. Away from her history. Away from her brother, her mother, her father, her stepfather. They were all dead. Their bodies had all fallen within a radius of about a hundred feet, and a quarter century, of each other.

But Pilar was free of it.

She checked in on her grandmother daily, and she helped with the planning of the service, but otherwise, she set Hugo to the side of her mind, with all of her unanswered questions and focused on the life she had made. She was still mostly numb, detached from almost everything except Connor. She could feel herself detaching.

Moore was on medical leave for three weeks. They made up a story about a climbing fall to cover for an unreported bullet wound. For almost their entire careers, they had been a team, and neither of them had been out hurt or sick in all that time. They'd even taken leave at the same time. So she'd never worked with anyone else. The captain rearranged the schedule to bring in someone from another watch to cover for Moore, and Pilar felt dislocated and territorial. She hadn't realized how much she relied on her easy symbiosis with Moore until she'd lost it.

So work was strange and unfamiliar to her in these weeks. Even the vibe at meals was off.

The vibe was off between her and Connor, too. Ever since the fire. They'd only been together a handful of times in the two weeks since, and they hadn't been really alone together at all. He was either doing club business, or he was at the hospital. If she wanted to see him, she had to go there.

And she didn't mind it; he belonged with his parents. His father remained unconscious, and his prognosis hadn't improved. They were all still, two weeks later, stuck at 'wait and see.' But his mother was recovering well and had been released after not much more than a week. Connor was bringing her to the hospital every day to sit at her husband's bedside.

He blamed Pilar. She could feel it. He said that he was working through it, that he loved her, wanted her, needed her, but she could feel the distance that was growing between them.

And she hated it. She had let him in, let him closer to her than anyone else, and now he was in there, rattling around like a ghost. She didn't know how to fix it, or how to go back to the way her life was before she'd met him. He was the only thing in her life right now that felt significant, but he was moving away from her, losing substance. She could feel him detaching.

As they stood at Hugo's graveside, listening to the priest intone the words of ritual, Pilar was thinking about Connor. Who was not there. She knew why, and yet she didn't. Hugo had torn his family up, and Connor had no grief over his death. But *she* did. She would have liked to have had his hand to hold as she buried her baby brother. The boy she'd failed. She would have liked the man she loved to stand with her. More than that—she needed it.

Instead, Moore stood at her side, holding her hand.

There weren't many mourners for Hugo. A couple of people Pilar didn't know, who might have been old school friends of his. Most of Pilar's crew. And their grandmother's friends. Usually, Chicano funerals were big, but there was no one left to mark Hugo's passing. Their parents were dead. Pilar and their grandmother were his only living family. He'd had few friends outside the Assassins, and they were all—all but Sam, who was still in jail—dead. So the mourners made a small circle around the grave. When the priest was done, they took their turns adding handfuls of earth to his resting place. And then they headed back to their cars.

It was done. Hugo was no more.

Pilar felt a small, shameful frisson of relief. She was free.

Moore had his good arm around her shoulders as they walked across the grounds. He gave her a quick squeeze, dropped his arm, and said, "I'll take Nana back to the house."

"What?" Pilar had been lost in thought, and she was confused. They were all supposed to ride together; the mourners, such as they were, were headed to Nana's house. When she turned to Moore, he tipped his head, indicating a point off to the front and side. She followed his gesture.

Connor was standing next to his bike, his arms crossed over a dark brown button-down shirt and a plain black leather jacket. No kutte, even though he was riding.

He had told her that he always wore his kutte when he rode, but she also knew enough to know why he wasn't wearing it today. Because he wouldn't show his colors at an enemy's funeral. Hugo had been an enemy. An Assassin. Knowing that the club had a lengthy and arcane list of rules and traditions, she assumed he wasn't supposed to be there at all. She was only assuming, however; he hadn't said one way or the other.

Even with his sunglasses on, he was telegraphing jealousy so strongly, watching her walking up with Moore, that she could almost see the hate beaming through his lenses. God, she was tired of that. But for now, she focused on her relief that he was there at all.

She needed him. So she kissed her grandmother's soft cheek, gave Moore a hug, and crossed the grounds to Connor.

"Hi. You came." She walked straight to him and leaned her body into his. He had unwound his arms as she'd approached, and now he folded her up and kissed her head. When he held her like this, she could feel that there was a chance they would get through all of this and be okay.

"Yeah. For you."

"Thank you. How's your dad?" They hadn't been together in a few days, and every day was a question with Hoosier.

"Same. Mom's picked up a fever and a nasty cough. They admitted her again. Pneumonia."

"Fuck. I'm sorry."

He only sighed.

She looked up into his handsome, somber face. His dark lenses obscured his eyes and made him inscrutable to her. "Connor, we have to fix what's wrong here. I'm losing my mind. I've never felt like this about anyone, I've never needed anybody like this. We're both going through some big shit. We should be dealing with it all together, but we're not. I feel so fucking lonely."

He looked over her head, and she knew—she just *knew*—he was looking at Moore. "Seems like you've got plenty of support."

And then Pilar simply snapped. She balled up both her fists and punched him, hard, in the chest. It hurt, but she was glad for the pain, and gladder still that he grunted and stepped back. "You have got to fucking stop with the jealousy. There's nothing between Moore and me, and I am out of ways to say that. I wanted it to be you holding my hand today. But you weren't there. So my friend held me instead. So fuck you."

She punched him again—and then she was tired and done. With all of it. "You say you love me, but between the blame and the jealousy, I don't know how you have room for any good feelings about me. All I do is piss you off. I can't deal with this anymore." She turned abruptly away from him, headed back toward the mourners, figuring she could catch a ride with another of her crew. Guzman, Perez, and Reyes were all lingering up by the cars.

She got three steps, and then his hand had her arm, and he was pulling her back and around to face him.

At first, he just stared at her, his shielded look intense and threatening. Then, in a voice gruff with controlled emotion, he said, "I want to go to your place."

"To talk? Can we talk this out?"

"I want to go to your place."

It wasn't an answer, but it was close enough. Choosing him again, even on this day, she set aside her grandmother, all that remained of her family, and nodded.

"Okay."

CHAPTER TWENTY-ONE

He was just so fucking angry. He was helpless and he was angry, and he could not get control of it. Every day, it got bigger. When they'd taken his mother out of his father's hospital room in a fucking wheelchair, down to the ER, and then up to her own room, he'd thought his head was going to explode.

It was all his fault, all of it. But it was too much for him to contain, so it flew out of him in waves. He was angry at *everyone*.

His father was gone. The small, frail sack that lay in that bed was *not* his father. Hoosier Elliott was the kind of man who filled a room. He wasn't an especially big guy, just average height and decently fit, but no behemoth by any stretch. And yet people always took note, stepped back, gave him room. He was a man you respected the minute you met him. You felt his strength, his power, his wisdom.

Yeah, he could be an asshole, too. What man couldn't? But he owned it. When he was wrong, he always made it right.

Connor had been a rebellious kid. He'd fought against every which kind of authority and had spent as much of his school life in detention and the principal's office as he had in class. But he had never rebelled against his father. From the time he'd been old enough to think what he'd wanted to do with his life, he'd wanted to follow his father. Never, not once, anything else. He'd never had a boyhood fantasy of being a cowboy or an astronaut. Or a firefighter. He'd wanted a kutte and a bike.

So he was angry, he was *furious*, at that pale sack of bones lying lifeless in a hospital bed, unable even to breathe for itself. That was not his father.

And if it was, Connor was responsible for what had happened to him. He had been falling in love, and he had brought somebody else's beef to the Horde.

And…God. His mother. If he'd admired his father his whole life, what he felt for his mother was adoration. She drove him crazy, meddling, always having an opinion, somehow knowing absolutely every damn thing about his life and being unabashed about throwing it in his face. It was a bizarre experience to have his own mother always in the know about his sex life, but somehow she always did know, and she was always there with that damn look that said she could read every single thought in his head. She *knew* him. He could tell her anything, because she knew everything.

Most of his brothers did not have parents like he had parents, and he knew how fucking lucky he was to have the father and mother he did.

And he had broken them both.

He was just so fucking angry.

~oOo~

Usually, riding with Pilar was an intensely erotic experience, but this time, Connor was so wrapped up in his head he barely noticed her. And she held him differently this time, with her hands on his hips instead of her arms around his body.

They should just stop. One of them should admit the obvious defeat, and they should break this off. He knew it, could feel the distance and withering happening, but it wouldn't be him who ended it.

Because he fucking needed her. Even in the anger and cold, that was true. He was being an asshole, treating her like shit, and he knew that was true, too, but he couldn't get control of himself. He didn't blame her. He blamed them. He blamed himself and the way his feelings for her—which had been seeded before they'd even gone back for their first fuck—had shifted priorities that should not have been shifted.

He should end it. He should never have let it start. But he couldn't stand the thought of losing her. So he was making her pay for his own weakness.

And she'd been letting him, accepting the guilt and blame he kept laying on her. As she unlocked her front door and they stepped into her living room, he wondered if she was finally done.

It would probably be for the best if she was.

She dropped her keys into the little bowl by the door, draped her jacket over the back of a chair, and kicked off the black pumps she'd worn to her brother's funeral. She wore a pair of simple black pants and a dark gold sweater that was the same color as her eyes. Her usual jewelry: gold hoops, the crucifix, nothing else. "You want a beer?"

Taking his sunglasses off and sliding them into the inside pocket of his leather jacket, he nodded. "Yeah." He shrugged off his jacket and laid it over hers. He loved this room. It was eclectic and warm, like Pilar herself. Today, though, it was dark: she had the heavy drapes drawn across all the windows. Instead of opening them and letting the autumn sun in, she turned on a few lights. When she went back to the kitchen, Connor sat on her sofa and stared at a cluster of three glass and metal lights hanging from the ceiling. They were shaped something like stars and threw intricate patterns onto the walls.

She came back and handed him a bottle of beer. Her own, he saw, was half gone already. So he put his to his lips and caught up.

Instead of sitting next to him on the sofa, she sat on the table in front of him. Her golden eyes were serious and sad. "Connor, what do you want?"

"What do you mean?"

"From me? Or us? I'm not giving you what you want, or need, I guess. I need to know if I even can. Because what we've been doing these past couple of weeks...I can't anymore."

"I need you." Even being sure that they should end, he couldn't get around that bald truth.

But she shook her head. "I don't know what that means. What is it you need? A scapegoat? An emotional punching bag? Because I can't be that anymore. I'm sorry for my part in all of this, and I've been tearing myself up about it. But the truth is, all I did was ask for help. I didn't drag you into it. I didn't force you or even manipulate you. I was honest about all of it."

He knew that, and he knew he should say so. But all he could do was stare into her eyes.

After a minute, she made a dry noise, like the opposite of a laugh. "And you know what? I need you. My family fell apart, too, Connor. I know you don't care about my brother. But don't you care about me?"

"I love you." Another bald truth that was lately more pain than anything else.

She finished her beer and set the empty bottle next to her on the table. Then she leaned in, resting her elbows on her knees. "Connor, I'm hurting. Whatever you feel about Hugo, he was my little brother. I loved him. I love Nana. And *I'm* hurting. But I'm afraid to feel it, because I'm doing it alone. You won't get out of your head and help me."

"You're not doing it alone. You're never fucking alone."

She made a violent, growing sound and raked both hands through her wavy hair. "MOTHERFUCKER. If you don't let that go, and I mean right now, then you need to fucking leave. Because I can't—I *won't*—fight about that with you ever again. I'm not giving up my best friend because you're an insecure shithead. I've told you a hundred times that he is not a threat to you."

There was a part of him that hated Kyle Moore even more intensely then he hated Hugo. He knew they weren't fucking. She said it, and he believed it. But that didn't even matter. His jealousy wasn't about that at all. Moore was always there, always at her side. She spent so much more time with her best friend than she ever would with Connor. And as the distance grew between them, Moore was filling it. Being a hero with her, being a hero for her.

And that was the thing, wasn't it? That was it.

That was it.

Moore was a fucking hero. Pilar was a hero. They spent their lives saving people, undoing other people's wrongs, their mistakes and their evils. Undoing even acts of God. What was Connor? A man who beefed with gangsters, who sat down with drug lords. Who planned assassinations. A killer. A drug runner. An outlaw. A man who brought violence into the world.

And that was all he'd ever wanted to be.

He could never be her hero.

Leaning forward, he set his half-finished beer next to her empty. Then he picked her hands up in his. "I love you. I've never felt like this about anybody, either. If there's such a thing as soulmates, I think you're probably mine. But I can't be what I need to be for you."

"I don't even know what that means."

There was no point in explaining. So he lifted one of her hands—so small to be so strong—to his lips and kissed her knuckles. "I'm gonna go. Take care."

He stood and crossed the room to pick up his jacket. As he reached the door, clasping his hand around the knob, she grabbed his arm in both hands and yanked him back. He was too big for her to turn like that, but he looked over his shoulder, and he let her keep hold of his arm.

She was crying. Yanking on his arm again, she said through her tears, "Fuck you! Just fuck you! You don't get to tell me I'm your goddamn *soulmate* and then just walk out of my life. I let you *know* me. I let you in! How do you just fucking walk away from that?"

"Cordero…"

At that, she went ballistic, shoving and punching, even going for his face. "Pilar! I'm Pilar! Fuck you!"

Acting on the instinct of self-protection, he fought through her whirling fists and grabbed her shoulders. Then he spun and shoved her against the wall, fighting until he had her pinned. Their sex had not infrequently begun in such a way, and his cock took notice, despite his mind's need to get clear of all of this.

They stared furiously at each other while the painful confusion of needing her and needing to be away ripped him up. Finally, he roared and punched the wall he'd shoved her into.

She didn't flinch. Instead, she turned her head toward the fist that was still pressed to the wall, and then she turned back.

"Hurt me."

His brain wouldn't make sense of that. "What?"

Tears had made her eyeliner or whatever it was run, and the effect made her look vulnerable. "You need to hurt me. So hurt me. I need it, too. But my body, not my feelings. I can't take that anymore."

"What? No!"

He'd let go of one of her shoulders when he'd punched the wall, and now her left arm was free. She hit him in the chest with the flat of her hand. "Yes! We can't talk it out, so let's fuck it out. Hurt me."

"Jesus! No!" He shoved away from her and crossed to the other side of the room.

But she was right on him, hitting him again, shoving him. "Yes! Come on! I know you want it. You're hard. So let's go."

Again, he grabbed her. This time, instead of putting her on the wall, he closed her up in a bear hug. "I don't want to hurt you. Stop."

She fought his hold. "All you've done since it happened is hurt me, asshole. I just want you to do it honestly." Her arm slipped free of his grip, and she slapped him. Hard. The whole side of his face stung.

For the past weeks, his control over anything going on inside him had been tenuous at best. At that slap, it broke entirely. "You want me to hurt you? You want to fuck it out?" he snarled, and then, almost literally, he threw her into the little side room off her living room, a tiny space she called her library.

She wheeled backward and landed on the worn area rug, and he followed after her, dropping most of his weight on her. She fought him, but he overpowered her, grabbing her arms and clasping them together, then tearing at her clothes, yanking her pants down and then flipping her over onto her stomach.

Snatching at his belt and jeans, he released his cock and then lifted her hips and shoved into her. It had been weeks since they'd fucked, and he shouted at the intensity of feeling as her wet pussy closed around him.

He fucked her furious and fast, his hands clenched hard around the parts of her body they held, his hips slamming brutally against her ass.

She came hard, silently, her body tightening fiercely around him, and he followed right after her, the orgasm ripping through his body and brain until he thought he'd die.

And then he did feel a little better.

But as he came back into the moment, as his clenched body began to relax, he realized that he had his hand around her throat.

Then he saw that her face, pressed hard, sideways, into the rug, was an angry, dangerous shade of purplish red.

"Jesus fuck!" He let her go and nearly jumped away, pulling out and falling back and away from her. She took a huge, strangled breath and rolled to her side, curling her body into a fetal ball.

He stared down at his hand as if it were a stranger, a parasite attached to his body. Then he looked back at Pilar. She was still in that ball, still taking big breaths.

"Baby. Baby, I'm sorry."

She didn't answer or even indicate that she'd heard him.

"Are you okay?"

After a second, she nodded. But she didn't unfurl her body.

That wasn't what she'd meant when she'd asked—demanded—that he hurt her. He knew that. He hadn't meant to do anything like that. He hadn't wanted to hurt her at all.

But he was a man of violence. He was no hero.

"I'm so sorry. Can I do anything?"

She shook her head.

"Should I go?"

After a beat, she nodded.

Of course he should. He should get far away. He stood and put his cock away.

Grabbing his jacket off the back of her chair, he stopped at the door. Without turning around, needing…something—just *needing*, he said, "I love you."

And then he left.

~oOo~

"Hey, Mom." Connor stepped into his mother's hospital room and shut the door. She was looking better, off the oxygen again. She still didn't look like herself—she looked old and pale and weary—but there was a light in her eyes he hadn't seen since before he'd left for Vegas. Three weeks ago. He'd seen her primary nurse at the station outside and knew that her temperature was down, too. "You look good."

"Liar," she rasped. But she smiled. "Did you see your dad?"

He nodded. There had been some improvement in his father's condition since the fire. The swelling in his brain was down. But he hadn't woken yet. "No change. Faith's with him." Though Hoosier was still in the ICU, they'd given up trying to keep visitors to five minutes. Somebody was in his room about twenty hours of every twenty-four. And somebody was in the hospital every fucking second.

She nodded—of course she knew that Faith was with him. Demon was sitting with her now. "Hey, Deme."

"Hey, brother." Demon stood up and leaned over the railing to kiss Connor's mother's forehead. "I'll get outta here. You need anything, Mama?"

Bibi put her free hand over Demon's. "No, baby. Thanks."

"You bet." As he headed toward the door, he stopped and put his hand on Connor's shoulder. "I'm gonna hang out in the waiting room awhile. Can we talk?"

Connor frowned. "Problem?"

"No. Just...want to talk."

Demon was not someone Connor had heart-to-hearts with. But he gave him a shrugging nod. "Yeah. I'll come out in a bit."

"Cool."

Curious, Connor watched Demon go, then turned back to his mother and smiled. "Hey, Bedelia Beth. You do look better."

There was an enormous new floral arrangement sitting on the table in the corner next to her bed. "Wow. These are gorgeous." He checked the card, which read: *Wishing you strength and health. Best regards, Dora.*

He chuckled, feeling cynical and tired. La Zorra was sitting pretty after all of this. The Horde had wiped an entire crew right off the map—not only crippled them but taken them completely out. The Fuentes cartel was now beholden to the Águilas cartel to get anything into Southern California—and that meant anywhere north of the border at all. Dora Vega now owned Mexico. Hers was the only game north of Colombia. And even Colombia had to go through her to get the western U.S.

If she wanted, she could declare herself Queen of Mexico, and Connor didn't think anyone in that country had the power to deny her.

The Night Horde SoCal had been powerfully instrumental in her success, and she was well pleased with them. She had sat down with Bart, Connor, and Muse, and they had formalized the agreement that Hoosier had wanted—they were partners, not employees, and they now had a vote and a profit share that reflected a partnership.

In only two years, the Horde had gone from a quiet, law-abiding club to reclaim the status the members had known as an outlaw powerhouse. They had wiped out a whole charter of the Dirty Rats, an infamous outlaw MC, and forced a truce, and now they had destroyed a decades-old gang and hamstrung the cartel that gang had been allied with.

And the price they'd paid for that power lay in two beds in this hospital.

Connor thought that price was far too high.

When he leaned down to kiss her cheek, his mother's arm came up and held him close. "I want to be with your dad," she whispered against his ear, her voice rough and breaking. She let herself be weaker for him than for anyone else.

He leaned back a little and brushed her hair back from her face. Then he caught a tear on his thumb. "I know. So kick this crap out of your lungs, then. You can't bring your germs around him. He was already sick when all this happened."

"I don't want him to die alone."

"Mom, shut the fuck up. He's not dying. He's going to get better. He just needs time."

She sniffed and nodded, then started on a coughing jag. He held her through it, then gave her some water and her breathing device.

Fuck, he hated seeing her like this, so wrinkled and weak. Gasping for air, looking like she'd blow away in a breeze. Her brown hair, shorter than he'd ever known it, since Faith had cut it to compensate for what had been burned away, was growing out, showing a line of white along her part. He hated it all, and he hated more that she didn't seem to notice. She had always cared about her appearance, and the thought that she'd given up now scared the shit out of him.

When she had collected herself, she patted the bed, and he dropped the side rail and sat next to her. He put his arm around her, and she leaned on his chest.

Connor sat like that, holding her, until she fell asleep. This old woman who used to be his mother.

He wanted his family back.

~oOo~

When Connor went out to the waiting room, Demon was sitting alone, staring up at the television on the wall. He stood when he saw Connor.

"What's up?"

Demon's face pinked up, which usually meant he was getting angry. Not knowing why he would be, Connor's adrenaline spiked a little. Had something happened with the club? No—he would know. Wouldn't he?

"Con, I…uh…fuck."

"Jesus, Deme. What?"

"Faith…" Demon huffed and started again. "Faith wanted me to talk to you."

"She okay? The kids?"

"Yeah, yeah. They're good. She's worried about you."

"What?"

"Yeah. You want to sit?"

He shrugged, and they sat.

Demon went on. "Look, I'm nobody to give anybody advice, so I'm just gonna say what she said, and then I can tell her that I talked to you, and you can tell her that I talked to you, and I can stop hearing about how I should talk to you, okay?"

"Jesus Christ. No offense, Deme, but—"

"Yeah, I know. None taken. She thinks that you're going off the rails and that I'm the perfect person to help you out with that, since, according to my wife, off the rails is where I lived until she fixed me."

At that, the anger that had been boiling up inside him cooled, and Connor laughed. "She's right. About you, anyway."

Demon grinned. "I know. Just…look. If you want to talk, I'm here. I don't know what I could do to help, but…you know. I'm here."

Before Connor could get out the 'thanks but no thanks' he had cued up, an image of Pilar curled up on the floor filled his head. He hadn't seen or talked to her since that day. Four days ago. The last thing he'd ever done to the woman he loved was hurt her. Because he was off the rails.

So instead of telling Demon, legendary club psycho, that he didn't need his help, the words that left his mouth were, "I hurt her. I lost my shit, and I think I really hurt her. I know I did."

Demon had been looking down at his lap. Now he turned to Connor. There was no condemnation there. Just…understanding. They hadn't even been talking about Pilar, but Demon was still right there with him. Understanding. "I'm sorry, brother."

"Sorry for me? Why? I'm the one who did the hurting, not the other way around."

"I don't know. Guess I'm sorry because I know what it's like. It hurts, too, doing something like that when you don't mean it."

Connor leaned back in the uncomfortable waiting room chair. "Everything is just fucked. I'm so fucked up. She's better off."

Demon laughed at that, his face lighting up with real humor.

Connor was deeply offended. "Fuck you. It's not funny."

"No, sorry. It's just…" Demon made his face serious. "Remember the day I went apeshit at Bart and Riley's? I went after Hooj and beat the shit out of him?"

"Uh, yeah. Hard to forget."

"I almost bailed on everything that day—the club, Faith, my kid. Everything. Muse was here—he'd been shot. I came to tell him goodbye. He called me on my bullshit. And he told me that if I wanted to be right, I had to deal with what was wrong. He said I needed to know what I wanted and then do what I needed to do to make it happen. It was good advice. You know, I haven't lost my shit since. It was a simple thing, but it never occurred to me, that most of what was wrong in my head was the way I thought about things. I never knew that I could fix that."

"Moron."

"Yep. But you, too, maybe."

Maybe so. Leaning his head back against the wall, Connor closed his eyes.

What did he want? What could he do to make it happen?

~oOo~

He hadn't called first; he wasn't sure how he'd be received, so he thought it would be better if he just showed up. He understood her work schedule now, and he knew when she was off and when she wasn't.

So when Connor pulled into Pilar's driveway, he saw her Element there, as he'd expected.

He hadn't expected to see Moore's truck behind it.

But okay. He took a breath. His jealousy was his problem, not hers. Not Moore's. He had to make it right in his head, because that was the only thing that was wrong about that friendship: the way he thought about them. If he wanted her, he had to get right with her life—her friends, her work, all of it.

And he wanted her.

So he dismounted and prepared to be civil to her best friend, who'd never been anything but civil to him.

Before he got to her porch, though, her front door came open, and Moore charged out at him. He landed a massive roundhouse right in Connor's face before Connor could even get his hands up. The blow took them both to the ground, and then Moore was astride him, pummeling him, all facial blows, back and forth, right and left, the force of the right-handed blows weakened by his injury.

Connor knew why it was happening, and he let him do it. He didn't fight back at all. After a while, winded and flagging, Moore sat back. "Fight me, you bastard. Fight back. I want to fucking kill you."

"No." Connor had to force the word through an already-swelling mouth. "I earned it."

"Yeah, you did. Get the fuck out of here."

"Moore, stop. Get up." Pilar's voice was rough, like she had a cold. But Connor knew she didn't.

"Cordero, no way." Moore looked over his shoulder. From his position on the ground, Connor couldn't see, but he'd heard her voice and imagined her standing in the doorway.

"Yes. Get up."

Moore glared down at him and then stood up.

Connor rolled to his knees and spat out a mouthful of blood. No teeth, thankfully. They felt surprisingly secure in his gums. He stood and turned.

Pilar was standing right where he'd imagined, wearing her favorite pair of sweatpants and an old, loose t-shirt with a stretched-out collar.

Her throat was mottled about every color of the rainbow. To get that kind of bruising—fuck, he'd almost killed her.

"Jesus, baby. I'm so sorry."

Standing between them, Moore scoffed dramatically.

Pilar moved her attention to her friend. "You should go, Moore. I'm fine."

"Oh, that is so much bullshit. I am not leaving you alone with him. Absolutely not."

"You are, because I'm telling you to go."

"Pilar—"

"Kyle. Go."

Moore turned to Connor. "You hurt her again, and I will hunt your ass down. I don't care how many biker assholes you hide behind. I will put my fist down your throat and pull your heart out."

Connor laughed a little at that—with respect, not derision. It was a good threat, all the more powerful because it was sincere. "Understood. I'm not gonna hurt her."

Then Moore turned to Pilar. "I'm calling every half hour. You pick up, or I am bringing the cavalry back here."

"Okay. Just go."

"I can't fucking believe this," he muttered, stomping past Connor on the way to his truck.

Connor stood where he was, and so did Pilar, until Moore had pulled out of the driveway and driven off.

And they were alone, staring at each other. His eyes fell from hers and focused on her throat. What had he done?

When he started toward her, she took a wary step backward and pulled the door close, so that it was only open the width of her body. He stopped. "I'm not going to hurt you. I've never wanted to hurt you."

She put her hand to her throat. "What do you want?"

"To make us right. I love you. I need you."

"You say that, but I don't know what that means to you."

"Will you let me in so we can talk about it?"

"The last time I let you in, this happened." Her fingers moved down her bruised throat.

She had fought him, asked him to hurt her, demanded that they 'fuck it out.' He'd been trying to leave. That thought, however, amounted to a rejoinder of 'you started it,' and even to himself, it sounded childish and wrongheaded. Yet the thought wanted to be expressed. "You…you said…"

She shook her head before he could get it out. "You know this wasn't what I meant."

Yes, he did. He knew what she meant when she wanted to be hurt, and strangled to death was not it. "I know. I'm sorry."

"So we talk. Only that."

"Only that. Mutual agreement."

She stared at him until the weight of the silence was oppressive. And then she stepped back and pushed the door all the way open.

"Okay."

CHAPTER TWENTY-TWO

"Sit. I'll get you some ice."

Connor sat on her sofa, as he had the last time she'd invited him in. He didn't bother to take his kutte off. Usually, it was the first thing he did, so Pilar had the sense that he was staying ready to leave as quickly as possible. For the best, probably.

"I don't need ice."

She laughed. "Yeah, you do. Just hold on."

In the kitchen, she collected her first aid kit and a clean towel and then got a bag of frozen corn out of the freezer.

Back in the living room, she sat on the table in front of him and opened the kit at her side. As she tore open an antiseptic wipe and began to clean up his mangled face, she said, "So talk."

He reached out, his fingers stretched toward her throat, and she flinched back; she didn't want him to touch her, not yet, and certainly not there. His hand froze, and their eyes met.

"I'm so sorry."

"So you've said." She believed him; even if she were inclined not to, the remorse in his eyes was deep and sincere. But he had hurt her—and terrified her. She'd thought she was dying. But it wasn't the worst thing he'd done that day.

She didn't say it, not yet. But the worst thing he'd done that day was leave. He'd walked away before she'd even known if she could get off the floor on her own.

He let his hand fall to his lap, and for a minute he quietly let her clean his bleeding face. As she dabbed antibiotic ointment onto a swab, he said, "I want to fix us. Is there a chance?"

Holding the swab, she looked hard at him. Moore had done a number on him—his lip was split, his cheek and nose were bleeding, and his left eye was swelling shut. "Why do you want to—and don't say because you need me. Or even because you love me. Why do you want me in your life?"

He didn't answer right away, and she dabbed ointment onto the gash in his cheek. If he didn't have an answer, then she wasn't sure what the fucking point of all this was. She could have answered; she'd thought a lot about the question. She'd argued with Moore about it. Fuck, she'd asked it of herself as she was stepping back and letting Connor in a few minutes before.

She loved him, wanted him, because when she was with him, she felt bright and alive. He was funny and bold, kind and smart. He challenged her, competed with her. He knew how to have a good time, but there was real depth to him, too—a depth he protected from most people. But he'd let her in.

The fact that he was about the most gorgeous man she'd ever known and they had blistering hot sex barely mattered in comparison to all of that.

"Do you know how amazing you are?"

At Connor's question, Pilar pulled away a little and focused on his eyes. "That's not an answer."

"Jesus, Pilar. I don't know how to say it. When I'm away from you, I want to be with you. When I'm with you, I don't want to leave. When something happens, good or bad, I want to tell you. I'm...fuck, I'm so fucking *proud* when I think about you or talk about you. Ow." He winced as she pressed on his cheek, closing the wound with a butterfly bandage. "Proud that you're mine. When I think about what's next, the future, I want you in it. I see you in my life. You are amazing. You're so much better than I am."

"What?"

"You're a hero. Your job is literally to be a hero—you even told me that, so I know you see it that way, too. Me—I'm an outlaw. You spend your life fixing the shit people like me fuck up. You and Moore, that's what you do."

"Oh fuck me, Connor. Not this again." She shoved back, but he grabbed her—not hard, but enough to make her tense.

"No. I'm trying to explain my trouble with him. I don't think you're fucking him. And if we're not over, then I will get right with him in your life. But there's so much in your life that's...fuck, that's *admirable*. I'm jealous of all of it. I'm like a black smudge in your life."

"Connor, that's nuts."

"Maybe. I never thought of myself like that before. I've been happy with myself. Loved my life. But compared to you..."

Her phone rang. Moore. She answered, "Dude, it hasn't been half an hour. And I'm fine. Everything is fine. Do not call again, because I'm not gonna answer. I will call if I need you. Okay?"

After a beat of silence on the line, she repeated, "Okay?"

Finally, Moore's voice filled her ear. "You better fucking call."

"If I need you, I will. Otherwise, I'll see you at the barn in the morning. Go kill zombies now."

"Shit, Cordero. You better know what you're doing."

"I do. Good night. And thank you."

After she ended the call, she picked up the thread of conversation. She'd been thinking about what Connor had said the whole time she was talking to Moore. "What you're saying is I make you feel worse about yourself? Then what the fuck are we doing? That's no way to be together."

He'd sat quietly through the phone call, and it seemed he'd been thinking, too. "No. I'm saying you make me want to be better.

You make me think deeper about shit I've been trying hard not to think about. I'm not saying I don't want to be an outlaw. My life is my life, my family is that life, and I don't want it to change. But being with you…I don't know. I want to be…better." He picked up the bag of corn and held it to his eye, then rested against the back of the sofa. "You wanted to know why I love you. All of that. So the question is, do you want me? Still love me?"

"That's not the question, Connor. Not yet. You say you want to be better, but you've been awful to me for the past few weeks. You blame me for what happened to your parents."

"I don't."

"Bulls—"

"I don't." He sat up. "I blame me. I blame the way I feel about you. But really, I just blame me. I wanted to be your hero. But I don't think it's even that. You were right to ask for help for your brother. I would've done the same thing. You go to the strongest source for help. And I was right to want to help you. Fuck, we would've helped even if I hadn't been wanting back in your pants. It's what we do. My dad has always run his charter with this idea that we should be good citizens. That we should do more good than bad. And we do. So we would have helped you if I'd never met you. What happened is not your fault."

He'd dropped the bag of corn to his lap, and Pilar heard a faint sound that made her look down at it. He was squeezing the bag so tightly she thought it was about to burst. "I've just been so fucking angry. Seeing my dad and mom both brought low by all this. Baby, my dad is probably dying. He definitely won't be the way he was. And I don't have anything I can do to make it right." The bag did burst then; little yellow kernels of half-frozen corn spilled out and rained down onto the sofa and rug. They both just sat and watched it happen.

Pilar recalled the feeling of his fingers doing that to her throat, and her own fingers went up to stroke the healing bruises he'd left behind.

His attention locked there, and again she saw remorse in his grey eyes. "I'm so sorry I hurt you. Not just that, but everything. Being an asshole. Not being what you needed. All of it. I don't have an excuse. But I am sorry."

"You left me laying there. You walked out."

His eyes went wide. "What? You said I should go. Why would you have wanted me to stay?"

"Connor…" Pilar stopped, not knowing how to explain how she'd felt, how she'd needed him to hold her and calm her, to help her, to take care of her, and how, at the same time, she'd needed him as far away as he could get.

It didn't matter.

She believed him, and she forgave him. What she wanted most to do right now was crawl onto his lap, to comfort him and be comforted. To erase the weeks before. But she needed to understand some things before she could move forward and trust him—or herself. "Connor, what do you want?"

He lifted his eyes back to hers. "I want you. With me. In my life."

"But what do you want your life to be? Or our life? What does that look like?"

"I want what my folks have. A partner, a house, kids." His expression became guarded. "I want kids with you. Is that even possible?"

Despite the heady blend of emotions she was feeling, which his latest words had kicked up into a froth, Pilar smiled. "I am capable of bearing children, yeah. As far as I know."

"You know what I'm asking."

"I do. I think it's weird to be talking about whether we'll have kids when this conversation started with me wondering whether I'd ever speak to you again."

"It's not. I was honest when I told you I thought you were my soulmate. That's where I feel you—that deep. So if I didn't fuck it all up, if we're still together, then I want it to be more. I want to be seeing the same things up ahead." He sighed. "I want the rest of my life to start."

"It's too fast, Connor. This month has been so fucked in so many ways. We have been so fucked up. I can't move from what happened four days ago to planning our family just like that." She snapped her fingers. "It's just too fast."

"Okay. Fair enough. Tell me this. Do you want there to be a future? Do you want kids at all? With your job, can you?" He looked down at his lap. He was still holding the now-deflated bag of corn. "Do you love me?"

One word could answer each of those questions, and Pilar almost answered with that single syllable. She was tired—of being sad, of being lonely, of feeling insecure, of feeling unfulfilled. Of being alone. Setting aside the first aid supplies, then leaning forward and taking the bag of corn from him, she brushed the stray kernels off his lap and climbed onto him, straddling him.

She'd shocked him. With his hands held out, in a gesture that looked like surrender, he said, "Pilar, what..."

"Yes, I love you. You *are* my hero, idiot. You helped me when I asked. You said you'd do it even knowing how it played out. It doesn't matter what side of the law you're on. You help. You try to do more good than bad. That makes you better than about ninety-five percent of the world. Yes, I want there to be a future for us. Yes, I want kids. Yes, I can be a firefighter and a mom. I'd go on admin or training duty while I was pregnant. But I'm not ready for that yet. In a couple of years, but not now. So let's go slow. But yes. That's what I want."

He grinned, then winced when his broken lip pulled and started to bleed again. Pilar put her hands around his face and leaned down to kiss him, licking the blood from his lip. "Fuck me slow. Right here," she whispered.

He grinned again, more carefully this time, and his hands held her head, mirroring her touch. "Just here to talk, remember? Mutual agreement."

"So we'll mutually change the agreement. I want to feel you love me. Not…whatever that was the other day."

His expression clouded over. "I'm so damn—"

She moved her hand to cover his mouth. "Stop. I know. So let's fix it. You be my hero, and I'll be yours." She brushed her fingers over his beaten face. "If you think you can."

"Oh, I can. Your buddy's not that tough. Nothing's broken." As if to prove his point, he kissed her, and the first, light touch of his lips to hers quickly became fiercely passionate. Pilar didn't even know which one of them had turned the volume up.

After a moment, he broke away. They were both breathless. He brushed her hair back, and she closed her eyes at the pleasure in that soft touch. Then he leaned in and kissed her throat. "I don't want to go hard," he murmured.

"I don't want you to. Just love me. I just want to be close."

"Then let's go to bed. I want to love all of you."

She smiled and got up from his lap.

~oOo~

They undressed themselves, and then they simply stood there, naked and awkward, as though they'd forgotten what they were supposed to do next. Finally, embarrassed and feeling stupidly shy, Pilar laughed quietly and turned to the bed.

And that was when Connor touched her. He stepped behind her, and she felt the rough-hewn texture of his palm as it skimmed over her hip. Tugging her back against his chest, he collected a handful of her hair and drew it to the side. Then his head came down, and she felt his beard brush over her bare shoulder. She expected him to kiss her, but he only turned his head side to side, letting the feathery touch of his beard caress her.

She moaned and put her hand on his head. His hand and arm went all the way across her belly, and he turned her around. She looked up at him, and even through his swollen face, she could see everything she needed to see.

His fingers traced a line from her chin to her chest, over her still-tender throat. As a response, she raised her hand and drew a finger across his split lip.

"I won't ever hurt you again. Body or soul." His voice was so low that if she hadn't been inches away, she wouldn't have heard him.

"Except the way I like." She smiled and hooked her arms over his shoulders, pressing her body to his.

He tipped his head to the side. "Except that."

"Don't hurt me now."

"No, I won't. I'm just going to love you." He stepped forward and took her down to the bed, moving her to the center of the mattress and covering her with his body.

They were almost never quiet like this. She normally would have laughed—she had laughed, at Connor, in fact—and said she wasn't into TV-movie sex. When he wanted to go slow, he had to hold her down. Or tie her down.

But now she felt too vulnerable for a rough, rowdy fuck. She was so tired. Her heart was tired. Her head. All of her. So when Connor began to kiss his way down her body, she lay back and let him.

He went slowly, his beard raising gooseflesh that his lips warmed away, his hands trailing his mouth, sliding tenderly over her shoulder and down her arm, then back up and over her chest, pausing to lave a nipple, then downward, steadily, all the way to her foot, then back up the other side. At the top of her thigh, he kissed the bare skin just above her folds. By then, she was quivering with need, but all he did was nuzzle her skin. When he moved away, up her belly, she arched and groaned.

"Shhh, baby." His lips and breath moved over her skin. "Shhh."

When Connor finally eased all the way back up, he settled his legs between hers, and he hovered over her, propped on his elbows. Pilar had closed her eyes, relaxing into his loving touch, but after a few seconds of his stillness, she opened her eyes and found him watching her.

Again, it didn't matter that Moore's fists had warped his face. Again, she saw what she needed from him. The blame and anger, the jealousy and hostility, all of that was gone. All she saw, in this room growing dark in the dusk, was the fire of his love.

"I love you," she whispered.

He closed his eyes and sighed deeply, and then he eased into her.

They rocked together for a long time, staring into each other's eyes. When Pilar came, it was the quietest, gentlest climax she'd ever had—no bursting sensation, no loss of control, no violent tensing of her body, just a complete, encompassing relaxation.

When Connor came, he made a quiet sound, a humming sigh, and then laid his body on hers.

It wasn't until he lifted his head again and brushed his fingers over her cheek that she knew she'd been crying.

~oOo~

"Let me help you with that, Mrs. Salazar."

"You should call me Nana, Connor. You're not the neighbor boy who cuts my grass."

"Yes, ma'am. Sorry." Connor took the glass serving dish holding a *capirotada* from Pilar's grandmother, and then offered her his elbow as she climbed out of the Element. Pilar laughed at his efforts to be gentlemanly and collected the bottles of wine in a cardboard holder from the back.

Then they walked across a wide, grassy yard toward Demon and Faith's house.

They lived out in the desert not far at all from Joshua Tree. They had what looked to Pilar like a little farm. Or a petting zoo. A little herd of five tiny goats wandered around. There were several cats, too, and a big, weird-looking dog, and chickens. All the animals seemed to have the run of the place.

If anybody was in charge, it was maybe a big, scruffy black-and-white cat. While Pilar and Connor led her grandmother toward the house, the cat chased one of the little goats away from the gravel where all the cars and bikes were parked and back toward the rest of the herd.

Did cats herd? Well, that one did, apparently.

As they got to the front door, it opened, and Demon stepped out with another little goat in his arms. Behind him, Faith's voice called out, "Dammit, Michael!"

"She's out, she's out. Sorry," Demon called back. He set the goat on the porch and patted its back end. It bleated and trotted away. Then he stood, grinning. "Hey! Happy Thanksgiving." He put his hand around Pilar's arm and bent down to kiss her cheek.

"Happy Thanksgiving, Deme. This is my grandmother, Renata Salazar."

"Happy Thanksgiving, ma'am. I'm Demon." Demon held out his hand, and her grandmother shook it.

"Demon?" she said. "Such a dark name for a handsome man like you."

He blushed a little and shrugged, and his eyes went to Connor, who grinned back. "Come on in. Things are getting out of hand already." He stood back, holding the door, and they all went in.

For the first time in Pilar's memory, her grandmother wasn't hosting Thanksgiving dinner. In the years before, even when their nuclear family had only been three, she had put out a spread, and some of Pilar's friends would join them. On the years that Pilar was on watch that day, they had a big meal on a different day. Those were often the best years, because everybody came, even those who had family to spend the actual day with when they had Thanksgiving free.

But now their family was only two, and her grandmother was still deeply mourning Hugo's death. She blamed herself, as Pilar had known she would, and she was closing herself off from the world, from even Pilar. She hadn't wanted to celebrate this day at all.

Then Connor had invited them both to the Horde Thanksgiving. She'd been surprised. His father was still in a coma, and had now been for a month. Most of Connor's attention was focused on Hoosier, and his slowly-recovering mother, and from what Pilar could tell, that was true for all the Horde. She hadn't expected them to have any kind of celebration—and she'd been concerned that there might still be blame directed at her.

But Connor had been insistent. There was no blame for her, he promised, and they needed to come together and be a family. His mother needed it. She spent too much time sitting in her husband's hospital room, alone with his unresponsive body. She needed to draw strength from all the love that surrounded her. She would have done the same for anyone else.

Pilar knew he was right—and thought maybe the same was true for her grandmother.

Nana didn't know the details of how Hugo had died. She knew the Assassins had killed him, but she didn't know the Horde were involved, and that was for the best. She had no reason to be suspicious or guarded around Connor's family, and she wasn't. She went into Demon and Faith's odd house with her best manners and her social smile firmly in place, and when she caught sight of the kitchen and the women in it, she grabbed the dish out of Connor's hands and walked straight toward it.

Connor watched her go with a laugh, then turned to Pilar. "I guess she's okay?"

Pilar smiled. "Yeah. That's good. She's too polite to be a bad guest. She'll slide right in. But I'll stick with her." She looked around—the men were sitting around a large, comfortable living room. A sliding glass door was open and leading to a patio, and other men were standing around out there. There were kids playing in the yard or climbing on the men. One of the men, Ronin, an older guy whom Pilar didn't think she'd ever heard talk, was holding Demon's baby daughter.

She turned back to Connor. "So this is still the whole 'women in the kitchen' thing, huh?" That social pattern seemed to transcend culture and generation.

He shrugged. "You want to stay out here and talk about bikes? Or football? Because I promise you, that's all we're talking about here. We are the most boring people in the world."

She lifted onto her tiptoes and kissed his bearded cheek. "Nah. I'll go gossip with the little women." Then she headed off to do just that.

Her grandmother and Connor's mother were sitting already at the kitchen table, both with cups of coffee in front of them. The *capirotada* sat on the table, nested comfortably into an array of pies and cakes.

"It's like a bread pudding," Nana was saying. "Usually, I make it at Easter time, because all of the ingredients are supposed to remind us of Christ's suffering."

Bibi frowned. "Christ's suffering in a dessert?"

"Yes," Renata smiled a smile that Pilar knew—she was pleased. Her grandmother liked to talk, and she loved to be able to tell a story. She turned to the dish of *capirotada* and stretched her hand out to touch the glass. "The bread is the body of Christ, and the syrup is his blood, thick with the suffering of his journey. The raisins are the nails driven through his body, and the cinnamon sticks are the wood of the cross on which he died to cleanse our sin."

Bibi stared at the bread pudding. "Gotta tell ya, Renata. That is the darkest story about a sweet I ever did hear."

At that, Pilar's grandmother laughed—her first laugh of anything like real pleasure in weeks. "Yes, it is. But it's a good sweet, and I wanted it today—like a comfort food, I suppose. It's very good, I promise."

Bibi, who still seemed a partial version of the woman Pilar had been getting to know, smiled and sipped at her coffee. "I believe you. It looks delicious." She looked up at Pilar and stretched out her free arm. "Hi, baby. I'm glad you're here."

Pilar bent down to accept the offered one-armed hug. "How are you feeling?"

"Better. Today is helpin'." She looked over at the bustle around the counters. "They won't let me help, though," she called in a louder voice. Pilar was glad to hear it—Bibi had been struggling to get her breath back since the pneumonia.

Grinning, Faith gestured toward Bibi, her eyes on the cast still covering Bibi's left arm. "You're on the bench this year, Beebs. But you're being plenty bossy, if that helps at all."

Bibi gave her an answering grin that looked mostly real. "Of course I am. I'm supposed to be in charge, y'know."

Faith came over. "You're always in charge, Beebs. Think of this as your throne." With her hand on Bibi's shoulder, Faith leaned down and kissed her cheek. "Love you."

"Love you, Faithy. But this throne sucks."

~oOo~

After dinner, while everyone was still recovering from food overload, the men were all slouched around on chairs and sofas, and Riley and Faith were trying to get their kids settled in a little playroom with a movie, Pilar went off and to find a quiet place to sit outside. It wasn't full dark yet, and the dwindling sunset was beautiful. She strolled over to a white fence and leaned on a post. The goats weren't around, but she could hear them bleating. Somebody must have put them in for the night. The dog, though, a big, shaggy mutt with one ear up and the other flopped over, came and sat at her heel. She couldn't remember his name.

She reached down and scratched behind his floppy ear, and he leaned on her leg with a sigh. Maybe he needed a minute, too.

She just needed to be quiet for a moment. Thanksgiving had been surreally normal, all things considered. A bustle of family, the constant rumble of laughter and friendly talk, children running about.

This whole month had been stuffed full of incompatible emotions and events. The hurt Hugo had done to Connor's family and to his own had left rubble in its wake. Loss was everywhere. But in the middle of it was this: family. Togetherness and contentment. No one untouched by loss, but everyone coming together, and welcoming Pilar and her grandmother in as members of the family.

Senses of loss and gain struggled in Pilar's heart and made her woozy.

"You okay?"

Pilar turned at the sound of Faith's voice. Demon's wife, Connor's somewhat sister, came over and stood next to her, leaning on the fence, one foot up on a whitewashed board. The dog shifted to sit between them, maximizing his opportunities for ear-scratching.

"Yeah. Just needed to turn the volume down for a minute."

She laughed. "We get pretty loud. How're you doing with…us? This?"

"Good. I like your family a lot." With the exception of her grandmother, and of Perez, with whom she had bonds of family or work, Pilar had trouble finding a way to talk to women. She didn't like small talk or aimless chatter, and she wasn't much interested in the things women seemed, at least from what Pilar could tell by her cursory attention, to be interested in.

She'd struggled at first today, helping out in the kitchen among these women she didn't know well, trying to be part of their group without horning into conversations she had no context for. But she'd eventually understood that she did have context. She was already sharing things with them. Connor had brought her that context.

The other thing she'd realized was that these women were all different. A movie star. A model. A teacher. An artist. A social worker. And Bibi, mother and guide to them all.

None of them had anything in common. And all of them had everything in common.

So when Faith, after a few moments of quiet, said, "From what I can tell, you're part of us now. You're family, too. You and your grandma," Pilar wasn't surprised.

It was true.

~oOo~

"You think your mom's gonna be okay?"

Before he answered her question, Connor shifted on the bed, sitting up and shoving pillows behind his back so he could rest on her iron headboard. Pilar settled against his chest and played her fingers over his belly. It had been a good day—as good a day as they'd had any right to hope for. Her grandmother had even enjoyed herself.

Especially with the little kids. Pilar had found her at one point sitting on a swing on the front porch, with three children around her, and she was telling the kind of folk tales she used to tell Pilar and Hugo when they were little. Some of those got pretty dark, but she'd been telling the more kid-friendly ones.

"Yeah, eventually. But I don't know if she'll be who she was. If my dad doesn't wake up..." He sighed, and Pilar knew he was forcing that thought away. He couldn't confront the idea that his father wouldn't get better. "But today she remembered that she's not alone. I think she's getting stale, sitting with Dad all day. But getting her to leave or do anything else is almost impossible."

"I understand that."

"Yeah. I do, too. I think she's mad that I don't sit with her all day."

"You're there every day. Almost." But he was back to his life, too—working, doing club business, being with her.

He shrugged and laid his cheek on her head. "I love you."

"And I love you. Move in."

"What?"

"You sleep here every night, even when I'm at work. You already live here. Just bring your stuff over." He was quiet, and that surprised Pilar. She'd thought she'd made an obvious offer. Because he did already live with her, and he had since the day they'd talked after Moore had beaten him. "Connor?"

"I hate that I don't have a place. My own mother had to move out to the desert to live with Demon and Faith because I don't have anyplace to offer her. I don't know how to feel about moving in here. I'm like a hobo. I'm thirty-six years old, and all I've got is a fucking dorm room. I could pack my whole life in the back of your car."

She sat up and turned to him. "So do that. Move here. And we'll look for a new place together, one that fits your mom—and your dad, too. In the meantime, have a spare room here, too, if you want your mom—"

"No. No, I don't want to make her move again. She's good out there. She's got the kids, and Faith's around all the time." He picked up her hand. "You want to get a place together?"

"Sure. We're seeing a future, right? So yeah. I want to stay in Old Towne, so I'm close to work."

"That's cool. I like it here. It's different from the rest of Madrone." His brows drew in and he cocked his head. "You sure about this?"

"Why wouldn't I be?"

"This is your last chance. If we make our life together like that, I'm not letting you go. My life, all of it—you're stuck with it."

"And you're stuck with mine. All of it. Moore, the job, all of it."

"Okay. Fair deal." He grinned and held out his hand. When she shook it, he pulled her close and kissed her.

CHAPTER TWENTY-THREE

Connor sat down next to Trick. Trick's hands were clenched together on his chest, and he was staring out toward the ocean. He looked like he was about to come out of his skin.

"Chill, man."

"I hate this shit," Trick muttered. "I don't want to be thanked. It was a job. I did it. End of story. And it was four months ago."

The murder of Allen Cartwright remained unsolved. No one had claimed credit, and the Feds had no viable leads. From what Bart and Sherlock could see, the Horde was not and had never been on the radar, and neither had Dora Vega. She had insisted that he was corrupt and had been trying to blackmail her. If that was true, then he had covered his own tracks exceedingly well. With no motive and no leads, it looked like his case would go cold.

La Zorra hadn't returned to California since her last meeting with the Horde, so now they were conducting business on several matters. Bart, acting President while Hoosier was laid low, and Connor, acting VP, with Eight Ball, the Brazen Bulls mother charter President, and the Presidents of the Nevada and just-formed Eureka charters of the Bulls, had all sat down with her already and plotted out expanded business ventures, adding guns to the cocktail of drugs they were moving.

The new structure was complicated, and the exposure for everyone was greater—and on both sides of the law. It was impossible to centralize this much power without gaining notice from law enforcement and from other outlaws. People everywhere would be looking to take the Águilas Alliance, as Dora had taken to calling it, down. But the upside was hard to turn away from. So they were in. They'd just have to look sharp.

Bart had stepped up in the weeks—nearly two months now—since Connor's father had been hurt. He was good in the lead.

But he didn't want it, and Connor was glad about that. His father still held that seat, and he would take it again. He would.

In the meantime, Bart's leadership was a lot like Hoosier's, and the club was in good hands.

When the business meeting had wound to a close, and everyone was standing around, eating and talking, Connor had gone looking for Trick, and he'd found him here, alone on the balcony of the hotel suite in San Diego. To every extent possible, Dora liked to conduct her meetings in comfortable style. She stayed in a nice hotel suite, and she always had food and drink for everyone.

It was a stark contrast to the way the Perro Blanco cartel had been run, back in the day. Julio Santaveria, the Perro boss, almost never met with his partners north of the border, and every meet Connor could think of had happened in some abandoned building, or out in the sticks somewhere.

"Come back in. Let her do her thing. Then we can get drunk and you can get laid."

At that, Trick laughed and stood. "The Conman, all settled down and domestic. How are all the little girls going to learn their lesson about bad boys now?"

"Fuck you, brother. Get inside. The Queen wants to knight you or some shit like that."

Dora was standing in the middle of the room, talking to Eight Ball, Bart, and Muse, who'd stepped into the SAA role for the time being. She smiled when Connor and Trick came in.

She held out her hand. "Mr. Stavros."

"Trick is fine." Trick shook her hand. Connor noticed that he'd squared his shoulders and picked up his military bearing, like an old habit that hadn't died.

Still smiling, she released his hand and waved at one of her men across the room. He stopped at a table and picked up a box, about the size of a business envelope, but half an inch deep, then carried it to her. She took it and turned back to Trick.

"You did me a great service, Trick."

He shook his head. "No, ma'am. I did the job my club asked me to do."

Dora's brow creased slightly, and she looked at Trick like she was trying to see something he wasn't showing her. Connor felt a tickle of apprehension. Trick was calm, and he was goodhearted, but he was not one to shiny up the truth.

"Be that as it may, I am grateful that you did that job so well. It was important to me. I give you this to express my gratitude."

Trick looked at the box but didn't take it. "You paid us for the job, and I got my cut. I don't need that."

"I'm sure you don't. But please take it. I put some effort into it."

With a deep sigh, Trick took the box and opened it.

Standing at his side, Connor saw that the box contained a folded piece of paper. Trick glanced up at Dora, then took the paper out. There was a key in the bottom of the box, under the paper.

Trick opened the paper. While he read it, Connor tried to read his face. What he got was confusion—and disbelief.

"What is this?" Trick returned his attention to Dora.

"The deed to your grandparents' home in Santorini. It's paid in full, and the back taxes, too."

"Losing that house killed my grandmother."

"I'm very sorry for that. Do you think your grandfather would not want to live in it again?"

"No, he would. He thinks he left her there." Trick looked down at the deed and then back up to Dora. "You bought my grandparents' house?"

"I paid for it. I don't own it. It's in your grandfather's name." She put her manicured finger on the deed and pointed to the name.

For a long, long second, Trick was silent. When he looked up, Connor thought his friend might have been on the verge of tears. "Thank you. I...I think I want to hug you."

Isidora Vega, the most powerful person in the entire country of Mexico, smiled. "I would like a hug."

~oOo~

Three days later, an early morning just days before Christmas, Connor paced back and forth across the main entrance at the hospital. The automatic doors kept sliding half-closed, then open again, over and over. He was probably driving the person inside at the information desk insane, but he didn't care. He couldn't be still.

When he saw Pilar pull in on her Victory, he followed after her. As soon as she dismounted and took her helmet off, he grabbed her.

She pushed back from him. "What happened? Is he worse?"

"No. He...he's awake."

"My God! That's great! How is he?"

"I don't...I haven't seen him yet."

"What? Why?"

"The doc talked to me and...he's not okay. He's awake and 'responsive,' whatever that means—"

"It means he's reacting to stimuli. Like light and sound. Voice. Touch."

"Okay, that. But he's not talking. They're doing a bunch of tests."

"But why aren't you in there?"

"I can't...on my own. I'm fucking freaked. What if he doesn't know me? And Mom's not here yet. Demon's bringing her. Faith's dropping the kids off with Riley and coming after."

"Connor. Should you see your dad first, so you can talk to your mom before she goes in?"

"It won't matter. She'll want in there right away. She won't slow down enough for me to talk to her."

She grabbed his kutte in her fists and shook him a little. "He woke up and there's nobody he knows around. Connor, think."

Oh fuck. Fuck. He'd fucked up. "Damn, damn. I'm such a fucking idiot. I'm a pussy. Fuck!"

She took his hand. "Beat yourself up later. C'mon, let's go."

Feeling far too full for his head to contain, Connor let her lead him into the hospital.

~oOo~

In the nearly two months that he'd been comatose, Hoosier's burns and other wounds had healed. His skin was scarred but intact. They'd taken him off the ventilator shortly after Thanksgiving. All his injuries had mended. Except for his head.

Part of his skull was still embedded in his belly; even though the rest of his wounds had healed, they'd left his skull open in case they needed to go back in, to minimize the trauma of further surgery. Connor still hadn't gotten used to the sloped gap in his father's head, or the idea that just below the skin of his scruffy scalp was his exposed brain.

He had taken to focusing on his father's hands instead of his head when he was there with him. There was too much weakness about his head. Connor hadn't been able to find hope there.

But when he and Pilar went into his father's room, the first thing he saw was his eyes. They were open and alive, and for a second, Connor felt overwhelming hope. That was his father in the bed, back in his body. He went to him and bent over the rail to kiss his forehead. "Hey, Dad. Welcome back."

Hoosier blinked but didn't react otherwise.

Still, Connor thought his father did know him. Maybe. It was hard to be sure. The doctor had told them on the way in that tests had shown that Hoosier had full feeling in his body, his pupils worked, and he could follow simple commands.

But he couldn't, or wouldn't, talk, and he hadn't reacted with any kind of emotion to anything anyone said. He couldn't hold a pen—he could grasp it, but not in the way he needed to be able to use it. Like he'd forgotten how. And he couldn't write. He seemed to have lost words completely, even the idea of them.

Connor didn't know how much of his father had come back.

But then the door burst open, and his mother was there. "I'm here, Hooj. Baby, I'm here. I'm here. You stay with me now."

Crying, she pushed Connor back and did as he had, leaning over the side rail and kissing her husband's forehead. Connor watched as she made a fist around Hoosier's chin—the way she always had, though normally she was taking hold of beard.

"I'm here, baby. Right here. Be with me, okay?"

And Connor's father smiled.

Connor felt hands on his back. He turned and wrapped Pilar up tight. She clutched him hard, and they stood like that. He didn't know what to think, whether he could stop being so afraid for his father, or whether there was more fear to be had, but he did know that the woman holding him now made him better and stronger.

~oOo~

"What are you doing?"

Connor glanced over his shoulder and saw Pilar wearing his t-shirt, and seemingly nothing else. Damn, he loved living with her. He had his own personal hottie on tap. Just for him. "Cooking you breakfast."

"For serious?" She came to his side. "Oh."

"What oh? These things are great." He turned and put into the oven the tray of orange rolls that he'd gotten out of a tube. Then he pulled her into his arms and slid his hands under that t-shirt. Yep. Nothing else.

"I don't think that exactly counts as 'cooking me breakfast.' But thank you."

He kissed her. "We have something like fifteen minutes."

"Barely time to get a good start." She scratched her fingertips over his bare chest.

"No, I don't want to…well, yeah, I do. I always do."

"I know." She grabbed hold of the waistband of his sweats, but he caught her hands in his own and held them.

"But I want to do something else first. I want to give you your Christmas present this morning, while it's just us. Before we go and it's crazy with everybody. I don't want a bunch of gawkers when I give it to you." They'd been to the Horde clubhouse party and the Station 76 party already. Today, Christmas Day, they were going out to Demon and Faith's and then to the hospital.

His father still wasn't talking. He just didn't know how. But he knew his old lady, and he knew his son.

The things he'd lost, he'd simply have to learn again. It would take time, but Connor finally felt the kind of hope that was confidence. His old man was a fighter. He'd come back.

Pilar smiled and patted his belly. "Cool. Let me get yours, too." Before he could stop her, she'd turned and left the room. Connor picked up the box he'd tucked at the back of the counter and went to sit at the table and wait.

She came back with a small box, wrapped in pretty paper. It was a little bigger than the one he had for her. When she sat, he pushed his unwrapped box toward her and said, "I want to go first."

"Should we flip for it?" She laughed, her gold eyes alight with humor and happiness.

"Just open the damn box, Cordero."

She did, and then she set it down on the counter and let her hands drop away. "God. Connor. Is this…"

He pulled the box toward him and took the gold ring out of it. "You don't wear a lot of jewelry, so I didn't think you'd like a big, flashy thing. If I'm wrong about that, we can take this back. This is a claddagh ring. It's a Celtic thing. The hands are friendship, the heart is love, and the crown is loyalty. My mom's is kind of like this."

"But different."

"Yeah. Hers is a traditional claddagh. And she likes bling, so the heart is a diamond. The chick at the store said this is a claddagh infinity ring. It's—I guess it's subtler. If you don't like it…"

"I love it. Are you proposing to me?"

"If you want that, then yeah. I don't need the ceremony. You know how I feel—I just want my life to be with you, and that's what the ring says to me. And I want to put ink on you that says it to everybody else. But if you want to be married, then we'll do that, too."

"Nana would want it. It would make her happy. A Catholic wedding. She'd feel that like something she did right."

Setting aside his discomfort with the idea of a big wedding like that, Connor smiled. He'd marry her wherever the hell she wanted, and he knew that giving her nana some peace was important to her. "Then we'll get married." He picked up her hand. Before he slid the ring on her finger, he said, "It's engraved on the inside. It says *anam cara*. It's Gaelic for 'soulmate.' Because you are that. Something was missing inside me until I fell in love with you."

Looking at the ring on her finger, she laughed, and Connor wasn't sure if his feelings should be hurt by that.

"What's funny?"

She pushed toward him the box she'd wrapped. "Great minds."

"What?" He tore the paper off the box and removed the lid. On a velvet bed lay two gold chains, one a little heavier than the other. From them dangled what appeared to be a broken gold pendant, one half on each chain. Engraved across the fragments, as if they were one whole, was a Maltese cross and the word 'FIREFIGHTER.'

"It's a mizpah. Each one is a half of the whole." She reached into the box and turned the pendants over, fitting them together. On the back was inscribed *May the Lord keep watch between us whenever we are apart. Genesis 31:49*. "We each wear one half. Because we're only whole together." She picked up the lighter chain and fastened it around her own neck, and the pendant lay at the base of her throat, with her crucifix, which had been her mother's.

Connor did the same with the heavier chain, and his half of the pendant lay with his crucifix, which his father had given him.

At first, they sat quietly. For Connor's part, he was too overcome with emotion to speak. He just wanted to sit for a minute and marvel.

Then Pilar laughed. "I feel like we should do something to mark the occasion."

Unbidden, the memory of the night they'd met rose up in his mind, and he grinned. "You want to go back and fuck?"

Her eyes lit up at that, but she asked, "What about your rolls?"

He shrugged. "I'll turn the oven off. I hear those don't count as real cooking, anyway."

"They really don't." She stood up. "C'mon, big guy. Tie me down and make me yours forever."

Connor stood. When she reached up as if to put her arms around his neck, he went in low. He picked her up and threw her over his shoulders.

Fireman style.

THE END

COMING SOON

Dream & Dare
A Night Horde Side Trip

*Bibi and Hoosier have been together a long time.
Their road has not always been smooth, but their love has always run deep and true.
This is the story of that long road and that abiding love.*

Printed in Great Britain
by Amazon